MT. PLEASANT

PLEASANTVILLE,

THE
LOST
VILLAGE

THE
LOST
VILLAGE

CAMILLA STEN

MINOTAUR BOOKS
NEW YORK

First published in the United States by Minotaur Books, an imprint of St. Martin's Publishing Group

THE LOST VILLAGE. Copyright © 2019 by Camilla Sten. English translation © 2019 by Alex Fleming. All rights reserved. Printed in the United States of America. For information, address St. Martin's Publishing Group, 120 Broadway, New York, NY 10271.

www.minotaurbooks.com

Designed by Steven Seighman

Library of Congress Cataloging-in-Publication Data

Names: Sten, Camilla, 1992- author. | Fleming, Alex (Translator), translator.
Title: The lost village : a novel / Camilla Sten, Alexandra Fleming.
Other titles: Staden. English
Description: First U.S. edition. | New York : Minotaur Books, 2021. | "Originally published in Sweden in 2019 by Norstedts ingår i Norstedts Förlagsgrupp AB."
Identifiers: LCCN 2020042041 | ISBN 9781250249258 (hardcover) | ISBN 9781250249265 (ebook)
Subjects: GSAFD: Suspense fiction. | Horror fiction.
Classification: LCC PT9877.29.T39 S7313 2021 | DDC 839.73/8—dc23
LC record available at https://lccn.loc.gov/2020042041

Our books may be purchased in bulk for promotional, educational, or business use. Please contact your local bookseller or the Macmillan Corporate and Premium Sales Department at 1-800-221-7945, extension 5442, or by email at MacmillanSpecialMarkets@macmillan.com.

Originally published in Sweden in 2019 by Norstedts ingår i Norstedts Förlagsgrupp AB.

First U.S. Edition: 2021

10 9 8 7 6 5 4 3 2 1

For Anna, who believed in this book long before I dared to myself

FOREWORD

When I first set out to write *The Lost Village*, I wanted to write a book just for me—a book I would enjoy writing. I never expected it to be more than a fun exercise, a way to get back to the thrill of writing after the slog of attempting to write a "serious literary novel" (which, as it turns out, is really not my genre).

Of course, things are never that simple. A book is, at the end of the day, always a reflection of its writer. Things you never intended to write about sneak into the story, worm their way into the text, and at the end of the day you're sitting with a very different book than you thought you were writing.

Don't get me wrong—it was still very, very fun to write.

The Lost Village is a book about a lot of things—isolation, fear, the terrifying power of groupthink, and how desperation can drive us to do things we never thought we'd stoop to. It is a thriller about a small, isolated, abandoned town and the horrors that take place there. But it's also a book written by a former psychologist-to-be (hi!) and, more importantly, someone who for years struggled with depression (hi, again!). And maybe more than anything, it is a book about how society views women suffering from mental illness.

We perceive women suffering from mental illness with a sort of paradoxical double-sidedness; both victims and monsters, simultaneously infantilized and feared. A certain level of dysfunction is accepted—after all, women who are suffering mild depression and starving themselves aren't going to leave their husbands or start revolutions, which is very practical indeed.

But beyond a certain point, it flips. Women are supposed to be gentle, devoted, loving and—above all else—rule-abiding. Undeniable suffering is bad, and anger is worse. A woman suffering from severe anxiety or untreated mania isn't going to have dinner on the table by 6 o'clock. No longer is she fulfilling that crucial, limited role she's expected to fulfill. No longer can she be a dutiful daughter, a picture-perfect wife, a devoted mother.

Throughout history, women suffering from mental illness have been hidden away, burned at the stake, lobotomized, and sterilized. I'm incredibly grateful I've been born into a time and context where my depression was viewed as a treatable illness, where I had access to the necessary care and the kind of support system that allowed me to eventually make a full recovery. But I'm also very aware that still, today, that is not the case for many people; that I am very privileged, and that my privilege had a huge part in my recovery.

Everything from degree of severity, to social status, race, level of financial stability, and ability to seek health care has an impact on not only how mental illness is treated, but how it is perceived. We view a depressed upper-class woman from a stable family background dealing with depression as "having the blues," while the homeless woman on the street corner battling auditory hallucinations is a thing to be feared, a threatening monster. Not a person in need of help. Not someone with thoughts, dreams, fears, and needs of their own. Not a fully formed human being with agency and identity, suffering from an illness and doing their best to function as well as they can.

There are three female characters in the book suffering from mental illness, and they are all perceived and treated differently. One of them has recovered, one is in recovery, and one was never given the chance. They are neither victims nor villains. They are just people, with differing needs and levels of functioning.

Recovered, in recovery, or struggling, we are still people. Sometimes that truth can feel like a fever dream. Writing this book helped me to accept that, my own undeniable humanity even while sick, filtered through the kaleidoscope of my own fictional characters. I hope it can do the same for someone else.

Or that you just enjoy the thrill and horror of the story.

That's the lovely thing about books, isn't it?

You can take whatever you want from it.

Camilla Sten

It was a stiflingly hot August afternoon, so much so that the breeze coming in through the open windows did almost nothing to lift the swelter inside the car. Albin had taken off his hat and was dangling his arm out of the window, careful not to let his hand brush against the searing-hot body of the car.

"How far now?" he asked Gustaf again.

Gustaf simply grunted. Albin took this to mean that he should check the map himself if he was so desperate to know. He already had. The village they were driving to was a place he had never been to before. Too small for its own police station, even its own hospital. Barely more than a hamlet.

Silvertjärn. Who had even heard of Silvertjärn back then?

Albin was about to ask Gustaf if he had ever been there before, but then thought better of it. Gustaf wasn't talkative at the best of times, that much Albin had gathered. For almost two years now they had been working together on the force, and in that time Albin hadn't been able to get more than a few words out of him on any one subject.

Gustaf slowed down slightly and looked at the map between them, then made a sharp left, down a road Albin had hardly noticed for all the trees. He lurched forward in his seat, and his hat almost flew away.

"Think we'll find anything?" he asked. To his surprise, Gustaf actually opened his mouth to reply this time:

"God knows."

Encouraged, Albin continued:

"Nah, sounded more like two dopes who'd had a few too many, if you ask me. Hardly worth the gas it takes to get out there."

The road they now found themselves on was narrow and uneven, and Albin had to hold on tight to stop himself from bouncing around on his seat. Outside, the tree trunks stood tall on either side of the car, but what little sky he could see was so dazzlingly blue that it made his eyes tingle. The journey felt like it would never end.

But then the forest started to clear.

The village looked exactly like the industrial backwater in which Albin had grown up. Without a doubt there would be some sort of mine or factory at which every man in town worked. It seemed like a pleasant, unassuming place, with dainty houses in even rows, a river meandering through the center, and a white stucco church spire that soared up over the rooftops, gleaming in the August sunshine.

Gustaf braked suddenly, bringing the car to a halt.

Albin stared at him.

Deep furrows had appeared across Gustaf's brow, and his cheeks hung slack in sloppily shaven resignation.

"Hear that?" he asked Albin.

Something in his voice made Albin stop and listen.

"Hear what?" he asked. All he could make out was the grumble of the car's engine.

They had stopped in the middle of a crossroads. Nothing much of note: a yellow house to the right, its front steps lined with wilting flowers, and an almost identical red house with white trim to the left.

"Nothing," said Gustaf, and it was the insistent tone of his voice that finally made Albin twig.

It wasn't that he had heard something.

It was that he hadn't heard anything.

The whole place was completely silent.

It was half past four in the afternoon on a Wednesday in late summer, in a village in the middle of the forest. Where were all the kids out playing? Where were the young women out on their doorsteps, taking fans to their shiny foreheads and wilted locks?

Albin looked around at the prim rows of houses that stretched out *on either side of the car. Every single one of them was neat and well kept. Every single one had its front door closed.*

No matter where he looked, he couldn't make out a single soul.

"Where is everyone?" he asked Gustaf.

The village couldn't just be deserted; they had to all be somewhere.

Gustaf shook his head and put his foot back down on the gas.

"Keep your eyes open," he said.

Albin gulped and felt it catch in his throat, which was now suddenly dry and swollen. He straightened up in his seat and put his hat back on.

The silence as they pulled off again felt just as stifling as the heat, and Albin's neck was already beading with sweat. When the village square appeared before them, Albin felt a surge of relief flood through him. He pointed at the figure in the middle of the square.

"Look, Gustaf! There's someone there."

Perhaps Gustaf's vision was sharper than his—that or his many long years on the force had given him instincts Albin had yet to develop. Whatever it was, before they had even reached the cobblestones of the square, Gustaf had stopped the car, opened the door, and stepped out.

Albin, still in the car, processed the scene in stages. At first he thought:

It's a very tall person.

Then:

No, that's not it, it's a person hugging a lamppost. Bizarre.

It was only when the stench found its way into the car that the pieces finally fell into place. Albin opened the door and stumbled out, trying to escape it, but out there it was only stronger. Sweet, overripe, nauseating; meat left to rot and ferment in the sun for long idle hours, untouched and unmoved.

No one was hugging any lamppost. It was a body, tied to a rough-hewn pole. Long, straggly hair tumbled down over the face, hiding it—a small mercy—but its swollen arms and legs were crawling with fat flies. The ropes binding the body had cut into its soft, spongy tissue, and its feet were black. Whether that was due to decay or to the coagulated pools of blood at the base of the post, it was impossible to tell.

Albin made it no more than a few steps before he bent double and brought his lunch up all over the cobblestones.

When he looked up again, he saw that Gustaf was almost at the body, peering at it from only a few feet away. He turned back to look at Albin, who wiped his mouth and stood up straight. Naked fear mixed with disgust in the bloodhound-deep wrinkles around his colleague's mouth.

"What in God's name has happened here?" Gustaf asked, his tone of voice betraying a hint of what could only be described as wonder.

Albin had no words. He let the silence of the empty village take over.

But then something cut through that silence—faint, distant, yet unmistakable. Albin had four younger siblings, and he had shared a room with all of them. It was a sound he would have recognized anywhere.

"What the . . ." Gustaf muttered, turning to look at the school on the opposite side of the square. A window was open on the second floor.

"I think it's a child," said Albin. "A baby."

Then the stench swam back over him, and he vomited again.

PROJECT DESCRIPTION:

The Lost Village is a documentary about Silvertjärn, Sweden's one and only ghost town. Our aim is to produce a six-episode documentary, accompanied by a blog on the making of the series, featuring any new leads we manage to uncover. Silvertjärn, a former mining village in the heart of Norrland, has stood more or less untouched since 1959, when all nine hundred of its residents disappeared under mysterious circumstances.

[More on the history of Silvertjärn]

The showrunner and producer is Alice Lindstedt, whose grandmother grew up in Silvertjärn.

"I grew up hearing my grandmother's stories about Silvertjärn and the disappearance. She had already left Silvertjärn when it happened, but her parents and younger sister were among the missing.

The Silvertjärn story has always fascinated me. So much about it just doesn't make sense. How can an entire village just drop off the face of the earth? What really happened? These are the questions that we want to try and answer."

We plan to spend an initial six days in Silvertjärn in early April to explore the village and film some test shots. As a backer, you will get access to our footage from these shoots—photos AND videos. We will also delve into some of the theories about the disappearance—everything from a gas leak that supposedly caused mass hysteria and delirium, to an ancient Sami curse.

[More on the theories surrounding the disappearance]

All being well, the team will then return to Silvertjärn in August, in order to shoot the documentary at around the same time of year that the disappearance took place.

WHAT YOU GET AS A BACKER:

- Immediate access to any footage shot in Silvertjärn in April
- Unlimited access to the production team's social media posts

- Regular progress updates via email
- The chance to see the first, director's cut of the finished documentary before it is cut for general release
- The chance to visit Silvertjärn with our team for the series premiere and blog launch

GOAL:

150,000 Swedish kronor

PLEDGED SO FAR:

33,450 Swedish kronor

CLICK HERE TO DONATE AND BE PART OF THIS PROJECT!

Like and follow us on social media!
Instagram: @thelostvillagedocumentary
Facebook: The Lost Village Documentary
(www.facebook.com/thelostvillagedocumentary)
Twitter: @thelostvillagedocumentary
#thelostvillagedocumentary #silvertjärn

TUESDAY

NOW

I'm woken by a shrill crackling noise that takes me from dozing to a dazed wakefulness in the blink of an eye.

As I sit up and bat the sleep out of my eyes, I see Tone reach out and turn off the radio. The crackling immediately disappears, replaced by the dull hum of the engine and the pent-up silence of the van.

"What was that?" I ask, running my fingers through my hair.

"The radio's been acting up for a few miles," Tone says. "It jumped from dad rock to dance band, and then it just started crackling."

"Must be the start of the dead zone," I say, feeling a fizz of excitement in my belly.

I take my phone out of my pocket, realizing as I do that it's much later than I'd thought.

"I still have signal, but only just," I say. "I'll post one last update before we lose it completely."

I log in to Instagram and take a quick shot of the sun-drenched evening road ahead.

"How does this sound?" I ask. "'Getting closer! Almost inside the dead zone. See you in five days, if the ghosts don't get us. . . .'"

Tone grimaces.

"Might be a bit much," she says.

"They're gonna love it," I say, clicking POST. Then, after checking that it has shared to both Twitter and Facebook, I put the phone back in my pocket.

"Our fans eat that stuff up," I go on. "Ghosts and horror films and shit. It's our best unique selling proposition."

"Our fans," Tone quips. "All eleven of them."

I roll my eyes, but can't deny that it hurts. The joke cuts a little too close to the bone.

Tone doesn't notice. Her eyes are still fixed on the road. It's empty and anonymous, a flat highway with neither bends nor turnoffs. Tall, impenetrable conifers enclose us on either side, and to our left the blazing sun drifts deeper into a bleeding sky that bathes us and the forest in its hue.

"The exit should be pretty soon," she says. "We're starting to get close."

"Would you like me to take over?" I ask. "I didn't mean to fall asleep. I don't know what happened."

Tone gives a tight, closed-mouth smile.

"If you were up till four a.m. going through everything then it isn't such a surprise," she says, without answering my question about taking over at the wheel.

I can't tell if she means it as a dig or not.

"No," I agree, "I guess not."

Still, I *am* surprised. I'd thought that same tingling, feverish excitement that has kept me up the past few nights would prevent me from falling asleep here, too.

I cast a glance in the wing mirror and see the other white van that Emmy and the technician are driving immediately behind us. Max's blue Volvo is just visible at the back of the caravan.

Is that excitement or anxiety I feel squirming inside me?

The intense light stains my white, cable-knit sweater a fiery red, and throws Tone's face into a sharp silhouette. She's one of those people who's more beautiful in profile than front-on, with her enviably chiseled jaw-line and straight patrician nose. I've never seen her wearing any makeup, which makes me feel both ridiculous and exceptionally vain, especially as I've just had highlights put in to turn my naturally matte, wastewater hair into a cold, lustrous blond. This, despite it costing almost nine hundred kronor that I don't have—not to mention the fact that I'm not even going to be in any of the footage we're shooting over the next five days.

I did it for me. To settle my nerves. And we do need photos, I guess, for Instagram, Facebook, Twitter, and the blog. To give our few—but enthusiastic—fans and backers something to whet their appetites, keep that fire burning.

I have a musty taste in my mouth after my nap. Eyeing up the plastic cup Tone got at the gas station in the cup holder, I ask:

"What's in there?"

"Coke. Have some if you want," she says, adding that it's Zero before I can even ask.

I pick up the cup and take a few big gulps of the flat, tepid drink. It's not particularly refreshing, but I'm thirstier than I thought.

"There," says Tone suddenly, and slows down.

The old exit doesn't exist on GPS, as we discovered when trying to plan our route. We've had to use old maps from the forties and fifties, cross-referencing them with the Swedish Transport Administration's archive on where the train tracks used to run when trains still puffed their way up to the village twice a week. Max is good with maps, and he guaranteed us that this was where the road would be. But it's only now, as Tone slows to a crawl to take the narrow, almost completely overgrown exit that was once the only road to the village, that I start to feel sure.

The van coasts along for a while and then comes to a halt. I look at Tone, thrown.

"What is it?" I ask.

She's even paler than normal, her freckles glowing against her wan skin. Her small mouth looks like a dash across her face, and her hands are clenched tightly around the wheel.

"Tone?" I ask, quieter this time.

At first she says nothing, just sits there staring quietly into the trees.

"I just never thought I'd see it," she says softly.

I put my hand on her arm. Under the lightweight fabric of her long-sleeved T-shirt, her muscles are coiled up tightly like springs.

"Would you like me to drive?" I ask.

By now the others have stopped, too. The second van is right behind us, with Max's blue Volvo presumably bringing up the rear.

Tone lets go of the wheel and leans back slightly.

"Might be a good idea," she says. And then, without looking at me, she undoes her seat belt, opens the door, and jumps out.

I follow her lead: I unfasten my seat belt, jump out of the van, and walk around to the other side. The outside air comes as a shock, clear and fresh and very cold. It cuts right through my thick sweater, even in the absence of any wind.

By the time I climb into the driver's seat, Tone has already fastened her seat belt. I wait for her to say something, but nothing comes. So I cautiously put my foot on the gas, and we pull off down the half-overgrown road.

An almost solemn silence descends on the car. Once we're swallowed up by the trees, which seem to stoop down over us on the narrow road, the sound of Tone's voice in the sudden semidarkness makes me jump.

"Plus it's only fitting that you should drive into the place. I mean, this is your project. You're the one who wanted to come here. Right?"

I snatch a glance at her out of the corner of my eye, but try to keep my attention on maneuvering the unwieldy van over gnarled roots and stones.

"I guess," I say.

It's a good thing we went for the extra insurance with the rentals; this is definitely not the terrain these vans were made for. But we needed them to get all of our equipment up here, and the cross-country vehicles were so eye-wateringly expensive that just one day's rental would have blown our budget several times over.

We drive on in silence. As the minutes pass and we go deeper and deeper into the forest, it hits me just how isolated this small community must have been. From what Grandma said, only some of the villagers had a car, so the train was their only real connection to civilization, and that only ran twice a week. If it's taken us this long to get here in our vans, it must have been a completely different world when the only option for getting out of town was to walk this entire stretch.

We drive past a small track that winds off into the forest. At first I wonder if I've missed a turnoff, but then I realize it must be the road that led to the mine. I carry on ahead, inching over undergrowth and fallen branches. The van grumbles and moans, but battles on.

Just when I start to worry that we've gotten it wrong—that this was just a forest path, a walking trail, and that we'll keep on driving further and further into the forest, until we get mired in the weight of our vans and equipment, our stupidity and ambition—the trees open up like a miracle before our eyes.

"There," I whisper, more to myself than to Tone.

It buoys me enough to speed up a little, just a little, and I feel the blood pumping through my veins as the fiery April sky swells before us.

We exit the forest onto a steep bank. And there it is, at the bottom of a valley that isn't so much a valley as a slight depression in the ground.

The church looms large over the small buildings on the eastern side of the village, its tall, proud spire topped by a slender cross that glistens, impossibly bright, in the light of the setting sun. The houses look almost as if they've sprouted from the church like little mushrooms, falling and moldering to form walls and silhouettes along the coppery-red river running down to the small woodland lake that gave the village its name: *silvertjärn*, silver tarn. It may well have been silver at one point, but now it sits, glossy and black, like an aged secret. The mining company's report stated that the lake had never been searched, nor had they been able to find any information on its depth. For all we know it could stretch all the way down to the groundwater. Bottomless.

Almost instinctively I undo my seat belt, open the door, jump down onto the soft wet spring topsoil, and look out over the village. It's

THEN

Elsa is on her way home from Agneta Lindberg's house when she realizes something isn't right.

The walk should take only fifteen minutes at a brisk pace, but rarely does Elsa make it home in under forty, there are so many people who want to stop for a chat.

Elsa has been visiting Agneta every week for the past few months, ever since the poor dear got the news. Elsa normally sees her on a Wednesday, as it's so convenient to pop by after one of the Wednesday lunches hosted by the pharmacist's wife.

Nothing much ever gets done at those lunches; in essence they're just a chance for some of the village ladies to get together and chew the fat, sip coffee from dainty little cups, and feel a fleeting sense of superiority. But it's all harmless fun, and goodness knows the women of Silvertjärn feel all the better for having something to do. Elsa can't deny that even she enjoys these sessions, although sometimes she does have to put her foot down when their chitchat becomes a little too barbed.

Insinuations about the paternity of the schoolmaster's youngest child won't do anyone any good. Elsa herself had been to visit him and his poor wife when the boy was refusing to take the breast, and she has rarely seen a father more doting—however red that boy's hair might be.

It's a hot afternoon, unusually close for April, and as Elsa walks she can feel herself start to perspire beneath her blouse. She likes to take the path down by the river's edge; it's nice and even underfoot, and if you look up you can see the lake shimmering in the distance. The meltwater has started to stream and ripple below the riverbank, and it's enough to make you want to stop for a paddle.

Not that Elsa does that, of course. How it would look if she were to pull up her skirt and start splashing around, like a little girl without a care in the world? That really *would* give the village women something to gossip about!

It's when Elsa smiles at this thought that it first strikes her that something is off, for when she looks around to see who might catch her would-be frolics in the river, she realizes that no one is there.

The river is lined with houses. It's the old heart of Silvertjärn, and Elsa has a soft spot for this part of the village. When she and Staffan first moved to Silvertjärn, back when she was scarce more than a child herself, they had lived in one of the new buildings the mine had constructed. It had been a cold, soulless place, and Elsa is convinced that those cracked white walls were the reason why her first pregnancy was so difficult. She had made sure that they had moved away as soon as they could.

The houses down here by the river are older, with more personality, and Elsa knows everyone who lives down this way. Without boasting or bluster, Elsa can honestly claim to know everyone in Silvertjärn, but the area between the church and the river is her own, which means she goes the extra mile for those who live here. She likes to pass by the house with the sloping roof on the corner to say hello to Pia Etterström and her twin boys; to stop outside Emil Snäll's porch and ask how his gout is treating him; to pause to admire Lise-Marie's rosebushes.

But today not one person has stopped or waved.

Despite the warm weather, there's not a soul to be seen in gardens or out on front steps, and not a single window is open. No one has bustled outside to say hello after seeing Elsa pass, even though she can see movements behind the kitchen curtains and closed windows. Everyone seems to have locked themselves away.

Her stomach turns.

In days to come, Elsa will wonder if some part of her already knows—before she sets off into a run, before she gets home, sweaty and disheveled, to find Staffan sitting at the kitchen table, his face empty with shock.

But no, she doesn't know. She hasn't realized, hasn't guessed. She could never have guessed.

So when Staffan says with the voice of a sleepwalker . . .

"They're shutting down the mine, Elsie. We found out today. They sent us all home."

. . . she faints on the spot for the first and only time in her life.

NOW

I've never seen Silvertjärn with my own eyes. I've pictured it, sure, based on Grandma's stories, spent late nights googling like a woman possessed, searching for some kind of description, but I've found next to nothing.

I turn around when I hear the click of Tone's camera. She's holding it up to her eyes, so half of her face is hidden.

What we should have done is filmed the view as we drove out of the forest. That would have made for a powerful, attention-grabbing opening, which is what you need when you're applying for funding. No matter how much we post on Instagram or try to direct people to the Kickstarter page, the hard truth is we'll need a grant to make the documentary I've envisaged. Without some form of state funding, we don't stand a chance.

But I'm convinced we'll get the money in the end.

I mean, who could resist this?

The light is pouring down onto the dilapidated buildings, steeping them in reds and oranges. It's surprising how well they have lasted, in spite of everything. They must have built things differently back then. Even so, the decay is still visible from up here. Some of the roofs have fallen in completely, and nature has started to reclaim the land in earnest; it's hard to make out where the buildings end and the forest begins. The streets are empty and overgrown, and the rust-withered train tracks jut out of the station and into the forest like a punctured artery.

It's beautiful, but in an almost obscene way, like an overblown rose about to shed its petals.

The clicks stop. I look back at Tone, who has lowered the camera.

"Get any good shots?" I ask.

"With a view like this, even an iPhone could get a good shot," she replies.

She walks over to me and pulls the images up on the small rectangular screen. We've agreed that Tone will be in charge of photographs. Unlike Emmy, Emmy's friend, and me, she has no background in film: she's a copywriter. But photography has been her hobby for a few years now, and her shots are better than anything I could come up with on the same camera.

It was also the easiest way to get her to come along. For a long time she tried to argue her way out of being here at all, saying she wasn't "essential." And all of my arguments as to why, as coproducer, she was in fact crucial to the project had done nothing to change her mind. It was only when I took up the photography angle that she started to cave.

She is essential to the project. Not as a photographer, perhaps. But she's part of the story, whether she wants to be or not. I just hope this trip helps her to see that.

I study the miniature village in pixels, then the silhouettes before me. The bright colors and sharp lines make it look like a painting.

The silence hangs compact. Not even radio signals make it out of here. They say it has something to do with the iron ore in the bedrock—some sort of magnetic field that jams the signals—but no one seems to know for sure. It doesn't exactly ruin the mystique.

"How are you feeling?" I ask, tearing my gaze from the buildings below us.

Tone takes a deep breath of the cool, fresh air, and purses her lips.

"I don't know," she says, looking at me. Then she does another one of her half smiles. "I guess I just never thought I'd actually get here—that it would go this far. It hasn't really hit me that we're here yet."

"But we *are* here." I say, almost as much to myself as to her.

And now, finally, she smiles for real, showing her white, slightly crooked teeth, and puncturing some of the tension that's hung between us since I woke up in the van.

"Yes," she says, "of course we are. Because you, Alice, are a fucking bulldozer."

I burst into laughter—ecstatic, euphoric—because even though my teeth are chattering with cold (my own fault for leaving my jacket in the van), we're here now. We're *here*. And all the planning, all those late nights, all those jobs I didn't get and those shitty ones I had to take, they've finally paid off. We're here. In Silvertjärn.

This is happening. *The Lost Village* is going to happen. The project that started as some sort of prepubescent fantasy is finally coming to life.

"Fuck me, what a place," Emmy says behind me, cutting my laughter short.

I turn around. Emmy and the technician have both gotten out of their van and walked over to ours. Emmy's leaning against the driver's side of the van, her misshapen white T-shirt seemingly melting into the paintwork. Her henna-red hair is tied up in a messy ponytail, and the jeans she's wearing are big enough to fit the guy standing next to her. Come to think of it, they might even belong to him. I'm not really clear what their relationship is, beyond the fact that they've worked together before, and that Emmy made a point of telling me that he's doing this as a favor to her and normally charges three times what we can pay for these five days.

The technician—Robin? No, that's not it, he introduced himself at our initial meeting and again at yesterday's team briefing, but I've never been good with names—is right beside her. He's a redhead in that way that makes you want to stare a little longer than you really should, with loads of golden freckles that crawl all over his face, down his neck and onto his body. If it weren't for that he could probably be pretty hot—he's tall and broad-shouldered—but the combination of his carrot top, indiscernible eyebrows and brown eyes make him far too squirrely to be taken seriously. He's quiet, too: I don't think I've heard him say more than four sentences in all, and that's including both meetings.

"So what's the plan?" Emmy asks, her eyes on me. I clear my throat.

"We set up camp in the main square," I say. "That'll be a good base, as it's right in the center of the village. We should be able to get there— it's on the other side of the river, but it said that the bridges are still stable enough for cars."

"Where did it say that?" Emmy asks, her eyebrows raised. "I thought there weren't any good maps of Silvertjärn?"

I hear another car door open further away. It must be Max, wondering why we've stopped.

"In the report," I say, trying to subdue a twinge of irritation.

You knew what you were letting yourself in for when you asked her to come on board, I try to tell myself.

"The report the mining company made in the late nineties, when they came to survey the land," I clarify. "There's a copy of it in the information packs you all have."

"And you're completely sure that information still stands? I mean, it's twenty years old. Just because the bridges were safe then doesn't mean they are now."

"We'll drive down and take a look," I answer sharply. "If they don't look safe then we'll make a new plan."

I see Max round the second van.

"What's going on?" he asks.

"Nothing!" I say.

Emmy glances over her shoulder, but seems to dismiss Max as soon as she's registered his presence.

Max's blond hair is flopping down over his forehead, and one side of his collar is standing on end. I've known him since back when he used to wear scruffy T-shirts with the names of obscure bands no one except him knew. And even though nowadays he's successful enough to be here as a project backer—wearing shirts that cost more than my entire ward-robe, at that—he still looks like he'd be more comfortable in those faded old T-shirts.

Tone looks up at the sky.

"We should probably get a move on," she says, and it's then I realize that darkness has started to fall.

"Down the bank," I say to Max, who has just made it over to us, and then, turning to the others, I add:

"Follow us."

Emmy nods without another word, thank god, and I hear her ask the technician:

"Robert, do you want to take the downhill?"

Max gives me a thumbs up and heads back toward his car.

I get in the driver's seat. Just before I close the door, I hear Emmy shout:

"But drive carefully—we don't want to damage the equipment!"

"As if she's even paying for it," I mutter, slamming the door shut behind me.

NOW

I bite the inside of my cheek in concentration as I try to negotiate the steep bank. There must have been a road here somewhere, but no matter how hard I tried, I couldn't find it on any maps. Clearly most of the deliveries in and out of the village came by train.

At one point I hear something shift in the back, which makes me grip the wheel even tighter. Tone looks back over her shoulder—not that you can see much through the middle partition—and when she looks forward again she asks:

"Are you sure you can work with her?"

I know she's asking out of concern, but it feels like criticism. Tact isn't always her strong point.

"It's not like I have a choice," is all I say.

We drive over a root, and the van lurches.

"No," she agrees. "Not now you don't."

Emmy was a last resort. I tried to pull in every contact I have in the industry, put out advertisements and announcements on social media, but it was no good. There was some interest, of course, but everyone backed out when they found out how tight we are for money and how little experience we have. One degree in filmmaking and the odd bit of production assistant work doesn't carry much weight when that's the sum of your entire production team's CV. It's not easy to put together a crew for an as-yet unfunded passion project, especially when it's people with talent and experience you need.

So, in the end, one desperate, exhausted night, after my last hope—an old schoolfriend's ex who, despite his terrible attitude and long, greasy hair, had been involved in a few big productions for TV4—called to turn me down because he'd landed another job that could actually pay, I caved and threw Emmy's name into the mix.

I had never mentioned Emmy to Tone before that night. But, despite my persistent efforts to pretend Emmy Abrahamsson had never existed, she had always been there at the back of my mind. I had checked her Facebook page every now and then, googled her the odd late night as the shadows crept up on me.

Things had gone well for Emmy since college, better than most of our former classmates. Half of the people we studied with had left the film industry within a few years of graduating, but not Emmy.

Not that this came as any surprise. Emmy had always been smart.

When I mentioned her name to Tone, she raised one eyebrow and asked why I hadn't suggested her before. Truth is, she sounds like a godsend—if you don't know who she is, that is. Or how she can be.

I shift down a gear as the slope starts to flatten out, and let out a long sigh I'd hardly realized I was holding in. Then I turn my attention to the houses that have now started to appear in front of us.

They are built in the classic Swedish cottage style, with gabled roofs and small windows. The first building we pass is small, barely bigger than a shed, and it's set back slightly from the other buildings, which start about a hundred yards up the road. Its walls were once Falu red, but the paintwork is now peeling off the clapboard in big clumps. The windows gape, black and empty, shards of glass dangling out of the flaking white window frames. The setting sun hangs behind it in the west, and the matte, sloping roof casts shadows too long for us to be able to see inside.

I slow down almost subconsciously.

"Is that . . . ?" asks Tone.

"Birgitta Lidman's house," I say. "It has to be."

I would love to stop and take a look, but we should really try to get camp set up before nightfall. According to our schedule, we start exploring the village first thing tomorrow. We won't start shooting any footage until day two or three, but we're going to need every minute of the five days we've budgeted for.

There's a lot to prepare: we have to figure out where we're going to shoot, and the scenes that will best convey how we want the finished documentary to look.

The short trailer we've uploaded to the Kickstarter site is surprisingly slick, given we had hardly anything to work with. Tone managed to get a freelancer from her advertising days to do it for mate's rates. But, slick as it is, it's still only forty-five seconds of generic sweeping shots of nature, spliced with old documents and an ominous voice-over. A real trailer with dramatic images of Silvertjärn itself would do a lot to get our Kickstarter going.

We should have hired a drone, I think, as I scan the small houses and cottages we're approaching. What an opener that would have been: Silvertjärn as seen from above—a picture-perfect village bathed in golden spring light—before swooping in toward the houses to shatter the idyll, reveal the decay: the collapsing walls, the sinking houses, the perfect little porches left to rot and crumble. . . .

I thought it wasn't essential at this point, that we could save the drone for the real shoot, but now that we're here I'm regretting that decision. I mean, there might never be a real shoot. Truth is, everything hangs on this trip; we only have one shot. If we can't get this to work then I can hardly expect Max to pay for another bite of the cherry.

"There," says Tone.

At first I don't get what she's pointing at, but then I suddenly see it: a wider gap between two of the houses ahead of us. A road. It isn't paved, but I hadn't expected it to be, either.

"Must be the main road," I say.

"One of them, at least," Tone replies.

Driving on the road is much easier going, although it's overgrown and full of potholes. Neither of us says a word. We're both too engrossed by the village we're entering.

The houses stand like accusatory skeletons, windows glaringly empty. Most of them are simple row houses painted white, yellow, or red, like the mummified ghosts of the Swedish welfare state dream.

Heather and shrubs have taken over most visibly, but there's also the odd thin, gnarled pine shooting up through cracked front steps and split fences. I wonder how long it will take before the foliage swallows up the village completely—another sixty years? One hundred?

For a moment I'm struck by an image so powerful it feels more real than the decay around us: these same houses, only with fresh layers of bright paint and lush little gardens; kids playing on the road we're driving down, without having to worry about cars or even bikes; women hanging stiff, freshly scrubbed sheets out to dry outside their homes; and sweaty, unshaven men heading back from the mine at day's end, washing themselves at a tap in the garden, and going inside to their bare but homely kitchens, to take their seat at a rustic wooden table with dinner ready and waiting. They would have eaten dinner early in a village like this—no later than five.

The van lurches as we drive over a rock, and I shake off my reverie, trying to focus on what is as opposed to what once was.

We drive across what must once have been a crossroads, and Tone silently points. I curse and stop the van, but leave the engine running. By now the last of the sun has disappeared behind the trees. We don't have much time before nightfall.

I quickly wind down the window and wave at the others, who have stopped behind us.

"What is it?" Robert shouts out of his window. In my wing mirror I can see the blue Volvo behind him. I can't see Max through his windshield, but his car seems to have made it down the bank without any major issues.

"The bridge," I say.

The mining company's report had led me to believe that the western bridge was made of stone, but it must have been made of wood. It seems incomprehensible to me that only twenty years ago it could ever have been deemed safe; all that remains of it are rotting blackened stumps on either side of the river. The water has burrowed down deeper than I'd imagined, and it surges down to the lake in a way that belies its dark, languid appearance.

"Shit," I mutter.

"What do you want to do?" Tone asks. She, too, has wound down her window, to get some shots of the remains of the bridge.

"I don't know," I say.

"We could set up camp somewhere else?" she suggests. "Just for to-night. Then we can find a way across tomorrow."

I shake my head.

"No," I say, "I don't think so."

I feel a shiver run down my spine. Out of the corner of my eye I can feel the houses watching me through their dark eye sockets.

"No," I repeat. "Let's check if the other bridge is still standing. If not we'll have to figure something out."

Tone raises an eyebrow.

"Didn't the report say that one was unstable?"

"I know what the report said," I say, cutting her off. "But it was wrong about this one, so it could just as well have been wrong about that one, too. Or confused the two."

Tone purses her lips but says nothing.

"I'll tell the others," I say curtly, getting out of the van. The stench of exhaust from the running engine follows me as I stride toward them.

Robert's window is still open, and he's sitting there patiently, looking completely unflustered. His eyes meet mine but he doesn't say a word.

"We'll have to try the other bridge," I say. "A little further on."

He nods to show that he's heard.

Emmy's eyes meet mine. Pale, gray-green eyes, somehow expression-less and angry at the same time, surrounded by short, dark eyelashes.

I stand up straight again and wave at Max, then gesticulate toward the river. I hope he knows to follow us.

When I climb back into the driver's seat, Tone's biting at her thumb-nail. She's staring at the house to our left, a small villa that at one point must have had a certain picture-postcard charm. It's one of the larger houses; perhaps it belonged to one of the foremen at the mine.

"What is it?" I ask, hoping she isn't mad about the way I spoke to her before.

She gives a start, then slowly puts her hand in her lap.

"Huh?" she asks. "What?"

"You . . ." I look at the house. It's in better shape than the others around it. The front door is slightly ajar, hanging from one lonely, rusty hinge, but the walls are still standing, the roof is undamaged, and most of the façade is intact.

"Just looked like you were looking at something," I say.

Tone watches me for a few seconds, her eyes empty and slightly con-fused, before pulling one side of her mouth into a smile that doesn't quite convince.

"I was somewhere else," she says.

I pause, then put it out of my mind. I know there's nothing to worry about, not really. Tone can be hard to read, and this whole trip must be difficult for her. She doesn't have the same unadulterated enthusiasm for Silvertjärn that I do.

The van edges along the road, and the river disappears again behind row upon row of empty houses with gaping windows. By now the shad-ows have really started to fall, long streaks of black silk.

A break in the houses on my left gives me a sudden glimpse of a very welcome silhouette, and the relief runs coursing through me.

"Hah!" I exclaim, pointing at a diminutive stone bridge.

Tone whistles quietly.

"Nice," she says.

It's an arched bridge made of speckled granite, like something out of a fairy tale. There's moss growing on and between the stones, but it looks stable. Older than the rest of the village.

"Must be the original bridge, huh?" she says. "From before the state nationalized the mine and started expanding."

"Exactly," I agree, continuing toward the bridge. "They must have gotten it wrong in the report. *This* is the bridge that's supposed to be safe."

Tone raises her eyebrows.

"Are you sure?" she asks. "If it's that old, it might not be stable. I don't know how solid their constructions were back then—it was built for horses and farmers, not vans."

For a moment I hesitate. But then I shake my head and tentatively put my foot on the gas.

"It'll hold," I say, driving onto the bridge.

For a few seconds I expect it to disappear from beneath us, that lurching, falling sensation. But it never comes. The bridge holds, and in a matter of seconds we're on the other side.

Tone shakes her head, but I smile jubilantly. I knew it would hold. It wouldn't dare try anything else.

I've fought to get here. Tooth and nail, for every little break. Nothing is going to stop me now.

The road runs straight up from the bridge to the main square, and we slowly make our ascent over heather and cobblestones.

On one side of the square there's a building with a grizzled stone façade that claims to be the village hall, and on the other, an old, Villa Villekulla–type building that can only be the village school. Its doorframes gape, the doors hanging open.

The square is smaller than expected, cobbled and overgrown. Dry yellow blades of last summer's grass poke up from between the cracks in the stones, and a few of the stone slabs have been completely overturned by particularly ambitious pine shoots that appear to have then succumbed to winter.

We drive into the middle of the square and stop. I put on the hand brake, and the engine goes quiet.

"Well," Tone says as we both look up at the church. The last rays of light give in to the blue dusk, throwing even the church spire into shadow. I hear Emmy's van pull up beside us and stop, and Max's Volvo right behind.

"We've made it."

I try to make a mental note of everything around me: that last buzz of sunshine, the artificial smell of spruce in the car, the feel of the cold air against my cheeks as I open the car door.

This is Silvertjärn.

This is where it all begins.

NOW

It's colder than I thought it would be. What little warmth the pale April sun gave off doesn't stick around long after darkness, and the chill of winter is still set deep underground, beaming up through the cobblestones to fill the night with the scent of frozen soil.

We have a little campfire going, and there's something perversely cozy about the whole setup. At Emmy's request, Robert has managed to hot-wire a small speaker to the generator we brought with us, which is now playing tinny dad rock. I don't know if it was Emmy or Robert who chose the music, but it brings back old memories of cold student dorms and warm beer. Emmy's head heavy against my shoulder. Tipsy, light-hearted pre-party chatter.

The camping mat I'm sitting on isn't really thick enough, so I can feel the heather beneath my thighs, the bumps in every cobblestone. Tone is sitting to my left, poking quietly at her hastily heated-up lentil stew. To be safe, we've brought enough food to last us a week, but this is no culinary master class; both Emmy and Tone are vegetarians, so we're mainly sticking to lentils and beans.

Max is sitting to my right, slightly closer than Tone, his shoulder brushing against mine. He's thrown a thick, gray knitted sweater on over his shirt, which is slightly too long in the sleeves. He's taken charge of the cooking, and every so often he gives the stew we've shoved on the fire a self-important little stir. Typical Max. He wants everything to be done just right, and he never seems to trust anyone else to know what that could possibly mean. That's why he insisted on driving up in his own car instead of riding in one of the vans, and I suspect it's also why he insisted on coming with us on the shoot, despite having no filmmaking experience at all.

We first got to know each other after I graduated, when we fell in with the same loose circle of friends in those confused, midtwenties years. He was a computer geek with a taste for indie pop and a never-ending supply of puns. And extremely pedantic, even then.

On the other hand, it's served him well. That meticulous side of him has meant that, by twenty-nine, he's been able to amass a small fortune from Blockchain transactions. It's also meant that he could put enough money into *The Lost Village* for us to actually be able to float it.

I look at Max and smile, and he smiles right back at me, his boyish, slightly asymmetrical face lighting up in the flicker of the fire.

"What?" he asks, and I shake my head.

"I just can't believe we're finally here," I say. "I can't believe I'm in Silvertjärn."

Out of the corner of my eye I see Emmy trail off midwhisper to Robert and look our way, so I'm only half listening when Max replies:

"Yeah, it's pretty unreal."

Emmy's holding a hip flask, which she sips from while looking around her at the square. The stars above us are like a trail of shattered glass through the vaulted skies, the slim crescent moon is a sliver of an eye. The wind is no more than a whisper through the village, but it still manages to find its way in under my clothes. I shiver. Max makes to take off his warm sweater to offer it to me, but I shake my head before he gets the chance.

"I'm fine, it was just a shiver."

Emmy takes another sip from her flask and hands it to Robert, who sees me looking and raises his eyebrows to ask if I want some. I almost accept, but then feel Emmy's eyes on me and lose my nerve.

"No, I'm all right," I say, a spark of irritation in my belly. "I'm running this thing, so I guess I'd better not drink while we're here."

"Smart," says Emmy, and I'm sure I can make out a hint of mockery in her husky voice.

"I think so," I say, as neutrally as I can.

Emmy doesn't answer back. Instead she says:

"So there's only one square in the village, then?"

Before I can get a word in edgeways, she goes on:

"This must be where they—"

"Yes," I interrupt. "This is the main square. Where they found her. Birgitta."

It was already dark when we finally got here, so there was no time to really explore the square. Still, I couldn't resist doing a quick sweep of the cobblestones once Tone and I had put up our tent. To take in the scents; the silence; the soil. To picture it all.

I didn't find the pole, but I hadn't really expected to, either. They would have had to cut it down to remove the body, and in the unlikely event that they didn't, a rough-hewn wooden pole would never have stayed standing for sixty years.

But I did find a hole.

"Where's she buried?" Max asks, dragging me out of my thoughts with a jerk.

"I don't know," I say. "I've looked, but I couldn't find that information anywhere."

"There was almost nothing about her in the packs you gave us," says Emmy.

I shake my head.

"Not much was written about her," I say. "Most of the information we have comes from my grandmother's letters, and that's hard to fact-check. I've checked the local records, and I found a Birgitta Lidman who was born to Kristina Lidman in 1921. But that's it. No medical transcripts, no school records, nothing."

"No, I guess you wouldn't expect her to have gone to school," says Max. "Not if it was as bad as the letters suggest."

"From the letters it sounds like she had some kind of autism," comes Robert's deep voice.

"Maybe," I say. I've spent hours googling Birgitta's symptoms. "Or some sort of chromosome abnormality."

"You can't just diagnose people like that," says Tone. The firelight casts deep shadows under her eyebrows and nose, making her face look full of holes.

"No, of course not," I say. "We're not going to try to."

The music has stopped; the only sound to be heard is the crackle of the fire. Most of the logs are already embers, seemingly glowing from within. It's almost hypnotic.

"Did you try to find out what happened to the baby?" Emmy asks me.

"She was taken into care," I say, hoping I sound just as matter-of-fact as when I was talking about Birgitta. "She was probably sent to an orphanage or foster home. That sort of information isn't made public."

"Did they ever test her to find out who her parents were?" Emmy asks.

"How, exactly?" I ask, only thinly veiling my sarcasm. "The sixties weren't exactly CSI. It's not like they had DNA kits lying around." I shrug. "Besides, who would they have tested her against? Everyone had disappeared."

"Well, your grandmother didn't, did she?" Emmy retorts. "There must have been others like her. People who had relatives here. Next of kin."

I do my best not to roll my eyes, and confine myself to saying:

"It's not that simple."

Emmy looks up at the school's gaping window frames, ignoring my tone.

"Did they find her in one of the classrooms?"

"In the nurse's office," I say. "But she wasn't there, of course. Just the baby."

I can't resist looking up, too. Searchingly, though I know it's pointless. It's not like the windows are going to speak.

"Pity you couldn't find her," says Emmy, her eyes back on me. "Would have been fucking cool to put her in the documentary. Made it more personal, you know."

"You're assuming she'd want to be in it," I say. "She'd be almost sixty by now. She could be anywhere. Or dead, even."

"Yeah," she says. "I guess."

"Plus it's already personal," I say. "It's not like we don't already have a connection to the village. Grandma's whole family disappeared."

My throat is dry, and the words catch as I speak. It makes them sound a little desperate.

I'm about to go on—*that's why we're here, it's all thanks to her and what she told me about Silvertjärn*—when Robert interrupts.

"Who was it that wrote those letters to your grandmother, again?"

I'm about to answer when Emmy jumps in, her green eyes locked on me:

"Her grandmother's little sister. Aina."

November 13, 1958

Dearest Margareta,

How's life down in the big city? And the new apartment? How I wish I could see it! Perhaps now that you and Nils have moved, I might finally be able to pay you a visit? I can sleep on your sofa! You know what a shrimp I am, and sadly it doesn't look like I'll be getting any taller. I know what you're going to say when you read this—the same thing you always do: "Don't be silly, Aina, I was hardly taller than a boot at your age, and then I shot up!" Which might have been true if I were twelve, but I doubt it now that I'm sixteen. (I'm sure you think I haven't aged a day since you left!) I haven't grown a single inch since I last saw you, and seeing as that was almost fourteen months ago now, I think it's time for me to give up hope.

I miss you terribly, Margareta.

Couldn't you just . . .

I wish you could come and visit us a little more. It's been so boring here since the mine shut down. At first it was almost exciting, as though every day were a Sunday: there were so many people out and about during the day, and Father was always at home. He said that something was sure to come up. But now it all feels rather odd. So many people have gone. The Janssons on the corner left last week, and just yesterday your old classmate Vera told Mother that she and her family are also going to try their luck elsewhere.

Father's so quiet nowadays. And Mother's so busy she hardly seems to have time for us. She asks me to do everything instead. It's driving me mad! As though nothing I might have to do could possibly be important. And if I tell her I'm busy, she just gives me that stare—you know the one I mean—and tells me that nothing is more important than helping our neighbors and fellow citizens. I hate it when she says that!

Today she asked me to take food over to Gitta. When I asked why she couldn't do it herself, she said that she and the school nurse were going to pay a visit to some sick old lady to hold her hand. I told her that the nurse was probably capable of doing that by herself, and that I actually had my own things to do. She asked what they were, and when I said that Lena and I had made plans to go to the river, she said that both Lena and the river would still be there after I'd been to Gitta's. I didn't know how to explain to her that Lena might not wait for me if I wasn't there when I said I would be. Obviously we weren't only going down to look at the water; it's where Vera's brother Emil and his friends go to smoke, and Lena's taken a bit of a fancy to him. But I could never say that to Mother! So instead I said that I had promised Lena, and Mother's always telling us how important it is to keep our promises, but clearly that wasn't the right thing to say, either, because then Mother puffed herself up and asked if I thought my promise to Lena trumped the promise she had made to Birgitta's dying mother to always look after her daughter, and then I felt so rotten and small that I didn't dare say anything. But I was seething all the way out to Birgitta's hut, thinking of all of the things I should have said.

It would be better if you were here, Margareta. I even used to enjoy going out to Birgitta's when we did it together. I think she liked you more than she likes me. Remember that humming noise she'd make whenever she opened the door to find you there on the doorstep? She never does that with me.

I know you and Mother have said she won't get angry as long as I follow her rules, but I have to say, I don't like being there alone. As soon as I see her hut, my heart starts to patter like a bird's, and my mouth goes dry. Mother says the only reason Birgitta got so angry at me that time is because I opened the door and stepped in without knocking—Birgitta's more afraid of me than I am of her, she says. But Birgitta's tall as a man and built like a bear! It took weeks for my scratch marks to heal that time. Part of me thought I'd be stuck with them forever.

Oh, now I'm sounding like I don't feel sorry for Birgitta, and you know that I do! I'm happy to report that she was looking well today. She had trailed some mud inside from her walk in the forest, and I wondered if I should clean it up, but I was afraid of getting her back up. Besides, Mother hadn't told me to clean—she probably thinks I'm too careless and would rather do it herself. Anyway, that's besides the point: Birgitta had some color in her cheeks, and she really devoured her chicken and gingerbread. She even did those funny hand movements that you say mean she's happy.

It's just . . . oh, Margareta, it's not just the scratch marks. I was afraid of Gitta even before then. She's just so big, and she moves so strangely, and the way her hair dangles down over her face makes her look like a forest troll from those fairy tales Grandmother used *to tell us. Perhaps that's a terrible thing to say, but it's the truth. She even smells of the forest. I've told Mother we should cut her hair and get her some new clothes—anything but those threadbare rags she goes around in every day. Perhaps then the other villagers wouldn't find her so strange. And then she could live in a real house, and we wouldn't have to look after her all the time.*

But Mother says it's not as simple as that. Sometimes I think she likes having Birgitta to take care of. It's not like Birgitta can ever answer back or get on Mother's nerves like I do, seeing as she can't talk.

Oh well. It did go okay today, and Lena wasn't too angry with me when I eventually got home. She even let me borrow some lipstick before we went to the river. I felt very stylish. Perhaps I can buy one just like it when I come down to visit you and Nils? What do you think?

Write soon!

Your sister, Aina

NOW

My sleeping bag rustles as I twist and roll over onto my other side. The tent is big and fairly spacious, but it's hardly a hotel room: it's cold and basic, and smells of a mix of plastic and something slightly nauseating that I can't put my finger on.

Still, it's better than sleeping on the back seat of a Volvo, like Max. It was his choice, but I'm sure he's going to spend our entire trip with a stiff neck and the makings of a bad back. Emmy and Robert didn't bring a tent, either, but Emmy said they're used to sleeping in vans. Maybe it is the done thing, but I'm glad I get to pass. Something about cargo compartments makes me claustrophobic. Even if we fixed the equipment securely in place, I wouldn't be able to shake the feeling that it was all going to collapse on us as we slept.

The sleeping bags we have are good, at least, so well insulated that the cold air actually feels nice against my cheeks. I normally like to sleep in a cold room under a thick duvet—even in winter I leave the windows open for a breeze—but right now I can't catch a wink, despite my exhaustion. My excitement sits like a vibration under my skin, keeping me awake.

"Can't sleep?" asks Tone, her voice cutting through the darkness.

I roll back onto my other side to face her, even though I'd need the night vision of a cat to make out anything but shadow.

"Did I wake you up?" I ask.

"No," comes her muted reply. "You know me."

Tone has sleep problems. It was one of the first things I ever learned about her, that first time we met, in an anonymous coffee chain by Odenplan just over two years ago. I'd stood waiting outside, unsure if she would show up and not even clear about what to look out for—her Facebook profile picture was four years old at the time and blurry, too (as far as I know, it still hasn't changed).

"It's like I can't wind down," I say. "My brain won't switch off."

"Maybe you should ask Emmy for some of her whisky," she says dryly. "That might help."

I roll my eyes, though I know she can't see me. "Who hits the bottle as soon as they arrive on a job?"

"From what you've told me about her, it doesn't sound like that should come as a surprise."

I hear a rustle as she changes position.

"No, I guess not."

I think for a moment.

"You don't have anything, do you?" I ask. "No sleeping pills or anything?"

"No," Tone replies, "I can't take them. Given . . . well, you know."

"Oh," I say. "No, of course. I'm an idiot. Sorry."

"It's OK," she says, sounding mildly amused. Her words seem to swell in the small space, though they're hardly more than a whisper. "I don't expect you to keep track of which pills I can and can't take."

"No, but still. I should know."

We go quiet. I prop myself up to rearrange the thick, folded-up sweater I'm using as a pillow, then lie back down to no noticeable difference.

"Does she know?" Tone asks out of the blue, all trace of laughter gone from her voice.

"Who? Emmy?" I ask.

She doesn't reply.

"I haven't told her anything," I say, as the silence starts to expand. "About anything. All she knows is what's in the information pack."

"Didn't sound like it," says Tone. "When she was talking about DNA-testing the baby, trying to find her . . ." She trails off, her voice taut as a violin string.

"I haven't told her anything," I repeat. "You asked me not to say anything, so I haven't." When she doesn't reply, I go on:

"Max knows, but he did from the start. And he's promised not to say anything."

"How much?" Tone asks, an unexpected edge to her voice.

"What do you mean? He knows your mom's the Silvertjärn baby—I told him I'd found you before we even met. He asked if you or your mom would like to be involved, and I said I didn't know but that I didn't think so."

"Mom would never do it," says Tone, as she has done so many times.

"I know," I say. "I never asked."

I've thought about it, of course. Wanted to. But I never have asked. Tone's made it clear that her mom has no interest in raking up that part of her past. She doesn't want to be the Silvertjärn baby, the mystery's sole survivor, the newborn found crying in the abandoned schoolhouse less than thirty yards from where we're lying right now.

It was Tone's mother I found first. What I told the others wasn't technically a lie: all the information on what happened to the Silvertjärn baby really is classified, impossible to access. I'm not even sure if the documents still exist, and if they do, they're probably buried deep in some archive.

But Grandma's letters aren't.

I didn't put all of Grandma's letters in the packs I gave to the others. I've kept a few to myself. Among them her correspondence with Albin Jansson.

Jansson was one of the policemen investigating Birgitta Lidman's murder—and, by extension, the Silvertjärn case. He and Grandma must have met at some point during the investigation, and for a while I wondered if there might have been something more between them—a secret affair, perhaps—but that's probably wishful thinking on my part.

I found six of his letters among her old papers, all of which are professional and to the point. It seems as though Jansson mostly just felt sorry for Grandma and wanted to keep her informed of their progress on the investigation.

And that happened to include the baby.

Grandma must have asked after her, or else Jansson just assumed she would want to know what happened to her, because he mentions her a lot in his letters: that she seemed hale and hearty, and that several hundred families across the country had offered to take her in, even if his personal opinion was that most of them were out after fame. In his fifth letter, he writes that they had found a family who had agreed to keep her identity a secret and "*. . . raise her as one of their own.*"

He goes on to give the family's name: "*. . . a family by the name of Grimelund . . .*"

And the name they had given the child:

"*You will be pleased to learn that they have named the girl Hélène.*"

Had their surname been Andersson I might never have found Tone. But Hélène Grimelund was unusual enough for me to track down.

It took me sending an unseemly number of emails to Hélène to realize that she was never going to reply. By that point I was close to giving up. My grief over Grandma had started to catch up with me, and everything felt like a dead end. I was having to do temp work to keep myself afloat after my speculative résumés hadn't had any takers, and I could hardly face social media anymore. It seemed as though all of my old classmates were racing up the career ladder two steps at a time, winning prizes for their short films and getting jobs in Paris or London, while there I was sitting my days out behind a reception desk, my fantasy project hardly more than a fever dream.

But then, on yet another late night spent scrolling hopelessly through Facebook, I noticed a photo on Hélène's timeline. It was right down near the bottom of her page, one that she hadn't posted—someone else had tagged her in it. It showed a gray-haired woman with a severe ponytail and a stiff, vacant smile, her arm around a girl in her late teens.

"Hélène and her beautiful daughter brighten up my birthday dinner! <3" read the caption.

The girl was tagged as Tone Grimelund.

Two years on, I still haven't met Tone's mother. I don't know how much Tone has told her about this project, and I haven't asked, either. From what little Tone has said and what I've read into Hélène's radio silence, my guess is she isn't too keen on the idea of digging up the Silvert-järn story.

My friendship with Tone is one of my life's more unusual relationships. For the longest time Tone didn't want anything to do with the project, either, beyond telling me what little she knew. But even from that very first day, when we made awkward small talk over cheap coffee, I could detect a reluctant curiosity there.

Would she have let herself act on it if it hadn't been for what happened?

That I don't know.

THEN

When Elsa nears the church doors, she is surprised to find them wide open. It's a cold day even for late November, less than thirty degrees, and over the course of the day only the odd isolated snowflake has sailed down from the bright sky. From midday onward the sun had started to break through the clouds, and as she walked to Agneta's house Elsa could even start to see signs of life on the streets. Elisabet Nyman had been out on an afternoon walk with her little girl, looking healthier than she had in a long time. After the birth, Elisabet had been bedbound for so long that Elsa had raised the matter with Elisabet's mother and the school nurse, Ingrid. Together they had agreed to help her out with the little one.

When Elsa had seen Elisabet earlier today she had looked genuinely happy, with rosy cheeks and a lovely winter hat. The baby was wearing a homemade crocheted hat, cooing through a toothless grin. Elisabet had said that they still didn't have a name for her, but they ought to get on with it: the girl is almost three months old, and children can't go on without a name forever. Elsa had offered to talk to Pastor Einar about a christening for the little one, since she would be passing by the church anyway.

It's never easy, the first child, especially when you're as young as Elisabet. Only eighteen years old, and four months along when she and Albert got married. Barely older than Elsa's Aina, and already a mother herself. It's no wonder she became a little melancholic when the child was born, especially with Albert being unable to find any work. As they have no ties to Silvertjärn they really ought to move, much as the thought pains Elsa. What will happen to Silvertjärn when all the young people just up and leave?

It has already started to happen. Just weeks ago the Engelssons moved up north to Kiruna in search of work. They didn't even wait to sell the house, so desperate were they to leave. It's just standing there in the middle of the village, its windows dark and its doors shut, like a bad omen.

Elsa briskly climbs the church steps, adjusting her hat with her free hand as she goes. If his drinking is so bad that Einar can't remember to close the church doors, then it's high time they took action. It's true he's always enjoyed a tipple—including one memorable evening when they were young, when he got it into his head to strip off and run into the lake—but he has always kept it somewhat under control. He's never had a wife nor children, so all he has is the church to tend to, but if he can't do that anymore . . .

"Einar?" Elsa calls through the open doors. "It's me, Elsa."

It's dark inside. The pews are cast in long shadows, and the carved Jesus above the altar looks unusually severe on his cross. Despite the gloom, she can make out movements up near the altar. She tries to discreetly kick the dirt off her shoes before stepping inside.

"Einar?" she calls again, but it doesn't look like Einar. He lacks Einar's shuffling gait and bulky figure.

The man now walking down the aisle toward her is neatly dressed in a casual shirt and well-ironed trousers. He's considerably younger than Einar—can scarce be more than thirty—with short blond hair that curls slightly over his forehead. A shy smile plays on his face.

"Fru Kullman?" he asks, taking Elsa's hand. His grip is steady, cool, and slightly dry, and as she shakes his hand Elsa tries to place him, but she has never seen his face before.

"I don't believe we've met," she says.

"Oh, I do beg your pardon," he replies, shaking his head. "But you are Elsa, are you not? Elsa Kullman?"

Elsa nods, extricating her hand from his.

"How . . . ?"

"Einar has told me so much about you," he says with another smile, wider this time.

"I'm pleased to hear that," says Elsa, a certain sharpness to her voice. "But you still haven't introduced yourself."

He blushes slightly, seemingly embarrassed; this says something good about his upbringing, at least.

"Oh, I do beg your pardon," he says. "Sometimes in my excitement I quite forget my manners. Mattias is my name. I'm the new pastor."

Elsa frowns.

"The new pastor?"

He nods.

"I shall be helping Einar. Times are tough, and Einar—well, when Einar . . ."

He stammers slightly and trails off, and Elsa shakes her head.

"I know about Einar," she says, to put him at ease. He seems to relax slightly.

"How long have you been in our village, Pastor?" she asks. He makes as though to reply but then cuts himself off, gesticulating at the doors.

"Won't you come in?" he asks. "I wouldn't want you to catch pneumonia for me having kept you here in this draught."

Elsa follows him inside the church. It looks as though he's been cleaning the altar, a task which, she admits, has been long overdue.

"Would you care for something to drink, Fru Kullman?" he asks. She starts to shake her head but then stops; she is actually rather cold.

"I was just about to put on a fresh pot of coffee," he says, as though reading her mind. She smiles.

"A cup of coffee would go down well," she admits.

Elsa has been inside Einar's study in the chapel many times, but as she steps inside now it looks different. It's clean and tidy, with everything in its rightful place, and the subtle yet unmistakable scent of schnapps that usually hangs in the air is gone.

The young pastor puts a pot of coffee on the stovetop and pulls out a chair for her. She sits down on the familiar, all-too-stingily stuffed seat and waits while he putters around the room, arranging papers and adjusting the curtains. She finds it rather endearing, the way he attends to the room with an almost matronly care.

"If you don't mind me asking, is this your first placement?" Elsa asks, as the young man pours coffee into Einar's small, chipped cups.

He smiles and places a cup before her.

"Of course I don't mind, Fru Kullman, there's no need for such formality with me," he says, before hastily adding, "unless, of course, you prefer it that way."

"In that case, you can call me Elsa," she says, then smiles. He can't be more than ten or twelve years her junior, but this young pastor inspires something almost maternal in her.

"Where's Einar?" she asks, lifting the coffee cup to her lips. It's good—strong and piping hot. Better than what Einar normally makes.

"He's asleep in the parsonage," says the young pastor. "I think— hmm . . . sadly I think he had a rather heavy night last night."

"Perhaps having you here to help him will do him good," she says.

"I hope to lighten his load wherever I can," says the pastor. His eyes are gray, Elsa now sees, with dark rings around his irises. Perhaps it's those eyes that make him seem so charming. They're big and round like a child's, and they make him look younger than he surely must be.

"What was it you wanted to see Einar about?" the pastor asks. "Perhaps it's something I might be able to assist you with?"

Yes, perhaps you can, she thinks.

Einar had used to help Elsa with any tasks that needed seeing to in the village; he would talk sense into men who didn't treat their wives properly, offer a shoulder to cry on to those who were bereaved and needed to talk. Einar had never been particularly sharp, it was true, but his heart was good and his faith sincere. In recent years, however, his drinking had worsened. Elsa had had to bear a greater share of the load.

"One of the older women in the village, Agneta Lindberg, is very unwell," Elsa begins. "I fear she may not be long of this earth."

He looks at her intently.

"How old is she?" he asks.

"Sixty-seven," she says. "She has cancer. Of the stomach. She's afraid, and I think she ought to speak to someone who can allay her fears. She isn't afraid of death; she's afraid of . . . well . . ."

He nods slowly. His big, light-gray eyes don't leave hers, and she feels something within her lift.

She can trust him. He can help her.

"She's afraid of what comes next," he says, finishing her sentence. "And you would like someone to hold her hand and soothe her fears. Tell her about the kingdom that awaits her after death, and God the Father who will receive her."

"Yes, exactly," says Elsa. "Just to calm her. Reassure her."

He gives a faint smile.

"If you feel it would be appropriate," he says, "then I would be most happy to do that in Einar's place."

Elsa returns his smile.

"I think that might be good," she says.

NOW

A loud scream yanks me out of my sleep.

Being woken by a scream is like the feeling of crushing glass with your bare hands: instantaneous, distinct, painful. My pulse starts racing and, still half asleep, I fumble with my sleeping bag, trying to make anything out in the darkness.

It's only once I've scrambled out of the tent that I realize I was the only one inside it.

The night air is still, the silence compact; for a few seconds the only sound I can hear is the frenzied pounding of my own heart. But then: the unmistakable sound of van doors opening.

By now my eyes have adjusted well enough to the weak moonlight to pick out Emmy as she stumbles out of the back of the van. Her hair is dangling messily around her shoulders, and she isn't wearing any pants—just a pair of underwear and the big, white T-shirt she had on yesterday. The cobblestones must feel just as cold to her bare feet as they do to mine. The dampness of the dewy moss between the stones is already working its way up between my toes.

"Did you hear it, too?" I ask her as I see Robert jump out of the van behind her. Emmy doesn't look at him. She has already marched off toward the front of the van and the school.

"Emmy?" I say, as Robert starts running after her.

I don't feel I have any choice but to do the same.

As I round the van, I see that Emmy has stopped after just a few steps. She's panting—shallow, scratchy breaths that echo my own—and her eyes are darting around the empty square. Bright and glossy in the cold light of the crescent moon, they flit from the blue Volvo where Max is sleeping to the school building, and then on to the greenery shooting up between the cobblestones.

Robert stops behind her and gently places his hand on her shoulder. Hesitantly, as though stroking a frightened dog. When he touches her, she doesn't recoil.

"Emmy, what is it?"

It's only then that it clicks.

"Was it you who screamed?" I ask.

I hadn't recognized the scream as Emmy's; every screaming voice sounds the same. But now, as she turns around to face us, I realize it must have been her.

"I saw someone," she says, and I can't tell if she's very pale, or if all of us look like monochrome ghosts out here in the square.

"There was someone there," she says, turning to look back at the school.

"Where?" Robert asks. "In the school?"

Emmy shakes her head, puts her hand on the base of Robert's spine, and steps toward him, seemingly subconsciously.

"No," she says. "Here in the square. In front of our van."

Her voice is thin and scratchy. At first I think it's from irritation or sarcasm, but then it dawns on me that it's fear.

She's afraid.

"What exactly did you see?" I ask, suddenly very conscious of all the dark windows staring down at us, of all the dark alleys winding out of the square like threads in a cobweb. So many empty spaces. So many walls to hide behind.

Stop, I tell myself. *There's no one here.*

Emmy looks at me.

"I woke up," she says. "I heard something, so I got up to see what it was. There was someone standing in front of the van, looking at me." She swallows.

"Did you see who it was?" asks Robert.

"No," says Emmy. "It was too dark. It was just a silhouette, but it was definitely a person. I could see their eyes. They were looking straight at me." She swallows again.

"Whoever it was, they *saw* me."

I shake my head, my skin crawling.

"It might not have been anyone," I say. "It sounds a little like sleep paralysis. People often see hazy dark figures watching them when they're just waking up and the brain—"

"I *know* what a fucking sleep paralysis is, Alice," Emmy hisses, interrupting me. "This wasn't it. I was standing up. I was awake. I saw them."

I open my mouth to reply, but then freeze. There, on the other side of the square. By the corner of the school. There's someone standing there.

A slim, dark figure. Unmistakably human.

I try to say something—anything—frenetically tell myself:

There's no one here. There's no one here. There's no one here.

But the figure doesn't disappear when I blink.

It starts walking toward us. I'm the only one who's seen it—both Emmy and Robert are facing me. And in that moment, I make an unexpected and unwelcome discovery about myself. I've always seen myself as the sort of person who would be proactive in a crisis—the one to run, scream, fight—but now, when it actually comes down to it, I can't even get a word out to warn the others.

But then the figure steps into the moonlight, and its features fall into place.

My knees turn to jelly, and I can't help laughing out of pure relief.

"What the fu—" Emmy begins, her face contorted in a mix of outrage and confusion, but I point over her shoulder.

"Tone!" I call out, just to make sure.

She replies:

"Oh. Hey."

She's bundled up in her jacket, her long, bare legs sticking out of a pair of rubber boots. When she stops a few feet away from us, I can make out the bleary look in her eyes, the shock on her face.

Tone looks at Emmy, and then me, and says:

"This some sort of midnight conference?"

I shake my head.

"I think you gave Emmy a fright," I say. "Did you go to pee?"

"Yup," Tone says. "But what do you mean?"

"She must have seen you walking across the square," I say. "She thought she saw someone staring at the van."

Emmy still hasn't said a thing. She studies Tone with narrowed eyes.

"Oh," says Tone. "Sorry. Didn't mean to wake you."

"Did you stop in front of the van?" Emmy asks, her voice hollow.

"No," says Tone. "Or—I don't know. I hadn't quite woken up. I might have been looking around to see where to go."

"You were right, Emmy," I say with a shrug. "It wasn't sleep paralysis. But it was no ghost, either."

I yawn into the back of my hand. The combination of the rude awakening, fear, and then relief has brought a new wave of tiredness rolling over me.

"I never said it was a ghost," Emmy says without looking at me, a certain roughness to her voice.

"What I saw was standing still," she continues, now looking at Robert. "It was staring straight at the van. At me."

My exhaustion makes me snap.

"Oh, come on," I say. "You'd just woken up, you saw Tone, freaked out, thought you were seeing some mystical being, and screamed. It's not so hard to explain. Now let's go get some sleep—we have a long day tomorrow."

Emmy's face is a mask of jagged shadows. I don't have the energy to hang around and let this turn into an argument.

When I'm almost back at the tent I throw a glance over my shoulder at the vans. Emmy and Robert are still standing there, shadows glinting in the night. Robert has put his arm around Emmy's shoulders, and it looks as though Emmy is saying something to him, but she's whispering so quietly that I can't hear. Both of them are looking up at the school.

I turn and climb back into the tent.

WEDNESDAY

NOW

I'm the first to wake up, although I can't have had more than a couple of hours' sleep. I've always been an early riser. It's worse when I'm hungover—then I can't even sleep past dawn. I just lie there with my eyes wide open, my mouth dry, and my heart pounding, until I eventually give up and drag myself out into the kitchen, ready for a long and restless day.

But not today. No: today I have butterflies in my stomach and a tingle in my palms and feet, despite the events of last night.

Today we explore.

I crawl out of my sleeping bag as quietly as I can, pull on the thick sweater I'm using as a pillow, and unzip the tent door. The air out here is colder than the heavy, sleep-stale air warmed by our dozing bodies in the tent; out here it's crisp and cool, like frosted glass.

I inhale deeply, drinking it in.

The sun has just crept up over the horizon, and the blush of dawn gives the village a pinky tint. In the light of this new day the village looks magical—playful and ethereal. Enough to make me wish I could use the cameras. It would have been nice to explore the alleyways by myself in this silence, to capture the village as I see it now, this first morning. Dormant and untouched. It's like a living photograph, a relic of a bygone age.

The campfire is by now nothing but ash and charcoal on the cobble-stones. I cast my gaze up at the derelict school façade, then on to the silhouette of the church as it soars above the roofs, its outline crisp and clean against the distant forest.

I feel a lump in my throat.

I can hear my grandmother's voice, like an echo in my ears.

"The last time I saw my sister, Aina, she was only seventeen."

When I was little, I used to think her tales of Silvertjärn were just that: stories like any other. It wasn't until much later that I realized not only were they real, they were the ruins on which she had built her entire life. She was a strong woman, my grandmother, with steady hands and broad shoulders, and eyes that would latch onto whoever she was talking to, no matter who that was. As though she wanted to make sure she always got the whole truth. Nothing made Grandma as furious as lies, however minor or unintentional they might have appeared.

"We're going to find out, Grandma," I say quietly to myself. "You and me."

She always looked you straight in the eye. Except, that is, for when she talked about Silvertjärn. Then she would look away, her eyes fixed on the horizon.

I was eighteen when I moved to Stockholm to train as a nurse. My sister, Aina, was twelve. At that point the Silvertjärn mine was thriving.

My family still lived in the same house I grew up in. It was a little yellow house by the river, just a few streets down from the church. All of the houses on that street were yellow, but ours was the only one with a green door. As a girl I was always so proud of that green door. It made me feel special.

I would go back and visit whenever I'd saved up enough for the train tickets. In those days people didn't fly around willy-nilly like they do now; there were two trains to Silvertjärn a week, and if the timings weren't convenient then you would just have to make do. The tickets weren't cheap, either.

She had beautiful eyes, my grandma. Light-gray and mottled, like polished granite. Until the cataracts came creeping over her corneas like misty white rot, taking her sight just as the dementia would take her mind.

"What did you say?" a voice behind me asks. I jump and whip around.

It's Max. He's wearing his retro knitted cardigan again, one hand massaging his neck.

"God, you scared me," I say. He smirks.

"Did you think it was the ghosts of Silvertjärn coming to chase us away?"

"Haha," I say, raising an eyebrow. "Very funny."

"This place *is* kinda spooky, though," he says, looking around as he steps toward me. He stops next to me and looks up at the school. "You can see why people think it's haunted."

"Apparently," I agree, shoving my freezing hands into the front pouch of my sweater. "Emmy got woken up when Tone went to pee in the night. She saw her through the windshield and thought it was an evil spirit or something. I'm surprised you didn't hear anything."

"Woah, shit," says Max, looking surprised. "No, I slept like a log."

I roll my eyes.

"Typical."

Max grins and then looks around at the fallen-in roofs.

"Weird no one's done this before," he says. "I mean, the story has it all, and you couldn't ask for a better setting. Don't you ever wonder why none of those ghost-hunter programs that were so popular a few years ago did a special out here?"

"Too far," I say. "There are plenty of supposedly haunted manors around Stockholm and Malmö."

"I guess," says Max.

Seeing me huddle up slightly, he puts his arms around me and gives me a rub to warm me up.

"Shall I try and rustle up some breakfast for us?" he asks. "Not meaning to boast, but my scout group voted me best campfire chef four years running."

I snigger, gently twisting out of his arms.

"Bullshit. Like you were ever a Boy Scout."

He grins.

"Maybe not," he says, "but I can probably put something together. I'm not just here to be your dead weight of a backer—I can help out, too."

"As camp chef?" I ask, and he gives a cheeky grin.

"Chef, eye candy, mother's dream," he says. "Whatever you need."

As Max gets a flickering little fire going and toasts us some bread, the others emerge one by one. Emmy's in a new T-shirt that's almost as shabby as yesterday's, under the same jacket Robert was wearing. I assume they're a couple.

I'm expecting a nod, some sort of lighthearted reference to last night to clear the air, but nothing comes. Emmy hardly even looks at me. I feel a twinge of disappointment, but then again this is nothing new. She was always pretty sluggish after those wild, late-night dorm parties. She would lie in late, while I would be there cleaning, doing the laundry, and making huge breakfasts that she would hardly touch, just to keep my restlessness at bay.

But at the time it never bothered me. We were in tune. In those days even our breathing seemed to find a shared rhythm.

When the memories come, I want to resist them. I've been trying my best to keep Emmy out of my thoughts for seven years now, and I've gotten pretty good at it, but it's harder to do that with her actually here.

Once we've eaten, and drank our thick, black instant coffee served in cheap white polystyrene cups, I clear my throat to get everyone's attention. By now the sun has crept up into the sky, and dawn has turned into morning. I do my best to calm my nerves, and sit up a little straighter on my camping mat.

"Are we all nice and full?" I ask, then immediately regret it; I sound like a perky kindergarten teacher. Emmy's raised eyebrow and the others' puzzled looks don't help, but Max nods and smiles, at least.

"I was thinking we could run through the schedule. Then we can assign tasks and get going. Sound OK?"

Emmy shrugs.

"Fine," she says.

"OK," I say, looking down at my papers.

The schedule I've drawn up looks so amateurish now that I see it again. Times New Roman, size 12, cheap A4 paper. I should probably have had it laminated.

I'll have to just try and own it.

"Today and tomorrow are all about trying to get a feel for this place. In your packs you'll find a list of eight key locations: the school, the ironworks, the church, the train station, Elsa and Aina's house, Birgitta's house, the parsonage, and the lake. These are the locations that we feel are the most relevant to the investigation, and the most important to scout. We'll take the lake on the final day, in case we want to give it a bit more time. As far as we know, no one has explored it before, so we've brought some diving equipment with us."

Robert sticks up his hand, and I lose my train of thought.

"Uh, yes?"

He puts his hand down and scratches his neck self-consciously. It makes me forgive him the interruption. Despite being Emmy's friend—boyfriend, fuck-buddy, partner, whatever—he comes across as a pretty nice guy; shy and polite, in an almost old-school way.

"How have you chosen which locations are relevant?" he asks.

I throw a quick glance at Tone, who looks unlikely to jump in and help me out any time soon.

"These are the places where we think we might be able to find something—any new information, leads as to what might have happened," I say.

Emmy raises her eyebrows.

"Actually, I've been wanting to ask you about that," she says. "In the pitch you say we're going to investigate what really happened to the people of Silvertjärn, but what are the chances of us actually finding anything? It feels pretty risky to promise something like that. I mean, the police investigated the disappearance, right? Seems unlikely we'll just stumble over evidence they didn't find. This isn't *Midsomer Murders*—it's not like we're about to suddenly discover Pastor Mattias's secret diary or something."

I can feel my cheeks burning, but it's because she's right—both about the situation, and about the secret hopes I've entertained, which she's now describing in her deliberate, mocking tone. Of course I'm hoping for a breakthrough, to find something no one knew about, to crack the Silvertjärn mystery. And of course I know that it's unlikely to the point of impossible. But it doesn't mean a girl can't dream.

"We aren't promising anything," I snap. "And the police investigation mainly focused on the forests. It's quite possible that they missed something."

Emmy says nothing, just looks me in the eye without blinking.

"In any case, the places we've selected are also the most relevant thematically," I round off, trying to sound like I haven't just lost my temper. "I think we should focus on the school, the ironworks, and the train station today. You should all have copies of the maps from the mining company report in your packs. I've marked the locations on each map. There are a couple we aren't completely sure about—the parsonage and my great-grandmother's house are educated guesses, based on information from the letters and my grandmother's descriptions, so we'll do them last."

I've barely finished my sentence when Emmy jumps in again. Her pack is lying open in her lap, and she speaks without looking at me. Her eyes are on the maps, and there's a frown on her face.

"Why isn't the mine on the list?" she asks. "Or, if it is, it isn't marked on the maps. We should try to get some shots in there. It should be pretty atmospheric, especially if we want to give some context as to how the community changed after it shut."

"It's not safe," I say. "The ground's too unstable, especially near the shaft. Apparently the ores in this area were very close to the surface, so the mine was shallow, and no one's maintained the passages since. There's a serious risk of collapse. That's partly why the surveyors who came here in the nineties didn't recommend reopening the mine."

I can't help adding:

"It's all in the report."

Emmy flicks through her pack. I swallow and continue:

"Apparently that's also why there's no signal out here, either."

Emmy looks up.

"Because the ground's been excavated?" she asks, her eyebrows raised.

"No," I say, "because the ores are so close to the surface. Something about . . . magnetic fields."

"Ah," Emmy scoffs, smirking. "Magnetic fields. Very scientific. Of course."

"Yes," I say.

I feel thrown, but I give my head a quick shake and look back down at my schedule.

"Yes," I repeat. "So let's see . . ."

Tone rescues me.

"Take a lot of pictures. We have three really nice system cameras to share."

Robert raises his hand again.

"Yes?" I ask.

"It would be good if we could get as many pictures as possible of the places we want to film in," he says cautiously. "Just so I can see how the light is and all that, what time of day would be best for filming where. I don't know if you have a more detailed schedule for the shoot, but if not then that could be good to have."

"He's right," I say to the others. "Tone, too. Take a lot of pictures. Both artistic, and anything that can help us with the logistics."

"Are we going to start shooting straightaway, or do you want to wait and have a day just for scouting?" Emmy asks. "And could we get a preliminary script and long-term production plan, too? They aren't in the packs."

I look at Tone. Our preliminary script and production plan are both very sketchy, essentially just rambling thoughts in a Word document—definitely nothing I have any desire to show Emmy. But Tone's eyes give nothing away: either she doesn't see my concern, or she's putting up a front so as not to show the others.

I look back at Emmy and say:

"We . . . don't have everything here with us. But you're more than welcome to take a look at what we do have."

"Great," says Emmy.

I tuck my hair behind my ear. Despite having washed it just before we left, it already feels flat and greasy.

"We'll pair up," I say. "I don't want anyone going into any buildings alone. They've been abandoned for almost sixty years, which means they could be extremely unstable. Be really careful with steps and basements; avoid them if you have even the slightest concern." I continue: "We have some basic safety equipment for everyone. The protective masks aren't particularly attractive, but it's important to wear them when you go inside any buildings. There's a pretty high chance there'll be asbestos in some of the houses, especially those built when the mine expanded during the war. We don't know what there might be in terms of mold and all that, either, so wear the masks, even if they're uncomfortable." I pause and think for a moment, but I'm pretty sure I've covered everything. I don't really know how wind up, so I say: "And, last but not least, have fun."

As soon as the words leave my mouth I realize how wrong they sound.

"How will we communicate with each other?" Emmy asks. "My phone's a brick, and I haven't had signal since we left the highway."

"Oh! Yes," I say. "Walkie-talkies. We have some walkie-talkies."

"How come they work when the phones are dead?" Emmy asks.

I throw a look Tone's way, and she gives a faint smile.

"Well, we don't actually know that they work here," she says. "But the guy we spoke to said they should. I didn't completely understand his explanation, but with them the connection is more local, so apparently the signal doesn't cut out in the same way."

"He said we can expect some interference, but they should work," I say. "And if all goes according to plan then we won't even need them," I add. "They're like the masks—we have them just in case."

Emmy nods.

"OK," she says. "Great. So can we choose our own partners?"

"There aren't so many to choose from," Tone remarks dryly. "Alice and I thought we'd start with the school. It'd be good if the other pair could take the ironworks and then work their way back here."

I turn to Max.

"Do you mind staying here with the vans and equipment?" I ask. "It would be good if someone could do that every day, I think. Just in case. We can take it in turns."

Max salutes.

"Your wish is my command," he says. "You're the producer."

I smile gratefully.

I look at the others, feel my smile grow, and let that tingling feeling spread across my whole body.

"OK," I say. "Then let's get our equipment on and get going."

NOW

I wish we had recordings of Silvertjärn as it looked in its heyday, before the mine shut. All we have are a few dim, shaky images in black-and-white and sepia. I plan to post them all on Instagram later, and to use them in any pitches to possible sponsors and grant applications, but it'll be hard to incorporate them into the documentary itself in a slick way. We'll have to hope that the material we get on this trip is strong enough to speak for itself. It should be.

The school's rough plasterwork has acquired a sickly, grimy, grayish hue, and the window frames are chipped and splintered, most of them gaping empty. It's hot and stuffy under my respirator mask, and the band chafes over my ears. I feel claustrophobic wearing it, but when we stop at the top of the crumbling front steps into the school I'm glad I have it.

Light floods into the hallway through the giant windows, revealing whirling specks of dust. Even through the air filter I can tell it smells of mold and old paper in here. We step cautiously into the little lobby, which, with its cream walls and sturdy wooden floor, is anonymous enough to belong to any Swedish institution. Were it not for the clumps of peeling paint and the bulging, warped floorboards, this could just as well be a dentist's waiting room.

I hear a jittery laugh and turn toward Tone. She's looking straight up at the imposing staircase leading up to the second floor.

"What are you laughing at?" I ask.

"Huh?" Tone asks, peeling her eyes away from the staircase to look at me.

"What are you laughing at?"

"I didn't laugh," she says. "I didn't do anything."

"Oh. I thought I heard something," I say, and her eyes narrow from the smile under her mask.

"Ghosts," she says, and I roll my eyes.

"Max was going on about ghosts earlier, too," I say. "Maybe we should forget about the documentary and make a horror film instead."

"You do look like you could be in a slasher film in that mask," she says, her teasing tone of voice audible even through her mask. "Michael Myers meets Darth Vader."

"That can be plan B," I say, taking in the staircase in front of us. "If we don't find anything interesting enough for a documentary."

"I doubt you'll have to worry about that," she mutters.

In the stillness of the abandoned building I can almost hear Grandma's voice again.

It was only a village, but it had everything you could need. There was a church that held services every Sunday—which was where my parents got married—a little grocery store, and a pharmacy. Twice a month a doctor passed through town to tend to any scratches or scrapes, but for anything more serious you would have to drive to the general hospital down in Sundsvall. And there was a school, of course.

The staircase before us is made of wood, not stone, which is a bad sign. On the other hand, it does look in better shape than the rest of the building. The steps are lined with what must once have been a thick, burgundy carpet, but which years of sun and rain and snow have faded and thinned to the extent that only a few ruffled patches remain, like the pelt of a mangy animal.

"Let's start down here," I say to Tone.

In preparation for this trip, I've spent many a long night on a forum for urban explorers. Most of them seem to be based in the United States and Germany, and they spend their nights and weekends exploring abandoned houses and buildings on the outskirts of cities. It's their tips I've used on which respirator masks to wear, what equipment we need to carry, and the safety rules to live by, namely: never take a staircase without checking how stable it is; always tread carefully; and keep an eye out for patches of damp or mold that could have weakened weight-bearing beams and walls.

The lobby gives out onto two corridors, one to the left and one to the right. I gesture to the corridor on the right with a quick jerk of the head, and Tone nods.

The first door we come to leads to a bathroom with four compact cubicles. Tone has the camera in her hand and takes a few quick snaps, but there's nothing too noteworthy here: tiles with dirty grouting; old-fashioned sinks in cracked porcelain; cubicle doors hanging off their hinges. I touch one of them but the hinge is more rust than metal, and the wood disintegrates beneath my fingers.

We move swiftly on into the first classroom. There are rows of desks with tiny Windsor chairs. For some reason the size of the chairs make the whole sight even more disconcerting. Some of the desks have lost their legs and collapsed, but most of them seem to be more or less intact. There's a large slate chalkboard on the far wall, but nothing is written on it.

The next two doors lead to an identical classroom and a small broom closet. Then the corridor ends. Tone takes a shot of the dead end without a word, and then we wander back along the row of shattered windows.

The corridor on the other side is exactly the same. In one of the classrooms the chalkboard has fallen from the wall and shattered into large black chunks on the floor. Tone lifts the camera to her eyes, but then lowers it again.

"Isn't it kinda weird?" she asks, without turning around. She takes a few steps into the room, toward the windows.

"What?" I ask from the doorway.

Tone tilts her head to one side.

"There aren't any insects," she says. "On the windowsills. No dead flies, no mosquitoes . . ." She looks around, her eyebrows raised.

I shrug.

"We're still coming out of winter," I say. "Maybe they got washed away by the snow."

Tone turns away and nods.

"I guess," she says. "Maybe."

She lifts the camera and takes a picture of the windows, while I try to shake the feeling coming over me.

"Shall we see if we can get upstairs?" I ask.

"Sure," says Tone.

Once we're back in the lobby, she looks up at the staircase with pursed lips.

"Ready?" I ask.

She gives a silent nod.

Having the rucksack on top of my jacket has made me start to sweat, so as I walk toward the stairs I unzip the jacket to let some air in. I look over my shoulder at Tone. She's standing still, watching me. Her gaze is steady, which should make me feel calmer.

"OK," I say, more to myself than to her.

I place one foot on the bottom step and slowly lean into it. The step creaks a little, but it doesn't sound like it's about to cave in. When I take my other foot off the ground I'm half-expecting the wood to give way beneath me, but now it doesn't make a sound.

"Seems stable," I say, still facing forward.

I take another careful step. My shoes sink into the carpet like mud, and the reddish fibers break away with my soles as I lift them.

I look over my shoulder.

"I think it's OK," I say, and Tone nods.

"Be careful," she says. "Stay near the wall. That's where it should be strongest, structurally."

"I know," I say.

The staircase spirals up to the second floor. I go first, and it feels as though I'm holding my breath the whole way up, half-expecting the floor beneath us to cave in with each step, for us to fall several feet onto the hard, warped wooden floor. But it holds. Some of the tension dissipates once I reach the second-floor landing, but my eyes stay glued to Tone as she slowly works her way up the stairs behind me. It's only when she's standing next to me that I actually relax.

"Be careful," I say. "Keep near the walls. We don't know how stable the floor is."

I expect her to say that she knows, but she just nods.

The floor is dusty and very worn, but you can tell that at one point the wood must have been beautiful. To our right there is a pair of large carved oak doors. Not only do they look miraculously undamaged; they are also still closed. I put my hand on the brass door handle and press it down, and the doors swing open on a creaking hinge.

Inside the room there are eight tall, narrow desks in rows, with a lectern and a slate chalkboard at the front. There are no chairs. The walls are lined with shelves, most of which are packed with neatly organized test tubes, glass bottles, and other equipment for basic chemistry experiments. The top shelf, however . . .

I step slowly into the room, my eyes glued to the jars lining the top shelf. They are filled with some sort of brownish preservative, giving the objects within them a sepia tone. Some contain plants and roots, others formless clumps that could be either fungi or organs. But at the far end of the shelf stand three jars of what can only be some sort of fetuses.

I hear something click behind me and glance over my shoulder. Tone takes a few photos of the shelves, then steps closer and zooms in, ensuring that the three far jars are in focus.

Then she lowers the camera and stares at them.

"Those are really gross," I say, trying to lighten the mood.

A frown line appears between Tone's eyebrows.

"Why would they even have these?" she asks.

"To teach kids about . . . anatomy and stuff, I guess."

One of the jars has cracked—or even split in the cold—and its dull, syrupy brown contents have dripped onto the shelves below. It must have happened a long time ago, because the stains have long since dried. I can't see what it might have contained.

She goes on staring at them so long that I say:

"I think we're done in here." My voice is louder than it needs to be. It seems to fill the whole space.

"We should come back at dusk," she says. "To film here. The light will be perfect then. Powerful images."

I can feel the timeless, hunched, unformed beings in the jars still pulling my eyes toward them, and a chill runs down my spine. But that has to be a good thing, really. Tone's right: it is powerful.

Once out of that room, we walk toward an identical set of doors to the left of the staircase. These ones are slightly aslant. One of the hinges on one side has come away from the wall, leaving that door slanting sharply toward the other. A golden streak of light shines through the gap between them.

I carefully pull at the door hanging from one hinge. I'm met by a cool puff of wind that, along with the sudden sunshine, makes my eyes water. I blink.

The room is big and almost empty, but the walls are covered in posters: everything from big printed letters like the ones they use in eye tests, to cross sections of the human body, and more detailed anatomical images of the eye and heart. The nurse's office.

By the wall next to the door stands an oak desk with a matching Windsor chair beside it. There's a dainty little corner cabinet to one side and, on the other side of the door, a heavy white porcelain sink with cobweb cracks in the enamel and a rusty tap.

Near the far wall stands a bier-like bed with a rumpled sheet that has yellowed with age. The window above it is the only open window in the room, and it hangs open in a way that looks intentional. As if it were opened to give whoever wrinkled up those sheets some air and sunshine.

Besides the old posters, desk, cabinet, and bed, the room is empty. It seems too big a space for so little furniture, and its emptiness makes it feel even bigger.

"This must be where they found her," I say. Without thinking, I've taken a few steps into the center of the room. I'm vaguely aware that my heart is beating hard, pounding in my chest.

"This must be where they found the baby—your mom," I say, looking over my shoulder. "Don't you think?"

Tone has stopped in the doorway. Her pupils have contracted in the bright sunshine, and there are beads of sweat on her forehead.

"Tone?" I ask uncertainly.

She lifts the camera to her eyes, but then lowers it again. Then she says, quietly:

"You take this one, Alice. I can't . . ."

She squats down, so quickly and so weightlessly that it catches me off guard, and places her beloved system camera on the dusty floor. Then she stands up and walks back into the hallway.

"Tone!" I call after her. I'm about to follow her, but then hesitate.

She wants some time alone, to compose herself, calm down. She isn't like me—she doesn't want hugs or attention in her weaker moments.

"OK," I mutter to myself. "Fine."

I pick up the camera and look through the lens. Tone has taught me the basics of how to use it, but if I'm honest, I never expected to need to.

I turn back toward the doors. Should I go after her, just in case?

I should have known this would be hard for her. Should have asked. But sometimes she can be such a closed book.

No, I tell myself. Take some pictures and leave her be. That's what she wants. In a few minutes she'll have calmed down and we can head over to the church.

I go further into the room and take a few random shots, knowing all too well that when Tone looks at them later she'll find fault with all of them.

The light is elegant and dainty, and bounces off the dancing dust particles that my footsteps have stirred up. No one has set foot in here in almost sixty years. The team the mining company sent here in the nineties were under instructions to survey the land and perform tests, but not to go inside any buildings. We have their findings on the state of the bridges, roads, and bedrock back then, but nothing about the village itself.

The April sun has started to climb to its peak. I hold the camera up to my eyes and take a picture of the village outside, breathing in the scent of the approaching spring. And something else, beneath it. Something like rust, but not quite.

When I tilt the lens to take a shot of the bed, I do a double take. My hand hesitates above the yellowing sheets. The top of the sheet has a simple lace edging, stiff and paper thin.

I pull it down sharply.

Beneath the sheets, the mattress is soiled with layer upon layer of rusty stains. Blood.

For a few seconds, I just stare at them, but then the resounding silence is broken by a sudden crash behind my back and the sound of something breaking. And a prolonged, ear-splitting scream.

NOW

L ean into me more," I say to Tone. "Don't put any weight on that
foot, I can support you."

Tone gives a steely nod. Her mask is pulled down so it dangles around
her neck, and I see the muscles in her jaw tense up with every short,
limping step her injured foot has to make across the cobbles.

Max sees us coming from afar. I wonder if he's been looking out for
us, because he's with us in just a few seconds.

"What happened?" he asks. His question is directed at me, but Tone
is the one who answers.

"Went through a step," she says sharply. "In the school. The wood was
rotten."

"Is it her foot?" he asks.

I nod.

"Can you find her something to sit on?"

Max sprints off in the direction of the vans before I've even finished
my sentence. He roots around in the back of our van and pulls out a
cooler box that he sets down on the cobbles. I help Tone to sit down.
Her forehead is shiny despite the cool air, and a twisting blue vein has
emerged on her temple.

I sit down on the cold cobblestones in front of her.

"We need to get your boot off," I say. She closes her eyes and nods.

"Wait," says Max behind me, and I turn around. He pulls a small, silvery pack of pills out of his pocket, then presses two out into his palm and hands them to Tone.

"What is it?" I ask.

"Tylenol," Max says.

Tone shakes her head and hands them back to him, the movement making her grimace in pain.

"We have to get the boot off now," she says firmly. "It won't kick in fast enough, anyway."

"But—"

"Could you fetch the first aid kit?" I ask, cutting him off. "It's in Emmy and Robert's van. Check the front seat."

Max is thrown for a second, but then he nods.

"Sure," he says. "I'm on it."

The moisture from the moss between the cobblestones has started to soak through the knees of my jeans. I look at Tone's chunky boot and then up at her face. Her lips are pale.

"We can check if there's anything else you can take," I say.

She shakes her head.

"I don't know what painkillers will work," she says. "Just get it off."

I start untying her tightly laced bootlaces, trying to ignore the short, choked sounds she makes when, despite my best efforts to be gentle, my movements cause her pain.

After loosening the bottom laces, I take the boot with both hands and look up at her.

"Ready?" I ask.

Tone nods.

I start slowly pulling the boot, and though she doesn't make a sound, her teeth are clenched so tightly that her jaws have gone completely white. But then, just as I'm coaxing the foot itself out of the boot, she can't hold out anymore. She lets out a long, drawn-out moan that's almost worse than the scream she made when her foot went through the step. I can still taste the adrenaline in my mouth from that moment; the fear still has my body in an iron grip. It hangs in my joints, like an ache.

I put the boot down and look up at Tone. Her eyes are wet, and when I wipe my face I realize my cheeks aren't dry, either.

"That's the worst of it over," I lie, and she tries to respond with a faint smile that, in its own way, is worse than the tears.

I peel the sock off her foot. She isn't bleeding, which is a relief, at least, but I can see that her ankle has already started to swell. The skin around it is crimson.

"I heard something," says Tone.

"It's probably just Max looking for the first aid kit," I reply.

"No," she says quietly, "in the school. I heard something below us. That's why I was on the stairs."

I look up.

"What did you hear?" I ask.

Her gaze is steady, but her lips are pale.

"Footsteps," she says. "There was someone walking around down there."

"But there was no one else there," I say, and Tone purses her lips.

"There shouldn't have been, no," she says.

Something inside me lurches. I think of Emmy's pale face last night, and can't help but ask:

"Are you sure that . . . I mean, are you sure what you heard was . . . real?"

Before either of us can say anything more, Max comes running back from the van with a white box.

"Here," he says, putting it down beside me. "It had fallen behind one of the tripods, so I had to move things around a bit."

"Thanks," I say as I open the box, and then pull out a roll of gauze. I am just winding it around my hand when, out of the corner of my eyes, I see Emmy and Robert running across the square. Robert is carrying their things, so Emmy reaches us first. She stops breathless in front of us, small spots of perspiration visible under her arms. Like Tone, her mask is dangling from her neck like a macabre necklace.

"What is it?" she asks, before her eyes land on Tone's rolled-up pants and swollen ankle. "What happened?"

"They're saying she went through a step," says Max.

"Were you the one on the walkie?" Emmy asks Tone.

Tone's eyes are shiny and confused.

"I haven't touched mine," she says.

"Someone was calling into their walkie-talkie. Moaning in pain." She looks at Robert.

Tone puts her hand into her back pocket, as though searching for something.

"No—I don't even have mine," she says. "It must have come out when I fell."

Emmy looks at Robert again.

"Could that have been it? Maybe she landed on the talk button when she fell."

Robert shrugs, his squirrelly brown eyes downcast.

"I guess," he says. "That or it broke. It could have sent out interference, or something."

Emmy steps forward and sits down at Tone's feet, so close that I have to shuffle back, thrown.

"All right if I take a look?" she asks.

Tone's voice is thin and exhausted:

"Alice was just—"

"I've had training."

My skin is rippling in irritation, but I can hear the pain in Tone's voice. Her ankle is now so swollen that it hardly looks like a leg anymore.

I swallow my pride.

"Go on, take a look."

Emmy carefully sinks her fingertips into Tone's swollen, red skin, then glances up at her, muttering a "sorry" when Tone whimpers.

"Have you taken anything for the pain?" she asks.

Tone shakes her head, and I add:

"She's allergic to painkillers. It's her stomach."

"Is that true?" Emmy asks.

Tone nods without hesitation.

"I have a little whisky," says Emmy. "You can take a few swigs, if you want. It's an old-school kinda painkiller, but it works."

Miraculously enough, this draws a wry smile from Tone. Emmy looks around at Robert, who sets off toward their van without a word. Then she picks up another roll of gauze and starts winding it tightly around Tone's ankle.

"I can't tell whether it's broken or sprained," she says. "But this should keep everything in place for now. It'd be better if we had something cold to put on it, but . . ."

She looks at me. "Did you bring any frozen foods we don't know of?"

I shake my head.

"Then we'll just have to make do with good old pressure and eleva-tion," she says, securing the gauze with a small safety pin from the roll.

"How does it feel?" she asks Tone.

"I've felt better," she replies. She's still pale, but is now regaining some color in her face, at least. She isn't sweating anymore. "But I'll survive."

Emmy smiles up at her.

"Great," she says.

Seeing the two of them interact gives me a strange feeling I wouldn't exactly call pleasant, a mix of anxiety and something uncomfortably close to jealousy. I bite the inside of my cheek.

Robert comes back with Emmy's small, chipped hip flask from the night before. Tone accepts it gratefully and takes a few big swigs. I'm not sure it's a good idea, but I don't want to say anything.

"OK, guys," says Emmy, standing up and brushing off her knees. "Why don't we take a break, settle our nerves a little? We can have something to eat and discuss what we want to do."

"Sounds good," says Robert.

It feels like those should have been my words, like she's taken something from me. I'm running this project, not her. But Emmy's already on her way to get us some food, and Robert has gone with her. The moment has passed.

I watch her walking toward the van, unease still festering in my stomach.

I don't recall hearing anything on my walkie-talkie—certainly not Tone moaning.

But if they hadn't heard something, what would bring them running back to camp like that? How could they have known she was hurt?

I heard something below us.

Could Tone really have heard something?

And could it have been Emmy and Robert?

But if so, why?

December 1, 1958

Dearest Margareta,

Wishing you a happy first day of advent! Or perhaps I should say second? After all, by the time you read this, the day will have already come and gone.

Ours was so lovely this year. Mother baked saffron buns for breakfast, and—you would have been so proud of me—I suggested we take one to Birgitta in the afternoon. It was all my own idea— Mother hadn't dropped a single hint! But then Mother said that Birgitta wouldn't eat it, advent or not: all she'll take is her cold chicken, gingerbread, and black-currant juice. But Mother smiled and stroked my cheek, and said that it was a lovely thought all the same. Besides, the gingerbread we normally take her is still rather festive. We went down to see her together. Even Birgitta seemed chirpier than usual. And when Mother and I sang her some Christmas carols, it almost sounded as though she was trying to hum along.

But enough! I can't keep it in any longer—I must tell you the big news! (Unless Mother has already told you? No, I'm sure she wouldn't have, she never writes about anything interesting.)

We have a new pastor!

I'm sure your first question will be why that would ever be news: everyone knows Einar's a drunk, and it's actually rather odd that he's been able to stay on as long as he has here. Mother gets angry at me whenever I mention it, says that he's a man of God and that we shouldn't speak ill of others, but it's only gotten worse these last years. Lena told me her father saw Einar asleep on the road a few weeks ago, and he'd forgotten to put on any pants! Surely it can't be speaking ill of someone if it's the truth?

But that's beside the point. What makes it such big news is not only that we have a new pastor, but that no one knew he was coming! Up here everybody normally knows everything about anything (a few days ago, Albert at the pharmacy asked me how you're doing in your new apartment!), but this came out of nowhere!

I'd already heard about him from Mother, who met him last week, but I thought the new kid she was talking about was some sort of assistant, not a new priest. Everyone was whispering and murmuring as they came into church. Last Sunday Einar had done the sermon, hissing and grumbling like a smokestack as usual, but for the advent service yesterday he just sat there nice and quiet in the front pew, while Pastor Mattias took to the lectern.

He's so dashing! Oh, forgive me, Margareta, can I say such a thing about a priest? It's the truth! He looks like a film star, with thick blond hair and light eyes. They're gray as fog, and his eyelashes are long and dark like a girl's. He isn't so tall—Mother's almost taller than him—but nor am I, so that suits me rather well.

Anyway, he said that he's been sent here from Stockholm, to help Einar serve the parish in these difficult times, and that he's looking forward to getting to know Silvertjärn. When he started his sermon, it was so beautiful. You know I've never been so good at listening when Einar talks (nor are you, for that matter!), but today I was completely mesmerized. His voice was so beautiful, soft and smooth as silk, and he spoke calmly and quietly, so everyone had to concentrate to hear him. You could have heard a pin drop! He spoke about the kingdom of heaven, but not like Einar usually does—about flappy angels and golden gates—but about heaven as a feeling. About creating heaven here on earth. It was so wonderful it gave me goose bumps.

And then he even came up to greet us afterward, when we were on our way out. (That was when I noticed his eyelashes!) He and Mother had something to discuss about some sick old lady, but he said hello to me, too, and looked into my eyes as he took my hand. And oh, Margareta, it had me blushing from head to toe! It was so embarrassing. But he didn't mention it, he just smiled and told me he thinks Aina is a beautiful name. He said it means "beauty" in Hebrew, can you imagine? I felt like I could have fainted!

Pastor Mattias said he's going to set up a small Bible group for young people, and that it would be great if I could help out. Obviously I said yes! On the way home Mother said it was good I would have something to keep me busy, and that it might do me some good. Oh, Margareta, I'm all aflutter! You must come and visit over Christmas, so that then you can see what I'm talking about. But be warned: you might just fall for him, and then you'll have to leave Nils, move back here, and marry the new pastor instead!

I have to go now, Mother is calling. Write soon! And lots!

Your little sister, Aina

NOW

Max throws back his head and shouts.

"Hello!"

His voice echoes off the vaulted ceiling and solid walls, as though sliced up, fragmented, by the broken glass in the windows. The station is small but strangely familiar; all Swedish train stations seem to have been built to the same standardized model, apparently even those in mining villages in the middle of nowhere. Tall windows and stone floors, with small benches in the middle of the room to sit and wait.

"Stop," I say to Max, who looks at me in surprise.

"What?"

I can't really explain why I want him to be quiet. Tone had understood intuitively in the school.

"Sorry," I say. "I guess I'm a little tense."

"No need to apologize," he says. "Of course you are. I'm impressed at how well you're keeping it all together."

I let out a small laugh. If he thinks this is keeping it together then I can only imagine what he was expecting.

It hadn't taken long for the alcohol to make Tone drowsy and muddle-headed, and she ate hardly any of the food that Emmy made for lunch. Once we'd finished eating, it was Emmy who assumed the role of leader again, posing the question. She directed it at the group, but her eyes never left Tone's face.

"Do we cut and run?"

Max has walked over to the door leading out onto the platform. He waves me over.

"Come get a load of this," he says. "You'll probably want a few pictures."

I stride across the dirty floor, feeling the rubble crackle under my boots as I step on the split flagstones. This afternoon light is softer than the sharp glare of morning.

Max has stepped through the doors and down onto the platform.

"Be careful," I say.

The platform is made of concrete slabs, which, like the steps up to the school, have cracked and started to crumble. There are two cast-iron benches next to the station walls, both of which so rusted that they're barely more than reddish-ocher husks.

I take a few pictures, the camera unfamiliar and unwieldy in my hands, then look up when I hear Max jump down onto the brushwood lining the tracks.

There's something instinctively unpleasant about seeing someone standing on railway tracks, even though I know no train has pulled into this station in more than fifty years.

Still, it's easy to picture the station full of people: bored kids bickering while waiting for the train; women dressed in their Sunday best to travel south to see relatives; my grandmother, impossibly young at eighteen, on her way to Stockholm to start a new life.

And, later: unemployed men with nowhere else to go, trying to drink away the uncertainty of their futures, only to wind up asleep on the hard station benches.

Raising his hand to shield his eyes from the sun, Max looks over at where the tracks disappear into the forest.

"Crazy to think this was their only way in and out of town," he says.

I sit down on the edge of the platform. Max holds out his hand and helps me down, but I land clumsily even with his support.

"They did have the road, too," I say, lifting the camera to my eyes again.

Through the lens the tracks look so distant, the forest almost an age away. The fading light makes the rust on the tracks shimmer, picking out the few pink buds that have started to shoot up amid the heather.

Max is wrong: it's not pictures I want of this place so much as moving images; to attempt to capture the stillness of it all, the unnatural silence. To let the camera linger while the absence of any sound makes the viewer aware of their own breaths, their own heartbeats. To make them feel like they're here in Silvertjärn with us, give them the same prickle along their spines that I feel as I stand here.

I turn and take a few quick shots of the station façade. With its rounded cornices and sand-colored stucco, it looks like a gingerbread house that's been left to the elements.

"At least that's one thing we don't have to worry about," I add. "We can get out of here whenever we want." The words leave a sour taste in my mouth.

Max hears what I want to say. He knows me that well, at least.

"Tone said she didn't want to go to the hospital," he says, his tone of voice clearly meant to sound calming. "She said she wants to stay."

"Yeah," I say. "So she said."

But her eyes had been heavy from the tiredness, pain, and alcohol, and she had looked at me long and hard before she said it. I wish I could say that she hadn't seen the tension in my face, the quiet prayer in my rib cage.

Truth is, this is the only chance we have at this. We've only hired the equipment for five days, and despite the money Max has invested, our budget is already being squeezed. Even if I stayed here, if Max were to drive Tone to the hospital it would mean losing two people for at least twenty-four hours. And going from five people to three would bring the production to its knees. We would never be able to keep to schedule.

Tone knows that, too. And I know she knows. So the razor-sharp relief I felt when she said: "It's a sprain. Let's stay," was tinged with something shameful and ugly.

"It's just a few days," says Max. "Tone's an adult. If it gets any worse, she'll say."

"I hope so," I say, not entirely sure if I mean it.

I climb back up onto the platform and go back inside the station. From here I notice a big clock hanging over the doors out into the village. The hands have stopped at nine minutes past three, and an ugly crack has cleaved the clock face in two. I automatically take a look at my watch—seventeen past five—before taking a picture of the clock on the wall.

"That production girl seems kinda bossy," says Max behind me, and I turn to look at him.

"Emmy?"

"Yeah," he says. He squats down on the dusty stone slabs, gets his water bottle out of his rucksack, and takes a big gulp.

"It felt like she was trying to take over," he goes on, wiping his mouth.

"Really? I thought I was just imagining things," I say, and Max shakes his head.

"Nope," he says. "I don't think so."

"She's always been like that," I can't help adding. "She just . . . she likes to be the one calling the shots."

"Always?" Max asks. "I thought she and the camera guy were just people you'd found for this project?"

Hearing the surprise in his voice, I hesitate. I haven't talked about Emmy to anyone but Tone—not for many years, at least. But the creeping discomfort I feel in my gut makes me swallow any resistance and say:

"Yeah. Or, they are, but we—I know Emmy from before. That's how I could get her for this. She's overqualified, really, she's done loads of great projects. She has some drama series for C More lined up after this."

"How do you know each other?" Max asks.

I sigh, rub my forehead with the back of my hand, and sit down on the floor next to him. My pants are going to get filthy, but right now I don't care.

"We studied together," I say. The words are sluggish, reluctant. I take a swig out of his water bottle to try to make it easier, to wash the resistance back down.

"She was my best friend," I say.

The unwelcome, overpowering memories come flooding back. Late nights and early, hungover mornings, in-jokes and peals of laughter. I used to always paint her nails, despite her complaining that she'd only ruin them. And she'd mix drinks for us to take to pre-parties: sour, foaming potions that tasted nothing of alcohol but had me soaring off into the stratosphere after only a few sips.

"You've never mentioned her before," says Max.

"No," I say. "I guess I haven't."

In my first and second years at college, I slept on Emmy's sofa more than my own bed.

But the third year I don't remember so well. What I do remember are blackened lights, darkness outside; silent tears streaming down onto the pillow; Emmy making toast and tea, rubbing my back with unpainted nails until I'd fall asleep, exhausted.

"We were very close," I say, slowly. "I more or less lived with her in the first two years. We were always talking about what we'd do after we graduated, about how we'd work together, revolutionize the Swedish film industry. You know. As you do."

I swallow again.

"You know that I had . . . problems . . . when I was at college."

I look at him, and he gives a quick nod.

"That I had depression—severe depression."

The word seems to hulk in my mouth. I hate saying it, hate how it sounds. It's a shapeless, gray word that implies something sad and pathetic. Someone who's lost control.

"When it started Emmy was there for me, but she got bored pretty quickly. I guess it can't have been much fun having a friend who just lay around crying instead of wanting to go out and party. After a while she couldn't take it. And then . . ."

The memory tastes bitter, a hum behind my forehead. My eyes start to burn, but I refuse to let it out.

The water coursing under the bridge.

My phone pressed against my ear.

"Please."

The laughter, the music in the background—"Hjärta," by Kent:

And by the riverbanks I left my tracks
Wrote my name in the water
So you'd know where I am.

I still can't listen to that song.

"I tried to kill myself," I say, quietly, so quiet it's barely more than a whisper. "I tried to jump off a bridge."

"Shit," says Max, softly. He reaches for my hand, but I move it away.

"I called Emmy," I say, "when I was up there. I called her and asked her to come get me. It was a Friday night. I guess she was at some party."

I swallow again. My throat is dry as sand.

"She said—" I begin, but then my throat constricts. I force it out, regardless:

"She said she didn't have the energy anymore," I say. "That I 'couldn't go on like that.' And then she hung up."

The last part is virtually a sigh. The tension is still there in my chest, but it feels nice to have gotten the words out, like the lightness you feel in your arms after dropping a dead weight.

Max shakes his head. I shrug.

"So what's she doing here?" he asks, quietly, without accusing me.

I shake my head.

"We had no other choice," I say. "We needed someone with Emmy's skills, someone with production experience. Emmy's good at editing and directing, and she has contacts. They're what we need."

"No, I mean . . . why did she show up?"

I open my mouth but then close it again.

"I don't know," I eventually say. "I assumed she'd turn me down. I'm still surprised she didn't."

Max spins a blade of grass between his fingers.

"You could have asked me, you know," he says, looking at me with wide, shiny eyes. I'm surprised by how thick and dark his eyelashes are. When we first met he used to wear glasses. I guess he must be wearing contacts now. At times I find myself missing those glasses, thick-rimmed and ugly as they were, in the same strange way I find myself missing the traces of acne across his forehead. It's a sense of loss that isn't anything to do with him: it's about me, about that time in my life. About who I was back then—peppy and fresh out of college—and who I am now.

"I know," I say. "But I didn't want you to find someone. I can't come running to you for more money as soon as anything goes wrong. I wanted someone with real skills, someone I knew was good, and whatever my personal feelings about Emmy are, this project is more important. This film is everything to me."

Grandma's story, my retelling; Silvertjärn is both my past and my future. I've lived with it since I was a child, and it's going to be my breakthrough. No more receptionist jobs, no more temping. No more sofa-surfing with friends, no more humiliating conversations asking my parents for money to pay my phone bill, even though I'm almost twenty-nine, even though all my old classmates are being offered promotions and raises, getting married and having kids.

The Lost Village is my ticket out of all of that.

Max nods slowly.

"I guess I just don't get how you can trust her after that," he says.

"I don't need to trust her," I say. "I just need to know that she'll do her job. And she will. She's a pro."

I swallow down the sudden sourness in my mouth. The languid light is shimmering in the brushwood.

I just wish I could believe what I'm saying myself.

NOW

Night falls soft as a sigh over the village. When Max and I get back to camp sunset has already started to lick its fiery tongues across the sky, and by the time I've transferred the photos from the cameras to the laptop the sun is already half-buried under the horizon.

I'm going through the pictures on the laptop while Max gets some food ready. Robert seems determined to help him out; I can hear them mumbling about boiling points and lead levels in food tins. With their red and blond heads hunched over the alcohol stove, they look like two bashful boys sharing their toys in the sandbox.

I smile to myself, then turn my eyes back to my laptop. I'm not expecting to get through all the shots now—I'm saving the bulk of that work for postproduction. I expect I'll have to work much closer with Emmy then. Before we got here that prospect hadn't seemed so unworkable, but now, less than twenty-four hours in, I've started to wonder if we could outsource some of the more technical stuff. Having her here is triggering things I hadn't anticipated.

Unfortunately, Emmy is a great director. A little too sure of herself, perhaps, a little too convinced of her own genius, but her belief in her own methods is often well-founded and she's extremely well-read. The first time I really noticed her was during our second seminar in Dramaturgy I at Stockholm University of the Arts. I'd seen the petite girl with the green eyes, tousled hair, and rocker clothes before, but I hadn't given her a second thought until I made a comment in class that I felt was both thoughtful and well-reasoned, only to watch in shock as it was cut to shreds by that very same girl. She had a dab of tobacco under her lip and looked as though she'd just rolled out of bed, but she went through what I'd said point by point, making mincemeat of my arguments against the conventional three-act structure.

Later that evening she had suddenly popped up again at the student bar, a beer in her hand and a mildly apologetic smile on her lips. She introduced herself as Emmy Abrahamsson and apologized for what had happened in the seminar. Said that she could "get a little enthusiastic at times."

I'm still not sure if I regret accepting that beer.

I've never been the same since that night on the bridge. I learned something about people that night. And something about myself.

Seven years have passed since then, almost a quarter of my life. And all this time she's been like a half-healed wound, a scab I can never quite seem to stop myself from scratching.

It was naïve of me to think I'd be able to put that to one side here.

I shake my head, try to focus on the images in front of me. They're good. The shots from the school are strong. Not all of them are completely in focus—Tone still doesn't seem to have completely gotten the hang of that camera—but the ones that are are crisp and striking. There's something so familiar, so Swedish about those classrooms: those chalkboards and desks, all broken and abandoned. A childhood memory contorted beyond recognition.

When I suddenly come to a video it takes me by surprise. I didn't even know these cameras could shoot videos.

"How's it going?" a voice asks, and I jump and look up. Max is looking down at me, his eyebrows raised.

"Shit, you scared me," I say, laughing to take the edge off.

"You looked pretty hypnotized," he says with a grin. "I was just going to say the food's almost ready."

"Oh, great," I say.

"Shall we wake Tone?" he asks, but I shake my head.

"No," I say. "Let her sleep. It's probably what she needs."

Max nods, and I turn my attention back to the computer. I click the small PLAY symbol on the video.

It looks as though Tone hadn't meant to film anything; the camera is swinging back and forth above the floor, capturing cracking, splintered wooden boards, shards of glass from the windows. Then I hear the soft tap of shoes against the floor, and turn up the volume. The camera is still pointing at the floor when the footsteps suddenly stop, and I jump when I hear my own voice say:

"Ready?"

The camera is pointed at a skirting board, above which the wallpaper is peeling away from the wall.

"OK," I hear myself say.

It's when the camera moves again to reveal a glimpse of steps and rotting carpet that I realize when it must have been filmed. It's from when we started climbing the staircase inside the school. That fucking staircase.

The video is almost over; only twelve seconds left. I see the camera swinging back and forth as Tone climbs the steps behind me, catching flashes of my clumpy sneakers and those treacherous steps.

Four seconds.

Then I hear something.

I frown and press PAUSE. I pull the video back a few seconds and press PLAY again.

The camera swings back and forth. Red carpet, splintered wood, damp walls.

There.

At four seconds.

There it was again.

I pause. Hesitate. But then I turn up the volume as high as it can go and rewind again.

Now I hear Tone's breaths on the recording, the creak of steps under our feet. And then . . .

Is that a cough?

Could I have coughed? It doesn't sound like a cough, not really. The sound seems to come from far away. It's tinny and muffled. And quiet, like . . . a chuckle.

It doesn't sound like a cough, no; it sounds like laughter. Husky and stifled, like a child hiding in a closet, trying to repress a snigger.

The evening chill has descended upon the square. I rub my arms, trying to ignore the shivers running down my spine. It's absurd.

And yet I'm suddenly, irreversibly aware that the school is just fifty yards away on the other side of the square, its doors hanging open like a gaping mouth.

It's all in my head. I'm probably just hearing my own breaths on the tape. These laptop speakers aren't particularly good, and you can make yourself hear anything if you want to enough. Like seeing faces in clouds.

But I still can't let it go.

I make to rewind and listen once more.

Then the screen dies.

I flinch and shout:

"Shit!"

"What is it?" Max calls from over by the fire.

I slam the laptop shut.

"Laptop died. Out of battery."

"Just as well," says Max. "Dinner's ready."

"Coming," I say and put it away in my bag.

I take one last, lingering look at the school and then walk over to the others to eat, doing my best to ignore the prickling sensation at the back of my neck.

NOW

The first stars are already shimmering as we finish eating, which is when Tone opens the van door and hops out gingerly.

"Tone!" I say, getting to my feet. "How are you feeling?"

Tone gives a cautious smile and rubs her face.

"Pretty hungry," she says.

Her eyes are puffy and heavy with sleep, and her short hair is unkempt. She takes my arm and I help her over to the fire.

"How's it going?" Max asks, throwing a travel rug over one of the cooler boxes so that she can sit down.

"I've felt better," she says, taking the bowl of soup I hold out to her. She tastes it and pulls a face.

"Canned minestrone?" she asks.

"Only the best," says Emmy, rolling her eyes.

I can't bite my tongue.

"I'm afraid we don't have the budget for the luxury catering you're more accustomed to," I say. "Sorry if you're missing your crayfish sandwiches."

Before she can respond, I turn to Tone and add:

"There's bread, too. I can toast some over the fire, if you want?"

Tone nods.

"Yes please. Thanks."

I take two slices of over-processed bread out of the bag, tie it up again, and skewer the bread slices while listening to the others.

"How did it go this afternoon?" Tone asks, eating the soup in tiny spoonfuls.

It's Emmy who replies.

"Good," she says. "We worked our way through the ironworks, and managed to squeeze in a few houses, too, just to scout them out."

"You did what?" I ask, whipping my head around.

"We looked in two of the row houses," Emmy says. "We had some spare time. It was insane—they really are completely identical, like the village just bought four hundred houses from IKEA and threw them all up next to each other."

"But isn't that pretty much how it was?" Max asks, looking at me. "Didn't the people who owned the mine build cheap housing for all the manpower they brought in during the war?"

"Yeah," I say, before a sudden smell of burning brings me back to my task at hand, and I turn the bread slices just before they catch fire. They're a bit burned, but it's probably OK. At least they'll taste of something.

"We got some awesome shots," says Emmy. "One of the houses had an apple tree growing in through one of the windows. It had taken half of the wall down. Really unsettling. In a good way."

I can't let it go:

"But the houses weren't on our schedule."

I feel like Emmy's about to clap back, but it's quiet Robert who says:

"It was my idea. I wanted to see how they looked."

"Oh," I say. "Right."

"Hard not to be curious," he says apologetically, scratching his neck. He has very big hands and feet. It adds to the clumsy, slightly awkward impression he gives. He looks like a teenager who hasn't quite grown into his body, even though Emmy's said he's only a few years younger than us. Maybe that's why it's hard to get annoyed at him.

"You can't help but wonder what happened," he goes on. "There was a cup on one of the kitchen counters. Like someone had just put down their coffee, gone out to pick up the paper, and then . . ."

"Disappeared," says Tone quietly, finishing his sentence.

"Yeah," says Robert. "Exactly."

I take the toast off the fire, coax the slices off the skewer and hand them to Tone. She looks at them and says, "Mmm, well-done," before taking a bite. Though the toast is practically charcoal, it comes as something of a relief: she sounds like herself, however tired she is, however much pain she's in. Sardonic rather than beaten.

"Are there any theories?" Emmy asks me. I pull my sweater sleeves over my hands and sit back down on one of the camping mats.

"It's in the packs," I say.

"Yeah, yeah," she says, "it's all in the packs. But you know everything about this place. Can't you tell us something about them?"

I clench my teeth, but then I see that both Max and Robert are watching me closely. I puff out the breath I've been holding in and relent.

"OK," I say. "Sure. Of course I can."

I search for a natural entry point, somewhere to begin. Scan my mind for the best thread to pull at. As I do this, I'm once again very aware of the square around us: the glaring, empty windows; the cold cobblestones beneath us; the impossibly high sky overhead. So many stars. Before Silvertjärn I'd never seen the Milky Way.

"The police investigation didn't really reach any conclusions," I say, fumbling around for the words. "You know that, it's in the . . ."

I see a pull at Emmy's lips, but then she purses them instead.

"Yeah. But anyway," I say. "Obviously there are theories. Most people seem to think it was some sort of mass suicide. Like Jonestown—you know, that cult in South America with the insane leader who forced almost a thousand people to commit suicide."

"If he forced them it sounds more like mass murder to me," Emmy mutters.

I ignore her.

"You can see the similarities," says Max. "A sect, an isolated location, a charismatic madman . . ."

"Except I don't know if you could call this a sect," I say. "I think most people have described it as a free church, if that. They never broke away from the Church of Sweden, so technically it was just a normal parish."

"There's no need to split hairs," says Emmy. "It was a sect—whatever they called themselves."

Before I can respond, Tone speaks up:

"Yeah, there are definite sect elements there. That comes through in the letters, if nothing else."

"Aina's letters, you mean?" I ask, and Tone nods.

"Anyway," I continue, "we don't know much about what happened in Silvertjärn in the final months. The last letter we have from Aina is dated May 1959. Except the very last one, that is. I've tried to track down other letters from the same period—there must have been other people who had relatives out of town—but I haven't found anything. People probably didn't save them, or else they've just been misplaced over the years. Some relatives gave witness statements to the police, but none of those give us much to work with. So all the theories about the church and the pastor are based on complete speculation."

"But it's got to have something to do with them," says Emmy. "Right? It can't be coincidence that they build up some fanatical movement around this guy and then just disappear."

"Oh, I wouldn't say that," says Tone, stony-faced. "Some people claim they were all abducted by aliens."

I smirk.

"I have to say, that one gets my vote," I joke. "So if anyone spots any UFOs tonight, be sure to let me know."

Emmy rolls her eyes, but I think I see a twitch at the side of her mouth. It gives me a strange feeling in my gut, an echo of a certain intimacy.

"No, of course it has to all be linked, somehow," I say. "The most banal theory is that it was some kind of voluntary migration; that the pastor convinced them all that God had commanded him to take them north, or something like that, but that they died along the way. It wouldn't be the first time something like that had happened; the history blog *Our Dark Past* compares it to the Children's Crusades in the thirteenth century. Religious fixation can make people do very odd things."

"Still, it's weird they never found anything," says Max. "You'd think they would leave some sort of tracks. Nine hundred people migrating would leave its mark—on the immediate surroundings, if nothing else."

"And it doesn't explain the baby," says Emmy. "Right?"

I shake my head.

"No, it doesn't," I say. "Nor the dogs and cats. Or the murder of Birgitta Lidman. Or why no one seems to have taken anything with them. Like you said, Robert: there are still coffee cups on kitchen counters, pots on stovetops. The police report said there was even laundry hanging out to dry on lines outside the houses. Whatever it was, it seems to have happened fast. If it were a mass migration, you'd think they'd have taken something with them."

"There are theories about mass hysteria," Tone adds.

I nod.

"There are historic examples of that: in the sixteenth century there was something called the 'dancing plague' in Strasbourg, where hundreds of people danced on the streets uninterrupted for over a month. Many of them died of exhaustion. They think it was a form of stress-induced psychosis, caused by starvation and general anxiety. If you think about how hopeless people here must have felt after the mine shut, it could have been something similar."

"But it still doesn't explain where they went," says Tone. "Just like the migration theory."

"No," I agree, "if they just took off then a lot doesn't add up. Some people have suggested it could have been a gas leak of some sort— methane gas in the earth's crust released by mining activity. But the mining company that came here in the nineties checked the air quality and found nothing. And, even if that did explain why everyone died simultaneously, it doesn't explain the baby, or why the only body they found here was Birgitta's, who clearly didn't die of suffocation. It was a hot summer that year, so if it had been a gas leak then there would have been corpses rotting on the streets when the police arrived."

Max grimaces slightly at the thought.

I look at Tone.

"Have I forgotten any?" I ask.

"Those are all the big ones," she says. "But I've always had a soft spot for the Russian invasion theory."

"Oh! Yes!" I say. "That's hilarious. Apparently the Soviet Union were doing some sort of dress rehearsal for a Swedish land invasion, and kidnapped the entire village." I shrug. "Though, I have to say, I can't pinpoint any actual holes with that one. I almost hope it's true. Just imagine the scoop!"

Emmy laughs. That same flash of recognition, of warmth.

I push it down.

"So what we're saying is there's no good explanation?" Robert hums.

"Yeah," I say. "Hence the mystery. Almost nine hundred people, lost without a trace. No one knows if they're alive or dead, or if they killed themselves, got sick, or left the place voluntarily. No one knows why poor Birgitta Lidman was stoned to death. And no one knows whose was the baby in the school, or why she got left behind."

A strange, heavy silence falls after I say this, as if the reality of the mystery hits us all at once. The wind that sweeps over the square isn't a spring breeze; it's still cold and raw from winter. It runs straight through my clothes, makes the hairs on my neck stand on end.

"But they must be dead, don't you think?" Emmy asks quietly, in a tone of voice at odds with her usual loud, defiant self.

I swallow.

"I think so," I admit. "But I don't know how or why. So I'm hoping we can find something. Some sort of indication."

A half truth. I'm hoping we can find more than some small indication: I want an answer. We aren't a courtroom, I don't need proof, just something that points in one direction. An unsent letter, fossilized tracks leading out into the forest . . .

I doubt we'll find it, but I can't quite bring myself to give up hope.

Max nods. Tone doesn't make a sound. When I look at her ankle, I can see that her pant leg has traveled up slightly, and that the skin above the support bandage is red and swollen. She hasn't eaten her toast; a sad, half-eaten slice of charred bread lies cooling on the ground next to her.

"So then we have a goal for tomorrow," Emmy says, sounding more like her usual self. She stands up and holds out a hand to Robert, who takes it and pulls himself up.

"I'm gonna hit the sack," she says. "See you tomorrow."

Robert nods at the rest of us and follows her off toward the van.

Max looks at me, his eyebrows raised.

"Jeez," he says, quietly, so that it doesn't carry to Emmy and Robert. "It's not even nine o'clock."

I look at Tone. Her mouth is a taut line, the dark circles under her eyes like the sweep of a dirty fingerprint.

"You know, maybe we could all do with some sleep?" I say. "It's been a long day."

Tone says nothing.

"What do you think?" I ask her, and she looks up, confused, as though hearing me for the first time.

"Sleep?" she repeats. "Yeah. That might be an idea."

I get up, roll up my camping mat and hold my hand out to Tone. It's not enough: I have to put my arm around her waist and hoist her up. It's harder than I had expected, and she leans into me heavily.

"Good night, Max," I say over my shoulder, to his lone silhouette by the fire. "Sleep well."

I see him watch us as we go, then put another log on the fire.

By the time I've helped Tone into the tent and zipped up the door behind us I can feel some sweat under my arms, but in the dim light of our electric lantern it's clear that Tone is dripping with it. My stomach turns when I see how bloodless her face is.

I brush my teeth while she silently pulls off her jeans and puts on long johns to keep warm through the night, every single movement sending a visible jolt of pain through her leg.

I stick my head out of the tent to spit out my toothpaste, and give a start when I find Max standing at the door.

"Sorry!" he says softly, a tentative smile on his lips. "Didn't mean to scare you."

"Don't worry about it," I say, wiping my mouth. "What is it?"

"Could I borrow some toothpaste?" he asks. "I can't find mine."

I look over my shoulder into the tent and fumble around for my and Tone's huge toiletry bag, which we've crammed full with everything from Band-Aids to toothpaste and shampoo.

"Knock yourself out," I say, handing it to him. "Wait, does that mean you haven't brushed your teeth since we got here?"

Max grins mischievously while rummaging around for the toothpaste. When he finds it, he squeezes half of the tube into his mouth, says a thick "thanks", and hands the bag back to me.

I laugh.

"Go to bed, you sicko," I say, then blow him a kiss before pulling my head back into the tent. I put on my thick socks and look up at Tone.

"Look . . ." I start.

"What is it?"

"Let's get you to a hospital."

I hate myself for saying it, but I would have hated myself even more if I didn't.

"Honestly, Tone, I know you're tough, but you're in so much pain. What if it's broken? Or if it heals badly?"

Tone purses her lips and shakes her head.

"It isn't," she hisses. "It's just a bad sprain."

"Are you sure?" I ask doubtfully. "It doesn't look so good."

"I can tell," she says sharply. "Look, I don't want to go to the hospital, and I don't need to, either."

She pokes around in the toiletry bag without meeting my eyes.

"I don't want you to stay here for my sake," I say. "My film isn't more important than your health."

Now she looks me straight in the eye.

"This isn't *your* film, Alice. You aren't the only one who's invested a lot into this project. You aren't the only one who cares about it."

It stings enough to silence me.

If a sprained ankle is the worst thing to happen on this trip, then I guess maybe it won't be so bad, after all.

THEN

Elsa trundles drowsily down the stairs and stops in the doorway to the kitchen. There's a twinge in her chest, a sinking feeling. It's an unfamiliar sensation, and it takes her a few seconds to put her finger on it.

Hopelessness.

On the table in front of *him* stands a half-empty bottle of schnapps.

Elsa has no idea where it could have come from: she refuses to have that stuff in her house, and he knows it. She hates the smell. The times he's stumbled home giddy and reeking from the Petterssons', she's made him sleep on the sofa in the dining room. That must be why he didn't even try to come up to the bedroom.

At least she hopes that's the reason.

When he wakes up he'll be hurting. His back has troubled him ever since an accident he had in his early thirties, but so long as Elsa massages him every evening it still works just fine.

Were it not for the thinning blond hair at the top of his head, he could be a boy lying slumped there on that table. He's still tall and lanky, with only the small pouch on his belly to suggest he's started to pile on the pounds. That has come on in the last few months. He eats more now, she's noticed. He doesn't have much else to do.

Elsa throws a quick glance behind her up at the staircase. Aina isn't awake yet—and a good thing, too. For once she's relieved her daughter has a tendency to sleep away her mornings. Though, it should be said, she has been getting up early of late—even on a Sunday, when she doesn't need to be in school. She gets herself dressed up for church. Elsa suspects she's taken a fancy to the new pastor. Which isn't so peculiar, really: he's a handsome man, and in Silvertjärn there's a dearth of men for a young girl to look at.

She walks over to the table and gently puts her hand on Staffan's shoulder.

"Staffan," she says quietly.

He doesn't make a sound. She gives his back a cautious rub.

"Staffan," she says again.

Now she feels him start to stir. He raises his head slightly, then, with a low groan, lifts it all the way off the table. It takes his eyes a few seconds to focus, but she can already make out the shame in them before he blinks.

Nowadays it always seems to be there.

He looks at her. His eyes are bloodshot, and he hasn't shaved. He looks like a drunkard, the way Einar always looked whenever she'd found him in the church and had to haul him back into the chapel to sleep it off.

She waits for the anger, as does Staffan—she can see it from the way he contracts beneath her gaze. But she doesn't have the heart. She feels no anger. Only sadness.

"Get up and go to bed, Staffan," she says quietly.

She strokes his head. Staffan purses his lips and gives a short nod, his eyes glassy.

As Staffan lumbers upstairs, Elsa's eyes stay fixed on his empty chair. It needs repainting. They all need repainting. The kitchen chairs are a brilliant turquoise, which always brings a smile to visitors' faces on entering the house. It's something unexpected, like their green front door. Elsa likes color. If it were up to her, the whole house would be fizzing with it—blues and purples and oranges and turquoise—but that would look a sight. So she's reined herself in to the odd splash here and there: the front door, the kitchen chairs. The flowerbeds in spring and summer, and the glossy apples in autumn.

She pulls a peeling flake of paint from the back of the chair. The gray, lifeless wood peers out from underneath.

It's as though the spark within him has died.

Elsa closes her eyes.

Elsa has always known what needed to be done. Even in her very darkest moments, she has always known what was required of her. She had looked after her mother when she was at death's door; spoon-fed her, held her over the chamber pot, changed her diapers. All without letting her see her shed a tear.

Elsa has always been able to give advice, has always been the kind of person others could lean on. *Ask Elsa*, that's what they say down in town. Be it for help or advice, or simply a kind ear, just ask Elsa. It's something she takes pride in.

But now she wakes up in the mornings with the feeling that she can't breathe.

What shall we do?

They still have a little money left, but nowhere near enough to buy a house elsewhere. It'll keep them going for a few more months if she asks to defer their bills, but after that . . .

There's no work to be had. Not in Silvertjärn. But there's nowhere else they can go. The world is closing in around them.

She opens her eyes. She doesn't have the time for this. It's no use thinking that way.

Elsa quickly takes the gingerbread, what remains of the cold chicken, and the last of the black-currant juice, and puts them in the basket. She needs to buy more. She tries not to think about what feeding Birgitta is costing her now that they hardly have enough for themselves.

The morning air is cold and crisp, with a late-winter sharpness. The village stands in stark relief against the brightening sky, which is high and clear. Only the odd bright cloud is hovering on the horizon, and the snow crunches underfoot as Elsa sets out toward Birgitta's hut.

It's empty down in the village. This time a year ago it would have been bustling, even before sunrise. The villagers on the Sunday shift would have been out on their way to work, and there would always be something to look forward to on the way out to see Birgitta; Elsa would share a joke with the boys heading off to the mine, ask after their mothers and sisters and wives. Now she almost fears these early morning walks, for if she does see anyone it'll be because they've spent the night on the streets, tired and befuddled, or that they're drifting around with nowhere to go, like listless ghosts.

It's colder out than Elsa had imagined—she should probably have put on a scarf just in case—but despite the cold it feels like spring is in the air. The river has started to course faster, and although the evenings and mornings are still dark, the midday sun is strong and warm. She can feel her heart start to lift as she walks. It's going to be all right; it always is. However bad things might seem, they always come good in the end.

By the time she reaches Birgitta's hut she can give the door her usual sprightly knock.

"Birgitta," she says. "It's me, Elsa."

Birgitta recognizes her voice and opens the door. She seems more timid than normal, and when Elsa steps inside she realizes Birgitta has been hurting herself again. There are bruises on her face.

"Oh, Birgitta," she says softly.

At times Elsa almost wishes she could take Birgitta in her arms and rock her like a child, even though Birgitta isn't so much younger than herself. But Elsa knows that Birgitta would panic if she even tried to. She dislikes physical contact, as Elsa has learned over the years.

As she watches Birgitta start to unpack the food according to her own special ritual, Elsa feels an echo of that horrible sinking feeling in her chest.

The house isn't the only reason why they can't leave Silvertjärn. For if they left, then who would look after Birgitta?

THURSDAY

NOW

The church is only a few blocks up from the square, but in Silvert-järn terms that's virtually the other side of town. The wind has picked up this morning, and the building looms ominously against a background of heavy, dark clouds.

The church is today's first port of call, but in the gray mist it feels like it could be almost twilight.

I've decided that the four of us will do the church together, and then we can split up afterward. Tone agreed. She's going to stay at the camp and go through yesterday's pictures while we're out exploring. She was looking better today; her eyes were sharp, and there was some color in her cheeks. I didn't feel the need to say anything, but at breakfast I saw her pop two Advil tablets and wash them down with her instant coffee.

The tall lattice windows above the church doors are still intact, except one small blue pane in the middle, which has cracked. The stucco walls are in surprisingly good shape, too—still a brilliant white—and the doors look alarmingly stable.

"Are they bolted?" Emmy asks when we stop at the bottom of the crumbling church steps. Those, at least, bear witness to the abandonment of the village: the concrete slabs are laced with fissures and pine needles.

I walk up the steps and tentatively push the church doors. I have to put some weight into it—the doors are heavy and seem to have swollen in the years of damp and cold—but with a creaking, slightly grumbling sound, they slowly swing open.

There's a faint, musty smell of mildew inside, but it's not as bad as in the school, presumably because most of the windows are still intact. The dampness hasn't been able to insinuate itself here like it has in the row houses. The dark wooden pews stand in silent rows, and the altar looms large at the front, apparently untouched. An emaciated, bleeding Jesus on the cross above the altar stares down at us with empty eyes. It's enormous, and hard not to stare at, much larger than the majority of crucifixes I've seen. The carved figure must be at least as tall as I am, and as heavy, too. It is also disconcertingly lifelike: the cheekbones seem to press up from under its skin, the contours of the ribs are clearly visible, and the stomach has sunken in, as though after many months of hunger. Unlike many other hale and hearty, inexplicably Aryan Jesuses I've seen on crosses throughout this country, this one has dark hair and is clearly in pain. Despite an untidy paint job, the eyes look bottomless, black and accusatory. Like the lake beneath the clouds.

"Fucking hell," Emmy says quietly. When I turn around, her eyes are also fixed on the figure.

"I can get that you'd start believing in a wrathful god if you had him glaring down at you all the time," she says. Her words are chipper but the tone rings false. She can't seem to tear her eyes from it.

A sudden click makes me jump. It's Robert, getting a shot of the cross. He takes some more pictures of the church as viewed from the doorway, then slowly starts walking up the aisle.

The ceilings are high. I look up to see thick wooden beams crisscrossing above us, yet not a single word echoes. I slowly make my way up to the altar.

I can picture him standing up there with his sleeves rolled up, those beautiful, angelic features red in animation. My image of his face is so clear that I'm sure I must have seen it somewhere before; it probably belongs to some innocent passing stranger, someone who happened to match the image I've formed of him in my mind. Smooth skin, a high forehead, piercing eyes and long eyelashes. Thick, pronounced eyebrows and a narrow nose. Like a renaissance painting of an angel—a Scandinavian prophet for the deep forests.

He was always what fascinated me most about Grandma's story.

He was a young man, scarce over thirty, with a smooth, boyish face. He wasn't particularly tall, but he had broad shoulders and a pleasant smile. The village women suddenly started wearing their best dresses to church of a Sunday, where they would sit in the front pews and listen, eyes gleaming, to Pastor Mattias's sermons.

I've toyed with the idea of trying to do a reenactment for the documentary, to bring in some actors and shoot here, on location. I've even scripted a few short scenes: a church sermon; a scene with Birgitta. We could even do something with the stoning. It would give the documentary something extra, sensationalize it. But it's just not realistic: we don't have the budget to make it look good enough. Better to stick to a straight documentary format and focus on making the story enough of a hook.

You have to do whatever you can to stand out. With Netflix, HBO, and a media market full to bursting point, we're going to have to throw everything we can at getting ourselves seen.

I look up again. I wonder how the pastor's voice sounded in here as it bounded up toward the ceiling. I tried to ask Grandma about his accent a few times, but she could never give me an exact answer, only something vague about it sounding different, like he wasn't from these parts. I could never get any more from her than that.

My eyes are drawn to the small, closed wooden door beside the altar. A closet of some kind? I walk around the altar toward it, take hold of the small brass doorknob, and twist.

There is a small but homely room behind it. The windowpanes have lasted pretty well in here, too, and the dull gray light from the spring day outside filters in through dirty glass panes. Beyond them I can see the blurred image of a pleasant little churchyard. It's perversely idyllic, lush and green.

The room feels most like a kitchen or living room, with a small kitchenette and a simple pinewood table. An empty glass jar with a few extremely crisp, faded dried flowers balances on the windowsill, and there's a small, old-fashioned coffeepot on one of the stovetops on the kitchenette. I walk over to it and lift the lid. The inside is thick with a black, dried-in slush. I smell it and, impossible as it may be, think I can almost make out the faint scent of coffee grounds.

Was this where the Bible group held their meetings?

He had an unshaking belief in the Bible, Pastor Mattias. He said that he had read it four times cover to cover, and thought that every good Christian should do the same. And so Aina started plodding her way through the Bible, too. She wrote that she read it every evening. Pastor Mattias had asked her to help him set up a youth group for Bible studies, and she was so proud she could almost have burst.

Grandma's voice always lost its color when talking about Aina. As though it were easier for her to put a lid on those feelings.

"What's this?" Emmy asks behind me. I look around, startled by her voice.

"I think it's some sort of meeting room," I say. "Or office," I add, as my gaze lands on a messy pile of papers on one of the corduroy seat cushions.

I pick them up cautiously. They are filled with dense, tight handwriting. The paper has yellowed and the ink faded with time, but the writing is still legible.

I hardly dare touch the pages for fear of damaging them; I don't know how brittle paper can get after sixty years. So I put them down on the table and lean in to read the top page.

He who is true and faithful to God need have no secrets.

"What is it?" Emmy asks as her eyes skim the writing.

"I think it's a sermon," I say, suddenly breathless.

Pure hearts have nothing to hide—neither from God, nor from each other. Standing here, I can see that you want to hide; that you want to flee His penetrating gaze and true light; to conceal the darkness within you; to suppress that of which you are ashamed. That is the Devil speaking, the rot within you that shuns the light, for your souls know no fear. But they are drowning, drowning from the weight of evil. They want to see, and be seen by, God.

It is only in completely submitting yourself to the Lord that you can become one with Him; only in giving up your worldly possessions, your petty worldly thoughts and concerns, that you can be pure. And only when you are pure can you be free.

You cannot move forward or change until you are pure. He who is pure does not sink down into darkness; he walks on water, like Jesus himself.

"Not particularly forgiving," Emmy remarks quietly.

"No."

There's a boom overhead. I jump, look up, and see the first raindrops start to land on the windowpanes.

"Shit," I swear, grinding my teeth so hard my jaws hurt. I had hoped that the rainclouds would hold out.

"We'll have to get back to the vans," I say, shuffling the papers into a neat pile and taking off my rucksack to put them inside. "Abandoned buildings aren't safe in heavy rain. It can be too much on the joints—the weight from the water can make them collapse."

Emmy nods.

"I'll let the others know," she says.

She walks over to the doorway without waiting for a reply.

"Guys," she shouts to the others in the church. "We have to get back to the vans."

"Why?" I hear one of the guys shout back.

"It's not safe in the rain," she says. "Pack up so we can get going."

They don't seem to protest. Of course they don't: Emmy said it. People do as she says because she expects no less.

I have always envied her that.

I close the zipper on my rucksack, and get it on just in time to see the sky outside the window flare up.

A real spring storm. So typical that it would happen on one of my five days. But with any luck it won't last long. They normally pass over pretty fast.

"Ready?" Emmy asks from the other side of the door.

"Yes," I reply, pulling up the hood of my jacket as the thunder rumbles above us.

NOW

The rain is clattering against the roof of the van. It's chilly here in the back, much colder than it has been, but I've wrapped myself up in a blanket. I'm sitting in the light of one of our small, battery-powered lamps. Tone's asleep in the tent, so I've started drafting a blog post about the first day. I wonder if she would mind us taking a picture of her ankle? I know it might not be in the best taste, but it gives everything credibility, makes it feel more tangible.

If not, the shots of the broken step will have to do. With any luck we can get them this afternoon, once the rain has stopped. We'll need to go back to the school to try to find Tone's walkie-talkie, anyway.

I've been staring at the same sentence for what must be ten minutes now. The sound of the rain lashing against the roof is strangely soothing, and I yawn into the back of my hand. I can understand why Tone's asleep. I would absolutely love to be, too. I'm not getting anywhere with this.

I feel the rucksack at my feet calling out to me.

Why not take a look at the papers from the church? I mean, they're part of the job, too. They're a story. Just because that's more appealing to me right now than writing blog posts and putting together a production schedule doesn't mean it's not important.

I close my laptop, reach for my rucksack, and unzip the bag slowly and carefully, so that the small raindrops on the outside don't make it onto the papers.

The sheets of paper are so thin between my fingertips that I'm almost too scared to take hold of them. Will they get destroyed by the oil on my skin? Archivists and librarians tend to wear gloves when handling old papers like this, but I don't have any with me. And I'm so eager to read them that my hands are shaking.

> The divine
> ~~To let the divine light in~~
> There is no fear before God. Only love.

The top few sheets match the one Emmy and I were looking at in the church. They look like sermons that Pastor Mattias has written, cut and edited, seemingly churning out draft after draft, polishing his ideas like any good writer. The language is turgid but compelling.

I turn the pages.

The next page must have been written at a different point in time. There are no crossings-out here; everything is written in one great sweep, and the handwriting is different, too. It's bigger, more sprawling, as though written in a rapturous frenzy.

> God has always demanded sacrifices of His own; salvation is neither cheap nor easy. The true path may lead us through darkness, but it is only in daring to walk through the valley of the shadow of death that we can be reborn, pure and new, on the other side; only by sinking down into darkness that we can find the light.
>
> The true path is neither sweet nor seductive. The true path is not straight, but winds. It is an arduous path, for it separates the faithful from the lazy and weak, the worthy from the unworthy.
>
> Meanwhile, beside that path, the Devil lies in wait. He walks among you, masked by innocent faces and gentle voices. And he will whisper in your ear: "Follow me. Choose earthly pleasures,

these gleaming, short-lived distractions. Who cares about eternity?"

You must find his servants among you. They will surely appeal to the evil within you, implore and beseech you, but you must temper your hearts and listen to God's voice alone. Heed not the lies that drip like honey from their lips, that coil around your hearts only to weigh them down. Steel yourselves against these lies, and follow the true light.

You are His warriors. You are his chosen ones. But you must choose Him. You cannot lie back and expect salvation; your place in the Kingdom of Heaven is not assured. You must let go of your worldly lives, dare to travel through the darkness in order to see the light. You must be willing to see his enemies for what they truly are, and strike them down with a divine strength and wrath.

I lick my dry lips and turn the page. Lightning strikes outside, and I see the bolt through the little Plexiglas window between the driver's seat and the back. I count slowly—*one Mississippi, two Mississippi, three Mississippi, four Mississippi*—then the rumble comes from above, quick and ruthless. The storm must be right over us.

The pages are muddled up, as though someone has just thrown them together. The next page isn't the continuation of the hastily written sermon. At first I don't even understand what I'm looking at. It looks like something a child has drawn. Incoherent scribbles. Some of the shapes look like clumpy stick figures.

It makes me uneasy to think a child could have been there in that room, with the person writing what was on those pages.

The words make me think of poor, battered Birgitta Lidman. An outsider, an outcast, even before Pastor Mattias arrived. Were these the words that turned them against her?

Grandma's voice echoes in my head.

Her name was Birgitta, but she was of meagre gifts, as we used to say in those days. At some point they started calling her names. Her mother had died a few years before, and on her deathbed she had asked my mother to look after Birgitta. My mother, being the sort of person who always wanted to help, agreed.

Birgitta was a tall, ungainly woman, with straggly hair and small dark eyes that never looked straight at you. Sometimes, before her mother died, you would see the two of them in the village together, but after her mother left her alone in this world, Birgitta stopped leaving her hut. Before I moved away, my mother and I would take it in turns to take a basket of food up to Birgitta each day. The basket always contained exactly the same things, for it was very important to Birgitta that nothing ever change.

Between her grunts, her evasive eyes, and her habits, Birgitta could be quite unnerving. At times she could fly into a rage, when she would get so frenzied that she would even do herself harm. I remember one instance, when Mother and I brought her a table and two chairs that Mother had managed to convince one of the village boys to make for her. They were a little crooked and uneven, but we thought them better than nothing (at the time the only furniture Birgitta had in her hut was a bed and chamber pot). But Birgitta was quite beside herself; she started shaking her head and rocking back and forth on the spot, and then her grumbling grew to a bellow, and she started flailing around wildly. She gave Mother a real wallop, but the one who came out of it worst was her: she smacked her head against the wall, giving herself a great big gash in the forehead.

Was her hut where Pastor Mattias believed that evil lurked?

Was it on these pages that it began, the process that would end with Birgitta Lidman being bound to a pole in the village square and stoned to death?

It's inconceivable to me that people would listen to that turgid, flowery language about supernatural and evil. But someone did listen.

Aina listened.

I make to turn the page, but lightning flashes across the sky, followed by a crack of thunder after only two counts. I flinch and then laugh, embarrassed, despite there being no one there to see it.

I put those sheets down beside me and reach for the folders that are wedged in at the top of my rucksack. I have to coax them out, and they're so heavy that they almost slip from between my fingertips.

Grandma's own research covered hundreds of pages. I've selected the most important information for the summaries I've given the others, but I had to leave most of it out: she had saved every single article ever written about Silvertjärn and the disappearance. Much of it is worthless: speculation, false leads, articles that just rehash what others had already written.

But some of it did surprise me.

NOW

I put the folders down on the floor next to me and thumb through them to find the one I want: MATTIAS ÅKERMAN. It lies beneath SKANDIJÄRN REPORT, '92.

I have no idea how Grandma managed to get hold of a copy of the mining company's report. The group that bought the company in the early 2000s rejected my request for a copy right off the bat, so when I found a yellowed but fully legible copy in Grandma's files, it felt like I had stumbled across a goldmine.

But that wasn't all I found in Grandma's archive.

The folder labeled MATTIAS ÅKERMAN is so old that the cardboard is almost fraying. I've copied and replaced most of the other folder labels, but Grandma hand-wrote this one, and I couldn't quite bring myself to throw it away. Her handwriting is neat and pragmatic. I run my fingers over the faded pencil text before opening it.

The first press clipping is short and almost illegible. It's the copy of a brief notice in a local newspaper.

Nils and Edda Åkerman are pleased to announce the birth of their son, MATTIAS ÅKERMAN, born September 12, 1928. The christening will take place in Forshälla Church on Sunday, September 23.

I don't know how Grandma tracked him down. I have no idea where she picked up his trail, or if she was even sure that she had found the right person. I only found her archive after her first stroke, and by then it was already too late.

I thought we would have more time. I guess that's always the way.

The next clipping isn't from the press. It's the copies of some hospital records for a Mattias Åkerman, then eleven years of age. According to these, a Mattias with the same date of birth was admitted to hospital three times in the years 1939 and 1940: once for a broken rib, once for stomach pains, and once for a broken arm. The cause of his complaints is never explained, simply that he was treated and then sent home.

In the first two records, Nils Åkerman is listed as the guardian present. In the third—the one relating to the broken arm—that field is left empty. I don't know if it's down to laziness, or if it means something. Grandma has written "Living with uncle?" in the margin beside it.

The next clipping is a death notice. It looks like it comes from the same local paper, from late May 1940.

EDDA ÅKERMAN has passed away after a short illness. She is mourned by her husband, NILS ÅKERMAN.

Her funeral will take place in Forshälla Church this coming Saturday, June 5.

The notice features a dark, blurry image of a washed-out face. The features are difficult to make out, and the eyes are simply two darker spots in a white oval. She doesn't appear to be smiling.

In the margin Grandma has written: "Already moved? No son mentioned." And then, underneath:

"Cause of death?"

That question is not answered.

After that comes the timeline. I have no idea whether these are simply educated guesses, or if Grandma based it on information that has since disappeared somewhere in her files.

09/12 1928: Born to parents Nils and Edda Åkerman in Forshälla, Blekinge.

1928–?: Early childhood spent with parents. Unclear when he moves, or why. Possible causes: Death of mother. Financial problems. Early violent tendencies.

1939–1940: Hospitalized at least three times for fractures and possible internal bleeding. No further investigations made.

1940?–1944: Leaves parental home and moves in with his uncle, Gustaf Larsson. Unclear when the move happens: mother's death notice suggests before her death in June 1942, but there is no concrete evidence of Mattias living with the Larssons before 1944.

June 1942: Mother, Edda Åkerman, passes away in early June. Mattias would have been thirteen. Unclear if still living with parents, or with uncle at the time. Cause of death unclear.

10/21 1944: First evidence that Mattias is officially living with his uncle Gustaf and his family. See national registration records. The same record states that Gustaf's wife, Berit, and daughters Linnea (b.1934) and Sofia (b.1936) both live at the same address. See also marriage license and birth certificates.

May 1946: Linnea admitted to hospital. Her mother, Berit Larsson, is the guardian present. The records state that she has previously complained of abdominal pains. She has bruises on her left arm and on both thighs, but does not want to state where these came from. The nurse deems no treatment to be necessary, and sends her home with a warning to be more careful in her play.

November 1946: Linnea admitted to hospital for the second time. Berit Larsson once again listed as the guardian present. Linnea is brought in after losing consciousness due to particularly heavy menstrual bleeding. When examined, the bleeding turns out to be an early miscarriage. Linnea refuses to give the father's name. She is kept in hospital for three days for observation.

July 1947: National registration records reveal Mattias is no longer registered at the Larsson family address, nor with his father, Nils Åkerman. No trace of him elsewhere.

02/16 1951: Mattias Åkerman is arrested in Stockholm for vagrancy, and fined. Fines don't appear to have been paid.

07/09 1953: A young man described as "of average height, with blond hair and gray eyes, wearing a ripped shirt and patched-up trousers" is arrested on suspicion of the sexual assault of a young girl in Falun. Gives his name as Mattias Larsson, but is unable to provide any formal identification. He is released the next day, after the victim claims to be unable to identify the perpetrator with any certainty. Exact nature of the assault not stated. Dubious as to whether this is Mattias Åkerman, but the physical descriptions match, and the name Mattias Larsson could be a nod to his uncle's surname.

June 1955: a Mattias Åkerman applies to study for the clergy. Application rejected.

June 1956: a Mattias Åkerman applies to study for the clergy. Application rejected.

Grandma's timeline ends here.

A few more documents follow after that—birth certificates for Sofia and Linnea, and hospital records for Linnea. The first of these features pictures of her bruises—no more than blurry, dark patches on thin white limbs.

I have scoured these documents many times, read the articles and national registration records, and studied the hospital records and the concise police reports. I don't know how Grandma came to be so convinced that Mattias Åkerman was the man who would later become Pastor Mattias. Perhaps she came across his name through his rejected applications to join the clergy, or perhaps she simply felt that he matched that profile. However hard I searched, I couldn't find any clear link to him in her papers.

Much remains unclear, but it would be easy to weave a story from the few reliable facts she did find: a violent childhood that appears to have culminated in him moving in with his uncle; a mother who died before her time; an unstable youth growing up with two younger cousins. Those girls must have idolized him—a beautiful older cousin, a sort-of older brother and secret crush in one.

One who took advantage of his status. And of them. Until it all came to light and he was cast out onto the street.

A few years as a drifter, small misdemeanors. The suspicion of another, albeit unspecified, sexual assault on a young girl in Falun. Unsuccessful attempts to join the clergy.

And then, one fine day, he turns up in Silvertjärn, with his exotic, lilting Blekinge dialect and mysterious past, to become the village's savior and prophet.

It's impossible to know if this is all true. But it feels as though there may be a grain of truth in there. And it's hard not to wonder what that might mean. What Aina's adoring, almost obsessive love might have led to.

I picture Silvertjärn on that August afternoon: the sweltering heat; that inexplicable emptiness; that lone baby in an empty room on the second floor of a deserted school.

I've scoured Tone's face for similarities to my grandma's, wondered if her narrow eyes could contain something of my grandma's steady gaze.

Could the baby have been Aina's daughter?

I've never quite allowed myself to ask that question.

The rain is still pitter-pattering against the windshield. How long can it go on for?

The sky above flashes again, and I see Max walking past the other van toward me, his figure doubly blurred through the windshield and the Plexiglas behind the driver's seat. He's wearing a thick jacket and walking fast, hardly more than a silhouette in the darkened storm light.

He's probably bored out of his mind and after some company, I think, and feel a twinge of irritation deep in my gut. We're here to work, this isn't a camping trip. I can't entertain him whenever he feels understimulated.

I hear footsteps approach and then stop by my back door. I realize I'm being harsh. For all I know, he might want to discuss the project or something.

I wait for him to knock, but none comes.

A few seconds pass. The rain starts to pound so heavily against the roof of the van that the noise is overpowering. All I can hear are my own breaths and the clatter of rain on metal.

Is he just going to stand out there?

I sit up and shuffle over to the back door to open it, but then wait.

The hairs on my neck are standing up. Why?

Something isn't right.

Why hasn't he knocked? Why is he just standing there in the pouring rain?

Deep at the back of my mind, my instincts start to murmur. My breaths have gone quiet and shallow.

Where was he coming from?

The Volvo is parked diagonally to the right of this van, but he didn't come from there. He was walking straight across the square. From the school.

It's as if time has slowed; I'm suddenly aware of how cold it is here in the van, of how much my fingers are trembling with the adrenaline.

Pastor Mattias's draft sermon is still lying on the floor behind me. For some reason, one phrase is drumming at the back of my head:

His servants walk among you

There's another flash of lightning, instantly followed by a clap of thunder. I jump, accidentally kicking the battery-powered lamp, which flickers and goes out. I have to cover my mouth with my hand to stop myself from screaming.

Yes, I saw that. I really did.

As the lightning flashed, I saw him sitting in his car. Max. Just a silhouette, his head bowed over something—a book or a phone—but it was him. It was Max.

But if Max is still in the Volvo . . .

It's Emmy, I tell myself. *Emmy's standing outside. She wants something.*

But if that's the case, then why is she just standing there?

I really wish Tone were in here with me; that I weren't alone in this small, enclosed space that suddenly feels like a cage.

The doors are unlocked.

The rain is pounding to the beat of my heart.

A sudden, deafeningly loud crackle fills the small space, and for one frantic, seemingly never-ending second I think it's someone clawing at the doors. Then I realize that the sound is coming from inside the van. It's coming from me. From my waistband.

The walkie-talkie. Fingers trembling, I fumble it out, press the button and say:

"Alice here."

It comes out as a shrill, shaky whisper.

That crackle returns, only louder, so loud that it grates. But then, amid the crackling, I hear a moan.

A child's voice, a woman's voice, distorted and metallic, emerges from the interference.

The doors open and I scream and drop my walkie-talkie. It clatters to the ground, sending the batteries flying.

The figure in the doorway pulls down its hood. Emmy's henna-red hair comes tumbling out.

"What is it?" she asks. "Relax! It's just me!" She climbs into the back of the van, leaving the doors open. Behind her I see the rain pouring down in big, hard drops into the puddles that have formed in the square.

"What is it?" she asks again. "Has something happened?" Her pupils look huge in the darkness.

It takes me a few seconds to find my voice again. My rational thought is still caged by fear and adrenaline, and the words burst out of me:

"What the fuck are you doing? Why were you just standing there? And that walkie-talkie game? That's fucking sick!"

Emmy recoils slightly at my rage, but then her features harden, and she hisses back:

"Since when is me coming over here something to get so fucking hysterical about? I just wanted to ask if you wanted some lunch!"

"I'm not mad about you coming over here, I'm mad about you hanging around outside like some psycho, zombie-groaning into your walkie-talkie! What are you, a child?"

My palms are sweaty, and I can taste blood in my mouth. My anger is so intense that my voice has transformed into something gruff and hacking.

"What?" asks Emmy, sounding genuinely confused. "What are you talking about? What groaning?"

"Don't even try it," I start to say in disgust, but Emmy shakes her head.

"No—Alice, I don't know what you think I did, but I don't even have my walkie-talkie on me." She turns the pockets on her hoodie inside out to show that they're empty, then points at her bare waistband.

"Look," she says.

I stare at her.

"And I wasn't hanging around out there," she goes on. "I literally just ran over from the other van. I wouldn't want to get any wetter than I had to."

Her hair is tousled, the skin around her bright eyes completely unsmudged.

Almost against my will, my eyes are drawn to the windshield, to the school looming over in the distance. Those big, open doors on their rusty hinges, and the silent void behind them.

The sky above us lights up again, but the thunder lags a few seconds behind. The storm is passing. The rain outside has started to slow, if only a little.

I look at Emmy. At her light-gray hoodie.

It's almost completely dry.

Her eyes are bottomless when she fixes them on mine and says, with a voice quiet and unflinching:

"You saw somebody, didn't you?"

February 9, 1959

Dearest Margareta,

I hope the journey went well, and that the train didn't leave you feeling too poorly! You did look a little peaky when we said good-bye at the station, but I didn't want to say anything in case I put my foot in it! Mother mentioned it today at breakfast. She told us how she had felt so ill when she was pregnant with you that she could hardly get out of bed for the first few months.

But how exciting it is! And, I know you're very busy right now with your work, the pregnancy, the new apartment and all, but you must try to write every week. I shall do exactly the same, to remind you!

Oh, and I've found such a beautiful name for the baby if she's a girl! Dagny was over for coffee when I came home today, and she said you're definitely expecting a girl, because apparently you always feel worse with girls. Mother just smiled when she said that, but as soon as Dagny left she told me it was all poppycock, if you can imagine! Still, I think Dagny might just be right—though perhaps

*that's just wishful thinking on my part. But how wonderful it would
be if it were a little girl! I can't wait. August can't come soon enough.*

*Oh yes, the name: what do you think of Ruth? Isn't it beautiful? I
know you mentioned Elisabet and Charlotta, but if you ask me, I think
shorter names are more elegant. (Besides, how important is it really to
have a "continental" name, whatever that means? Father said you've
started to sound like big city folk. Did he say that to you, too? Perhaps I
shouldn't have written that. I don't think he meant anything by it.)*

*Anyway, I found the name in our Bible group yesterday. Ruth
has an entire book named after her in the Bible, and Pastor Mattias
had selected a passage from it to read for the meeting. The group has
already become quite the crowd—even Lena has started coming to
meetings, though I think that may be less to do with her interest in
the Bible than her crush on the pastor. Yesterday she wore that blouse
with the pleated front that she says gives her a real waspish waist.
But the pastor didn't seem to pay it any notice; he just smiled warmly
and said it was lovely to see so many new faces in the group. And
that was it! In fact, he gave her no extra attention at all—I almost
think she was a little put out by it.*

*We talked about Ruth and her family, and how hard it must
have been not to have a home, and then Karin Änglund started to
cry. The room went quiet—none of us knew what to say—but the
pastor just sat down next to her, waited for her tears to start to settle,
and then asked her what had made her so sad. Karin said that her
mother and father might not be able to stay in Silvertjärn, that they
might have to leave to find work elsewhere, and she didn't know
where they would go. She said that she would be homeless, just like
Ruth. But then the pastor reminded her that Ruth found a new
home, and he told her that she needn't worry, for we and the church
would be her home, and that he, and God, would always take her
in. Then Karin started to cry even more, and when she whimpered,
"thank you, thank you, thank you," then my chest started to hurt,
too, and I thought even I might burst into tears.*

Mother thinks I haven't noticed, but I can see her getting more tired and anxious by the day. She didn't want to let on while you were here because she didn't want to worry you, but I heard her tell Dagny that they're short of money and that Father's struggling to find a job. If things don't get better soon then maybe I'll be in the same boat as poor Karin Änglund.

But do you know what? It was almost a miracle, for no sooner had I thought that than Pastor Mattias looked me straight in the eye, and it felt like he could read my mind. He told us—though it felt like he was talking to me alone:

"Everyone has a home in the house of God. None of you need ever worry about losing your way. If your families lose their houses then the church shall be your home. If your parents and siblings leave you then we shall be your family. God looks after his flock."

He sounded so truthful and confident, and I believed him utterly. And, for the first time in many months, I felt calm.

I hung back slightly after the meeting, and Pastor Mattias thanked me for all my help with the group, and for managing to bring in so many other youngsters. He even said he could never have done it without me! Can you believe it? Me! I hardly knew what to say, but he seemed to understand (he always understands), and just smiled. And then he said I could choose our passages for the next meeting! He said I could choose whatever I wanted, but that I should look at the Song of Songs, as he was sure I would like it. I haven't managed to do it yet, but I'm certain he's right. He always is.

But anyway, do have a think about the name! Ruth! I know it may not be so "continental," but despite her hardships Ruth did become a queen in the end. So it is a royal name, and I think that's even better!

Now, I'd best go read the Song of Songs, to try to select some passages. Write soon!

Your little sister, Aina

NOW

I wake up.

My heart is pounding, but I blink and sit up in my sleeping bag, trying to shake off the nightmare. I stretch out, let my fingers brush against the edge of the tent. I'm not in that van anymore.

What woke me up?

It's pitch black in here. I have no idea what time it could be, but the dawn light hasn't started to filter in through the thin fabric of the tent. It smells of humans and sleep in here, with a faint hint of rain.

I hear Tone roll over in her sleep, and say her name quietly.

No reply.

When I focus on Tone's curled-up figure, I almost think her eyes are glinting at me in the darkness; that she's lying there, silent and unmoving, staring at me. It makes my heart pound even faster, but the next second I'm convinced it's all in my head. It's just the lingering shrouds of sleep over my eyes, that's all. She's asleep.

I'm not used to waking up in the middle of the night. Staying up late for work, sure, but not the feeling of being wrenched out of sleep, the kind of unpleasant stillness that comes of being awake against your will, while everyone else is asleep. My hearing seems keener than usual, and however hard I try, I can't stop myself from listening out for something.

Footsteps.

There's no one there, I tell myself. *You know there's no one there.*

But I don't believe it.

There's no sound outside.

I had denied what I thought I had seen and asked Emmy to leave the van, but even once the doors were shut that lingering fear had lived on in my body. I felt uneasy well into the evening, even after the clouds had dispersed enough to reveal an ethereally pink sunset. The ground was too wet to get a fire going, so instead we made grilled cheese sandwiches on the alcohol stove. I didn't say much while we ate, just watched the others as they made full-mouthed small talk, spraying bread crumbs over the cobblestones.

I watched Emmy.

She was the one who was there, despite everything—the one who opened the door. And even though her hoodie was dry, that could have been some sort of setup: she could have had it in a plastic bag, for example, then put it on to make it look like she had run straight over.

But why?

Tone said she'd heard someone downstairs in the school before she fell through the steps, and Emmy and Robert did make it back to camp suspiciously quickly.

It feels ridiculous to picture Emmy behind all this, though. It would go against everything I thought I knew about her. However dim my opinion may be of her now, there's no denying she has always taken her work incredibly seriously. At college she was just unbearable, so nitpicky that no one ever wanted to do group projects with her. She would edit and re-edit until her eyes were tired and bloodshot, her fingertips numb. She always had her eyes on the prize, results over all else.

I can't believe that she would sabotage this project.

But then . . .

I *have* wondered why she agreed to come on board—despite us paying peanuts, despite having to work under me. . . .

No. I shake my head. The thought is insane. Emmy may be selfish, pragmatic, and cold, but she isn't unhinged. She isn't trying to ruin my chances, or my film. It's all in my head. Silvertjärn is just getting to me.

I really wish Tone were awake. A familiar voice in this darkness. She would tell me to stop being ridiculous, remind me, in that deadpan voice of hers, that the most we have to worry about is a hungry bear fresh out of hibernation wandering into the village one night and deciding we look like a tasty breakfast.

But Tone's sleeping soundly, and I'm the only one awake.

It's a very lonely feeling.

I can't help thinking about Grandma. Grandma, alone in a narrow bed in Stockholm, heavily pregnant and beside herself with worry. What she said about the last letter.

It arrived at the end of August, just before my due date. It had been a cool summer, but a heat wave had swept in at the end of July, and August had been just terrible. The air felt completely static, and I could hardly breathe, let alone move. It had been almost a month since I'd heard anything from Aina or Mother, which had worried me, but the pain and the heat had taken up more of my attention.

The letter was short. The handwriting wasn't Aina's usual style, which everyone had always praised for its elegance. It was written in a jerky, slip-shod hand, on ink-stained paper, and was both incoherent and incomprehensible. She wrote that the hour was nigh, and that I must return to them before it was too late.

This made me frantic with worry, as I'm sure you can imagine. I begged and pleaded with your grandfather to let me go to Silvertjärn. Even he started to worry when he read the letter, but I was in no state to travel: I was in my ninth month, and practically bedridden.

So your grandfather went there himself.

He roped his best friend into going with him, in case he should need any help. They took the 09:13 from Stockholm Central Station to Sundsvall, where they changed to the train for Silvertjärn. It took them eleven hours to get there in all. Trains were slower back then.

It was already dusk when Grandpa and Nils got off the train, and the station was completely deserted. There wasn't a soul in sight.

They made their way toward the center of town, the shadows drawing in, the houses empty. They knocked at doors here and there for directions— your grandpa hadn't been there in a long time and couldn't find my parents' house, especially with the cottages looking so alike—but no one opened up.

It was only when they crossed the river to the main square that they saw it.

A pole had been raised in the middle of the square, and from it hung a limp body bound by ropes. Gitta must have been there for many long days, for the flies were swarming around her, and she had swollen in the late summer heat. Her face was bloody, beaten beyond recognition, and the stones they had used to execute her lay strewn around her body. Smooth, round river stones that had been gathered from the riverbed and blunted of any jagged edges. They were peppered with blood and hair.

Your grandfather and Nils were petrified. They had no idea what to do. At first they wanted to try to get her down, but it was soon clear that Birgitta was beyond saving. She had been dead for days. So they ran into the nearest house, in search of someone who could help.

It was empty. As was the next one, and the next. The doors all stood ajar, the rooms vacant.

By this point they were so scared that they were at their wit's end. They ran back out into the square. Darkness had started to fall, and Birgitta's body was still hanging from the pole. But when they looked at her, your grandfather swore—on the name of God the Father himself—that he saw her turn her head to look at them.

They ran all night through the forest to reach the nearest town, some sixty miles away. Nils collapsed from exhaustion on the edge of town, but your grandfather held out. He told them something terrible had happened in Silvertjärn and that they had to send help, before he, too, collapsed.

When the police arrived they found Birgitta's body in the middle of the square, just as your grandfather had said. The village was completely silent. But in the midst of that silence they heard a baby's cries.

They found the baby naked on the floor of the school nurse's room. It was no more than a few days old. There was no trace of whoever had left it there—nor, indeed, whoever had given birth to it.

The police searched every building, cottage, and villa, but they couldn't find a single soul. It was as though every one of the 887 residents of Silvertjärn had disappeared into thin air. Doors had been left open, windows ajar. The river ran peacefully down to the lake. And the village was empty.

They combed the forest but found no one—not a single track. Aina, my mother, and my father were gone, like the rest of our neighbors, friends, and acquaintances. Gone. As though they had never existed.

FRIDAY

NOW

The morning that dawns is clear and almost lavishly beautiful. The air zings with that fresh smell of pine and wet earth that comes only after a real spring downpour, and the sky feels enormous overhead. Light blue, without a cloud in sight.

The river water is freezing but surprisingly clear. From what I've read, it comes straight from the mountains. We've washed with an all-in-one shampoo that the woman in the camping store assured me was organic and biodegradable. I stand up and wring out my hair, watch the current carry the small white bubbles off toward the lake. Its glassy surface sparkles in the morning light. Perhaps we should have washed down there instead—the water would probably have been marginally warmer—but Emmy said it probably wouldn't be as clear, as it's still. To be honest, I was relieved when she said it. Those unfathomable depths look anything but inviting.

By the time I climb back up onto the riverbank and wrap myself up in my ugly, burled Coca-Cola towel, I'm so cold I can barely feel my feet. The air feels almost warm after the ice-cold water, and despite my long, anxious night I feel wide awake.

Everything seems easier in the daylight, and the night's worries feel far away. Not that my suspicions have completely disappeared, but as I watch Emmy shivering and cursing as she rinses the lather from her hair,

I find it hard to see her as the shadow lurking in my nightmares. I glance at her out of the corner of my eye as she scrubs out her shampoo. She has a tattoo on her hip I don't recognize—a small stylized owl—and she's more muscular than I remember her being.

A sound makes me turn away. Tone is struggling to get out of the water. I give her my hand and help her to pull herself up. She's so heavy on my arm that I almost lose her, but I manage to regain my balance. And when I take a closer look at her foot, I can understand her difficulty: her throbbing red ankle is so swollen it's as wide as her calf.

"How's the foot feeling?" I ask. The question is redundant, really. I can see how it feels. I just want her to tell me something else.

Tone nods.

"Oh, it's fine," she says. Her lips are blueish with cold, but her hand feels like it's burning up. "You just haven't seen it without the strapping before."

I hear Emmy get out of the water behind us and start getting dressed.

Tone sits down heavily on her towel and, still wearing her wet underwear, starts strapping up her ankle again.

I open my mouth to say something—what, I'm not sure—when I hear Max's voice from the buildings.

"Are you guys done already?" he asks.

I shut my mouth.

"We're ready," Tone shouts back, her voice unwavering. It doesn't sound like she's in much pain. She sounds normal.

I hastily pull my clothes on over my wet underwear. My jeans cling to my thighs and hips as I pull them up, and my top bunches up stubbornly as I try to put it on. I've just got everything in place by the time Max and Robert arrive.

"How was the water?" Max asks.

"Cold," says Emmy, pulling her loose T-shirt over her head. "Really fucking cold."

I smirk at him.

"Your sweater's on inside out," I say.

Max looks down, sees the label flapping under his chin and blushes.

"Ah, who cares," he says. "I'm about to take it off again."

I smile.

Robert's just a few steps behind him. His hair is a dazzling gilded red in this early morning light, and with his invisible eyebrows he has an almost androgynous look.

"It'll have to be a quick dip, guys," I say. "We have a lot to get through today, after losing all of yesterday."

Max gives me a thumbs up.

"Quicker than lightning."

Tone, Emmy, and I start making our way back to the square—slowly, so that Tone can keep up. At this time of day we could almost be in any sleepy old Swedish town; a Saturday morning, perhaps, when everybody's still asleep and the daily bustle has yet to begin.

"Wait," I say, slowing down.

Birgitta's shack is just ahead, to the left of the road we've taken. From this angle the bare, leafless tree at one corner of the house looks almost burnished, and the broken window panes are calling out to me.

I turn to Tone.

"Shall we take a quick peek?" I ask. "I know we're going there this afternoon, but, I mean, it can't hurt to take a look now."

Tone nods.

"Sure," she says. Emmy frowns and looks at Tone.

"Are you sure you feel well enough?" she asks.

Tone nods.

"Might as well do it now," she says. "Make the most of our time."

I hesitate, but my curiosity overcomes my bad conscience. I support Tone as we walk over to the little hut. It's more out of the way than I'd first thought, and I imagine how it must have felt to come out here every day with a basket on my arm, seeing the closed curtains, knowing who waited inside.

The front door isn't locked. In fact, it's ever so slightly ajar, but that's only visible when we're standing right by it. I give the door a careful nudge, and it swings open on a creaky hinge.

The hut is even smaller than it looks from the outside; the three of us will barely be able to get in without difficulty. Despite the broken windows and the bright, clear morning, the inside is also dark and dim: the windows are small, the slant of the roof blocks much of the sunlight, and the dead tree casts a large shadow from the west.

The bed is small and shabby, and has lain unmade for sixty years. One small, lone pillow lies at its head, and it's strewn with blankets in drab, clashing colors. There is no sheet on the faded, striped mattress, which is marked in a few places by indistinct light brown stains. The bed can only be two and a half feet wide, but it takes up almost half of the room.

"You'll need to move in a little," Emmy says behind me.

Tone squeezes past me, hobbles over to the table with its two Windsor chairs, and sits down on one of them. I would have stopped her, but she does it before I can say anything. Despite a creaking protest from its uneven legs, however, the chair holds.

With the three of us in here there's hardly any space to move. Emmy looks around the room.

"No tap," she says. "Or toilet."

I wonder if we're all thinking the same thing. Standing here, in this tiny, dark space, the distressing reality sinks like a weight on my chest.

"What a life," says Emmy, quietly, making my own thoughts echo between the narrow walls. "What a fucking life."

I'm surprised she cares. On the other hand, I guess she's always enjoyed taking care of people, so long as it comes at no cost to her. It's easier to sympathize with dead people, tragic victims long gone. They aren't nearly as demanding. As compassion goes, it's cheap.

Or perhaps it's just that, when standing here between these four closed walls, it's almost impossible to remain cold to how bleak Birgitta Lidman's life was.

Tone's breathing has calmed. Sitting down seems to be doing her good. She leans over the table and runs her fingers across it.

"There's something here," she says. I edge my way over to the table, lean in, and squint at the dark wood.

It looks like a finger painting, as though someone has scrawled something in thick, clumsy streaks with their fingertips. The color has dried and faded with age, sunk down into the bumpy wooden surface, but I can still see what it is. Stick figures: uneven, clumsily drawn scribbles, like the restless doodles of a child. The figures' mouths are furious, like black holes, and the crayon has been pressed so hard it has crumbled.

Suddenly I can't take it anymore.

I don't say anything, just push past Emmy and out of the door. The outside air should make me feel better. I look over to the forest's edge, try to breathe in the fresh air and make that dark, distressing hut leave me alone. I try not to think about the innate naïvety of those small scrawls on the tabletop; about that child trapped in a grown woman's body, a grown woman's strength; about how scared she must have been, the anxiety of not knowing what was happening as she was bound to that pole; about that first stone. . . .

Someone puts their hand on my shoulder, and I turn around.

I'm expecting Tone, but it's Emmy who's standing there behind me. I know the look on her face; I've seen it a thousand times: every late night I came to her dorm with anxiety gasping at my lungs, every time the black spilled over and she would sit there, taking it in with calm, unyielding eyes, holding my gaze until my heartbeats started to settle, until my breathing calmed.

"We should get Tone back to camp," she says. "Get some breakfast in her."

This throws me.

"Yes," I say, once the words sink in. "Yes, of course."

I look back at the hut. Tone's still bowed over the table. Her hair is hanging forward, covering almost all of her face, and her bad leg is stretched out in front of her.

When I step back over the threshold, I can hear her muttering something. But it doesn't sound like she's talking to herself; it's as though she's responding to something, a disjointed piece of a longer conversation.

"Tone?" I ask. My uncertainty makes her name shrink in my mouth.

She doesn't look up. Her gaze is glued to the tabletop, where she jerks her hand once, and then again, as though re-creating some sort of pattern. It's only when I take one step more that I realize what she's doing.

Transfixed, she's tracing the outline of one of the small figures on the table, over and over again.

"Tone?" I say again, louder this time, and she stops and looks up.

She blinks repeatedly, as though forcing her vision into focus. Her eyes, normally steady as flint, have the look of an autumnal fog. Out of focus. Like Grandma's toward the end: half-blind and veiled by cataracts.

My skin starts to prickle. I clear my throat.

"We thought we'd head back for breakfast now," I say, conscious that I sound like I'm talking to a child. "Are you hungry?"

Tone nods and makes to stand up, but grimaces when she puts weight on her foot.

"Shit," she says, and it's as though something clicks. She looks normal again—a tired, wet-haired normal.

"Here, you can lean on me," I say. "We're going to the parsonage later on—maybe we can find you a cane or crutch or something there."

"If not, I'm expecting you to whittle me one from an old pine," Tone mutters with a weak smile. "I mean, what good is all that research of yours if you can't do that?"

NOW

By the time we get back to camp, Tone is hobbling, leaning heavily into my arm.

"Why don't you go rest in the tent?" I say, less a question than a command. "We can make breakfast."

Tone purses her lips. I expect her to protest, but instead she nods. Her short blond fringe has stuck to her sweaty forehead.

"Might be a good idea."

I help her into the tent and then walk around to the back of Emmy and Robert's van, where Emmy is on her knees, rooting around in one of the boxes of tinned goods.

"Could you pass the alcohol stove?" I ask.

Emmy jumps at the sound of my voice, but then reaches in and pulls out the box containing the stove. She hands it to me with a glance over her shoulder, and a firebolt anger in her green eyes that makes me start.

I stand there holding the box for a few seconds, then back away to the middle of our little campsite. I get out the alcohol stove while Emmy continues to poke around in our food stores behind me. When she walks over and puts the open packet of instant coffee, the coffeepot, and water down in front of me, I look up.

"Alice, we need to talk," she says, then sits down cross-legged on the cobblestones. She does it smoothly, in a single movement. She never used to be so agile. She used to be stiff and a little lazy, slow in the mornings and energized by night; used to yawn like a cat, wide-mouthed and red-tongued.

How many times have we eaten breakfast together? One hundred? One thousand? Her with hair wet post-shower, like now, me with yesterday's makeup still clinging to my eyelashes. But this time my face is bare, and hers is closed.

The alcohol stove stands like a wall between us.

I light it.

"What is it?" I ask as the little blue flames appear, then wave the match to put it out. I try to keep my voice cool and professional. I'm her producer, after all. Her project manager. Her boss.

Emmy drops her forearms to her knees. There are grass stains on her jeans.

"I know you can see Tone's sick," she says bluntly. "And I can get why you wouldn't want to call off this trip, but this isn't sustainable. She needs to get to a hospital, now."

Her words aren't aggressive, just direct. Like a hand thrusting into my stomach and squeezing my organs.

"She says she doesn't want to," I say, then reach for the coffeepot and put it on the little stove. "She's an adult, she knows what's best for her."

Emmy rolls her eyes.

"Come on, Alice," she says, her voice somehow both irritated and unfeeling. "Don't try that shit with me, you can see she's not well. We both saw her in Gitta's house—she was raving, for fuck's sake! She's probably delirious. She needs to see a doctor—now."

"But she doesn't feel like she has a fever," I say, clenching my jaw so hard I can feel my muscles strain. Strangely enough, Emmy's words make my own anxiety start to ebb away. I mean, I practically carried Tone back to camp, and she didn't feel so hot to me. "She says herself it's just a sprain."

"Sprains don't look like that, Alice."

By now I can't bite my tongue any longer. I snap:

"What are you, a doctor?"

"You don't need to be a doctor to see she can hardly walk, and it's only getting worse!" Emmy replies. Her hands are now clenched into small, hard fists.

"It's not like I'm her mom!" I say. "Do you think I haven't talked to her? Do you think I haven't asked? I've asked her time and time again, but she's insisting she wants to stay. So what am I supposed to do? Throw her into the back of the van, lock her up, and drive away? She's a grown woman—we have to respect her wishes."

"If you say so," says Emmy. In the space between her words I hear everything she isn't saying. The curse of knowing someone's rhythms. Of being able to intuit her meaning, rather than her words.

"What are you suggesting?" I ask. I can hear I'm overarticulating, letting the syllables draw the lines I can't.

Emmy stands up and brushes off her legs. I can't take having her look down at me, so I scramble to my feet, too.

"Nothing, Alice," she says, a rusty edge to her words. "I'm not suggesting anything. I'm just saying it's weird that Tone's fucking sick and that you, as her friend, don't seem especially concerned."

Her accusation knocks the wind out of me. I'm so angry that my teeth ache.

"Don't you dare say that to me," I bite. "Don't you dare tell me I'm not worried about Tone. And don't you dare talk to me like that."

Emmy raises her eyebrows and opens her mouth, but I cut her off before she can speak. I'm feeling that delicious sting of being able to say what's been hanging over me since I first saw her at our recruitment meeting, since I first noticed those delicate little laughter lines that had started to form around her eyes, the new highlights the henna had brought out in her hair, the strangely familiar lines of her ears. The shock and rage and sadness I felt at all of them.

"It's great that you're so worried about Tone," I say, "you've never struck me as someone to worry about someone else's well-being before. But I'm guessing it's not Tone that's the issue here, is it? It's more about you getting the chance to tell me how self-obsessed and demanding I am. It's like gold dust to you, any excuse to say that."

I've heard the expression of someone's eyes turning black with anger before, but never before have I seen it. Emmy's pupils dilate, and I take a small step backward.

She says nothing, and suddenly I'm very aware of how alone the two of us are. Tone's asleep in the tent, which leaves just Emmy and me; Emmy lithe and muscular, her eyes black with rage, her fists clenched.

My breath catches in my throat. I try to swallow, only to find that I can't. Time seems to have stopped still.

"Hey, how's it going?" The unexpected break of the silence almost throws me off-balance. I don't think I've ever been so relieved to hear Max's voice.

"Fine!" I shout, my voice rough, as I throw a final glance Emmy's way. She has run her fingers through her hair, all trace of her furious mask gone—all but a lingering streak of stiffness in her face.

"How was the water?"

Max and Robert are walking across the square, all wet hair and clean, refreshed faces. When they arrive I can't resist giving Max a hug out of pure relief.

He hugs me back and laughs.

"Whoa, what a welcoming committee!" he says. "A hug *and* coffee."

When I step back I see that Emmy has poured some instant coffee into the pot of boiling water that she has taken off the stove.

"Would you get the bread?" she asks Robert, who has stopped next to her. "And the oil, and a skillet."

Robert gets out the equipment and ingredients for beans on toast, then helps Emmy to prepare them. I'm still a little shaken up, but the semblance of normality is so convincing that I almost feel like a fraud. The sunshine warms me up through my jacket, and the thin wisps of cloud on the horizon serve only to accentuate just how high and clear the sky is.

When we sit down to eat, Max asks what the plan is.

"We'll do the rest of the church," I say. "I'd like to finish scouting and do some filming in there. And the parsonage. After that we'll have to see how we're doing for time."

"In pairs?" Max asks, but before I can answer, Emmy jumps in, her mouth full of half-chewed bread and beans:

"I'm staying here."

Robert looks at her in surprise. I stop short.

Emmy looks me straight in the eye and says:

"I think it's a good idea if someone stays here with Tone. Plus I'd like to go through the material we have and put together a more detailed production schedule for the next few days."

Her gaze is steady and completely shut off. Eyes like green marbles.

The moment seems to last an age, but I find myself nodding. Sure: if it gets her to calm down and drop the issue then it's a small price to pay. We can finish scouting in a couple of hours without her, and she's right that there's work for her to do here. And maybe it is a good thing if someone stays here with Tone.

"OK," I agree.

THEN

Elsa shifts restlessly in her seat. The church pews are hard and worn, and in recent years her hips have started aching whenever she sits in the same position too long. Her mother had always complained about her hips, knees, and ankles, but Elsa had never thought it would happen to her, too.

Oh well. She isn't so very old. Nor is it so strange that she would get a sore backside after sitting on a dry wooden plank for an hour.

". . . how many people actually give thought to Jesus's deeds in their daily lives?" she hears the pastor ask the congregation. "Many of those who call themselves Christians do little to live up to the name. It is easy to let oneself be distracted by the toils and troubles of everyday life, and to forget . . ."

This sermon seems to be dragging on a bit. The church is full to the rafters, which is, of course, nice to see—many of the people she can see in the front pews are faces she doesn't often see in church, a happy mix of youths and single older men—but she is concerned that Pastor Mattias is being too long-winded for their tastes. Einar tends to always keep himself to forty, forty-five minutes—short and concise. He realizes that Sunday isn't a day of rest for anyone in Silvertjärn, whatever the Bible may have to say on the matter.

Although, it has to be said, nowadays most days are days off for folk in these parts.

Elsa can feel her stomach tying itself in knots. But she shakes her head: she can't think like that. It's going to be all right. She will figure something out, just as she always does. She'll sit down and write to her cousin down in Skåne. You never know—he might be able to find Staffan a job at a factory or the like.

As unbearable as the idea of leaving Silvertjärn is, Elsa has also noticed herself beginning to fall prey to the gloom hanging over the village like fog.

It's rather cold in the church. Spring's raw, biting chill has found its way in through the large windows. Elsa wraps her shawl around herself more tightly.

". . . it is not that Jesus loves only the worthy; but that the only way to prove one's worthiness is to merge with Christ. Every human soul has the opportunity to merge with the divine. What sort of person would renounce such an opportunity? One who has already turned their back on God. One who has already chosen to surrender themselves to mortal filth, mortal pleasures. The soul that chooses to follow the true path is pure and clear as water, but he who allows himself to be tempted and seduced becomes dark, dirty, and coarse, like ash."

Elsa frowns. The pastor's voice has started to intensify, and his impassioned words soar up to the ceiling and echo back down. When he raises his voice and throws out his hands he sounds almost bewitched. But the color of his face is even and light, and his eyes gleam bright and silvery.

Elsa leans in to Staffan and whispers:

"Rather hard in tone, don't you think?"

But before Staffan can answer, Aina shushes her sharply. Elsa recoils at her daughter's blazing look: Aina's eyes are brimming with a concentrated rage. Elsa scrabbles to find a response, but Aina has already turned back to the altar, her face transformed from rage to adoration. She looks completely spellbound.

Elsa looks wide-eyed at Staffan, but he simply shrugs and shakes his head. Didn't he see what just happened? Perhaps not. Staffan never has been the most perceptive of men.

She looks around the church. On closer inspection, she realizes that Aina isn't the only one gazing at the pastor with a look of spellbound devotion; a number of the people around her look exactly the same—in fact, many seem to be hanging on the pastor's every word.

The knot Elsa now feels in her stomach is different from the one she feels when thinking about the mine, or about Staffan, or about moving away. It's sharper. More alarming.

Perhaps she ought to pull the pastor aside for a quick chat. They have had a fair bit of contact now, after all, since he helped her with poor Agneta Lindborg in her final days, and with Pär Nilsson when he was left to raise little Elinor on his own, and no idea what it meant to be a parent.

Pastor Mattias does seem a reasonable man. Aina has taken something of a fancy to him, yes, but she's young, and he is rather dashing. It isn't his fault that his handsome face and natural charisma have turned a few heads among the congregation.

Elsa will ask him to tone things down a little—perhaps even let Einar take the next sermon. That will probably be enough. Just a small change of course. She has helped many villagers to make those over the years, for the sake of keeping the peace.

The sermon seems to be finally reaching its conclusion, thank goodness. They sing a quick psalm together, and then the congregation stands as one. Elsa touches Staffan's arm.

"I'll just have a quick word with the pastor. Take Aina home with you, I shan't be long."

Staffan nods, but when he turns around he raises his eyebrows quizzically.

"Where's the girl got to?" he asks.

Elsa looks around. She spots Aina's long dark hair in a group that has formed around Pastor Mattias at the altar. There must be twenty or thirty people crowding into that space.

She's never seen anything like it.

Or has she? Small observations start to stir in Elsa's mind; things she has seen and heard but never given a second thought until now.

Aina's behavior has been slightly strange of late, hasn't it? Quieter, more abrupt? And there's been rather a lot of talk of Pastor Mattias, hasn't there—of how good he is, how much he's doing for the parish, how he's driving the evil from Silvertjärn? *Evil.* As though that were something one might discuss of a normal afternoon.

Elsa pulls back her shoulders and shakes away her worry. It's all fine. She can handle this. She always does.

She walks toward the altar only to find herself stuck at the back of the group that has gathered before Pastor Mattias. Elsa clears her throat politely, but no one budges; no one even looks at her. She can't hear what the pastor is saying; he's having some sort of quiet, whispered conversation with one of the young ladies up at the front. Then he places his hand on her head.

It's little Lena, Elsa realizes with a jolt. Aina's friend Lena. And she's crying silent tears, staring up at the pastor in wide-eyed enchantment.

Something inside Elsa breaks.

"Pastor Mattias!" she says loudly. Her voice sounds shrill, but it cuts through the murmurs and babbles before her.

The pastor looks up and sees her. It's rather odd: the corners of his mouth are pulled up into his usual mild smile, but his eyes are cold as stone.

"Might I be able to have a word, Pastor?" Elsa asks, not allowing herself to feel intimidated. When all's said and done, she has nothing to fear from this boy or his little flock. Elsa knows every single person in Silvertjärn, and Pastor Mattias has only been here a few short months. She just needs to show him how things are done in Silvertjärn, that's all.

At first the pastor doesn't respond. The silence expands. Elsa becomes uncomfortably aware that every eye between her and the pastor is glued on her.

"Of course, Fru Kullman," he says eventually. "What is it that you should like to discuss?"

"Shouldn't we perhaps go into the chapel to talk?" Elsa asks.

The pastor watches her, his gaze calm and unbroken.

"Here is fine," he says.

Elsa swallows. She refuses to let herself be intimidated, but it's hard not to be affected by all the eyes that seem to be tracking her every move.

"I just wondered if it might be nice to have Einar do the sermon next week?" says Elsa. "He's been with us so long, after all, and, as engaging as you are, it would be good to hear from Einar, who has been our spiritual guide all these years."

Pastor Mattias pulls that strange, cold little smile again.

"Einar has chosen to step down, Fru Kullman," he says. "He has moved south to live with his sister. For the sake of his health."

Elsa blinks.

"His—his s-sister?" she repeats, hearing herself stutter but unable to stop doing it.

"Yes," says Pastor Mattias. "We shall all miss him dearly, of course. But before leaving, Einar assured me he had every confidence in me."

Elsa can't think what to say.

"Was there anything else, Fru Kullman?" the pastor asks.

"Yes," says Elsa, and swallows again. Her throat feels dry as dust. "I—"

The pastor interrupts her.

"In that case I wish you a good day, Fru Kullman," he says. His eyes are glistening. "See you next Sunday."

It isn't a push, just a shift. As though the crowd takes a small step backward, and Elsa suddenly loses her footing.

She gropes around for something to say, but everyone has turned their back on her. No one is looking at her; no one even seems to notice she's there. Not even the pastor.

And no, not even Aina, the back of whose glistening, dark-haired head is a stronger, more painful statement than any shove could ever be.

NOW

When I step out of the church, I pull my mask down to feel the April sun on my face. It's strong today, could almost be called blazing, and the warmth it radiates makes the village smell of spring.

"OK," says Max. "Was it the parsonage next?"

"Yeah," I say. "If that nineteenth-century map is right, then it should be around here somewhere." I pause.

"You can take off your respirator masks out here if you want," I say. Robert shrugs, but Max pulls his down and smiles. It has left a red mark around his mouth, which makes me wonder if mine has done the same.

This part of the village—the area that was built up between the church and the main square—is older than the identical row houses on the other side. The houses here all vary in size and shape, and they're also lower, more stout. Hefty clapboard façades painted a faded sunny yellow or Falu red, with peeling white trims. They have resisted the ravages of time better than the row houses, despite being many times as old.

We managed to do some filming inside the church and get a lot of photos, catching the details we missed the first time around. All in all, it took less time than I had expected. The stress has started to ease a little, even if it's still a nagging twinge at the back of my mind. No matter how efficient we are today, we've still lost twenty percent of our scheduled time, which means we need to prioritize. I'm guessing the contextual shots of the ironworks will have to go. The sad truth is that a deep dive into the collapse of a small mining village won't quite have the same appeal as the more sensational aspects of the story. The murder. The baby. The pastor.

At the end of the day, we aren't here to make a film: we're here to show why we deserve the money and support we need to make a film. To pique the internet masses' curiosity enough to make them want to see the final product. It's all about generating interest—about questions, not answers.

After today we only have two days left, which feels insane. How has it gone so fast? At the same time, I'm—cautiously—starting to hope this is a sign we might actually do this.

Two more days. Two days to keep Tone as pain-free as possible; two days to keep an eye on Emmy. Two days to get material that'll hopefully give us enough traction to find someone to take Emmy's place on the project. More than one, if need be.

I can last two days. We can last two days.

When I see the neat little house it doesn't look very different from the surrounding cottages, but I can still feel the pulse in my fingertips. I double-check the printout of the old map. Every site has been marked with an ornate-to-the-point-of-illegible hand, and the proportions seem slightly distorted—the river looks longer than it is, and the square lies further east—but the neat little rectangle labeled the CLERGY HOUSE seems to be in exactly the right place to be the building before me.

"I think this is it," I say and stop.

It's a yellow building with a small porch. The door is shut, and the few wooden steps leading up to it look completely rotted through.

"I'll go, Alice," Max says, then walks around me and puts his foot on the bottom step.

"No, wait—" is all I can get out before he crashes through it with a cry of shock.

I put my hand on his shoulder.

"Are you OK?" I ask.

"Be careful," Robert adds, as Max starts to extract his leg from the hole in the step.

"You can't put your weight in the middle," I tell Max, my voice sharp with worry. "That's where they're weakest."

"So I see," says Max, attempting a laugh as he pulls up his pant leg to check his thin, white calf. It doesn't look hurt.

"Are you OK? Don't scare me like that," I say.

I walk past him and test out the step above the one that has just given way, then cautiously climb, keeping next to the bannister. The stairs creak, but hold.

I don't wait for the others before reaching for the door handle. It's in an ornate, forged bronze style, old-fashioned but beautiful. The house itself may not be big, but it's clear that someone influential once lived here.

I pull my respirator mask back on. It feels hot and damp on my face. I push the handle. The door is heavy, but it opens.

Behind me I hear the click of Robert's camera as I step into the hall. The ceiling is surprisingly high, with one light—a small, dusty chandelier—hanging from it.

Once we're inside the front door, as if by silent agreement Robert turns into the little kitchen, while Max and I go through the door opposite. A bedroom, timeworn and a little cold. There's nothing in there but a bed with a starched, yellowed sheet and a large wardrobe. There aren't even any curtains over the slanting window frames. When I kneel down and look under the bed, I see two empty, brown glass bottles.

"Must have been Einar's," I say, taking a picture.

"Einar?" asks Max, as I stand up and brush off my knees.

"The pastor before Mattias," I reply. "I haven't found any trace of him. He must have disappeared along with the rest."

We walk back into the hall, where Robert meets us.

"Anything interesting?" I ask him.

He shakes his head.

"Pretty cold," he says. "The bedroom?"

"Empty," I say. "Is this something we should be spending time on? In terms of filming?"

Robert rubs his chin so that the stubble scratches against his fingers, then shakes his head.

"Maybe later," he says. "Could be some nice background for the film. A nice detail. But I don't think it's worth using in the preliminary pitches."

"No," I agree, relieved to have had my own suspicions confirmed. "I'll let the others know. We can always have an early lunch and take another look at the schedule."

I snap my walkie-talkie out of my belt and lift it to my lips.

"Alice here," I say, pressing the talk button. "Emmy, are you there?"

I hear my words echo robotically from the walkie-talkie in Robert's pocket. I release the button and wait, but nothing comes.

"Emmy," I repeat. "This is Alice. Can you hear me?"

Nothing.

"Emmy?" I ask again.

"Could be the walls," says Robert, squinting up at them. "They seem to work in here, between the three of us, but maybe the signal can't get outside? That can happen sometimes."

I nod, even if my worry doesn't quite want to give in. It sounds plausible enough.

We walk back to the front door, and as soon as I have one foot on the porch I try calling her again.

"Emmy," I say. "Hello? Can you hear me?"

Nothing—nothing but the weak, melodic murmur of the line.

I swallow.

"Could she have put it down somewhere?" I ask Robert.

I'm hoping he'll shrug and tell me not to worry in his steady, humming voice, but he doesn't. A line has appeared between his eyebrows, and he pulls his own walkie-talkie out of his pocket.

"Emmy?" he says.

No reply.

"Do you think something happened?" Max asks, giving voice to what we're all thinking.

I shake my head, trying to convince myself when I say: "I'm sure it's nothing, it's just—I mean, they've been acting up ever since we got here. It's probably like the phone signal."

I look at Robert. His eyes meet mine, and I'm sure we're thinking the same thing.

"I think we should head back," he says quietly, and I nod.

"OK," I say. "There's nothing more to see here, anyway."

I should really stay behind to get some more shots of the exterior, but the sudden clump in my belly makes me shove my phone back into my pocket and start walking briskly back toward the square. It's only when the straps start to chafe against my face that I realize I'm still wearing my respirator mask. I pull it down sharply.

We pass a road sign. It's rusted and paper-thin, and only parts of the name are visible.

So treet

I hear Max panting behind me, jogging to keep up. The road we're on turns in toward the main road, and the square appears before us. The well-trodden, overgrown country road turns into a cobbled street.

"Where—" I say, stopping still. Then I start to run.

One of the vans has gone. It's the first thing I see—the asymmetry makes it stick out like a sore thumb: suddenly there's only one where once there were two.

"Emmy!" I hear Robert call out, his voice cracking slightly on the last syllable.

No reply.

I slow down as we reach the square and look around, in the vain hope that they've just moved it.

"Where the fuck are they?" Max asks behind me.

Robert runs over to the other van and tears the door open. I manage a few split seconds of hope before I see there's nobody in there.

When he turns around, the naked fear in his once so calm and collected exterior makes him look like someone else. His freckles blaze against his pale skin.

"Where are they?" he asks me helplessly.

I look around at the empty square. At the heather between the cobblestones, the white stucco walls of the village hall, the wide-open school doors.

"Shit," I splutter, wiping my forehead. What an idiot. I should have seen this coming.

"Emmy must have taken Tone to the hospital," I say.

Robert looks baffled, but relief has already started to smooth out the desperation between his eyebrows.

My jaw is tensed, but I'm trying not to let my anger come through. I can't lose control. Not now.

"Without saying anything?" Max asks.

"They probably tried to," says Robert, sounding more confident with every word. "But if the walls blocked the walkie-talkie signal . . ."

"We know they didn't," says Max. "I don't think—"

"They were probably in a hurry," I say, interrupting him.

My anger is wrestling with my relief and bad conscience.

Gutless, so damn gutless. I've thought many things of Emmy in my time, but never that.

At the same time, she's always been blessed with a winner's mentality. For her, it's goals over everything else. She wanted to get Tone to a hospital, and I wasn't playing ball. So she put herself in a position where I'm out of the way. Simple.

But who knows, maybe it's a good thing. I can't deny I was worried. And, much as I try not to let it, the odd thought had crossed my mind.

Is she still taking her meds?

We can do this without Tone, I tell myself. We can shoot without her. We can get enough material to keep the project afloat without her. What does it matter if she goes home a few days early? She won't like it, but it's better that way. She can be with us for the real shoot instead.

When I first hear the sound, I don't understand what it is, but then I look up at the road. Out of the corners of my eyes I see Max and Robert do the same.

It's the sound of an engine.

When the van appears on the other side of the square it looks almost animated, so out of place against the still backdrop that it seems to belong to another time entirely. Which, I suppose, it does.

I see Emmy in the driver's seat. She turns the wheel and slows even more, so that the van's jostle over the broken cobblestones turns into a slow trot. She pulls up and maneuvers in perfectly next to the other van, then undoes her seat belt.

"OK," she says as she slips out of the van. "I'm sorry. I can explain. I . . ."

She looks at us and then around. Her eyes land on the other van and its gaping back doors. Slowly—slowly—they pan back to us and stop on me.

"Where's Tone?" she asks.

NOW

It takes me a few seconds to find my voice. Max gets there before I do.

"Isn't she with you?"

Emmy stares at us blankly, as if expecting us to say it's all a joke, or Tone to jump out from between us and tell her she's been pranked.

"No," she says, shaking her head. She looks at the other van. "No, she was . . . she was here, she . . ."

I blink and look from Emmy to the van, then the rest of the square.

"What do you mean?" I ask. "Didn't you go to the hospital?"

Emmy licks her chapped lips and looks at us.

"No, I . . ." She looks around. "She was here when I left, it was less than two hours ago."

I know it's just a vain hope, but I stride over to the tent and fling open the door.

It's empty. Of course it is.

I stand up, the seriousness of the situation hitting me like a hammer to the head. I almost buckle under its force.

"So where the fuck have you been?" I ask Emmy.

Emmy doesn't reply. She steps back from the van and, raising her voice as though she doesn't quite trust it, says:

"Tone? Hello?"

The silence rings in my ears.

"Emmy," I say. Just uttering her name makes my teeth ache. "If you didn't take Tone to the hospital then where have you been?"

Before she can respond—if she had even intended to—Robert asks her:

"How long did it take? How long were you gone?"

Something about his voice doesn't sit. The way he's standing. The way his chin is pulled in toward his chest. The absence of surprise in his voice.

"What have you guys done?" I whisper.

"What had to be done!" Emmy cries. Her eyes have gone from glassy to wild, and her red ponytail is gleaming like a traffic light in the sun.

"And what was that?" Max asks.

Emmy doesn't look at him when she replies. She's looking at me.

"Someone had to do something, Alice," she says. "You wouldn't listen."

I just shake my head. A short, gnarled laugh slips out of me.

"Of course," I say. "Clearly this is all my fault. Right?"

"There's somebody here, Alice!" Emmy hurls out of her mouth.

Her words make me stop short.

"What?" I ask, staring at her.

"There's something wrong with all of this," says Emmy. "Fucking wrong. I know you saw somebody yesterday when you were in your van. And I saw somebody staring at me that first night. And other stuff, too—both Robert and I have heard things."

She shakes her head.

"And now with Tone only getting worse . . . I didn't want to force her to get help, but I couldn't sit by and do nothing. We're completely cut off here—I had to do something."

Emmy purses her pale, determined lips.

"I wasn't even gone two hours. OK? Tone was asleep when I left. We had more than enough gas—I didn't waste anything. I just wanted to get out of the dead zone to make a phone call."

"To?"

The short word bulks in my mouth.

I see Emmy swallow.

"My mom," she says. "You know she's a nurse. I wanted to ask about Tone's foot. And to have some contact with the outside world. Just in case anything happens. We're so fucking helpless here—no phones, no way of calling for help. . . ."

"So what you're saying," I say, articulating slowly and carefully, "is that you were so worried about something happening here that you just took off and left Tone sick, alone, and asleep? For a few hours?"

This may be the first time I've ever left Emmy speechless. Her hands are dangling at her sides, her palms facing out, pale and exposed.

It gives me no satisfaction.

"And now she's gone," I finish, both a judgment and statement of fact.

"Maybe we're overreacting," Max offers. "You know, she might have just needed the bathroom."

"Then she would've heard us," I say. "We've been here almost half an hour."

"But her foot's hurt," says Max. "What if she just went to pee somewhere, lost her balance, and can't get up again? That wouldn't be so strange."

He puts his hand on my arm.

"Come on," he says. "Let's go look for her. I'm sure we'll find her in no time. I'll go with you." He cups his hand gently around my elbow, as if to hold me up.

I shake my head.

"No," I say, nodding at Emmy. "Go with *her*. Keep an eye on her. Someone has to stop her from taking off with one of the vans again."

I'm expecting anger, but Emmy just stands still. Then she looks at Robert.

"It's OK. You go with Alice," she says. "The important thing is that we find Tone before she does herself any harm."

NOW

T one!" I shout, turning off down an alley. Robert takes my arm. His grip is cautious, but I still feel myself recoil.

"It'll be easier if we do it systematically," he says. "Check street by street. Otherwise we might miss her."

His voice is mild. It feels like a provocation.

I stop and look at him.

"Did you know Emmy was going to take off?"

He hesitates, shifty-eyed. His pupils look tiny in his hazelnut irises.

The feeling that comes over me is something close to disgust.

"Of course you did," I say.

If only Emmy hadn't offered to stay. Max or I could have stayed with Tone. If only Emmy had just told me she wanted to go call somebody, told me she was worried. I would have said yes.

Wouldn't I?

The sunlight stings my eyes. The walls of the buildings feel like they start to close in, tightening and contracting. Soon we'll be completely swallowed up. We'll sink down into the soil, grow into the walls, coalesce with the decay and the silence. Like Tone. Like Aina, and Elsa, and Staffan.

There won't be any trace of us.

I try to shake off these thoughts. They're morbid; they won't help.

"Tone!" Robert shouts. His voice is clearer and less desperate than mine, but maybe that's a bad thing; maybe that means it doesn't travel as far.

My nerves feel brittle as singed hairs, shriveled and tender under my skin. My ears seem unnaturally sensitive. It's as though each distended second is the one before I'll suddenly hear her cry: "Here!" weakly and pitifully, her voice flecked with pain.

She must have fallen on that foot and hurt it even more; she's probably lying on the ground somewhere, tears in her eyes, teeth clenched.

As soon as we find her we're getting the hell out of here. Getting her to a hospital. Leaving this damn place behind.

The buildings rise up on either side of us, deceitfully idyllic. I scamper across the road, ruthlessly trampling down the shoots of blue scilla and crocuses that have painstakingly set their roots in the dusty, compressed earth. The rusty mailboxes stand crooked and warped on thin wooden posts, like speared shrunken heads with metal numbers for faces. 16. 17. 18.

"Tone!"

My voice has started to falter. Do I really think she's going to respond?

Where could she be?

Against my will, I hear that strange laugh from the video echoing softly in my head; see the figure in the rain in my mind. And there it is—the thought I don't want to acknowledge.

We're not alone here.

I can't even approach the idea that Silvertjärn, my desolate, deserted Silvertjärn, may not be so deserted after all. That something has been lying in wait here. That that something—or someone—has taken Tone and is lurking in the shadows, perhaps even watching us right now.

The exposed skin on my arms starts to prickle.

Robert catches up with me, and I stop outside a grayish white cottage. The white plastic window box that once hung from the windowsill is cracked and lopsided.

When I close my eyes, the frenzied April sun shines straight through my eyelids.

Robert puts his hand on my shoulder. I flit it off and shake my head.

"No," I say.

"She didn't mean any harm," says Robert, and I open my eyes.

"What?"

"Emmy and I did talk about it before," he says, quietly. There's a hesitancy in his voice.

"I knew what she was going to do. She was worried. She said she didn't know if you'd listen to her, so . . . She was just worried about Tone, I swear."

He looks so sincere, so nakedly honest. I don't know if I believe him, but he has the sort of face that makes you want to trust him, want to believe him.

I don't reply. Instead I look up at the street, take a deep breath, and shout:

"Tone! Tone, can you hear me? It's Alice! TONE!"

Not a sound; nothing but the wheeze of my breaths and the whistle of the wind through the broken windowpanes.

I can't keep still. I look up and down the street, and then start heading back toward the crossing. When the sun hits my eyes I shield them with my hand, then stop and squint down the other street.

That's when it happens. Right then, in that saturated silence.

For one instant, reality freezes. Time shatters into milliseconds. One frame where I stop. One where I raise my hands to my ears. One where I crouch down low, hunch my back. One where I screw up my eyes, trying to close off my senses to the overwhelming noise. A bellow resounding through the village.

It's an explosion. And it's in the square.

NOW

I smell the smoke before I see it.

The harsh, piercing odor makes me cough as we run. I'm pretty fit, but I'm soon left breathless and lagging behind, and Robert isn't waiting for me.

Up ahead of us the thick, black smoke is soaring up over the square.

Robert doesn't care about me, or Tone, or himself. He's running to Emmy.

I take a few deep breaths, cough into my hand as the smoke sinks deep into my lungs, then try to catch up.

The square looks like something out of a war film. The sooty, black remains of one of the vans lie strewn across the square.

Our things are still burning; it's from them that the puffs of smoke are surging up into the sky. The second van has flipped onto its side. Its white body is flecked with black soot, and the wheels appear to have melted in the heat.

The shock waves have thrust Max's Volvo into the side of the village hall. Its crumpled blue body looks like it's been squeezed by a giant's hand.

Most of the heather has caught fire, and it burns in shifty, slight flames that seem to be gasping for air.

My ears are still ringing.

Across the square, I see Emmy and Max run up and then stop in their tracks. Emmy's hair has fallen out of its ponytail and sprawls, red and ruffled, around her head. Even from across the chaos, I can tell when her eyes meet mine.

Our things are still burning steadily, but by now they have started to blacken and shrivel in the flames. I can barely make out what's what.

"Emmy!" Robert cries, her name tearing out of his throat.

Emmy takes Max's arm and says something to him. Then they cautiously start edging around the square toward us, keeping their distance from the flames still licking the cobblestones.

When they near us, Robert runs forward. He hugs Emmy so hard that it looks like she's about to snap. Emmy hugs him back, her eyes closed. Neither of them says a word.

I feel a strange ache inside me, made only worse when Max gives me a hug. It feels weird, and wrong, and I pull back.

Emmy lets go of Robert and locks her eyes on me.

"We can't stay here," she says. "The other van could blow."

"What the fuck is happening?" I ask. I don't know if I'm directing this at Emmy, one of the others, or at Silvertjärn itself.

"I don't know," says Emmy. "But we've got to get to safety first. Then we can try to figure it out."

She sweeps her hair behind her ears and looks at Robert, who nods.

There's a sound of metal cracking as something in the burning van gives out.

I don't know how explosions work. All I know is I that want away from that van. I've heard that it isn't the fire you need to worry about but the shock waves; that they can make soup of your internal organs.

I don't let myself dwell on that thought.

Emmy starts running, and I follow her.

THEN

"Elsa!" she hears Dagny calling behind her. She hesitates, almost considers pretending she hasn't heard, but plain, simple good manners get the better of her. She turns around.

Dagny is, as usual, rather well dressed for a stroll through town, wearing a tight skirt, an ostentatious brooch on the collar of her coat, and dark lipstick that has smudged slightly at the corners of her mouth. She used to be the village beauty—and is of course still very elegant—but the years have taken their toll on her. She and her husband have no children, and Elsa suspects that it isn't for want of trying. Sadness has made its mark, giving her a hard, lacquered appearance, like a beautiful vase in brittle porcelain.

"Good afternoon," says Elsa when Dagny catches up with her. "How are you?"

Dagny gestures at the cold gray sky, more fitting for January than April.

"Oh, you know. The weather's just frightful," she says, as though it were a personal affliction, rather than one felt by the whole village. "And how are you?"

Elsa isn't sure what to say. How is she, really? Her youngest daughter is refusing to speak to her, her husband has turned to the bottle, her firstborn is laid up with preeclampsia hundreds of miles away, and she can't be at her side because she doesn't dare leave her charge alone, not even for a few days.

"Fine," she says. "Just fine."

"Have you seen the Axelssons' dog?" asks Dagny. It appears she's planning to walk with Elsa all the way back to her house.

"No," Elsa says. "Should I have?"

Dagny shakes her head.

"Ran away a few days ago, apparently," she says. "That's what they're saying, at least. Personally, I think we have bears in the forest."

"Bears?" Elsa asks.

"Yes." Dagny nods insistently. "Klaes Ekman's dog disappeared a few weeks ago, too. Ran away, he says. Not so cut up about it all, though, is he, as it was mainly to keep the rats at bay, but I think the bears took them. I have a cousin up in Lapland who lost a dog to bears last winter. Because they're short on food, you see."

"But surely that happens mainly in winter?" Elsa can't help but ask. "Not spring?"

"Eh," Dagny says with a dismissive wave of the hand. "With weather like this I suppose it makes no difference."

Elsa is itching to tell Dagny why she's wrong, but she doesn't have it in her to explain bears' responses to the seasons to Dagny today.

By now they are approaching Dagny's house, and she slows down. Elsa feels compelled to do the same.

"Now, there was something I wanted to talk to you about, Elsa," Dagny says, looking slightly discomfited. "You see, there's been rather a din coming from Birgitta's hut of late."

Elsa's heart starts to pound.

"A din?"

"Late in the evenings and at night—we can hear it all the way from our house," says Dagny. She purses her lips, turning them into a plum-colored line across her thin face.

"Well, you know I'm not one of those who—I'm not one to run around spreading nonsense about Birgitta," she says. "And I daresay some of the things people in the parish are saying about her are outrageous. She's sick. It's not her fault she's the way she is."

Dagny looks so pious as she says this, so sanctimonious that Elsa almost wants to give her a piece of her mind, but she forces herself to bite her tongue.

"But please, do try to make her understand that she must keep the noise down," says Dagny. Then she lowers her voice and looks around.

"The way people are talking . . ." She shakes her head. "I think it would be good for her to be careful," she says, casting a long, anxious look in the direction of Birgitta's hut.

NOW

Emmy doesn't stop running until we're almost three blocks away. She takes a right behind some buildings, and I follow her. All I can hear are the hard slap of soles against the cobblestones, the ringing in my ears, the swish of Emmy's jeans, and her hair flicking with every step.

She stops a little further down the side street, then bends double and starts hacking and whooping. The smoke has embedded itself like a film across my tongue and down my throat, but the coughs don't want to come. My lungs feel constricted, pressed to shriveled kernels in my chest.

I hear Max's and Robert's footsteps behind me and stop. I bend double and allow myself to close my eyes for a second. To make the world stop. Ground myself in my body. Everything feels so far away. Numbed.

A strange tingle runs up through my rib cage. In detached curiosity I let it rise in my throat, until it comes out as a shrill giggle. I open my eyes and put my hand to my mouth to hold it inside, push it back down. Kill it.

"What happened?" Max asks.

Something about his flat, reasoned tone helps me to get my insane giggle under control, and I drop my hand again. I see Emmy cough one last time, then spit on the ground before straightening up.

What happened?" I hear someone ask. In the distance I realize it's me.

"How could it just explode? Vans don't just explode!"

I want somebody to do something. To take me by the shoulders, shake me, slap me. Force me to get a grip.

But none of them move. We just stand there, speechless and breathless, staring at each other.

"The lighter fluid," Emmy says quietly.

I look up to see her staring at the wisps of smoke still coiling their way up over the rooftops.

"What?"

"The lighter fluid," she says again. "There were containers of lighter fluid in there, for the campfire. And we had an extra can of gas for the vans. It was on the list."

Oh, right.

"Someone must have set fire to them. Somehow. It's the only explanation."

We all look at each other, one of those rare moments when three or four people are hit by the same thought at exactly the same time. I look at Robert, and then Max, who says:

"Emmy was with me," just as Robert says:

"I was with Alice."

"It wasn't one of us," Emmy says. "It can't have been one of us four."

There's an added weight to the final word.

"Tone."

It's Max who says it.

I stare at him, fear and surprise forming a sickening whirlpool in my belly.

"Max . . ." I start.

"Come on, Alice. They have a right to know."

"Know what?" Emmy asks sharply.

Max gives me a lingering look. His lips are narrowed, his asymmetrical features tense. When he turns to Emmy, I already know what he's going to say.

"Tone's mom is the baby they found in the school," he says. "That's how she and Alice first met. Alice found her two years ago while she was doing research for the film."

"Is that true?" Emmy asks, her voice subdued but sharp.

"You didn't need to know," I say. "Tone didn't want to say anything, and I respected that. It was up to her to tell you, not me."

"But that wasn't the only thing you didn't tell us, Alice," Max says.

The smell of fire, soot, and burning steel still hangs in the air; a sharp, piercing odor that makes my eyes water. We've carried it with us, haven't made it far enough to lose it. It clings to our clothes and makes my nose itch.

"Max, please," I say. Like a prayer.

"I saw the pills, Alice," he says.

I don't even recognize him. Max, my Max, my friend. The guy who's always put a smile on my face, who's always up for getting a beer, listening, shooting the breeze. Who always has my back, in every situation.

He doesn't look like he's enjoying this. He looks like I feel: about to burst into tears. Maybe he really means it when he says he thinks they have a right to know.

Maybe he's right.

"I saw them in your tent," he goes on. "In the toiletry bag, when I was borrowing your toothpaste. Abilify." He pauses. When he goes on, his voice is heavy. "Abilify is an antipsychotic. Right? That's what it said on the packaging."

I don't reply, so he says, both clarifying and aggravating:

"Tone has a psychotic disorder."

I shake my head.

"No, it's not like that," I say, blinking frenetically against the tears that are about to brim over. "She's just had one episode, and that was over a year ago. She's not psychotic and she's not dangerous! She's depressed, and she's had *one* psychotic break, once, it's not like she experiences it the whole time. And she's feeling much better now. She didn't want anyone to know—and no, I didn't think it was my place to tell. So long as she takes her medication she's . . ."

I want to finish my sentence, but can't.

The silence expands.

"But is she taking her meds?" Emmy asks slowly.

My throat contracts.

Maybe you should take some painkillers anyway?

I see the small packet of Advil in her hands. That staring, inscrutable look in her eyes as she swallowed two pills and then pursed her lips.

I knew why she didn't want to take any painkillers—that she didn't want to take anything that might interact with her medication. But I didn't get it. I didn't know what might happen.

Tone's an adult. She knows what she's doing.

But she was in pain. So much pain. And she knew I didn't want to leave, knew how much this meant to me. She could see it in my eyes whenever I asked if she wanted to go to hospital.

"When did she stop taking her meds, Alice?" Emmy asks, her voice thin and clear.

And then it dawns on me, light and brittle and clear, like day-old ice.

This is my fault.

I visited her at the hospital. Once a week. In the run-up to the break, Tone had stopped responding to my calls and messages. I never dropped by her place to check in on her, as I took her silence as a sign she just didn't want to talk to me. It hadn't even occurred to me that something might be wrong, even though I, of all people, should have known. I, who knew how impossible it can feel to so much as open an email when anxiety has its spindly black fingers around your neck.

At the hospital Tone was quiet, even quieter than normal. She hardly even responded to my chatter. Which of course made me talk even faster than normal, trying to fill every second to avoid hearing the silence. At times I wondered if she even wanted me there.

But then whenever I left she would always hug me tightly, as though I were a lifebuoy and she were drowning. So I kept on coming back, until one day she called me on her cell and said she was home. Like nothing had ever happened.

I never saw her during the episode itself, and she never said much about it. The few times it did come up she just said she had felt "... *confused. And scared. Sometimes I thought I was my mom and I was in Silvertjärn. Sometimes I heard voices, voices trying to tell me secrets.*"

But she hadn't mentioned it in forever—other than to check I wasn't going to tell anyone, that is.

I mean, she felt better. She was doing well.

So long as she just took her meds.

The image of Tone at Birgitta's table lumps in my throat, forcing those nasty, unwanted tears back to my eyes. I didn't want to see, didn't want to understand what it might mean.

She said she was OK.

She said it.

Why didn't I listen to her?

No one says anything for a while. I try to bite back my tears and find my voice, wishing one of them would say something, fill the space.

"We need to get out of here," says Emmy. Her voice is flat. "We can't stay here, we need help."

"How?" Max asks. "You saw the vans and the car—what was left of them."

"We can walk," says Emmy, but Robert clears his throat.

"It's at least twenty miles of rough terrain to the nearest road. And there were no cars there. Where was the nearest gas station? Another ten, twenty miles, right?"

"We don't need to find anyone," says Emmy. "We just need to get out of the dead zone."

"How far was that?" Robert asks.

"Forty-five minutes," says Emmy. "But I had to drive really carefully through the forest, so it was slow going. I don't know how far it is as the crow flies."

I look up long enough to see her fish her cell out of her pocket. She tries to turn it on but shakes her head.

"That call took the last of my battery," she says. "What about yours?"

Robert just shakes his head. I don't need to check mine to know it's dead.

"Mine's out," says Max.

"Where was your charger?" asks Emmy. "In the Volvo or the van?"

"The Volvo," says Max.

"Do you have a car charger?" Emmy asks him nervously. "One that you plug into the cigarette lighter?"

Max's eyes flicker.

"I think so," he says. "In the glove compartment."

Robert shakes his head.

"But the engine's shot," he says. "You saw the car, there's no chance—"

"But not the generator," Emmy interrupts. "That was in the other van. It could still work. If we can plug Max's charger into that outlet then we can charge his phone. Then hike twenty, twenty-five miles till we get signal."

"Is it safe though?" Max asks. "We don't know if the other van could blow."

Emmy looks up over the rooftops.

"It's stopped smoking," she says. "And vans don't just explode. If it's the gas can that blew then there's no reason the other van would be dangerous."

"Not the van, no," Robert says quietly. He doesn't need to say anymore.

"There are four of us," says Emmy. Her face is tense, won't accept any arguments. "What's one against four? We don't need to be there long. We'll just go there, find the charger and generator, plug in the phone and let it charge. We'll keep a lookout. And we can get whatever we need from the back of the van—food, water, whatever's left."

I know I should keep quiet, but I can't.

"It wasn't Tone," I say, my lips cold. "It can't have been. She isn't crazy. She isn't violent, never has been. She's just . . . sick."

Max, his voice subdued, asks the question:

"But Alice, if not her, then who?"

I can tell he doesn't mean it as a question so much as a way of shutting down my rambling, but it hits me straight in the chest. I think of the figure in the rain, of the shadow of a laugh on the film, of Tone whispering:

I heard something below us.

Of Emmy and her probing green eyes.

You saw somebody, didn't you?

It's to her I turn now.

Emmy's lips are so pinched that they're practically just a dash on her face.

"That doesn't matter," she says, to my surprise. "What matters is that we get help and get out of here. And to do that we have to get back to the square."

"What if it doesn't work?" Max asks. His mint-green cable-knit sweater is flecked with soot.

Emmy scratches her neck.

"Worst case, we wait it out," she says. "My mom was worried, so I told her that if she hasn't heard from me in forty-eight hours then she should send in the police. That was when I thought I'd just be coming back here to put Tone in a van and take her to the hospital, but now . . ." Emmy shrugs.

"It's best if we try to charge one of the phones and call for help today," says Robert.

My voice dull and subdued, I say, "We have to get back to the square."

NOW

I lag a few feet behind the others as we slowly but surely make our way back to the square. My eyes stray down the alleys, search the shadows, the heavy clump in my belly making me slow and lethargic.

Tone. Tone. Tone.

I want to believe she didn't set the van alight; want to be as sure as I'm trying to make myself sound. But however hard I think about it, I can't find a better explanation.

Could it be spontaneous combustion? Some kind of manufacturing flaw? A leak, an engine left running, a spark at the wrong time?

Maybe.

Maybe it's the curse of Silvertjärn. Or ghosts, or aliens.

Or maybe it was my friend, my friend who's sick, who hasn't been taking her meds. My friend who's paranoid, and confused, and who thought she was defending herself against something that isn't there.

My anxiety is cold, and its nails are sharp.

I don't want to believe it.

The others have stopped ahead of me at the edge of the square. I catch up with them, and we still ourselves. Listen.

"OK?" Emmy says to us.

I look at the others. None of them says a word, but Robert nods.

For a second I'm struck by the absurdity of the situation, how impossibly cinematic it is.

I'm not ready for this. I don't want this.

It makes no difference.

Emmy steps out into the square, and we follow her.

Most of the fire has waned and died out, leaving only the blackened remains of the vegetation on the sooty cobblestones. There are no alarms, no spinning wheels; the wreckage of the vans lies where we left it, the remains of our equipment still strewn across the square.

I can't remember if our insurance covers bizarre accidents. Or arson. Surely this must count as arson?

I creep across the square, trying to go as quietly as possible. I can't explain why I'm doing this: anyone close enough to hear my footsteps would surely be able to see me, too. But my primal instincts aren't interested in logical arguments. Their primary concern is to make me as small and quiet as possible; to crouch, sneak away, disappear.

Prey.

The Volvo is standing on the far side of the square. It was set back slightly to begin with, which is probably why it wasn't as badly affected by the explosion as the vans. The force of the explosion has pressed it into the wall, but it hasn't been flipped or burned, or marked by the fire. It looks more like the work of a drunk driver who's made an unfortunate turn off the road. Crumpled and by no means roadworthy, but still in one piece.

"Do you hear something?" Emmy asks quietly, her face tense. I shake my head.

"Nothing," Robert says, just as quietly.

Max stops beside me when we reach the car, but I hold back. I can't even bring myself to look at him. I step back as he reaches for the door handle, and then turn away as I hear the click of the door.

"OK," says Emmy. "Great. While you get the charger I'll try to fish the generator out of the van."

I don't want to stay with Max, so my feet follow Emmy over to the van: the least bad alternative. Its position makes it look vaguely menacing, a wounded animal lying on its side to regain its strength.

"I don't know how we'll get inside," says Emmy, her voice flat but pragmatic.

I know what she means. The van had been parked with its rear angled toward the other van, so its back doors took the brunt of the explosion. It's so dented and blackened that I'm seriously doubting if we'll ever get them open.

"I can try," I say, against my better judgement. "If not I can try to climb in from the driver's seat."

Yes, the one up in the air.

I'm expecting a protest, but she just nods.

I reach tentatively for the handle, which is still hot. I try to pull it, but it won't budge.

"OK," I say to Emmy—no more, no less. No more is needed.

I walk around to the front of the van. The side is higher than I'd expected. There's no chance I'll be able to get up there myself.

I look for something to stand on, but Emmy is already lugging a semi-charred tire my way. Once she's next to me she turns the melted clump of rubber onto one side and holds out her hand for me to take.

"Thanks," I say, my eyes lingering on hers a second too long. I hadn't meant to; I just get stuck, somehow, and she does, too.

I don't know what we're saying to one another.

I put my foot on what's left of the wheel and lift myself up. I almost lose my balance, but manage to get a hand on the door handle. Then I pull myself up, kicking the tire for an extra push. The side of the van is smooth and covered in soot, which smears itself all over my clothes as I somehow manage to haul myself up so that I'm sitting next to the driver's door.

I get onto my knees and pull at the door. With gravity working against it it's surprisingly heavy, but at least it isn't stuck in its frame. Using both my arms, I lift it high enough for the door hold mechanism to kick in, then worm my way down inside.

It's like a fun house for grown-ups in there: a normal, familiar setting turned ninety degrees the wrong way. There are things scattered everywhere, and the hatches have flown open, sending trash and debris raining down in the van. The passenger door is strewn with old stumps of pencils, and the coffee cup from the journey up. And there, beside them, lie the papers I found in the church. For just a second I hesitate, but then I fold them up as carefully as I can and stuff them into my back pocket to take with me.

The small window between the driver's seat and the cargo compartment has been blown out—either in the explosion or when the van flipped—but the empty window frame is completely blocked. Something has wedged itself up against the opening, and it doesn't want to shift. I assume it's a tripod or something.

Is this all that's left of my dream?

No. I can't think like that now, can't let the sadness set in. Because with that will come the fear. The shame. The anxiety. Black, oozing tar.

I have to focus on what needs to get done.

I shift backward so the dashboard is against my back, then put my feet up against whatever it is that's blocking the opening, and press as hard as I can. For a moment I think my back's about to give way—my muscles are strained to the point of snapping, and the sweat is beading on my forehead—but then a split second later the whole shebang suddenly shoots out of the way like a cannonball. There's a huge clatter as the heap blocking the empty window frame subsides, and I instinctively curl up with my arms over my head.

"Alice!" I hear Emmy cry outside.

"I'm OK!" I call back, surprised she would raise her voice.

I squeeze in through the hole and feel my way around the piles of equipment. The windshield cracked in an elaborate star pattern in the blast, and was then covered by a layer of soot from the fire, so it lets hardly any light into the back compartment. I can't tell what it is I'm crawling over, only that it's plastic and metal, sharp corners and wires. I wonder how much of it held in the explosion. Presumably very little.

The generator is a small, sturdy cube, and I do my best to grope around for something of that shape. One of my feet slips, and my knee knocks against something sharp, so hard that I see stars. I whimper quietly and grab my knee. My pants have held, at least. The knock can't have broken the skin.

I wish I could see better.

I consider getting out my cell to try to use the flashlight, but then I remember my dead battery. That's why I'm in here, duh, to try to get out the generator to charge Max's phone. To get out of here. Away from this fucking place.

And then, in the darkness, I hear it.

At first it sounds like no more than the echo of my own breaths on the walls, but then I hear that slight, oh-so slight, disparity; the other's breaths are shallower and slightly faster, falling out of step with mine until the rhythm becomes something dissonant.

My feet have started to fall asleep in the awkward position I'm in, but I don't dare move. It's all in my head. I know it's all in my head.

My body is acting without me.

I hold my breath.

Still I hear them, those scratchy, shallow breaths.

I feel a tiny thread of urine run down my thigh and wet my jeans.

Slowly but surely my eyes start to adjust to the darkness. There's too little light to be able to see anything clearly, but some contours start to emerge. Something lies by the broken doors. Something with soft, elongated lines that isn't a camera tripod or a generator or a cooler.

Something moving.

"Tone?" I whisper.

And then I hear it—there, in the darkness.

A short, muffled laugh that whisks against my eardrum.

An icy, blazing shock of survival instinct runs through my body like a tornado, snapping me out of my paralysis. It tears out of me as a bellow and pushes me backward, fumbling, scrabbling, beating, as I fight and kick my way out, away, back to the driver's seat, struggling with a desperation I've never felt before. I'm senseless, frantic, an animal fleeing for its life, and there's not a single thought in my mind, only the mortal fear that has commandeered my instincts and is threatening to burst from my skull.

I squeeze my way through the hole between the seats and pull myself up out of the door with a strength that makes my muscles strain and burst, a strength I didn't know myself capable of. I shuffle and slide off the edge of the van and onto the ground, landing on the cobblestones with a jolt I feel right up my spine. I shouldn't be able to move—I can't, really—but somehow I scramble back to my feet and start running.

I only make it a few feet before I'm grabbed from behind.

NOW

A lice! What are you doing?"
    I try to wrest back my hand, but the grip around my wrist is tight. Slowly my pulse starts to calm. I turn to see Emmy staring at me.

"Alice?" I hear Max call from by the Volvo.

The world begins to fall into place around me again.

"Alice, what is it?" Emmy asks, letting go of my wrist. She studies me, her eyebrows slightly furrowed.

"What happened?"

I swallow and look at the van. It's lying exactly where it was, a sooty, wounded giant. I realize that my foot hurts; I must have landed badly when I jumped off the van.

"There . . ." I begin, my voice thin and distant.

There's someone in there.

The words are on the tip of my tongue, but they don't want to be articulated.

I heard something in there. Someone.

That wasn't Tone.

I did, didn't I?

My courage flails in my throat, then deserts me.

I swallow.

"I . . . couldn't find the generator," I splutter. "But everything was in pieces. I think it must be broken."

Emmy curses under her breath, then looks at me, hesitates.

"Are you OK?" she asks. Her eyes feel like they're grilling me.

What will they say if I tell them I heard someone in there? Someone laughing? Someone who isn't Tone?

Or . . .

Was it all in my head?

I've never experienced psychosis, not like Tone. But her symptoms started as depression, and that I have had. I've been severely depressed. And Emmy didn't listen to me then, either.

There are no sounds coming from the van.

I could ask them to check; to open the doors, crawl inside, and take a look for themselves. But I can just picture Emmy coming out again and saying, in her usual, measured tone:

"There was nothing there. She was just seeing things. Hysterical."

I swallow.

"I . . . got stuck," I say. "Upside down. It was horrible. I didn't think I'd get out."

"How did it go?" Robert asks behind me. By now he has also reached us. When I turn my head I see that he's holding a long, white charger cable.

"She says it looked like the generator didn't make it," Emmy says.

He purses his lips.

"Shit," he says.

"We should set up camp somewhere," says Emmy. "Somewhere stable, sheltered. Then we can figure out what to do."

"Somewhere with doors," Robert adds.

Doors to shut out. And in.

He doesn't need to say it.

Emmy squints up at the midday sun, then looks out over the village. The rays catch and gleam on the church's cross, Silvertjärn's highest point and polestar.

"The church," she says. "Let's go to the church."

NOW

We have to barricade the doors," Emmy says to Max and Robert. She doesn't just say it, but walks up to one of the pews and takes hold of one end. She can hardly shift it—it looks like it's solid oak—but Robert adds his weight, and together they manage to get it all the way over to the doors, with a horrible screech that echoes off the high ceiling.

Robert takes a few steps back and looks at it.

"Should be enough," he says.

"So what now?" Max asks.

It's Robert who answers.

"If your mom was going to call the police after forty-eight hours, and you called her a few hours ago, they should be here in the morning of the day after tomorrow," he says.

"But that's two days," says Max. "And we have no food, or water . . ."

"We can get water," says Emmy. "From the river. At this time of year it'll be meltwater, so it should be clean."

"We could try to walk," says Robert, some doubt in his voice. "But we have no compass, no proper shoes . . . we can try to follow the road, but it's at least twenty-five, thirty miles to the nearest busy road. Further still to the nearest town."

"What about gas stations?"

"The one we stopped at was a few hours away by car," says Robert.

Max isn't looking at Robert. He's looking at the oak pew barricading the church doors.

My eyes are drawn to the carved Jesus above the altar. His eyes, deep-black and matte, almost look like they're jeering. And his lips . . . don't they look twisted into a disgusting, slick grin?

"We can't just leave her out there," I say.

I tear my eyes from the figure to look at Emmy. She shakes her head. Neither of the others say anything.

"She's probably scared. Terrified. And she's all alone. She could hurt herself, she could . . ." I gulp.

"What do you want us to do, Alice?" Emmy asks. "Comb Silvertjärn? We won't find her if she doesn't want to be found. And she's dangerous. It isn't safe."

"She's not dangerous!" I explode.

Some small, logical part of me knows this isn't the best way to convince them, but I can't help it. How can they just leave her out there? How can they see a monster in a sick, lone woman who doesn't even know what she's doing?

"She blew up our vans, Alice!" Emmy says. Now she seems to have lost her patience, too. "It's because of her that we're stuck here!"

"You don't know that," I say, shaking my head. "You don't know that, you're just guessing."

"Well, we wouldn't have to do that if you'd cared to tell us your partner's disturbed."

"She's not disturbed," I say. My voice is shaking. I try to swallow it down, steady myself. Hold in the anger, anchor myself to it. "She's not disturbed. She's sick. This is just an episode, and it . . ."

It's my fault.

Emmy just shakes her head.

"We're staying here," she says. "We're waiting it out."

My teeth are clenched so hard my jaws hurt.

"No," I say.

"OK," says Emmy. "Then we'll take a vote."

She looks at the others.

"Hands up who votes to stay here till the police arrive."

I look at the other two. Robert raises his hand slowly, almost timidly. Max furrows his brow when he looks at me, but then raises his hand, too.

For a moment I'm about to say something about the breaths I heard in the van, the ones still echoing, shallow and scratchy, in my head.

But would they even listen to me now? Even if Emmy thought there was someone here before, why would she listen to me now, when I didn't listen to her then? Or would they just think it was Tone in that van, even though every fiber of my being is telling me it wasn't?

I don't even know that there was anything there myself: it could have been a moment's madness, a figment of my imagination, born of Silvert-järn's whispers in my ear.

I say nothing.

"So there we have it," says Emmy.

NOW

I'm slumped down on one of the old Windsor chairs in the chapel. The seat cushion is moldy and half-disintegrated, and only the traces of a once-dainty floral pattern remain. The legs creaked when I dropped down onto it, but they held.

Outside the window the sun has started its listless voyage down to the horizon, and my tired eyes have been following its journey. I don't know how long I've been sitting here, but it can't be more than an hour.

I closed the door behind me when I came in, and so far no one has come after me. I'm not sure if I'm disappointed or not. The stillness in here is soothing, comforting; there's nothing for me to rage against here. But at the same time this silence offers nothing to distract me from my thoughts.

My thoughts of Tone. Of Silvertjärn. And, ashamed as I am to say it, of my film—the one that will never get made now. Perhaps that shouldn't be playing on my mind when my whole world has capsized and nothing makes sense anymore, but it is. That one dream has been pushing me on for almost twenty years. And to suddenly lose it, when I was so close to making it happen, is like looking down at my legs only to find a bloody stump where one once was.

The creak of the door behind me is enough to make me start and look around.

"How are you holding up?" Max asks.

He's holding a half-empty bottle of water. Before I can answer, he comes in and closes the door behind him.

"I thought you might want some water," he says, taking a few cautious steps toward me.

I feel uneasy being so much lower than him, so I get out of my chair. Max stops and gives me a quick smile, then holds out the water bottle.

I hesitate but then take it, and drink thirstily. It's warm and tastes of plastic, but it rinses the dry film from my mouth and throat, making me suddenly aware of how hungry I am.

"I had it in my rucksack," says Max. "A couple of protein bars, too, if you want."

I put down the bottle.

"What do you want, Max?" I ask.

My question comes out harsher than I'd intended, but I don't regret it.

"I just wanted to check you were OK," he says.

"No," I say. "I'm not OK. None of this is OK. You can go now. Here."

I try to hand him the bottle, but he refuses to take it. There's some tension around his mouth, and his big, sorry cow eyes look out at me from under a furrowed brow. His eyebrows are very thin, I notice. I've never realized that before. They look expressionless, like the painted lines on a doll's face.

"Are you mad at me?" he asks.

All I can do is stare.

Mad?" I say, with a scratchy laugh that edges toward a sob.

"Alice, please," he says, taking a few steps toward me, but I shake my head.

"Mad doesn't even come close," I say. "I don't get how you could do that, Max. Of everybody here . . ." My lips sting and fail me. I swallow.

"Of everybody here I thought you were the one I could trust, Max. OK? I thought that no matter what, at least I'd have you."

When Max speaks, his voice is soft and reasoned. It's a sharp contrast to my unsteady, emotional words.

"I had to say something, Alice," he says. "I had no choice. You know I'd never want to hurt you, never. But the others deserved to know." The corners of his mouth turn downward.

"It wasn't my secret to tell," I try to say. Again. Every time I say it, the words feel flimsier. Like paper folded over and over, until the fibers start to wear and tear along the fold.

"But they deserved to know," he says. "That's why I said it."

Some of the things he's saying make sense. Or at least partly: the others needed to know that Tone was sick, that she wasn't well, wasn't herself.

"But now they think she's dangerous. They want to just leave her out there, and she must be so *scared*. . . ."

I shake my head.

"It's too dangerous, Alice," says Max. "I know you say she isn't dangerous, but she isn't herself. And Silvertjärn is obviously having an effect on her. The best we can do for her is to get out of here and get help."

He takes a cautious step toward me.

"I didn't mean to hurt you, you have to know that. I only did what had to be done."

I don't want to hear this. However reasonable his words sound, I can still feel his betrayal all over my body. But, then again, how can I trust my instincts? So far nothing I've thought has proved true.

"Come on, Alice," he says, drawing my stiff body into a hug. He's hot and sweaty under his dirty sweater, and the remnants of his deodorant find their way up my nose.

"We'll be out of here in no time," he mumbles into my shoulder while squeezing me hard. "Soon all of this will be over. We'll get through this."

I let myself be hugged, but can't quite bring myself to hug him back.

Eventually he lets go, then steps back, looks at me, and smiles.

"Hungry?" he asks. "Let me go get you one of the protein bars."

I swallow and nod.

"Yeah," I say. "Thank you."

He leaves, closing the door behind him.

I go back to my chair and sit down. The distaste I've just stifled has coagulated into something stiff and cold that makes my stomach ache. That or it's just the hunger.

Something pricks me from below. Cursing, I stand up and feel the seat. Nothing there.

Then I realize I can still feel the same pricking feeling. It's in my back pocket.

I reach around and pull out a bundle of messy, crinkled sheets of paper.

Oh. Of course. The papers from the chapel, the ones I found at this very table, half a lifetime ago. The ones I took from the van. My fingers blunt and unwieldy, I unfold and inspect them. At the top is that strange scribble, those clumsily childish doodles of spirals and stick figures. The papers have been practically destroyed by my rough treatment, and, as absurd as it is at a time like this, it pains me to see how badly they've fared.

I hear the faint sounds of Max chatting to Robert out in the church, but in here everything is quiet. The light has shifted, from an afternoon sharpness to a golden early evening glow.

Wait.

I force myself to focus on them, those clumpy stick figures. They look like they were drawn in crayon, with an awkward hand. I stare at them.

One of them has a big, black mouth like a hole. A void.

The windows above the sink face east, toward the slowly setting sun. Over the graveyard.

I look from the papers to the nondescript table by which we found them, vaguely aware of a mumbled conversation out in the church, and of an angel-faced man who sat at this very table some sixty years ago, writing and rewriting his sermon.

How could that drawing have gotten bundled up with his papers?

I know where I've seen those drawings before. That clumsy style that looks like a child's, but isn't.

I saw these stick figures this morning, on Birgitta's table. She must have drawn these.

But as far as we know, Birgitta never strayed more than a few yards from her hut.

So what was one of her drawings doing in the church?

THEN

Elsa knocks at the door. Her knock is harder than usual, but her hand is trembling and she's finding it hard to keep her voice steady.

"Birgitta!" she says, trying to sound as cheery as she can. "Birgitta, it's me. Elsa. I've brought some food."

She does have food, in the normal picnic basket, but it's all wrong—it's been scrabbled together too hastily. Elsa's still completely beside herself. Her heart is racing, and she's sweating, despite the cool summer day.

It has been a dark start to the summer, cloudy and cool, with a constant smell of rain in the air. Elsa's senses feel stale and insipid, and the villagers have been drifting around town like ghosts, wandering the streets without purpose or feeling. The churchgoers blaze like torches among them.

Something is afoot.

"Birgitta," she calls out again, louder and more shrilly, and bangs on the door. "Open the door!"

It can't be anything serious, she tries to reassure herself. She was here just a few days ago. And Birgitta was looking perfectly normal then.

Though perhaps she had been a little wan? Not that Elsa had picked up on it. Or let herself pick up on it. She was too preoccupied with other things: Staffan and his drinking; Margareta and her latest letter. More than anything she wishes she could be there with her now, that she could hold her hand and help her through her pregnancy. Her heart is bleeding for her.

And, with all of this on her mind, she hasn't seen what has been happening to Birgitta.

To Aina.

Her girls.

Elsa can't even curse herself anymore; the anger fails her. She drops her hand, puts her forehead to the door and whispers, though she knows Birgitta won't open it:

"Please, Birgitta, open the door."

The worn wood feels smooth and cool against her forehead. It soothes the heat in her face.

Her right hand is still banging on the door.

And then she hears footsteps.

She manages to straighten herself up just in time for Birgitta to open the door.

Her first feeling is one of relief. Despite knowing that it couldn't possibly be the case, she had a crippling fear of finding Birgitta dead—that or gravely ill. Three days untended is a long time for someone like Birgitta.

But the relief soon fades, replaced by something that could almost be called horror.

Birgitta's eyes are downcast as usual, but they are flitting around in frenzied terror, and she is humming quietly while rocking to and fro. It almost sounds like she's crying. Elsa has never heard Birgitta cry before.

"Oh, Birgitta," she says. She puts down the basket and reaches out to hold her, but Birgitta's hums grow to a moaning roar, and she lashes out at Elsa. One of her arms meets the side of Elsa's head, forcefully, and Elsa stumbles backward, seeing stars. It hurts terribly, but she manages to catch her balance just in time. She touches her cheek: it's burning but not bleeding, and nothing appears to be loose or broken.

Birgitta has backed a few steps into the hut. She is still making her plaintive, sorrowful moans, but they now sound almost resigned. She didn't want to hurt Elsa. Elsa knows that.

"Forgive me, Birgitta," she says. Her head is still spinning. "That was wrong of me. I shouldn't have done that."

Elsa doesn't know if Birgitta can hear her. She approaches her cautiously, her hands at her sides. She wants to show her she won't try to touch her again. Then she picks up the basket of food from the ground.

"Can I come in? I've brought some food. You must be very hungry."

Elsa makes sure to stand very still while Birgitta makes up her mind.

Eventually Birgitta takes another step back, just enough for Elsa to be able to squeeze in through the doorway.

"Thank you, Birgitta, that's very kind," she says politely, as though Birgitta has just invited her in for a coffee. Elsa makes sure to wipe the mud off her shoes on the threshold before stepping inside. After the long, wet summer they've had, Silvertjärn is virtually one big swamp.

She steps inside and looks around. To her surprise, the musty stench is no worse than normal—quite the opposite, in fact. The summer sun filters in through the slender branches of the young oak and down onto the kitchen table.

There's something there.

Elsa takes a close look at Birgitta before going further in, but Birgitta shows no signs of agitation. She appears to have calmed down. Elsa puts the basket on the chair, as usual, and looks down at the tabletop.

Crayons.

Four small, cheap crayons, the sort a child would have, and clearly well-used. There are four colors: red, blue, yellow, and black.

Elsa leans over the tabletop to see what Birgitta has drawn, but finds nothing. Her eyes scan the room. Nothing.

Then her eyes land on the floor next to Birgitta's feet.

Faint traces of mud.

Footprints, in the same mud that surrounds the hut.

Elsa looks at Birgitta's feet, but she already knows the footprints can't be hers; they're too big to come from Birgitta's surprisingly dainty feet, and they're shaped like a pair of shoes. As far as Elsa knows, Birgitta doesn't own any shoes, and she shakes her head and flails around if anyone so much at tries to get her to wear anything other than the big, shapeless dress she's lived in since her mother passed away. Anything else seems to cause her pain.

"Birgitta," she says slowly, turning her eyes back to the crayons. "Who has been here?"

Elsa wants Birgitta to look at her and answer the question. But she can't. She just mutters to herself, sounds without context or meaning.

It can't have been Aina. Elsa knows it can't have been her, for Aina's defiant, contrary voice is still ringing in her ears, along with those strange, wicked words that she could never have imagined coming from her daughter's mouth.

"You have no power over me! I'm one of God's chosen ones. You can't tell me what to do, and I have better things to do than look after that monster!"

Elsa has never hit one of her children before, has never raised her hand against anyone in anger. Her hands have always been ones that comforted and soothed, that sought to help others.

But her palm is still burning from where it met Aina's cheek.

And what haunts Elsa now is not the lie, nor Aina's defiance, nor even the slap that rang through the room.

No—it's the spark that had flashed in Aina's beautiful dark eyes as she slowly raised her hand to her cheek, her gaze locked on Elsa's. A look that resembled triumph.

Elsa feels sick.

Birgitta has started to rock back and forth on the spot again. She moves one foot, places it over the dried-on footprint, and rubs until hardly any of the shape remains, just a brownish patch of dust on the floorboards.

As she does so, through Birgitta's swaying, straggly curtains of hair, Elsa catches sight of some dark patches at the base of her neck. Patches shaped like fingers.

Far away, like a rumble from the underground, Elsa hears the faint sound of hundreds of people singing in chorus.

Evensong has begun.

NOW

I open the pantry doors and look at the contents. Nothing to eat here, either, just shriveled paper bags of mummified flour and oats, small tins of spices, and glass bottles with coagulated, calcified contents.

"Nothing here, either," I say to Robert as I close the doors. The hinges creak, but they still do their job. He nods, a furrow appearing between his transparent eyebrows.

This is the fourth house we've checked, and I've started to give up all hope of finding anything.

Max was the only other one of us, apart from Robert, who took his rucksack with him from the square, and the three protein bars he had in there didn't go far. By the time darkness started to draw in, we were forced to make a new plan.

I didn't say much while the others discussed what to do. All of our provisions were in the van that blew, so Emmy said the best solution would be just to do the rounds of the nearest houses and check the pantries. Surely there would be something: some foods don't go off, and it doesn't need to be gourmet. So long as we get some nonpoisonous calories in us, it doesn't matter where they come from.

When the others nodded I sat up and said I could go.

Emmy told Robert to go with me, and he nodded without protest. We've been told to contact them every fifteen minutes so they know we're safe.

I wonder if Robert would ever challenge Emmy; he seems to view her authority as absolute. I wonder what it feels like to have that sort of power over another person. My relationships have never been like that. Either they're not interested and I'm left pining, or I'm not interested and they get angry; somehow I always end up losing. Pathetic or cold-hearted, nothing in between.

Still, I'm glad I have Robert with me. It's nice not to be here on my own—not that the others would have let me go alone. They don't trust me. Knowing that rubs a bit, but at the same time they're absolutely right: I don't think we'll find any food, I just wanted a chance to look for Tone. Dragging Robert around with me is a small price to pay to be able to keep an eye out for her—for a trace, a hint, anything that could tell me where she might be.

"On to the next one, then," says Robert, and I nod.

When we come back out onto the street, the sun has disappeared completely. All that's left of daylight is the fiery spectacle playing out above the treetops, but even that will soon fade. We're standing on the street that runs along the river, and from here most of Silvertjärn is visible: the teeming roofs, the river that cuts through the center, and the lake, dark and deceitful like a promise.

Robert looks at his chunky black wristwatch.

"It's been fifteen minutes," he says. He takes his walkie-talkie out of his belt.

"Robert here," he says into the microphone. I hear a tinny echo of his words from the speaker in my jeans pocket. "We're on our way to—Alice, what are you doing?"

I've already taken a few steps before I realize what I'm looking at.

That has to be it. No question.

A little yellow house by the river.

It's a cottage, like all of the others, on the middle of a small patch of land that has long since been overrun by the vegetation jostling along the riverbank. It seems to have held out better than the other houses on the street: the roof hasn't fallen in, and the door is intact.

202 • CAMILLA STEN

A green door.

All of the houses on that street were yellow, but ours was the only one with a green door.

The green paint has faded and started to peel. At one point it must have been a bright emerald green, but years of sun and wind and snow have turned it into a washed-out bottle green that's peeling away from the grayish wood underneath.

Still.

I look up and down the street, to make extra sure. Yes, every other house is yellow. But none of them has a green door.

It made me feel special.

"Alice, what are you doing?"

Robert sounds unexpectedly nervy, so I turn around to look at him. He's let go of the talk button and is staring at me.

"It's my grandma's house," I explain.

Robert blinks. He looks at me, then the house.

"Oh," he says. "Oh shit."

He studies the house with the green door for a few seconds, but then he shakes his head.

"You know what we said. Water, food, back. We're safer as a group."

"There could be food in there," I persevere. "We can just step inside. Quickly."

Robert shakes his head.

"No," he says.

I look back at the house.

"Robert, she could be in there," I say, quietly. "Tone knows which house it is. She might still recognize it—it might even feel safe to her. There are two of us, and she . . . she isn't dangerous, I promise. Can't we just go take a look?" I start rambling: "Plus we were going to check one more house, anyway. This is one more house. There might be food!"

Robert looks at the house, and I can see the doubt storming over his freckles. I say nothing more. I just look him in the eye, trying to seem stable and sincere. I can't let my desperation show.

Then he gives a short, sharp sigh and brings his walkie-talkie to his lips.

"Robert here. We're OK. We may be a little longer than expected."

He waits for Emmy's quick, tinny: "OK," and then gives me a faint smile.

I could kiss him, but I make do with a simple "Thanks."

Robert reattaches his walkie-talkie to his waistband.

"But if we don't find her there, how about we don't mention this to Emmy?"

I nod.

"Of course."

The house is in a worse state up close. Something that must be some sort of lichen has grown over most of the front steps. The door handle on the faded green door glistens in the dying light.

I put my hand on it and push down. The door opens without a creak.

It's dark inside. We come straight into a small, low hallway with wall-papered walls. On the right there's a staircase to the second floor, and straight ahead there's a small, anonymous door that must lead to a bath-room. The kitchen is to the left.

The same layout as in the other houses. Nothing remarkable.

Still, it feels like it unlocks something inside me.

I walk hungrily into the kitchen, my eyes like target-seeking missiles. Tone, to my shame, is temporarily forgotten: I'm soaking up all I can. This was their home; where they *lived*. Here, on these eccentric turquoise Windsor chairs, is where they would sit, talk, and eat; around this rustic table, with a round burn mark at one of the ends. Elsa. Staffan. Aina. Grandma.

I squat down and run my fingers over the rag rug, which has so many colors that they all run into each other, making a meaningless slush.

"Alice?" Robert says quietly behind me, and I turn around and stand up again.

"So this is where they lived?" he says.

I nod.

Robert steps over to the sink and opens one of the cupboards. His rectangular body blocks the contents, so I see nothing.

"Well, would you look at this," he says softly, reaching up to the cupboard.

He pulls out a jar of honey. It's almost full. He reaches up to the top shelf and finds a tin labelled "tea," which is empty, then feels around the obligatory paper packaging on the middle shelf before finding three metal tins of what must be sardines in tomato sauce.

"You think they're OK to eat?" I ask him.

"Honey doesn't go off if it hasn't been contaminated," he says, his chestnut eyes glinting in the last of the evening light. "It doesn't look like this has. And I don't know about the sardines, but we can take them with us anyway. That'll have to do for dinner."

I smile at him.

"See?" I say. "I told you it would pay off."

Thanks, Grandma, I think.

She's still looking out for me.

I step out of the kitchen and back into the hall, let my eyes wander along the floral wallpaper running up the stairs. The damp has run in thin, sporadic rivulets down the turgid, painted leaves.

I know what must be up there. I've seen the other houses.

The bedrooms. Staffan and Elsa's. And Aina's.

I walk toward the staircase. It looks stable, not rotten like some of the others. The handrail is essentially held up by one narrow spindle on one side, but when I test it out with a little weight it doesn't give way.

"Are you sure going up there is a good idea?" Robert asks. "Maybe we should call first. See if she replies. You don't know if the steps are stable."

"I don't want to scare her," I say quietly.

Robert has put the food in his rucksack, which he places on the wooden floor beside him. The patterned parquet is scratched, worn, and dry, but it's clear that at some point it must have been beautiful. That someone scrubbed it and polished it to keep it shining. That someone took pride in their home.

Not someone. Her. Elsa. My great-grandmother.

"We'll be careful," I say. "If she's up there she might be hiding."

June 23, 1959

Margareta,

I don't understand why you sounded so angry in your last letter? It hurt me to read it, but I can see that what I wrote must have been hard for you to hear, too. It isn't always easy to open your eyes to new truths, especially when you're so tied to the old. That's what Pastor Mattias says. Here in Silvertjärn it hasn't been easy to open people's eyes to God's light, but when it does happen—ah! I'll leave you to experience that for yourself. I'm sure you will.

It's like a new world, Margareta; it feels like I was blind my entire life, running around worrying about petty, unimportant things, feeling small and scared and powerless, but Pastor Mattias has shown me the true way. I know you have felt the same! When you were new to Stockholm and no one wanted to talk to you, when they laughed at your clothes and the way you spoke, didn't you feel lonely then? You said it like a joke, but I could tell it made you sad! And though you claim to be happy and content now, that old feeling will never leave you, Margareta. It's there because you've distanced yourself from God.

But it isn't your fault! It's Mother and Father's fault. You say that you felt the same way at my age, and that it'll pass, but have you ever considered that you might have disliked them because they're bad parents? They haven't taught us about God. They've never truly cared about us, Margareta! Only as pairs of helping hands, no more. That isn't true love. True love is boundless, unconditional. It is the sharing of both body and soul, nothing withheld. When you live in love, you learn to never say no.

But how many times has Mother said no to you and me?

Thousands! Because she has never seen us—not you, nor me, nor even Father. Why do you think he was driven to the bottle? Because he slumped into godless depths, and because she wasn't there for him.

Perhaps you would understand had you seen it, Margareta. I know you remember Mother as a good person, for you are a good person yourself. But you haven't seen her now! All she does is scold Father and try to undermine the church. She hardly wants me to go there anymore. How can you call her a pious person when she doesn't even want me to visit the house of God?

You'll see. When you come here.

Pastor Mattias has explained it all. He's helped me to see why I always felt so lonely. He's given me answers I never even knew I wanted!

You may not believe what I'm saying about Birgitta, but you will understand once you hear Pastor Mattias. He told me that pure, blessed people are more sensitive to evil than others. That's why I've always felt so uncomfortable around Birgitta, for I've sensed the darkness within her. Pastor Mattias says that the demon inside Birgitta may be what has corrupted Mother. But he says he will try to save Birgitta nonetheless—and Mother, too.

Now do you see what a good man he is? That he lives his life for God? That's how much he is willing to sacrifice to save the rest of us. He has shown us the way. He is our light in the darkness.

Just come home, Margareta. I would dearly love to show you our new church. Then you will see. You will understand it all.

Aina.

NOW

The air upstairs is still. I'm in a small hallway, barely more than a landing, that leads to two doors. Both are shut.

I hear the creak of Robert's steps behind me and turn around, nervous that he'll go straight through them. He may be slim, but he's still heavier than me.

At the top of the stairs is a small window, with four panes that let the dusky light inside. Dust particles are dancing around in the air. I'm uncomfortably aware that we don't have our respirator masks, but push the thought from my mind. Asbestos and black mold will have to be another day's concern.

Robert takes the last step, and gives a curt nod when he reaches the landing. I take a deep breath, hold it, step forward, and open the door on the right.

"Tone?" I say quietly as I scan the room.

It looks like a sweet girls' room from a classic film. It's sparingly furnished, with two beds, each less than three feet wide. Grandma must have shared the room with Aina before moving south.

The wallpaper has yellowed, and it's impossible to tell what color it must have once been. The pattern, however, is still clear: plump little rosebuds on supple vines.

There isn't much else in the room: a bookshelf and a desk, and a ceramic flowerpot full of dried earth on the windowsill. The window is one of the few that has simply cracked, rather than shattered completely. Through it the sun sinks over the forest in the distance. Its flame-red light makes the cracks in the glass gleam.

I take a few steps into the room and look around. Empty as it seems, it still feels like there's a presence in there. The short, sweaty hairs on the back of my neck are standing on end, and the skin on my exposed wrists feels more sensitive than normal.

"Tone?" I say again.

She isn't here. There's no one here.

I gulp, then quickly kneel down next to one of the beds and look underneath. A split-second vision of a piercing gray eye staring out at me from the darkness makes my heart skip a beat, but in reality there's nothing under either this or the other bed.

"No one here," I say, hushed, to Robert.

He nods and steps back into the hall, but I don't follow him. Instead I get up and walk further into the room.

The desk is calling me to it. It's small and dainty, with carved wooden knobs on its oblong drawers, and slender white legs. I slowly open each of the drawers, afraid that they might stick.

There isn't much inside: blank sheets of paper, an almost completely used-up pencil. Not the diary I now realize I've been subconsciously fantasizing about—the slender volume filled with Aina's neatly hand-written musings.

"Alice," Robert says quietly, a clear request.

"Coming," I say, though I can't quite tear myself away. I want to stay in here, soak up the house. Sleep on these mattresses, and wander these rooms.

They're like mythical figures to me, Elsa and Staffan and Aina. I've grown up with them like with a fairy tale. Even in the midst of every-thing else, it's almost impossible to believe I'm actually here.

I lift one of the mattresses. It breaks in my hand, spilling hard stuffing out onto my fingers.

"Alice," Robert says again, slightly louder this time. I nod, let go of the mattress, and follow him out.

I think he's going to tell me off, but instead he just puts his hand on the other door handle and pushes it down.

The other bedroom is larger. The windows in here have shattered inward, spewing glistening shards across the floor. The wooden planks around them are rotten and splintered. There are two narrow beds beside one another in here, too—no double bed—which strikes me as strange. I wonder if that's just a fifties thing, or if the drinking and the joblessness drove Elsa and Staffan apart. Or if Elsa was just as cold and distant as Aina describes her in her letters. I find it hard to know what to make of Elsa. Grandma always said she was strong and driven, tenacious in a way that wasn't always the norm for a woman of those times. The sort of person—and mother—whose love was brusque and pragmatic, but also sincere, and deeper than most people's.

But that image doesn't fit with the woman in Aina's letters.

I've always believed Grandma's version, seeing Aina as a confused teen, but perhaps that's wrong of me; perhaps Grandma's memories were just muddied by time and loss.

I'll never know. They're all long gone, and with them the truth.

"Tone?" Robert says.

Not a sound.

He looks at me.

"There's no one here."

The desk in here is bigger and clearly more expensive, made in a dark, lacquered wood with a green leather inlay. The lacquer has developed an ugly white sheen from exposure, but it clearly must have once cost a lot of money. Elsa's pride and joy, surely. Or Staffan's. A first step toward a life that never came.

"Seems not," I say, opening the desk drawers.

It's full of papers I don't immediately recognize. I don't know what they are, but their official appearance makes me think they're some sort of bills, important documents that mean nothing to me. Still, I pick them up.

I should turn around now. We should go. But instead I walk to the wardrobe on the other side of the room and open the doors. They're stiffer than the drawers, must have set in their frames, and I have to give them a good pull to get them open.

Inside, damp-stained clothes lie in disarray, in crisp fabrics that have slipped from their hangers and been soiled by time and water.

"Did you think she'd be hiding in there?" Robert asks. I can't tell if he's joking or not. In any case, I start opening drawer after drawer, rifling through coarse wool and thin underwear in horrible, synthetic fabrics, feeling around for something, anything—

And then I feel it.

Sheets of paper at my fingertips.

I pull them out, and for a split second I think the sound I'm hearing is the rustle of old paper on dry fabrics, but then it continues, gains in volume. Confused, I turn around to see Robert pick up his walkie-talkie.

It's a strange, dissonant noise that sounds like interference yet isn't. It rises and falls, then ascends in key until it starts to sound both cleaner and rougher at once. I almost think I can make out words—babbling, distorted words—but then it intensifies to a bellow, one so loud and so unexpected that it makes me shrink away and Robert drop the walkie-talkie.

It thuds to the floor and goes abruptly quiet.

Robert and I stand rooted to the spot, staring at the innocent yellow-and-black device in the shards of glass between us.

When it crackles to life again, I instinctively want to cover my ears, but the voice that comes out of the speaker is Emmy's. It sounds tinny and shaken.

"What the fuck was that?" she asks.

Robert picks up the walkie-talkie and presses the talk button, his pale fingers trembling slightly.

"You mean that wasn't you?"

"No," she replies, almost before he's even released the talk button. "We thought it was you."

Robert looks at me, his eyes dark holes in his white face. I just shake my head.

"I have no idea," I say. "Not a fucking clue."

Robert raises his walkie-talkie again.

"We're on our way," is all he says.

We take the steps quickly and carelessly, faster than is safe, but my heart's rattling in my chest, and suddenly I want nothing more than to be back behind the church's heavy brick walls with the others. The sheets of paper are still under my arm, and Robert grabs his rucksack as we go. We race out onto the porch and down onto the street.

Darkness has started to fall, the sky a velvety-soft shade somewhere between indigo and blue. The first stars have started to twinkle to life above us, pinpricks from another world.

We start walking up toward the church, going as fast as we can without running. I hug the papers to my chest like a security blanket, feeling the bite of the cold air against my cheeks. The blood is roaring through my veins.

Then something makes me stop short. Robert makes it a few steps down the overgrown road before he realizes I'm not beside him.

"Alice?" he says, his voice half an octave higher than usual.

"Did you hear that?" I ask.

Robert looks around, then shakes his head.

"Hear what?"

I scan the houses. The collapsed walls and peeling paint look soft and cuddly in the falling dusk. The windows seem to be calling out to us.

"It sounded like . . ." I can't bring myself to finish the sentence.

Robert shakes his head.

"She isn't there, Alice," he says, in a tone that suggests even his apparently endless patience is beginning to wear thin. "And even if she is . . . Just come! We have to get back to the others."

I don't protest, simply nod and follow him. When Robert breaks into a jog, so do I.

The words I don't say.

It didn't sound like Tone.

It sounded like someone else.

It sounded like someone . . . singing.

SATURDAY

NOW

I can see through my eyelids when the light begins to change.

I don't think I've slept at all. Dozed, yes, but I've barely slipped beneath the surface of my consciousness all night. Each time I have done, the delicate patter of drizzle on the roof has woken me up with a start.

It doesn't help that the floor is cold and hard, or that the few blankets we've managed to find are scratchy and paper thin. All of me feels raw and tender. I've heard each of the others get up to take over at the lookout: we agreed to keep watch in shifts, and drew lots to decide who went when. I got the last one.

The silver-gray dawn light turns my eyelids into networks of thin veins. I open my eyes, and sure enough, darkness has started to recede. The rain has stopped, and the fragment of sky that's visible from where I'm lying has that washed-out non-color that comes between night and morning.

I sit up, grimacing at the stiffness of my body and the rank taste in my mouth. Turns out a dinner of water, honey, and tinned fish makes for some pretty spectacular morning breath.

I look toward the doors. Emmy is sitting on the floor, her back to the pew that's serving as our barricade. One leg is pulled in to her chest, and her hair is falling in stiff, red tufts over her head and collarbone.

"Emmy," I say quietly, walking to her. "I can take over."

Emmy looks up through her tousled hair. Her eyes are bright and focused.

"OK," she says. She stands up and walks over to the bundle that is Robert, kneels down behind him on the blanket, and then curls up into his back. The pew isn't any softer than the ground, but at least it's marginally more ergonomic. I lean forward and grab the water bottle, which still has an inch or two left at the bottom. I hesitate for a second, but then drink the last of it, reasoning that I can go and refill it once the others have woken up. I savor the feeling of rinsing away the rank taste of night. Then I put the papers I've been holding onto my lap, lean back, and wait for the light. If I'm going to sit here awake, I'd rather do it with the papers from Grandma's house than alone with my thoughts.

In the light of day, the top few pages turn out to be pretty much what I had expected. They're bills. Someone has annotated them with a "paid" in a narrow, compact hand—that someone probably being Elsa—and I find myself staring at them longer than is probably reasonable. My great-grandmother.

I've only seen one picture of her before: a family portrait that Grandma took with her to Stockholm. In it, Aina is still just a sulky little girl on the verge of puberty, with straight, dark eyebrows and short, dark blond hair, wearing a checkered dress that makes her look younger than she probably is. She's squinting at the camera defiantly, a stiff and unconvincing smile on her lips. Under her left eye she has a birthmark that almost looks painted-on, like a French lady-in-waiting or a silent movie star. It must have given her an air of glamour when she got older. Perhaps she filled it in to accentuate it—or else powdered it over so it wouldn't be seen.

Grandma—sixteen or seventeen in the photo—is no surprise beauty, as elderly relatives can so often seem in photos of them from their youths. She has a square jaw and slightly flyaway hair, as well as that powerful, competent look that she would still have in her seventies. What always surprised me about that photo is that beautiful smile; how she seems to be laughing straight at the camera. She has the open aura of a teenager

with boundless self-confidence and a future that seems to promise the world.

Staffan and Elsa stand behind them, in a classic familial pose. He is tall, with a fairly undistinctive face except for his wide, charming smile. His arm is wrapped around Elsa in a way that feels surprisingly affectionate, and his head tilts in toward her, as though his entire being is striving to be near her. He isn't a handsome man, my great-grandfather, but he definitely has a certain charm. Elsa is the photo's unmistakable axis, the person the entire family seems to be built around. Like my grandmother, she doesn't seem a great beauty: a stout woman of just over forty, she is wearing a skirt and blouse which, with their girlish fifties silhouette and mismatched florals, make her look like a child playing dress-up. She looks as though she would be more at home in pants and practical shoes, clothes to help her where she had to be going.

Her face has the same distinctive squareness as Grandma's, with surprisingly full lips in the middle of her face—the same lips that, on closer inspection, you can see an inkling of in Aina's. A small, almost mischievous smile plays on Elsa's lips, which stands out because it feels so at odds with the rest of her appearance. Her hair is styled in stiff curls that seem to be there for the sake of the photo alone, and below her fluffy fringe her light, steady eyes look straight down the camera, firm and direct. Her hands sit on Aina's shoulders. My great-grandmother's hands, almost identical to my grandma's, with a simple, silvery wedding ring on one finger.

Those very same fingers marked every bill paid with a neat little "paid." May 1958. July 1958. November 1958.

Then other notes start appearing.

"Late."

"Deferred."

"Deferred."

"Cancelled."

On the final two bills there are no notes at all.

I sit and stare at the thin, sepia-brown sheets of paper spread out on my lap. My fatigue is making reality throb.

Below the bills are the three sheets of paper I found in the underwear drawer. They're in pristine condition.

The handwriting on them is the same as the small notes from the bills, but it looks different. The letters are smaller but more spaced out, the lines are flurried and uneven, and the ink is smudged in a few places.

There's no date at the top of the page, nor any greeting, so it's only when I hunch over to squint at the words that I realize it's a letter.

Margareta, I'm writing this to you for I feel I must. I see no other option.

I know that you are busy and have a lot on your plate, with a baby on the way. I know that you don't have much space. But please: take your father, your sister, Birgitta, and me in with you in Stockholm. I hope it will only be for a short while, but I am asking you, as your mother, to help us in our time of need.

The situation here is worse than I could ever have imagined. The entire village is all but entranced, your sister included. They are treating the pastor as though he were God the Father himself, although I'm starting to suspect he's more a demon in human guise. He has stirred up the congregation to the brink of madness. I have heard them speaking in tongues during services, and every evening at sunset the drone of their songs rings through town.

There are only a few of us left who have not fallen in thrall to him. Your sister is his right hand. I'm losing her. She has moved in to the church, where she now sleeps. I fear that the venom he has filled her ears with has turned her against us completely. I must get her out of here before it is too late.

I understand that you must have your concerns about Birgitta. I know that it's an additional burden, especially given the way she is, but I refuse to leave her here. Pastor Mattias and his congregation hate her. They say that she is a witch and succubus, that she is possessed by demons and serves the devil. I fear what they will do

to her if I leave her here. She would never be able to defend herself.
God knows if any of the rest of us could.

I'm not even sure if they follow the Christian doctrine anymore.
They have started holding mass in

Here the letter comes to an abrupt end. No period, no sign-off. As though she were interrupted mid-sentence, then shoved the letter at the bottom of her underwear drawer and never cared to finish it.

Or never could.

THEN

S he hesitates, her pen poised, before lowering it again.

I'm not even sure if they follow the Christian doctrine anymore, she writes. When the words finally come, they do so in a swinging, flurried hand that is quite unlike her own. She doesn't know how much she should tell Margareta.

Margareta has always been like Elsa: decisive. If Elsa says too much she fears it will bring Margareta storming up to Silvertjärn herself, but at the same time she has to say something. She must tell someone what has been happening. She can't take this anymore.

Until a few short days ago, Elsa had thought she could get through this herself, that it would pass.

But then she had come home one day to find Staffan waiting for her at the kitchen table. He wanted to talk to her, he said. His eyes were glassy but he didn't smell of drink, and initially that had been a relief. For a moment Elsa had hoped it meant he had pulled himself together, grasped the seriousness of their situation.

Elsa feels almost physically sick when she recalls the hope that budded within her as she sat down opposite her husband at the kitchen table, her hands clasped in front of her, the air thick with the heady scent of the late summer heat.

When Staffan told her that it had to stop, Elsa couldn't agree more.

She was about to say that they had to do something about Aina, to get her to see sense, but he went on before she could get a word out:

"You must be reasonable—stop challenging the pastor," he said. "Folk have started talking, Elsie. Enough, now. Enough."

In that instant she had felt her heart split in two. He had looked at her with flat, angry eyes, as though looking not at her but at a stranger. Someone who meant nothing to him. Someone he scorned.

The next night he hadn't come home at all.

When evensong had swept over Silvertjärn, Elsa had thought, impossible as it was, that she could hear Staffan's voice among them.

They have started holding mass in

The front door slams downstairs, and she stops writing.

"Staffan?" she ventures to ask, but his name sounds flimsy and washed-out on her lips. Her voice falters.

Elsa hears steps and stands up. Quickly shuffling the letter together on the desk, she looks for somewhere to hide it.

She opens the wardrobe and shoves it down the side of her underwear drawer, then closes the wardrobe door just as someone calls her name.

She steps away from the wardrobe. The bedroom door bursts open.

It's Dagny.

Her face is shiny with sweat, and her hair is in disarray. She is holding her sunhat in her hands, and her yellow shoes are covered in dust and muck. She looks like she's been running.

"Elsa," she says, her voice rough and scratchy from exertion. "It's Birgitta. You must come."

NOW

I wake up slowly, my consciousness cloudy with sleep and confusion. Then I sit up and look around. It must be late morning—ten or ten thirty, judging by the warmth of the light outside. It's a beautiful morning that lends the church a magical aura, despite the mud and dust on the checkerboard slate floor.

Oh God. I must have fallen asleep, even though it was my watch. Yet another thing I can't do right.

Luckily enough, none of the others seems to have woken up and caught me sleeping on the job. Small mercies.

I blink and yawn into the back of my hand. Some of my papers have fallen to the ground, so I quickly bend down and sweep them together into a small pile. It's quite peaceful in here, with the sunlight streaming down on the others as they sleep. The only thing to taint the image is the glowering Christ above the altar.

When I take a closer look at the others I give a start. Robert's eyes are open.

"I didn't want to wake anyone," he says, so quietly that I almost have to read his lips.

He sits up, slides carefully out of Emmy's arm, and gets up.

"Is there any water left?" he asks.

I look down guiltily at the empty bottle next to the pew and shake my head.

"Sorry," I say. "I drank the last of it."

He nods.

"Hard to make it stretch to four people," he says.

"We can sneak out and get some more," I whisper. "The river isn't far. I would have gone earlier, but it seemed stupid to go alone."

Robert glances at sleeping Emmy, who has curled up into a little ball under the thin blanket. Her face is soft in sleep; it looks younger, strangely familiar. When I used to sleep over at her room I would usually wake up first—she wasn't a morning person—and sometimes I would just lie there and watch her sleep. It was the sort of friendship that can only exist in those few brittle years between teenage life and fully fledged adulthood, before you've set your limits as to how much you let others in.

"OK," Robert whispers. "But we'll have to move the pew. We should try not to wake them."

I jump off the pew and take hold of one end. We try to lift it but don't manage to get it far—I can't keep my end up—and it slips out of my hands and scrapes loudly against the floor.

I glance at Emmy, but she hasn't even moved. Max is still lying where he was, snoring in thin whistles.

I pull open the heavy door. The fresh air streams into the room like a gasp, and I take in the smell of morning after the rain. The light is of the clean, white type that seems to only exist in April and May.

I stride out onto the steps. It's completely still. Not even the blades of grass are swaying.

Robert comes out behind me, and I hear him close the door. I look around.

"Ready?" I ask. My voice sounds almost perky.

But Robert isn't looking at me.

He's staring past me, down at the steps, with an almost thoughtful look on his face. I turn to follow his gaze.

The rain has turned the dust on the steps into mud. It has started to dry up again in the morning sun, but the ground is still sticky and wet.

And dotted with smeared, muddy footsteps.

My mind runs through the possibilities in less than a second. The prints are clear enough to visibly be footprints, but it's hard to tell if they were made by shoes or bare feet. They could possibly have been made by an animal with elongated paws . . . but no. We haven't seen any animals since we arrived.

Someone has been here. In the past few hours.

I look at Robert. His face is completely calm. He walks past me and down the steps, stops by one of the marks, and squats down for a closer look.

"What is it?" Emmy asks, giving me a start.

Clearly she wasn't so sound asleep after all. She's standing in the doorway behind me, looking at Robert. It seems to take her a few seconds longer than us to register what we're looking at, but then her eyes widen, and some of the color drains from her cheeks.

Without a word, she walks out and down the steps, too. I hastily look up and out at the countryside around us. All I can see are empty houses and swaying greenery revived by the night's rainfall, but that doesn't make me any calmer. One thousand empty windows stare back at me on every side. I look left and right, try to catch some sort of movement, spot something out of the corner of my eye, but everything is quiet and still.

Meanwhile, Emmy has squatted down next to a print, which she studies intently. She reaches over and picks something out of the mud. It looks like a small, light pebble.

"Chalk," she says quietly.

"What?"

I'm barely listening to her, so preoccupied I am with our surroundings. My paranoia is making everything both slow down and speed up at the same time.

"It's a piece of chalk," she says. She lifts it up at me.

"It must have gotten caught in the sole of her shoe," I say.

My lips start to tingle.

"It's from the school," I continue. "There was crushed chalk on the floor in the classrooms."

"Do you think it was . . . ?" Emmy asks.

"If it was Tone we heard last night over the walkie-talkie," I say, interrupting her, "then she must have gone back to the school. It's where she lost it, when she went through the step."

I look out over Silvertjärn. From up here it looks almost like a normal village in bloom. If you squint, that is.

"It's where she hurt herself," I go on. "And where her mom was found. It wouldn't be so strange for her to feel a pull back there."

"Back where?"

Max hasn't come out onto the steps, but stands half in shadow.

"Tone was here," I say. "Last night. I think she's in the school."

"We don't know it was Tone," says Emmy. "It could have been one of us. It could just as easily have come from your shoe, Alice."

"But that wouldn't explain why there are crumbs of chalk in the prints," I say, hearing the impatience shining through my own voice.

"And even if she was in the school, we can't be sure she's still there," Emmy says.

"But it's the best lead we have," I say, looking at the others. "We have to at least try."

"This changes nothing," says Emmy. "I know it might feel like it, but it doesn't. Not really. We voted that it's safest to stay here."

I look at the others. Robert's lips are pinched. Max's eyes don't meet mine.

She's right. They all are. I can feel it in my bones, that fear, like a sour taste on my tongue. I want nothing more than to stay there, to give in to their reason. I've seen the movies, too—I know what happens to the person who leaves safety to head out into the dark forest, the haunted psychiatric ward, the abandoned school.

But what those movies don't show is the guilt surging like a current through my skin; how it feels to know someone you care about is already there, alone and vulnerable and terrified.

What the moviegoers don't see is that the shame of staying can weigh heavier than the fear of going.

"Then I'll go alone," I say.

The sun stings my eyes. I turn around and walk past Max, back into the church.

NOW

It takes a few seconds for my eyes to adjust to the darkness of the church, and I hit my thigh on one of the pews we've shoved to one side. I curse under my breath—ugly, explosive words I wouldn't normally use—but hobble on into the chapel.

It's warm in there. I close the door behind me, sit down on one of the chairs, and bury my face in my hands. Try to take slow, deep breaths. In and out.

Can I do this?

I have to. Even though the stress is making me sick. Even though the sound of that walkie-talkie is echoing through my head, off the inside of my skull. That inhuman, many-edged roar.

It must have been Tone. Just like it must have been Tone in the van—if there really was anyone there. Just because it didn't sound like the Tone I know, doesn't mean it isn't her. The Tone I know probably isn't the same person who's hiding out there now.

But at the end of the day it doesn't matter. I have to go. If there's a chance she'll be there I have to look.

When the door opens, I say quietly:

"Do you want to come with me?"

I'm expecting Max's voice. I'm expecting a no. It's only when I hear nothing that I look up.

Emmy has already closed the door behind her. Her eyes are looking at the window, out onto the graveyard. The sunlight plays over her face, washing away the tiredness and dirt.

"You can't stop me," I say, even though some small part of me really hopes she can.

"Oh no," she says. "I probably could. If I tried."

She sounds so naturally confident that it grates on me like flint on steel, lights a spark that turns fear to anger.

"I don't get how you can just sit here," I say to her. "If you hadn't taken off this would never have happened—you do see that, right? If you'd been there, like you said you would, she would never—*never*—"

"I know," Emmy cuts me off. "OK? I know. I know."

This stuns me into silence.

"You're acting like you're the only one here who cares about Tone," she says, looking straight at me for the first time, her eyes devastatingly green. "Like you're the only one here with any sense of responsibility, the only one who's worried. Don't you get how fucking frustrating that is?"

She throws her arms out.

"Everyone wants to be heroes, Alice! Everyone wants to run around fixing everything, but this isn't a movie! It isn't one of your grandma's stories! Just because we're in Silvertjärn doesn't mean we know how the story ends. Tone blew up our vans. You say she isn't violent, that she's sick, and I buy that she doesn't know what she's doing, but you have no idea what she's capable of right now! What do you think is going to happen? That if you whisper softly and sweetly to her, appeal to her inner goodness, that she'll just snap out of it? That isn't how it works!"

Emmy runs her fingers through her hair in frustration. I get to my feet and open my mouth to reply, but she starts again:

"I'm just trying to be pragmatic, Alice. I'm trying to be an adult. Because one of us has to be, OK? One of us has to have a foot in the real world."

"Yes," I spit out, seven years of poison in my voice. "Pragmatic and adult. That's always you, isn't it? It's never worth fighting for anyone, sticking your neck out. Trying to save them. No, way better to just give up and move on—right?"

Emmy is staring at me.

"What the fuck are you talking about?" she asks.

"I knew this was a mistake," I say, chuckling impotently, hopelessly, to myself. "It's my fault, I know. Because I knew what you're like. I knew, and still I asked you to be part of this project. I thought the worst that could happen would be you doing a bad job. Look, I get that you don't give a shit about this movie, and I can live with that. But I can't sit back and let you try and make us abandon . . ." My voice cracks. I shake my head and try to go on, but for a moment my vocal cords betray me.

"But that's just what you do, isn't it? You abandon people when they need you most. I don't even know why I'm so surprised. But you can't make me do the same thing, Emmy. You can't make me be like you."

It should feel good to finally say this. But all I feel is tired, tired and sad, and when I wipe my eyes with the back of my hand I realize I'm crying.

When Emmy speaks, her voice is dry.

"Is that really how you remember it?"

I shake my head.

"How else should I remember it?" I whisper. "Please, tell me. Tell me about this *real world* of yours. You were always good at that—at telling me whatever I felt was wrong."

Emmy shakes her head. When she looks at me, her eyes are glistening.

"What do you think I should have done, Alice?" she asks. "Please. Tell me what I could have done that I didn't do. I tried everything. I loved you, Alice." Her lips quiver as she says it. "You were like a sister to me. Do you have any idea how painful it was to see you like that? To see you contract, shrink down until you could hardly get out of bed? Do you even remember that you slept in my bed for three weeks, refusing to shower because you said the water hurt your skin too much?"

"Are you really telling me it was hard *for you*?" I ask, half laughing, abrasive.

"Of course it was!" she says, an outburst that bounces off the walls in the small room. "OF COURSE it was hard for me, too! You were my best friend, and you were wasting away, and I didn't know what to do! I booked you appointments at the health center, but you refused to go! I spoke to the student counselor to stop you getting kicked off the program! I did everything I could, but it was never enough. Nothing worked. You didn't want to talk to anyone, didn't want any medication. You didn't want to get help. Didn't want to . . . live."

She stumbles over the last word, as though it's too big for her mouth.

"Alice, the first time you said you wanted to die, I called my mom and just cried. I couldn't even speak. I just cried. I was so tired. I was only twenty-two. I was so tired, and I didn't know what to do. I didn't know how to save you. Mom said you were drowning, and that I was getting pulled down with you. She told me I couldn't help someone who didn't want to be helped. But I tried anyway. Because I loved you. All I wanted was for you to get better."

She shakes her head. Her thick, hennaed locks graze her shoulders.

"But in the end I just couldn't go on," she says. She dries her eyes with her arm, a big, sloppy motion. "OK? And I've never forgiven myself. Never. Clearly you haven't, either. I get it. But when you contacted me about this project I was so happy, because I knew how much it meant to you. I thought that you wanting me to be involved meant that maybe you'd forgiven me. That you wanted to let me be part of your dream."

She shakes her head again.

"Mom told me not to take the job. But Robert said he could tag along as a cameraman, and I—I wanted to believe I was right. I wanted to believe you meant it as an olive branch."

She swallows.

"But from that very first meeting it was clear you still hated me. So I tried to keep myself to myself. Do my job."

She shakes her head. And then she smiles, a shaky smile with tear-stained lips, one so unlike her.

"I really believed in the film, Alice. Just so you know. I think it would have been fantastic. We could have made something really special."

My mouth tastes of blood and salt. I can hardly see her anymore. The sobs sit like a tremor in my body, an approaching earthquake I do all I can to keep under control.

"I didn't hate you," I choke, the words so thin and strained that they twist out of shape. "I don't hate you. Or maybe I did. Once. Because I hated myself. And because I was so lonely. When you disappeared I had nothing left but myself. No one."

I dry my eyes again, roughly; push my fingers up against them so I can rest in darkness for a few seconds.

"That's why I can't leave her there. Don't you see? It's not that I want to be the hero, to run in and save the day, it's that she's out there all alone. And you're right—it is my fault. I'm guessing she stopped taking her meds so she could take painkillers, because she saw how much I wanted her to stay. It's my fault she's sick again and I can't . . . I can't just leave her there."

Something in my chest has slackened. Old scar tissue, hardened and petrified. I'm not sure if that means it's bleeding or healing. Emmy closes her eyes, then opens them again. The green in them flashes brighter when they're red with tears.

"OK," she says. "Then let's do it."

"You don't have to come with me," I say.

Emmy gives a faint smile.

"Yes," she says, "I do. And you can't stop me."

"I probably could," I reply, smiling back at her with trembling lips. "If I tried."

Emmy opens the door.

"Come on," she says. "Let's get our boys and go."

I walk up to her and stop.

This isn't a movie. In a movie we would have hugged and been best friends again, now and forever. That's never going to happen. I think I'll be living with this dull pain for the rest of my life. I'll never get back what we used to have.

But maybe that doesn't have to be such a bad thing.

Maybe we can still live with each other, in some way, shape, or form.

"I'm glad you didn't drown with me," I say.

She nods slowly.

"I'm glad you didn't drown," she replies.

NOW

The square hits me as a shock, even though I know what to expect. The blackened car parts and sooty, withered greenery are an open wound in the silent village, a postapocalyptic vision in the middle of a tattered postcard.

The smell of ash and burning metal still hangs in the air. The school looms like a monster on the short edge of the square. The explosion was clearly the last straw for one of the doors, which seems to have fallen off its hinges completely.

We stop at the bottom of the front steps.

"Wait," says Emmy.

She steps forward and stands completely still. Listens intently.

I do the same. Try to hear something, anything.

Footsteps.

Laughter.

Breaths in the darkness.

Not a sound.

Emmy looks around.

"We'll stick together," she says. "No one goes anywhere alone. No one goes off to look around. Not even in pairs. OK?"

I look her in the eye and nod.

"OK," I say.

She gives me a quick, closed-mouth smile, surprisingly sincere.

"Then let's go," she says, and I follow her up the steps and into the school.

It's warmer in here than outside—inexplicably so, given all the empty window frames and open doors. Beyond the pat of our soles on the broken glass, it's so quiet you could hear a pin drop.

When we open the door to the first classroom, it swings open quietly, no arguments. The classroom looks like it did the last time I was here. With Tone. The desks in neat rows; the alphabet posters on the walls, with letters in capitals, lowercase, and cursive; a slightly smaller chart of times tables next to the blackboard at the front.

Empty.

We move on through the other classrooms without saying anything. They're almost the same as the first, only with different charts on the wall.

When we reach the last classroom, Emmy stops abruptly in the doorway.

Suddenly I'm struck by an image of Tone crouching under a desk, stony-faced, her head twisted to one side and her wild eyes fixed on us—or else hunched on a desk, her back bent, eyes glimmering under a dirty fringe, like something dangerous and alien. A monster.

I hate myself for thinking it, and even more for the fear that those crystal-clear images inspire within me; how they make my heart race and my mouth dry.

I can't let myself fear Tone.

"What is it?" I ask Emmy quietly.

I swallow down my acrid fear and look past her shoulder. Someone has tossed the chairs around and flipped the desks. One of the little wooden chairs is completely destroyed.

Emmy takes a few steps into the room. She stops by the smashed chair, then turns. When I follow her eyes, I see a mark on the wall. It's dark and uneven, a browny-red sweep over the peeling light yellow paint. It looks recent.

A slender, writhing chill plants itself at the pit of my stomach. My eyes sting.

What has she done to herself?

It's impossible to fend off the image that pops into my head; of Tone, her ankle wounded and bleeding, her eyes empty, clumsily smearing throbs of blood over the wall.

Emmy turns to look at me. I clench my teeth as hard as I can and just nod.

None of us says anything, but we keep much closer together as we walk back along the corridor to the classrooms on the other side. We try to dodge the shrapnel on the floor, sneaking through as quietly as we can. There's still no sound to be heard, beyond our own anxious breaths.

The rest of the classrooms seem untouched. But I start to notice something. The way the glass is lying on the ground looks almost as though somebody has already walked on and through it: some shards have been crushed and trodden down into the ugly green linoleum floor; others lie swept to one side in piles. Together they make an almost invisible, meandering trail.

I say nothing. I'm not even sure what I'm seeing.

We get back to the entrance and stop at the bottom of the staircase. The hole that Tone fell through sits, big and ugly, halfway up. The rest of the steps still look somewhat stable, but it'll be hard to get past there.

"I'll go first," I say. "I've done this before. And you guys don't have to come up with me. I understand."

Emmy shakes her head.

"No, me first," she says. "I'm the smallest. It's best if I test them."

Robert and I both start to protest, but Emmy shuts us down.

"Honestly, you both know I'm right," she says.

I look up at the staircase again. The steps are wide and flat. The light, splintered wood looks OK, except for the part that has fallen in.

"If you stick to the sides . . ." I say, doubtfully.

"We're going together," Emmy says. "Follow in my footsteps. Like walking on ice."

She ties her hair up into a high, messy bun and nods at us.

"OK," she says. "Follow me."

She puts her foot onto one of the steps and cautiously tests it. It neither creaks nor breaks.

Taking a firm hold of the brass railing, which, with its sturdy bolts in the wall, looks considerably more trustworthy than the steps, she cautiously starts to climb. I follow her slowly. Despite the cool day, the sweat beads on my neck. I imagine I can feel the wood bending beneath my feet, but so far it doesn't worry me too much.

When we pass the hole, I don't let it out of my sight. Out of the corner of my eye I see Max edging up behind me nervously, his jaw clenched, and behind him Robert with a furrowed brow.

Now I'm two steps above the hole, Emmy four. Only five steps until the second floor.

I turn my head to tell the others to tread carefully around the hole—both Max and Robert are much heavier than Emmy and I—but my voice is drowned out by an overwhelming crash.

The ground disappears beneath me, leaving me hanging in the air for a dizzying split second. A thousand thoughts run through my head, none of them connected. For a second it's as though I'm trying to run in the air, and when I lurch forward to try to grab the step in front of me, that one disappears, too. I fall.

I hear someone make a short, surprised yelp, the sort of instinctive cry that's gruff and throaty rather than high-pitched or light, and I can't tell if it's coming from me or someone else. My body is weightless. Then I land hard on my back, so hard that the breath is knocked out of me and I see black and red flash before my eyes.

In a few seconds my vision contracts to a single white point. Breathe, I have to breathe, but my lungs don't want to cooperate, and my rib cage won't move. I feel sick, and lie there opening and closing my mouth like a fish.

And then a lick of breath slips inside me, delicious and not enough.

I gasp for air, pull it in again and again, until my throat begins to open and my rib cage expands.

Then I roll onto my side and retch. Thin saliva and honey, sweet and watery.

It slowly sinks in that I'm lying on the broken remains of the steps, my back in dazzling pain. We're inside what used to be the staircase, the hole above us an open chasm through which the cracked paint on the ceiling gazes down at us. The staircase can hardly be more than splinters now; the entire thing has collapsed.

I dread looking at the others, but I have no choice. I pull myself up to sitting and look around.

Max is struggling up to all fours only a few feet away from me, his face frozen in a pained grimace. His nose is bleeding, and the blood is running down his chin. Robert is lying on his back, one leg bent, unmoving. My heart skips a beat, but then I see him start to move with a groan.

I look around.

Max. Robert.

Where's Emmy?

NOW

Robert rolls over onto his side with a low groan. Max pulls himself up to sitting and wipes his nose, inadvertently smearing the blood across his face. He blinks his dazed eyes in shock.

"Emmy!" I shout. My voice swings up toward the ceiling, but dies out before it takes flight.

Could she have been thrown out of the door somehow?

I scrabble over the debris of rotted wood and out onto the hard stone floor, both hoping and dreading to see her there. But there's no one.

This time I manage to suck the air right down into my lungs and shout:

"EMMY!"

And then it comes, like a blessing, thin and small up above.

"Here. I'm up here."

The relief swells over me, temporarily subduing the throbbing pain in my back.

"Emmy! Where? Where are you?"

It takes a few seconds, and when it does come, her voice sounds choked as it drifts down toward me.

"Upstairs." And then, a few seconds later:

"Jumped when the steps fell."

By now Robert has emerged, and he shouts, too:

"Are you OK?"

His red hair is covered in splinters, and there's a nick in his eyebrow. The blood has already started to dry.

The pain in my back has started to sharpen, a dull stab to the time of my heartbeats, but there's no time to think about that.

"Broken ribs," Emmy says. "I think. I landed on them."

Her voice is strained.

"Don't move!" Robert shouts, his voice surprisingly shrill. "We're coming up to get you!"

I hear something that sounds like a cross between a laugh and a moan, and I feel like I can almost read her thoughts:

How will we get her down?

But right now that doesn't matter. The important thing is to get up there.

Robert turns back and starts jogging down the corridor in long strides, and Max follows him, his arm pressed to his bleeding nose. As Robert runs, I see him limping slightly on one foot.

He looks around, then turns back.

"Shit," he spits.

"Is there a supply shop or something?" Max asks.

I shake my head.

"Not so far as I know."

Max nods. Robert looks out of the window. The muscles in his neck look tensed, and a small vein has appeared on his temple.

"Come on," I say. "Let's look outside. There might be some way to climb up. We'll get up there, don't worry."

When we step outside I squint up at the sun, which has passed the midday point at the top of the sky. It's after twelve. Less than twenty-four hours until the police arrive.

This helps to loosen the hard knot that has formed in my chest. I can almost breathe again.

One day. We can make it.

We just need to get Emmy down, then carry or drag or support her back to the church—it's not far, it should be fine—barricade the doors again and wait it out. We have water and honey. We can do it.

I can't even think about Tone right now.

Max has walked straight out onto the cobblestones, and he studies the building up and down. What he sees doesn't seem to encourage him, and I soon realize why: the façade, gnarled and ugly as it is, offers nothing to climb.

"Around the back," he says. Robert just nods and sets off at a trot, with me hard on his heels.

I can't even look him in the eye right now. I know what he must be thinking.

If only I hadn't insisted on coming here, if only I'd just listened to them, if only I hadn't persuaded Emmy to come with me . . . Then none of this would have happened. Then Emmy wouldn't be lying hurt up there right now.

But I can help. That has to mean something.

As we round the corner I run straight into Robert's back. He's stopped abruptly at the start of the alley.

The back of the school plot is small but strangely sweet, a square patch of land that was presumably once trampled down by games and sports. The skeletons of four neat picnic tables stand in a row next to the building. The wood has shriveled and contracted down to their metal legs, which have rusted into a deep red and started to disintegrate.

But it isn't the tables Robert's looking at.

It's the fire escape behind them.

Of course. Obviously there had to be a fire escape.

Robert starts heading toward it, but I stop him with a hand on his arm.

"It won't hold you," I say.

"It'll hold," he says sharply, but I don't let go. I shake my head.

"Look at it," I say, "it's rusted. You must weight what, a hundred and seventy pounds? A hundred eighty?"

At first Robert doesn't answer, but I see his shoulders droop slightly.

The steps on the ladder are rusty, but they don't look broken to me.

"I'll go," I say.

I give myself a quick shake, try to force myself to focus as I step up to the fire escape. It looks less stable up close. Some of the steps are thin as pencils.

It's OK. It'll be fine.

Behind my back I hear Robert shout:

"EMMY! We've found a fire escape! We're on our way!"

I pull myself up onto the first step, expecting it to snap under me, but it holds. Then the next. That one holds, too.

My heart is pumping in hard, powerful thuds. It's just like the bridge again, only crystallized into something else, something smaller, weaker, worse. The water coursing beneath me.

I'm trying not to look down, but my feet have already passed the first row of windows. A faint breeze against my back stirs up my sweaty, ruffled hair and makes the small hairs on my neck stand on end. I stop.

My breaths are coming in short, sharp stabs, but whether that's the exertion or the fear talking I can't tell.

"Alice!" Max shouts below me. "Are you OK?"

I don't reply. My mouth is dry.

"Alice!" he shouts again, louder this time. "Do you want to come down?"

That's all I want to do.

I can already feel it: the step cracking beneath me, the first split second of shock. The fall, short and frozen and beautiful, and then the smack of me hitting the ground, that absurd shift from speed to stillness. The crack of my skull as it smashes against the stones.

But Emmy's up there and she can't get down. Emmy, who held me when I would cry until my whole body shook, who picked up the phone again and again and again, who listened to me and looked after me and loved me, until me and my anxiety wore that love down to nothing. Emmy, who's lying up there all alone, her ribs broken, because I asked her.

"It's OK," I shout back, my voice shaky, and then I start climbing again.

I take the last steps faster, refusing to think about the height or the rust on my fingers. When I come level with the next window, I see it's already completely free of shards. A small blessing.

I grab hold of the window frame and heave myself in over it. The relief is greater than the effort it takes, and I manage to pull myself into the room and get my feet down onto the floor reasonably smoothly.

I dry my palms off on my jeans, leaving ugly rusty marks on my thighs, and look around. It isn't hard to figure out where I am. It's the school nurse's office; that tall, empty room with the bed in the far corner.

"I'm in!" I call out of the window to Max and Robert, and then I call inside:

"Emmy? It's Alice! I'm here!"

I stride across to the big, stately doors, which are already slightly ajar. I open them.

Emmy is lying flat on her back by the door to the science room. The gaping hole where the stairs once were comes as something of a shock to the system.

"Emmy?" I say, walking over to her.

She's staring up at the ceiling, I see as I come closer. She isn't looking at me. Is she angry? That wouldn't exactly be surprising.

"I'm sorry," I begin, now beside her. "We've found a fire escape. We'll get you down some—"

I stop short.

She says nothing.

In fact, she isn't reacting at all; she's lying completely still.

Her chest isn't moving.

Her eyes are empty, the whites strangely bloodshot.

"Emmy?" I try to say, but my voice sounds odd, as though coming from far away. "Emmy, can you hear me?"

She doesn't reply.

I look down at her. Her white T-shirt is dirty and dusty, and her jeans are ripped and stained, too. The small gold heart pendant she usually wears around her neck—a baptism gift from her grandfather—has fallen out of the neck of her T-shirt.

I put my hand on her arm and her skin is warm, and I think that she must be OK, that she's just in pain, that that's why she isn't replying, and I shake her and say her name again, and again she doesn't reply, and I shake her harder and her head starts to loll from side to side like a doll's, and now I shout at her because all I want is for her to reply, to just say something—say something.

"EMMY, FUCKING SAY SOMETHING!"

Silence.

"Please," I whimper, and now someone tears me away and shouts:

"Emmy?!"

I didn't even hear him coming. He's shoved me aside but it doesn't matter, because the whole world is shut in a giant bubble and I hear nothing and see nothing, and my field of vision has shrunk to a pinprick and in it all I see are her empty, staring eyes.

"Emmy?" Robert whispers, and he stops shaking her, and when he says her name again it's the worst sound I've ever heard.

Because his voice just . . .

. . . breaks.

He can't turn around.

I can't see his face.

"What . . ." I hear from behind me as I sit there kneeling on the dusty wooden floor. It seems to be coming from very far away.

"Oh," is all Max says, and it's such a small sound. He says it again.

"Oh."

We all go very, very still. As though we're trying to imitate Emmy as she lies there.

I reach out and touch the exposed gap of ankle over her muddy white Converse sneakers.

Her skin has started to cool now.

NOW

It's Max who reaches out and closes her eyes.

Something about the gesture seems so final that it bursts the bubble around me. The world surges back into me.

Robert stands up sharply and walks off, throws open the doors to our right, and disappears into the classroom. I make to follow him, but Max stops me.

"Let him . . ." he starts, but he doesn't finish the sentence.

I look at Emmy again. I can't stop looking at her. It's like a disgusting instinct I have, a need to always confirm what I already know, again and again.

"I don't understand," I whisper to myself. I say it again and again, probe it. "I don't understand, I don't understand."

Is this what shock feels like?

I reach over and grab Max's arm with a desperate strength that I know must hurt, but his expression doesn't change. It's vacant, just as expressionless as his voice, and I'm struck by a sudden need to make him react, make him feel what I'm feeling. To scratch him, scream in his face.

He looks at me with a sleepwalker's eyes.

"I didn't realize this would happen," I force from myself, hoarse and snotty-nosed, and now I retch: "I didn't realize, I don't get how this could happen, I didn't see how badly she was hurt, that—that her ribs had punctured her lungs, or that she'd damaged her spine, or hit her head, or whatever it was, I just . . ." I let go of his arm, feel my body start to shake like it's cramping up, and now he seems to finally wake up, and through the fog I see him moving, feel him gently take hold of me, and I want to shake him off me but at the same time I just want someone to hold the pieces of me together.

Like Emmy always used to do.

"We should . . ." Max begins, his voice shaky and thick with tears, "we should cover her with something, so that she isn't just . . ."

I dry my eyes. Try to force my breaths to calm, then pull back slightly from Max.

"I'll check," I say. I don't look at her; I can't anymore.

I walk over to the room I came in through. The doors are wide open now, after Robert and Max stormed through them. I look out of the window, and for a split second I picture myself jumping out of it, but the image has no real power.

Is it possible to turn back time? Just a few weeks. To delete that email, stop myself from finding her new email address.

To go back to that moment when I paused, unsure, my fingers hovering over the keyboard, and whisper in my ear:

Don't ask her to get involved. Don't offer her the job. Just tell her you're sorry. Tell her you're doing better now. Tell her you'll always be grateful for everything she did.

My bottom lip trembles and I bite it hard, bite until I feel the skin break and the taste of blood fills my mouth, until that little red bead of pain gives me something to focus on.

My shaky legs take me over to the bed in the far corner of the room. The sheet is still pulled down, and the faded, dried-on bloodstains make the nausea rise in my belly.

I can't cover Emmy with those, I just can't. Nothing with blood, nothing to remind me of what's happened, of the brutal reality of our bodies. I don't care if it's blood from a child's nose after tumbling in the playground, or the blood of that newborn's mother.

Emmy deserves to be shrouded in something clean. And whole.

Shrouded.

My mind catches and sticks on the word, while my eyes land on the small cabinet in the corner. It looks like it could contain sheets. I walk up to it and look at the elegant door, but there's no handle. A small lock gleams mockingly at me.

For one frenzied second I want to kick the cabinet to pieces, but I calm myself down. It's solid. Kicking it will do nothing.

I walk over to the desk instead, kick away the chair, squat in front of it, and start tearing open the drawers.

There's nothing in the top drawer. It's empty except for a pen and a small coin with an unfamiliar face.

I have to give the next drawer down a good pull.

It opens in small jerks, as though something is stuck. It's full to the brim, mainly old-fashioned paper folders, brown and thin, labeled in neat, boxy handwriting.

I pull out the top one.

KRISTINA LIDMAN

I open it automatically.

For a few seconds my eyes stare, unseeing, at the contents. My stiff, bungling fingers flick through the perfectly preserved, square Polaroid images.

A sound rises in my throat. I put my hand over my mouth to stifle it. The insane laugh tears and scratches at my mouth, trying to force its way through my fingers. I'm afraid of what'll happen if I move my hand, if I let it come swinging out.

Here it is. Finally.

The breakthrough I've been looking for. An unparalleled scoop.

I just never could have guessed the price I would have to pay.

THEN

S he hears it before they even make it to the end of the street.

It's a terrible sound, like an animal in unbearable pain, a muffled bellow that hardly seems like it could come from a human throat.

But Elsa can hear where it's coming from.

It's coming from Birgitta's hut.

Dagny has slowed her jog slightly. She looks around, breathless and red in the face.

"It started a few hours ago," she says, in response to the question Elsa has not yet asked.

"At first I thought it was just one of her outbursts, but then it got worse. And when she started making those noises I thought it was best to fetch you."

Elsa nods. Her mouth feels dry as dust and her heart is pounding, but still she manages to say:

"You were right to do so. Thank you."

Dagny has never helped her with Birgitta, has never offered, but Elsa still feels a wave of gratitude that she has come to her. She is one of the few left.

Elsa doesn't know what would have happened had the pastor's followers got there first. Perhaps they're already on their way.

Elsa stops sharply outside the door.

"Birgitta?" she cries.

No reply. The bellows have quietened.

There's no time for the normal ritual. Elsa opens the door. Birgitta is curled up in the fetal position on the bed, her arms clasped around her stomach. Her bellow has sunk to a whimper. She is turned away, and her hair is covering her face. This isn't one of her outbursts. Nothing is broken. The table is where it should be, as are the chairs. Yesterday's basket is standing exactly where Elsa left it. She doesn't seem angry or upset; she doesn't even seem to have noticed Elsa come in.

"Birgitta?" she says.

The whimper dies down to nothing.

The fear in Elsa comes into full bloom.

"Birgitta, may I come closer?" Elsa asks cautiously. "It's Elsa."

Birgitta doesn't reply. She's lying completely quiet and still.

Elsa goes to Birgitta's side. She doesn't want to scare her. She has been standing there for a minute or so when Birgitta starts up again.

It starts as a low humming sound, then Elsa sees her clasp her stomach tighter and fold her head down into her chest. In the dim light of the window it's difficult to see much, but Elsa squints and leans in a little.

The edge of Birgitta's loose brown dress is darker. She has soiled herself.

"Birgitta," Elsa says, putting her hand on her side.

That's when she feels it.

Elsa snatches her hand back in horror and pulls away. Birgitta curls up even tighter. Her guttural moan rises in volume.

"What's wrong?" Dagny asks anxiously from behind Elsa's back.

Elsa just shakes her head.

The space seems to have contracted down to Birgitta's dark figure and her rolling, muffled laments.

Elsa leans in over Birgitta again. How could she not have noticed? How could she not have realized?

Such a thing would have been impossible to imagine. Unthinkable. It can't be.

Elsa puts her hand on Birgitta's belly. Beneath her palm she feels those familiar contractions.

"Dagny," says Elsa, and her voice sounds almost strangely calm to her own ears. It shouldn't be audible over Birgitta, but somehow it reaches Dagny anyway. "Birgitta is giving birth. We must get her to Ingrid."

Elsa hears Dagny inhale sharply behind her.

"But how . . ." she says, and Elsa just shakes her head. She reaches over and strokes Birgitta's sweaty hair. Normally Birgitta would recoil at Elsa's touch, but this time she doesn't react.

Her voice has started to quiet again. How far apart were the bellows coming? Not long. Four, five minutes at the very most.

They don't have much time.

"I don't know," says Elsa. "But her waters have already broken. We must hurry."

NOW

I'm still sitting on the floor when Max comes in.

"Alice?" he says.

"Over here," I reply.

I'm holding the photos. The top one now bears my thumbprint, which stands out on the shiny surface.

The light outside has started to change in character, grow softer, warmer. It rounds out the room's corners and glistens in the shards of glass in the windows. When I look up at Max, he, too, is more beautiful than he was in the hard glare of the morning sun, despite his deep, sunken eyes, despite the cut on his jaw, despite the grubby clothes hanging from his slender frame.

"Look," I say listlessly, spreading out the images like a fan in front of me.

There are four Polaroids. The child in them appears to be a newborn. Two of the images are sharp, and two are blurred. You can tell that the baby has been dried off, but there are still traces of something dark and sticky on her chubby arms. In one of them she is naked, shot clinically from above. In another she is lying in familiar arms.

Elsa's face is visible up to the hairline. She looks like she has aged thirty years since the photograph Grandma left me; her eyes sit deep in her face, her mouth just a limp dash between her cheeks.

A bit like Max looks now, come to think of it.

Me too, I'm sure.

"What is it?" Max asks, a hint of confusion in his voice. He stops behind me, and I feel his shadow fall over me when he leans in to take a look.

"Kristina Lidman," I say. "Birgitta Lidman was the mother of the baby they found here. Birgitta Lidman was Tone's grandma."

"Who . . ." he begins.

"Gitta," I say quietly. "Look. It's dated August 18, 1959."

I look at the two blurry pictures. Though they aren't in focus, I can still see what they show.

One of them is the same child again, shot from the side. The other shows her lying on a naked breast. The figure she is lying on is large and shapeless, and her face is turned away. Her long, dark hair winds down over her shoulders and chest.

"Where did you find that?" Max asks.

I nod at the desk.

"In the nurse's records," I say.

The folder is still lying open in front of me. The scrawls on the lined paper float in front of my eyes. I didn't want to read them, but I couldn't help myself. Anything to distract me from the throbbing, pulsating truth hanging over me like a red mist:

Emmy is dead and it's my fault. Tone is gone, lost, insane, and it's my fault.

The scrawls don't offer much. The birth weight and length. I don't know what's healthy for an infant, but it looks normal to me. And the name. Kristina Lidman.

So that was her first name. Before she became Hélène Grimelund.

I wonder what Tone's mother would say if she could see her own baby pictures. What Tone would say.

Another note, jotted right at the bottom:

FATHER: UNKNOWN.

I shut the folder. It's a breakthrough. Explosive. It would have made the documentary a success.

But that doesn't matter anymore, none of it does. There will never be any documentary. No one will ever get to know.

And none of it matters because Emmy is dead.

"I really believed in the film, Alice. Just so you know. I think it would have been fantastic. We could have made something really special."

"Have you found anything to cover her with?" Max asks quietly.

There it comes, barging in again. The truth. The real world.

"I was going to check the cabinet," I say quietly, pointing limply at the one in the corner.

He doesn't say anything, just walks over to it and looks at the doors.

"It's locked," he says.

I open the bottom drawer of the desk. There it is, neat and compact, a small brass key on a twisted string.

I pick it up and walk over to the cabinet. The key glides in and turns so effortlessly that it feels as though my hand is following the key rather than vice versa.

The cabinet is unbearably tidy, with bandages and Band-Aids sorted into small compartments. The lower section is taken up by towels and sheets. I pull out the top sheet and hold it for a second.

It's white, cotton. It has yellowed slightly with age, and is stiff in that way that sheets only get from mangling. An embroidered trim of dainty white flowers lines its edge.

Emmy will like it. She has always liked old things, flowery vintage pieces that contrast with her ripped jeans and ugly T-shirts.

Emmy *would have* liked it.

She will never like anything again.

What would Emmy have done?

She would have pulled herself together; she would have taken charge.

The floor is steady underfoot as we leave the room. Robert hasn't come back yet, and she's still lying there, small and still.

Reality wavers here, but I force my feet to keep moving.

Max and I stand on either side of her, like in some sort of ritual. I unfold the sheet to its full length, while Max straightens out her legs and arms.

I carefully take the golden heart around her neck and lift the hem of her T-shirt to slip it back underneath, where it should be, but Max stops me.

"Wait," he says.

"What?"

My voice is rusty. Unfamiliar, unused.

Max leans in over her and pushes my hand away from her neck. I flinch at his touch, pull back as though burned, but he doesn't seem to notice.

His eyes are fixed on the base of Emmy's neck. On the dark marks on her pale skin.

It's beautiful, somehow: the suggestion of a bird, ghostly dark tracks winging out and around her neck.

I want to ask *what is that,* but the words don't come because they don't need to. Because I already know the answer.

They're hand impressions.

Max straightens his back a little. Then he reaches out and puts his hands over her eyes. He opens them again, and that more than anything feels wrong, somehow, and I want to turn away because those still, staring eyes are worse than her stiffening limbs and cold skin, but Max looks for the both of us, he leans in and stares.

"They're bloodshot," he says, his voice strange. "I've read that the whites go bloodshot if a person's been . . ." He swallows the last word.

Strangled.

No broken ribs that pierced soft, vulnerable tissue. No unlucky fall.

No accident.

The marks of someone's fingers, like a necklace tightened around her neck.

Rage and horror combined have a sour, stale taste, I learn.

I look for Max's eyes, but he isn't looking at me. Suddenly tense, he

254 • CAMILLA STEN

scrambles to his feet and looks at the doors to his right. The realization of what he's thinking drops into my lap just as I hear him shout:

"Robert!"

Someone managed to do that in the ten minutes that elapsed between Emmy answering our last question and me climbing through the second-floor window. Someone was either following us or waiting for us.

Someone who might still be here in the school.

Here upstairs.

And Robert is alone in the classroom.

THEN

The afternoon heat has given way to a cooler evening air. They haven't been able to open the windows in Ingrid's office for fear of the baby's cries being heard, so some trace of the day's oppressive heat remains. Between that and the stench, the air in the room feels thick as syrup.

Elsa leans against the basin and, for the first time, allows herself to feel her exhaustion. Her knees are almost shaking, her hands are sore and tender, and tears she doesn't remember crying have left salty trails down her cheeks.

"Here," says Ingrid. Her voice sounds just as flat as Elsa feels, and when she walks over to the basin to fill a chipped pewter mug with water, Elsa notices that her skin is sallow and droops from her face. Her normally so neatly curled hair is straggly and damp with sweat, and all she is wearing is a vest and slip.

It's only when Elsa looks down at herself that she notices that she has taken off her cardigan and shoes, too. It must have happened at some point in the last few hours. Bruises have started to blossom down her left arm. During the worst of the labor pains Birgitta had started to flail and struggle; she must have hit Elsa when she tried to hold her to calm her down.

Elsa drinks in large gulps. The water tastes flat and metallic.

The twilight that has started to sneak in through the windows colors everything a mild blue. Birgitta is still curled up on her side on the bed. Her face is turned away, and her hair is a bird's nest of dirt and sweat. She isn't making any noise now; perhaps she has fallen asleep.

Dagny is standing over by one of the windows. The light behind her throws her silhouette into sharp relief. You can barely see the baby in her arms.

She's beautiful; a perfectly formed little girl with thick, dark hair, albeit slightly smaller than what Elsa remembers her own as being. She has the cloudy blue eyes and strangely shaped head of a newborn, and she had showed off a good set of lungs when Ingrid had clapped her on the behind.

Elsa had held her while Ingrid cut the umbilical cord. Neither of them are doctors, but in the past Ingrid has helped Silvertjärn girls in childbirth, if the doctor wouldn't make it in time. Elsa has never been present at any other deliveries than her own, and had she imagined being at one, she would have thought it would be Margareta's, or even Aina's, one day.

A bustling sound swells outside the window. At first it's so quiet that it scarce seems real, but then, slowly but steadily, it grows. Words begin to emerge from the mass, from the hymn rising over the village. It breaks the flat spell that has settled over all of them.

Dagny looks up from the baby. The girl has started to whimper slightly at the sound of the congregation's evensong. Perhaps, tiny as she is, even she understands the danger.

Dagny looks terrified, as though she's been caught out. From the look on her face, Elsa can tell she won't be of much help.

Ingrid straightens up. Her glasses have started to slide off her nose, but she pushes them back up with the back of her hand. She looks Elsa in the eye, then at the curled-up figure on the bed by the far wall.

"What shall we do?" Ingrid asks.

The helplessness that hits Elsa in that moment is like nothing she has ever felt before. The apparently unending hymn seems to be whispering, intimating to them that it's hopeless, that there's nothing they can do. The congregation is so great, and they are so few, and Birgitta can't even help herself. Even less so the tiny, new human lying in Dagny's arms.

"We must try to get them out of here," says Elsa. "Away from the pastor and his congregation. Away from Silvertjärn."

Ingrid nods. She doesn't ask how they will manage any such thing, nor does she need to; she knows Elsa is wondering the same thing.

Dagny looks back down at the girl she is holding in her arms. Her face has relaxed slightly, and she is rocking her gently, lulling her softly to quieten her down. In her eyes Elsa thinks she can make out a trace of a longing that Dagny has buried deep within.

"We must give her a name," says Dagny.

Ingrid looks over at Birgitta again.

"Do you think she can name the child?" she asks Elsa quietly.

Elsa shakes her head. "I'm not even sure if she understands it's her daughter," she says with a heavy heart.

"How about Kristina?" Dagny asks suddenly. "Isn't that what her mother's name was?"

"Yes," Elsa says, "it was."

Elsa mostly remembers Kristina as she was in her final days, tired and bloated. The fear in her strained, red face, and then the relief once Elsa had promised to look after Birgitta.

But she has failed her. Just as she has failed her Aina.

"Kristina Lidman," Elsa says quietly to herself. She puts the mug down next to the sink and walks over to Dagny. The cold water has lifted some of her flatness.

"Kristina," she repeats to the little one.

The baby has settled slightly, and now her cloudy eyes look up at Elsa. There's something about looking into a newborn's eyes that's like nothing else. Elsa isn't a superstitious woman—not even a particularly religious one, truth be told, though she wouldn't dream of saying that out loud—but yes, newborns do have a look that suggests they know something. That they have seen something others can't see.

"It's a good name," Elsa says to Dagny.

"The next train leaves tomorrow at three, no?" says Ingrid behind her back.

Elsa doesn't need to look at any schedule to be able to nod in confirmation. With two trains a week it isn't hard to remember the departure times.

She knows what Ingrid is thinking, and remembers the half-written letter lying buried in her underwear. There'll be no time to finish it or send it now. Elsa will just have to hope Margareta understands. She will; she has to. Once they're in Stockholm they can try to make a plan.

They just have to get out of Silvertjärn first.

NOW

When we race into the room, Robert is standing stock-still at the window. He doesn't turn when we enter.

"Robert?" I say cautiously, and then he turns his head.

I don't know what I was expecting, but this isn't it. His face is still, and his index finger is raised to his lips.

My first thought is that he's lost his mind (*him too*), but that passes just as soon as it comes. He doesn't look crazy.

Max starts to walk over to the window, and Robert nods slowly. I follow him, creeping across the floorboards. My heart is pounding.

Max reaches the window before I do. Then Robert lowers his finger. He doesn't point, but makes a subtle nod straight ahead.

The window looks out onto the road running down to the river. From up here I can see the houses' gabled roofs stretching down and away from the square, these set in a slightly more organic way than the poker-straight lines of the row houses further out of town. At first I don't understand what I'm supposed to be looking at, but just as I'm about to ask I see it, and the words die in my throat.

Something moving.

I only catch a glimpse of it. Something peeks out from behind the corner of a house, then disappears again.

"She's been doing that for a while," Robert says quietly, without moving his lips. "Peeking out and then disappearing."

There it is again. A head; a flash of sunlight on blond hair.

Perhaps she can sense our eyes on her, because suddenly she disappears—there one second, gone the next.

"Is it . . ." says Max, peeling his eyes from the window. He stares at me.

I nod.

"She's been moving around between the houses a little, but no further than that. It's her," says Robert.

"What is she doing?" asks Max.

"It looks like she's hiding," says Robert. "Or looking out for someone."

Max looks out of the window again, and I do the same, try to pick her out.

Then he straightens his back and looks at me, and something in his face changes.

I know what he's thinking; not so much because I see it on his face as that the same thought hits me simultaneously. But everything in me balks at the idea. I shake my head.

"No," I say. "No."

"What?" Robert asks.

"Robert . . ." Max begins, and I see him falter at the thought himself, then try to swallow it down. But he goes on anyway.

"We looked at . . . at Emmy."

How much time has passed? How long has Tone been out there for? Forty minutes? One hour?

How can it be that Emmy was alive an hour ago but not anymore?

"We were going to cover her with something, a sheet, and when we were adjusting her we saw she—she had bruises. On her neck. They looked like handprints."

Robert's eyes look like black-and-white marbles. In the light of the window, his pupils are no more than pinpricks.

"Someone must have done it while we were trying to get upstairs," Max goes on.

"Tone . . ." He licks his lips and goes quiet.

I shake my head, tossing it from side to side like a defiant child.

"No," I say.

Robert turns to me. His eyes are blazing, but I can't tell if it's from grief or rage. Maybe even hate.

"You," he says, swinging that single syllable like a weapon. "You said she wasn't violent, that we had to come and get her, that she was sick. She . . ." His voice sticks. ". . . she wanted to stay there, where it was safe. But you forced us here anyway. To save *her*." He nods at the window, out at the being that was Tone.

Then he looks straight at me. His eyes are wide, vast and bottomless.

"And now she's lying out there," he whispers. "She's out there lying on the floor, and she's dead."

His eyes narrow and focus on me again. The impact of his rage feels like I've stuck my hand in an open flame.

"Don't try to defend her again," he says, biting off each word. "Don't say that again, don't tell me she isn't violent. Don't. Tell. Me."

I stand completely still. The air prickles against my skin. I think he's about to fly at me. Hit me, kick me. Hurt me.

As though he hears what I'm thinking, he turns abruptly and walks out the door.

Max and I are left alone. He doesn't look at me, but stares out of the window as though hypnotized.

My hands are shaking. I want to sit down, but I can't persuade my knees to obey me.

It's all falling apart.

I want to try to do what she would have done, but how? How do I even start to come to grips with this? What do rationality and pragmatism help when the world is turning itself inside out, and none of the old rules still apply?

"We should probably go after him," says Max, and I look up.

"What?"

"If he goes after Tone now, I don't know what he might do," Max says. His lips are pale and his face is flat.

"Oh God," I say, and start running to the doors, feeling a stab in my back every time my feet hit the floor.

I throw open the doors.

There he is, sitting by Emmy's body, kneeling as though in prayer. His head is bowed.

He has covered her in the sheet we left beside her, and she looks so small under the white, no more than a silhouette. The only thing not covered is her small, thin hand, with its short fingers and bitten-down nails. Both of his hands are clasped around it in a tender, delicate hold, as though not wishing to hurt it.

He doesn't look up straightaway. It takes him a few seconds to come back to us.

Then he puts her hand down, slowly and carefully, and pulls the sheet over it.

NOW

As we round the school toward the road, it takes me a few seconds to orient myself: I've only seen the houses from above, and I'm not completely sure which one she's hiding behind.

"There," says Max behind me. He isn't speaking quietly enough. She could hear him and get scared.

"I can't see anyone," I whisper to him. It's a little red house he's pointing at, one with a black roof and black trim.

"She could have moved," he says. "Maybe she heard us coming."

He takes a few slow steps forward, but I grab his arm.

"Wait," I say, then turn to look at Robert.

"I won't hurt her," he says.

His face has lost something of its flatness—deadness—but I'm still not sure I can believe him.

I go first. I don't want to let him take the lead. No matter what happens, I want my face to be the first one she sees. Perhaps that could calm her, somehow.

I make straight for the front of the house, then creep toward the corner, keeping close to the peeling red clapboard. I stop at the corner, the blood pumping in my ears.

I step out.

She isn't here.

The narrow, cobbled passageway between the houses is completely empty. There's nothing there but shadows and heather.

But then I see a flash of movement at the corner ahead of me.

"Tone!" I say, taking a few steps forward. "Tone, it's me. Alice."

It's too fraught, too loud. The little glimpse I caught of her instantly disappears.

"Shit," I hear Max mutter, and there's too much adrenaline in my body for me not to react instinctively. I take off after her.

The passage is so narrow that my shoulders scrape against the walls on either side. It almost feels like I'm elbowing my way through them, and I practically fall out onto the street on the other side. But now I see her.

She's running as fast as she can down toward the river, but that isn't quick. There's something wrong about the way she's moving—it's a lumbering, hobbling gait, and one leg drags behind her.

Of course. Her ankle.

"Tone!" I call after her again. I can't help it, pointless as I know it is.

I keep on running toward her, and it doesn't take me long to catch up. Her breathing sounds strange, too; it's more than a pant, it's like a muffled hum. I hear Max and Robert running behind me.

I close the last of the distance between us with a few powerful strides and grab her arm, feel her skin and bone under the sleeve of her dirty knitted cardigan.

She erupts. With a loud, moaning wail of sheer panic she wrests her arm free, then flings it out as she twists, knocking me square on my temple and throwing me off balance. I manage to break my fall, but the blow is so powerful that I see stars, and I bite a gash into my lip on impact.

I lie there for a few seconds, trying to make my head stop spinning. I've never been hit before. I roll onto my side and blink away the spinning and the pain, and see that Max and Robert have managed to get hold of her.

Tone is struggling like a wounded animal, kicking and trying to bite at them. Her eyes are flitting around, unfocused. I try to meet her gaze, but there's no recognition there, only mindless anxiety and rage.

Her hair is ruffled and stiff with dirt, and her lank, blood-encrusted fringe is stuck to her forehead by a dirty, smeared scab. She can't put any weight onto her bad foot, but time and again she tries to step on it. Finally she kicks out and yelps in pain when it hits Max's thigh. I shudder—as much from Max's gasp as from the sight of the abnormal bend in her ankle.

"Stop!" says Max. "Tone, stop, try to calm down, we won't hurt you, we don't want to hurt you, we want to help you."

I want to tell him he sounds too angry, too worked up, too agitated; to tell him to try to speak calmly, softly; that she might not be reacting to his words but his tone; that he has to show her he means her no harm. But I can't get a word out.

"She can't hear you," Robert says thickly, then, linking his arms around her, he just sits down.

Tone is slight in build, with narrow shoulders and hips, and however hard she flails and fights, she can't escape his firm grip. She gives up after a few seconds, stops kicking and squirming, and drops that awful, raw moan. It turns into a heavy pant.

It's only then that I realize my entire body is shaking.

I squat down in front of them, partly to be at Tone's level, and partly to hide the fact that my legs can't hold me.

"Tone!" I say, trying to meet her eyes. "Tone, it's me. Alice."

She doesn't look at me. She's staring down at the ground, still panting breathlessly.

The blood on her forehead has run down to her eyebrow, clumping her fine strands of hair into strange, lumpy forms. I try not to let my eyes drop to her hands, but I do.

She's too sick, I think, trying to convince myself over the pounding of my heart in my ears, over the taste of iron on my tongue and her raspy, panting breaths.

Emmy's much stronger, it wouldn't have been possible, Tone could never have overpowered her.

But the voice of logic is impossible to turn from.

And if her ribs were broken?

If Tone was out of her senses, like now, and she had no means of escape?

I think the tears are about to start again, but they don't. That blessed, welcome blurriness never arrives. Tone's contours remain sharp, and I stare at her in the dirt and sunlight with dry, swollen eyes, unable to escape the recognition growing within me.

NOW

At first I suggest taking Tone back to the church—which seems like the most obvious thing to do—and neither of the others make any objections. But as soon as Tone catches sight of the place, she starts going wild again, kicking and struggling enough to almost topple Max. It's only when we back off into a side street that she calms down again.

"What is it about the church?" Max asks. He directs the question at me; we have all given up trying to communicate directly with Tone.

"I don't know," I say, completely drained. All I want is to sleep. "But we probably won't get her in there."

There's something horrible and disturbing about the sight of skinny little Tone suspended between the two bigger men, something that triggers a sort of primal fear in me—not for her, but for them. I want to tell them to let her go, to leave her alone. Despite having just seen her swinging, roaring, and kicking; despite her unfocused gaze and that awful, bloody mask she's wearing.

And those hands. Those thin, dirty fingers that my eyes keep being drawn to, that I can't stop staring at.

I've reached some sort of limit. I'm so tired I don't even feel heartbroken anymore, just resigned.

"What do we do?" Robert asks me. I see my own state of mind reflected in his face. His skin is gray.

"I don't know," I say again. "I don't know. We just have to wait it out somewhere, just find somewhere to . . ." I trail off and look around.

"My grandma's house," I say. "It should be on the next street. It wasn't in such bad shape—we might be able to wait there."

The other two don't think about it, they just nod.

We cut across the gardens of the houses to reach the next street. I see Grandma's green door straightaway. It's still hanging slightly ajar, after Robert more or less dragged me out of it.

"There," I say to Robert and Max, but Robert has already seen it.

Was it just yesterday that we were here? Less than twenty-four hours. One day and one night.

I press up against the wall to let Max and Robert pass with Tone, then close the front door behind them.

The air in here is mustier than outside, but warmer. To our left, the kitchen cupboards are still hanging open after yesterday's plundering.

I hope there's something left in there. Although I don't feel like I'll ever want to eat again, my body is crying out for food all the same. Food and sleep and darkness. The most basic things.

"What do we do with her?" Max asks. He says it quietly, as though afraid Tone will hear. I can understand. She sways slightly, then leans into him, away from her injured foot. I can barely look at it.

"Lock her upstairs," I say. The words sound foreign. "I think there was a lock on one of the bedroom doors."

"OK," Max says with a nod.

I watch them take Tone upstairs. I'm scared that she'll fight or protest, fall and hurt herself, but she goes along without any resistance.

The compact living room is the only room I haven't been inside yet. It's straight ahead, through the kitchen, with an eye-wateringly ugly floral sofa suite in a thick throw fabric just past the door and a small ornamental dining table to the right with a faded, embroidered tablecloth. Two of the windows have broken—one from an apple tree that has forced its gnarled branches in through the frame—and big, black spots of mold bloom from the center of the tablecloth, like a morbid imitation of its embroidery.

I sit down carefully on one of the two puffy sofas. They, too, stink of mold, but I can't tell if it's coming from the tablecloth, or if the stuffing has gone the same way. Perhaps both. The cushions are stiff but strangely spongy, and at first I think the fabric is going to rip under my weight, but it holds. I lean back onto the hard back and look at the wall in front of me.

In the middle of the bloated, discolored, delicately floral wallpaper hangs the photograph.

It's the same picture, I'm sure of it.

I always thought Grandma's copy was the only one, but here they are staring back at me through a painted gold frame: Grandma with her laughing smile, Aina with her sulky look, birthmark, and tight braids, Staffan with his slightly bulging nose and swollen jaw, and Elsa. Elsa with that straight, uncompromising gaze that seems to see straight through time to me here on this sofa.

All I wanted was to tell your story, I think.

All I wanted was to know what happened. Was that so wrong?

I hear the faint sound of a door closing upstairs. A mumbled conversation between two male voices.

Elsa stares down at me from the wall. I close my eyes to escape hers.

I don't know when I fall asleep.

NOW

I wake up to a hand brushing against my cheek.

My neck feels stiff and immobile. I make a quiet groan as I try to
sit up, but it gets louder when Max puts his arm on my back. When his
hand touches my deep bruise, it feels like he might as well be stabbing
me between the ribs with a kitchen knife.

"Ow ow ow, shit! Ow!"

"Sorry," says Max, quickly moving his arm away. I shake my head
and lean back slowly onto the stiff cushions. When the pain begins to
pass I realize that I also have the beginnings of a splitting headache, and
that my swollen airway is itching.

I glance over at the small windows that look out onto the garden. It's
still light out, but the day has started to take on the overripe, glowing
hue that comes with the approaching dusk.

"Hi," I say to Max once I'm sitting up. He gives me a half smile. Thin
lips under sunken eyes.

"Hi. Fall asleep?"

"Yeah," I say. Weird question, seeing as he's just woken me up.

Reality has started to seep back in, thick and viscous like tar. Images
returning. Emmy on the floor. Tone's unseeing eyes. Her light hair a
caked-on pile of blood and dirt.

"How are you feeling?" Max asks.

I shake my head, choosing to answer the more innocuous side of the question.

"My back really hurts," I say.

"Let me take a look," he replies.

He doesn't exactly have any medical experience, but I don't mention that. Instead I just twist away slowly and let him pull my top up over my back and the bruise. He whistles quietly when he sees it.

"Looks like someone's painted you with purple watercolors," he says, running his fingertips gently over the skin above my ribs. I gasp when he presses slightly too hard.

"Does that hurt?" he asks, without lifting his hand.

"Yes," I say. I pull away slightly and roll my top down again. "How are you feeling?" I ask, tucking my hair behind my ear.

Max shrugs.

"Empty, somehow," he says. "Does that sound weird? I feel completely blunted."

"I know what you mean," I say. My eyes wander the room in the over-ripe afternoon light.

"It doesn't feel real," I say slowly. "None of it does."

"No," says Max.

"How is . . ." I have to swallow before I can say his name. "How's Robert?"

"I don't know," says Max. "He's not saying so much. Not that he was so talkative to begin with, but now . . ."

"Where is he?" I ask. "He isn't outside on his own, is he?"

"He's in the kitchen," says Max. "Not that that matters now. I mean, she's locked upstairs."

She.

As though she were a monster, a ghost. A shadow without a name.

"Hey," Max says softly, then reaches out to stroke my cheek with his thumb, and I realize it's because I'm crying. The tears spill over without me being able to stop them. I try to wipe them off, shake my head.

"It's OK," I say.

"No, it isn't," says Max, and then I crumble.

I bawl, a sob that runs so forcefully through my body that it feels like I'm cramping up. Max wraps his arms around me and holds me to his chest. The tears run out of my closed eyelids as I cry a hacking, ugly cry, like a blubbering child, uncontrolled and uninhibited. The words I'm muttering make no sense.

I think I say "Emmy." Or else "sorry."

Max is rubbing my back hard, and it hurts—so much that it makes me whimper every time he touches my bruise—but he doesn't seem to notice.

"Shh," he says, petting me like an unruly cat. "It'll be OK. I'm here. I'm here."

I feel my snot running into his T-shirt and try to sit up, but he won't let me go.

"I'm here," he says again.

"I never meant for this to happen," I whisper into his top, where my words dissolve unheard. "It wasn't meant to be like this. It wasn't meant to be like this. I didn't know."

Max kisses my head. Dry lips on my sweaty scalp.

"We're going to get through this, Alice," he says into my hair. "We'll get through this, we'll get past it. I promise. I've got you. It's going to be OK."

He keeps on rubbing my back, and my sobs have started to calm. I try to pull away again, and this time he lets go of me.

I dry my nose. Max looks at me and half smiles again. Up close, his pupils are huge.

"I'm here," he whispers, and touches my cheek.

His caress turns into a light grip on my neck, and he pulls my face into his and kisses me.

His lips are rough, and his mouth tastes rank and too sweet, of blood and sugar. I try to pull back but he moves with me, forcing his tongue into my mouth. It's only when I forcefully twist my head away that he stops.

"What the fuck are you doing?" I ask, staring at him as I wipe my mouth with my hand.

His small, warm smile gradually slips off his face.

"What do you mean?" he asks, defensiveness already creeping into his voice.

"What are you doing?" I repeat, standing up. I feel like I need to get to my feet, take a wide stance to steady the ground beneath me. My head is spinning.

"I thought it was what you wanted," says Max. "I was trying to comfort you."

"By shoving your tongue down my throat?" I splutter. I almost start to laugh. It's so absurd—with everything else that has happened. In the middle of this terrible, broken situation.

"So then why did you kiss me back?" he asks. "You didn't seem to be hating it."

"I didn't kiss back," I say. "I . . . I was shocked."

Now Max stands up, too. He gives his pants a good brush to get the dust off the denim, despite the blood and tears on his top, despite the dust and wood chips all over his body.

"Maybe it wasn't the right time," he says.

Reasonable. Always so reasonable.

I shake my head.

"Emmy's dead, Tone's sick—so sick we've had to lock her up—and you—" I say, my voice getting shriller with every word until he cuts me off.

"I'm sorry! OK? I said I'm sorry! This hasn't been an easy day for me either, OK? I guess I lost my self-control. It was stupid. I get it." He throws up his hands, then rubs his face and sighs.

I shake my head, trying to get my breath back under control.

"We're all in shock. These things happen. Let's forget it."

He looks at me. Something flickers in his eyes.

He opens his mouth, but at first he says nothing. Then:

"So when is the right time?"

His voice is soft. I don't know what to say.

"What do you mean?"

"Come on, Alice," he says, with an almost resigned laugh. "You know what I mean. I've been waiting seven years. Waiting, and listening, and being there for you. Waiting for you to wake up and realize. So when is the right time?"

I swallow.

"I didn't know," I say, trying to keep my voice as quiet and nonconfrontational as possible. "I'm sorry, Max, but I'm not . . . I mean . . ."

He looks up at the ceiling.

"No," he says. "You *cannot* tell me you didn't know. I know you saw it. Why do you think I sponsored your little film? It's not like I'm getting that money back."

"I thought you believed in the film," I say helplessly.

"I did it because I believed in *you,* Alice." He shakes his head. "I saw the look on your face when I said I'd come here," he says. "Come on. We both knew it was going to happen here."

All I can do is stare at him.

"Alice," he says softly, taking a step toward me. "Come on. I know you know what I mean." He smiles to one side, twisting his whole slanting face.

I take another step back and look down.

"The police will get here tomorrow," I say. "It's going to be OK, Max. We're not going to die here. It's going to be OK." I swallow.

When I look up again, Max's teeth are clenched hard, then he swallows, sending his Adam's apple bobbing up and down in his neck. A vein is pounding on his temple.

"Max . . ." I say, pleading, the tears welling up again. My jaws ache. "Please, don't do this to me. Not now."

"You're so fucking selfish." He shakes his head, and says it again: "You're so fucking selfish."

Then he turns and walks out of the room, slamming the door so hard behind him that the doorframe shakes.

NOW

I drop back down onto the sofa. I don't know how long I'm sitting there before I stand up, my feet slightly unsteady, and step out into the hall.

No one there.

I sense Robert before I can fully see him, a shadow in the corner of my eye, and when I turn into the kitchen he's already looking up at me.

He's slightly too big for the chair he's sitting on, and the sharp contrast of his red hair, the turquoise blue kitchen furniture, and the thick rag rug gives the entire kitchen a Wonderland feel.

At first I hesitate, but then I pull out one of the chairs and sit down. I choose the wall closest to me, so that there's a chair on either side between us. The chair leg scratches lightly against the floor as I scoot in under the table.

A clock hangs on the wall above the doorway, with a white face and boxy white numbers. The minute hand has fallen off, and it lies like a dividing line at the bottom of the clock. The hour hand has stopped on three.

"Have you seen Max?" I ask.

He nods.

"He said he was going out," he says. "He was going to go to the church to fetch what was left of the honey."

"Oh," I say.

Seconds pass.

"How are you doing?" I ask.

He seems to mull over his response. Or perhaps he, like me, doesn't quite know how to answer. He opens and clenches his fist a few times on the table, looks at it thoughtfully. His knuckles are red and bloody.

"I tried to punch a wall," he says, sounding almost taken aback. "For some reason I thought it would help," he goes on. "But I didn't feel that, either."

"Here?" I ask.

"Nope," he says. "In the school."

Silence.

I lick my lips. They are dry, and still taste of Max. I swipe the thought away, and say:

"I don't understand."

I don't know if it's a statement or a question, but it's the truth. I test saying it again, and this time it sounds like a prayer.

"I don't understand."

Robert puts his hands flat on the table, palms down. His hands are big and bulky, disproportionate to his slender wrists. Faint freckles run all the way up his forearms.

"No," he says. "I don't, either."

I don't know if we're talking about Tone or Emmy or Silvertjärn. Perhaps we're talking about all three; perhaps none.

My lips tremble, and I press them together.

"There's water," he says, nodding at a ceramic pitcher on the counter. I raise my eyebrows.

"I found it in the cupboard," he goes on. "It seemed the best option."

"Where's the water from?" I ask.

"I went down to the river. An hour or so ago."

I hear something upstairs, a creaking plank.

"Has she had anything to drink?" I ask.

"No," he says, without looking me in the eye. His voice is strained,

THEN

Elsa wakes up when Ingrid opens the door to her office. She had dozed off in the chair, her head against the wall. Her mouth must have dropped open, because her throat is dry, and her breath tastes revolting.

"How have things been?" Ingrid asks quietly.

It's still dark outside, and there's hardly any light on the horizon. It must still be night. Ingrid is no more than a shadow among shadows.

"Fine," Elsa replies, quietly, so as not to wake the others. "It's been fine."

The girl has slept better than either of her own ever did: she woke up and whimpered twice, but went back to sleep when Elsa rocked her.

"Has she fed her?" Ingrid asks, looking at Birgitta's sleeping form.

Elsa shakes her head.

"I haven't dared wake her," she admits.

Elsa feels trapped between the two of them. The little one must surely be starting to feel hungry by now. Elsa has given her a towel dipped in milk from the school canteen to suck on, but she knows that won't be enough. At the same time, she's wary about even going near Birgitta, let alone waking her.

Birgitta has slept all through the night, and Elsa can't deny that she's afraid of what she will do when she wakes up. How much will she understand?

squeezed. "I can't think about her being up there, I just can't. Because then I think about what she did, and Emmy, and I just want to—"

He clenches his fists so tightly on the table that one of the cuts re-opens. Sharp little drops of blood emerge from under the broken scab, like jewels.

I don't know how long I'm holding my breath for. All I know is that I feel the seconds as heartbeats, and that my chest starts to hurt before Robert breaks the silence:

"You take it up to her. She has to drink something."

I waver.

"If you hear me stamping on the floor, come up."

Robert nods slowly.

"OK."

His fists are still tightly clenched.

Elsa can't make out Ingrid's face in the darkness, but she sees that she nods.

"No," says Ingrid. "That I can understand."

Elsa hears the weight on her own chest reflected in Ingrid's voice.

Ingrid sits down on the floor next to Elsa's chair, and looks over at the little sleeping bundle lying a few feet away. They have layered some sheets up to create something of a cot for her. Dagny had rambled on about bringing over an old cot, but Elsa had put her foot down. They can't do anything that might attract unwanted attention.

"How will we get them to the station?" Ingrid asks.

Elsa shakes her head.

"I don't know," she says. "I think all we can do is walk them there as though there's nothing wrong. It's not so far. If we go just before the train leaves there'll be no time for anyone to stop us."

Ingrid sighs softly. The night makes it sound bigger than it is.

"Will you go with them?" she asks.

"Yes," says Elsa. "I'll take them to Stockholm. My daughter lives there."

"Margareta," says Ingrid.

Elsa nods, though she doesn't know if Ingrid can see it.

"And what about Staffan?" Ingrid asks.

"I'll write to him," Elsa says. "Once we've arrived. When they're . . . when we're safe."

Far from Silvertjärn.

Far from Pastor Mattias.

"I don't understand how this could happen," Elsa says softly, vulnerable words she would never have let herself utter in the light of day.

"Nor I," Ingrid replies quietly.

Neither of them mentions the name Elsa knows they are both thinking. Neither of them mentions Aina. Aina, who throbs in Elsa's chest with every heartbeat. Her beloved, her baby. What sort of mother abandons her own daughter?

The baby starts moving and whimpering again, and Elsa gets to her feet. Her knees are shaky and her neck is stiff; she's too old to be sleeping on anything that isn't a bed.

Elsa leans in over the girl, picks her up and rocks her gently, but this time the baby won't be soothed. Her cries are only getting louder. Elsa is always amazed by infants' cries. That such a small body can make such a noise.

She tries to calm her, cradles her and hushes her, but the baby won't stop. If she doesn't quiet down soon it might draw prying eyes to the school.

Elsa blinks at a sudden light. Ingrid has lit a bare candle in her hand.

"Where's the rag?" Ingrid asks, looking around.

"We're out of milk," Elsa says, nodding at the corner where she left the empty bowl.

"Perhaps she can suck on the rag," Ingrid suggests, but Elsa shakes her head.

"She's hungry," she says. "That won't help."

Elsa's stomach begins to tie in knots. She looks around and gives a start when she sees that Birgitta has woken up. Of course she has; only the dead could sleep through the shrill wails filling the room. She has sat up slightly in the bed, her eyes fixed on the girl.

Little Kristina starts up again with renewed voice, and Elsa makes a decision. She cautiously steps over to Birgitta. Birgitta doesn't look at her. She's looking at the baby.

Does she understand who she is? Does she see that she's her daughter?

Elsa can't imagine that she does.

But still.

When Elsa reaches the edge of the bed Birgitta does something inconceivable: she holds out her arms. At first Elsa hesitates, but then she places Kristina in Birgitta's outstretched hands.

Her hold is awkward and uncertain, presumably uncomfortable, and although Elsa is afraid to correct her too much, Birgitta holds the baby gingerly—cautiously—while Elsa adjusts her arms.

When Elsa unbuttons Birgitta's dress she can see her stiffen, but she lets Elsa continue. Elsa is ready and waiting to sweep Kristina away at the slightest hint of agitation, but Birgitta doesn't make a sound.

Elsa folds back the front of her dress, exposing a swollen, blue-veined breast. Then, placing her hand under Kristina's back and heavy head, she lifts her to the nipple.

The baby keeps on crying. By now Elsa can sense how tense Birgitta is, how close she is to breaking point.

But then something happens. Kristina's little mouth finds the nipple and latches on. The cries stop, replaced by the muffled sound of her starting to suck.

Elsa's shoulders drop. She lets go and takes a step back.

"Ah," she hears Ingrid say. Nothing else. When Elsa turns around to look at her, her eyes are twinkling with tears.

Elsa quickly dries her eyes and forehead with the back of her hand. She doesn't know what she is witnessing. She doesn't know if Birgitta understands what she is doing, or what is happening.

Perhaps this might be something resembling hope. Elsa isn't sure. All that she is sure of is the quiet instinct that rises up inside her when she sees Birgitta nurse her daughter.

She can't leave Aina in Silvertjärn.

NOW

I slowly open the door to the girls' bedroom.

Tone is sitting in the far corner of the room. She's chosen not to lie on either of the two beds, or to sit on the padded seat at the desk, but to huddle up below the fallen wardrobe, in the small triangular space formed between the wardrobe, wall, and floor.

She doesn't look at me when I come in, just rocks back and forth on the spot, her forehead pressed to her knees.

"Tone?" I say quietly, against my better judgment.

She doesn't reply, but makes a quiet, drawn-out sound that is muffled by her thighs. I take this to mean she can hear me.

My body is tense and my armpits sweaty, but when I look at her like this it's hard to be afraid of her; she looks more like someone to pity than fear. As I stand here looking at her, it dawns on me that she hadn't seemed threatening in the alleyway, either. She had run away from us, not toward us—fearful, not aggressive. And even when kicking and trying to break free, she had seemed more like someone fighting for her own life.

"I've brought you some water," I say. I take a few steps into the room and around the bed, but then she hunches up even more.

"Don't worry," I say. "It's OK. I'll put this down here, see?"

I try to keep my voice calm and neutral.

I put the water jug on the ground a few feet in front of her, then raise my hands to show I'm not dangerous. I take a few steps back and sit on the desk chair. The seat is hard, but it's more comfortable than the floor.

She hesitates for a moment, then lets go of her knees and reaches for the water. There are still traces of her lilac nail polish on three of her nails.

She clutches the jug awkwardly—practically hugs it with both hands—and lifts it to her face. When she drinks, she does so feverishly, in big gulps.

It's like watching a stranger.

"What has happened to you?" I ask. It's formulated as a question, but I'm not expecting a reply.

To my surprise she puts down the jug and looks in my direction. Her eyes don't meet mine, but it's me she's looking at—just my left arm rather than my face.

She shakes her head.

That's something. It's not much, but it's something.

I have to ask her, I have to try.

"Was it you who blew up the vans?" I ask.

She says nothing.

It's harder to look at her face than the rest of her. That terrible scab. It's not just blood, I realize as I come closer, but dried-in soil and dirt, which have made a hard cake of her hair. The skin around it is red and looks slightly inflamed.

"How did you get that?" I ask. I stick to that practiced voice, stable and calming. I don't know if it's having any effect on her, but I'm almost managing to calm myself.

She still doesn't respond. She has started rocking slightly again, making a sustained, quiet, guttural sound.

"Tone," I say, pleading and slightly frustrated, because she's right there in front of me but I can't understand what's going on inside her. I can't align what I'm seeing in front of me with my friend. I can't align her with what she's done. It just doesn't fit.

"Please just say something," I say, my voice cracking slightly. "Just talk to me, for fuck's sake. We can try to . . ."

Yes, what can we try to do?

Try to fix this?

It's too late for that. Some things can't be fixed.

I turn away and stare out of the window for a few seconds. The sun is nearing the horizon. In half an hour the whole sky will burst into flame.

One of the desk drawers is still half open. There's nothing inside it but a few pencils. I pick one of them up. It has a classic yellow grip, and its tip is still sharp. On an impulse, I put it down on the floor and roll it over to Tone.

It stops just in front of her. She picks it up clumsily and holds it. Her grip is strange, her whole hand clenched around the pencil like a fist. The way a child would hold it.

Then she leans forward and presses the tip to the floorboards, so hard that it gouges out a trail in the wood.

"It'll break," I say. "Be careful, or it'll break."

I don't know why I'm even trying; I know she's not going to answer.

The pencil tip runs in sharp lines over the planks. A Y with two legs, topped by a head.

A human.

She draws hair around the head in gawky strokes, long, tangled lines that score the soft planks, then she places the tip in the middle of the oval face and starts moving it in a circle. Around and around and around. A mouth like a black, bellowing circle.

The tip of the pencil breaks, and she goes still.

She starts making that wordless hum again, the one that seems to come from somewhere deep in her chest.

She doesn't look straight at me: her eyes are fixed somewhere to my side, which seems to be as close as they can come to my face. It feels like she's trying to tell me something.

And yes, I know that figure. It's a monster I've seen before. On a piece of paper and a worn tabletop.

She draws just like her grandmother.

"Just like Birgitta," I say.

I don't know if I'm saying it to myself or to her, but when Tone hears the name she looks me straight in the eye.

THEN

Elsa knows Aina won't be home. It's been days since she's so much as seen her.

She races through the house like a whirlwind, hastily shoving clothes into a little bag without even looking at what she's grabbing. She can't take too much; it can't look like she's on her way somewhere.

By now they have hardly any money left, but Elsa grabs two necklaces she inherited from her mother. The chains are thin and silver, but they must be worth something. She should be able to sell or pawn them in Stockholm.

Elsa pauses over the half-written letter in her underwear drawer, but there'll be no time to send it now. She leaves it where it is.

It's when Elsa takes the little tea tin from the top shelf in the kitchen that she hesitates. She can hear her own heartbeats in her chest, fast and rattling and guilty.

It doesn't feel right to take it.

The tin contains all that is left of their savings; almost one thousand kronor, in different denominations. If she takes it then Staffan will have nothing to live on.

But they will go with her, she tries to persuade herself; Aina will go with her.

It isn't theft. It's her money, too.

Elsa takes seven hundred kronor, folds the bills up neatly, and stuffs them in a sock in the mess that is her bag. She leaves the rest in the tin. It feels better this way, but it also feels like capitulation.

She casts a quick glance at the clock over the kitchen door. It's almost 7:00 A.M. Which means Aina should still be in church.

When Elsa locks the door behind her and starts walking, she wants nothing more than to turn around and go back. She can hardly get her head around the fact that she won't be coming home tonight to cook dinner. That she won't be opening that green door as dusk approaches, stepping inside to hear Aina and Karin monkeying around upstairs, giggling over God knows what. To see Staffan in the kitchen with his feet on one of the chairs, and berate him for not taking off his shoes.

Elsa promises herself that she will come back, one day. She and Staffan and Aina, together. Her family will return to this house with its green door. Once all of this is over.

They might even bring Kristina with them, too.

Elsa sets off toward the church. She must keep up appearances, look like everything is normal. Everything could depend on it. She has always been proud of her ability to keep a cool head and take control of situations, but now, when it really matters, she's trembling like a leaf.

The day that is breaking is beautiful, warm and bright. But despite the light sky stretching out over the village, the church looms ominously. The doors are wide open, as they always are nowadays. The pastor often sermonizes about having no secrets before God or the congregation.

The thought of him and his cold, gray eyes in that young, strangely sexless face sends cold shivers running down Elsa's spine.

She must be strong.

She walks briskly up the steps and into the church, striding like someone who has nothing to hide or no reason for shame. But the scene before her makes her stop short.

They are lying in circles around each other, curled up like children on their sides, on top of thin blankets that can only offer scant protection from the cold floor. The pale sunlight streaming in through the tall windows washes out their colors, giving them the look of stone angels. Cold, eternal, and perfect.

Elsa freezes on the threshold. There must be over a hundred people on the floor: old and young, men and women. She can see children among them, curled up with their mothers. She knows them all.

Maj-Lis with her bad knees. Karolin, whose oldest was born at almost the same time as Margareta. Back then they had knitted together as their due dates approached, chattering and gossiping about nothing and everything, giddy with nervousness and joy.

Göran, who had been on the same team as Staffan at the mine. He would always stutter when he was nervous, and had tended to blush whenever Elsa was in the room. She had always suspected he had a liking for her when they were younger, but then he had met his Pernilla and stopped stuttering when they talked.

Pernilla. She's three rows away.

And two steps from her lies Staffan.

Staffan. Her beloved husband.

Elsa has lived with him so long now that she hardly sees him anymore; he's as familiar to her as the back of her own hand. Elsa was scarce more than a child when they married, younger than Margareta is now.

Elsa has seen him sick as a dog, and so drunk that he can only mumble. She knows that his eyes tear up when talking about his dad, and that his big, heavy face softens when he looks at their girls. She has seen him as a beardless nineteen-year-old, a new father at twenty-two, and bereft as a fatherless thirty-two-year-old. It was Elsa who had found the first gray hairs on his temples, who had held him when the mine shut down, promising him that they would get through it together.

He has been her entire adult life. He is the father of her daughters. And now he's lying there among them, a frozen angel, and she realizes that she has lost him.

Elsa has never hated anyone—has never understood how one human could hurt another—but in that instant she wishes she could kill Pastor

Mattias with her own bare hands. She would like to press the life out of him, see the fear in his eyes.

One of them stirs slightly in their sleep, and Elsa tries to pull herself together. She can grieve later. She has to find Aina, that's all that matters now.

But, try as she might, she can't see her.

If Aina isn't here then where could she be? Could she have come to her senses?

Elsa doesn't let herself hope. She knows that can't be.

Then her eyes land on the door on the other side of the church. The door to the chapel.

It's closed.

Elsa creeps along the wall so as not to wake any of them. A few of them stir or sigh in their sleep, but they must have grown used to the sounds of people creeping around, after days or weeks of sleeping next to each other, breathing each other's breaths.

Elsa reaches the chapel door and puts her hand on the handle. The metal feels cold against her palm.

She prays a silent prayer not to find what she fears most of all.

But Elsa is no longer convinced anyone is listening.

She opens the door. It swings in without a sound.

The first thing she sees is Aina.

Her thick, dark hair hangs like a veil across her face. She is lying curled up on the floor, in front of the little sofa. Elsa doesn't recognize the dress she is wearing: white and shift-like, like an old-fashioned nightdress, with neither embellishment nor embroidery. It makes Elsa contract.

Pastor Mattias is sitting on the sofa.

His beautiful gray eyes are fixed on Elsa, and he looks completely relaxed. As though he's been expecting her.

"Good morning," he says.

Elsa stands completely still. For a long time she doesn't know what to say.

"Good morning," she eventually replies.

The pastor's eyes move to her bag and then back to her face. Elsa sees there's no point in trying to lie.

"So the day has come," he says calmly.

Aina stirs slightly. The sight of her there, asleep at his feet, fills Elsa with a fury she hadn't known herself capable of.

"Aina's coming with me," she says, her voice like ice and steel in her throat. "Aina's coming with me, and you can't stop me."

"Aina is a grown woman," says the pastor, while Aina rubs her eyes and props herself up on her elbows. "She can do as she chooses."

Aina sits up and stares at Elsa, as though she has seen a ghost.

"Mother?" she says, confused.

"Aina," says Elsa, her eyes still glued to the pastor. "We're going to Stockholm. To Margareta."

Aina's eyes flit from Elsa to the pastor in confusion. He places his hand on her head. It isn't the sight of his big, bony hand against her silky-smooth crown that cuts at Elsa's chest; it's the look she gives him. As though he were the sun itself.

"Don't touch her!" Elsa exclaims. She can hear how shrill and hysterical she sounds, as though she's lost all reason. A mad old woman.

When Aina looks back at Elsa, her gaze is blank and dead.

"This is my family now," she says, and it isn't Elsa's Aina speaking, not the Aina who begged, cried, and pleaded for one of the neighbor's kittens when she was four, not the Aina who huddles up to Elsa so that she can brush her hair, not the Aina who keeps binders of bookmarks under her bed.

She's a stranger.

The pastor's hand is still on her head. He looks completely relaxed.

"I take it she has had the child?" the pastor asks Elsa, and she can't understand his words. Can't register them.

"Had . . . h-h-had the . . ." Elsa stutters, just as Göran once used to do. Her mouth is completely dry.

"Has the witch given birth to her devil-spawn?" he asks again, calmly and quietly. As though enquiring when lunch would be served.

His eyes. Those damned tempest eyes.

They are laughing at her.

"Did you think we didn't know?" he asks.

She doesn't understand—doesn't understand how they could possibly know. They had done everything right. Has somebody told them—Dagny? Ingrid?

Elsa can't believe that of either of them. She refuses to.

A sound outside the church makes her jump, and she looks around. The sound is familiar, as familiar as her daughters' voices.

"Ah," says Pastor Mattias. "They have returned."

It's Birgitta, and she's howling in panic. Elsa can hear it through the church and the closed door.

She whips around. The pastor has stood up, and their faces are level. Something terrible is lurking in the corners of his eyes.

"I'm afraid we can't let you leave for Stockholm just yet," he says to Elsa. "Not while you're so upset. It would be better if you calmed down a little first."

"You can't stop me," she says, trying to find strength once again in her rage. But all she can find is the start of a bottomless fear.

The pastor doesn't reply. He just smiles. A small, cruel smile.

Fear snatches hold of her, and Elsa feels herself give way to it. She looks at Aina, begs her:

"Aina, don't do this, don't let them do this to Birgitta. She's innocent, she hasn't done anything wrong. Let us go, please."

Aina just looks at her. There is no life in her eyes.

And then she smiles. The carbon copy of his little grin.

Elsa flies around and tears open the door, but the Sundin boys are waiting outside. Frank and Gösta, standing silently side by side. They both have the same straggly brown hair and small eyes. Broad shoulders, big hands.

Behind them the congregation is waiting. A sea of staring eyes. Panic floods into Elsa's pumping blood, merging them all into a single, malevolent mass before her eyes. An impenetrable wall of hate.

She backs into the room, looking around wildly. There's no other exit in there, only the shell of the girl who had once been her daughter, and the pastor.

One of his hands is resting on the table, where a few stray sheets of paper lie. Elsa's eyes catch on the top one. It's a drawing, in crayons. Clumpy figures in different colors. And then spirals, jagged and uneven, running into each other.

The room starts to spin.

Elsa looks up.

"It was you," she says, but hardly any sound comes out. It's no more than an exhalation.

"Frank," the pastor says softly, "Gösta. Would you please take Fru Kullman to the cellar under the parsonage? So that she can calm down."

All that Elsa can see is little Kristina. Little Kristina and her newborn, cloudy dark-blue eyes.

Will they darken to Birgitta's bottomless brown? Or will they slowly but surely fade to her father's light storm-cloud gray?

"It was you," Elsa says again, and this time it's audible. But it makes no difference. Rough hands have already locked on her arms, restraining her.

Elsa's eyes flit across the horde of faces, angels no more. They look like evil spirits, quiet and glaring.

For a second she finds Staffan in the crowd.

Her lips form a mute: "Please."

He looks down.

She hears Birgitta's cries grow to a scream outside the church.

Then it cuts off abruptly, and silence is all that's left.

NOW

I'm still bent forward on the seat when I hear a knock at the door.

I sit up quickly and throw a glance at Tone in the corner. She doesn't seem to have paid it any notice.

"Come in," I say.

It's Robert. He looks around the room and then at me.

"Alice," he says. He stops in the doorway, a touch too big for it, and I get up and walk over to him.

He herds me out of the room and carefully closes the door behind him.

"What is it?" I ask.

"Max has been gone a really long time," he says.

"OK," I say.

"The church is only five minutes away." The corners of his mouth draw stiff lines that will one day be etched permanently into his cheeks.

"He's probably just . . ." I shake my head. Think of the look on Max's face. The disappointment verging on disgust.

You're so fucking selfish.

"I think he just wanted to be alone," I manage to squeeze out. "To process everything. Calm down."

"Yeah, I guess," Robert says, but that stressed, anxious look doesn't shift from his face. "I just thought . . ."

He shoves his hands deep into his pockets.

"We can go look for him anyway," I say. "If it'll make you feel better."

"Yeah," he says and nods. A hint of relief. "I just think . . . it'd be better if we were all here. Together."

I put my hand on his arm and nod.

"Let's go get him, then," I say.

"What do we do with her?" Robert asks, nodding at the door.

"We can . . . lock the door," I say, even though the thought of locking Tone up makes my stomach turn. "It's not like we'll be long. Like you said, the church is just around the corner."

I turn the doorknob carefully and open the door.

"Tone?" I say. "We're stepping out for a little while. But we'll be back soon, OK? With something to eat."

She neither moves nor responds.

I swallow.

"Birgitta," I say.

This gets a response. A flash of eyes through her fringe. A short, vague sound that seems to come from deep in her throat.

My stomach turns. I remember what she said about those weeks when reality was shut off, like a drape pulled over her mind, when she disappeared inside herself, into her own world.

I thought I was in Silvertjärn. I heard voices. Sometimes I heard Birgitta.

Her grandmother, though she didn't know it at the time.

Is she hearing her voice now, too?

Or does she think she's Birgitta?

The question vibrates on my lips, but the moment passes.

I close the door again and turn the key.

"OK," I say to Robert. "Let's go."

He hangs back slightly, a small furrow between his light eyebrows.

"What did you just call her?" he asks.

I meet his gaze for a second and then look away.

"Come on," I say.

The sun is almost skimming the horizon as we take the road down to the church. The air is cold, despite the warm light, and it feels like there'll be frost overnight. Some of the most pioneering clusters of the newly budded spring flowers seem to be wilting.

When we reach the church the doors are ajar.

"Max?" I call into the darkness, though my voice doesn't really want to carry.

No reply.

I look at Robert, who slowly pushes the heavy doors. The hinges grate as they swing open.

The pew we shoved in front of the door is still standing diagonally across the entrance a few feet in. One of our water bottles is sitting next to the remnants of our fire, and the thick, mildewy blankets we slept on are strewn over the floor. It looks as though we've come in, occupied, and desecrated the church. The only thing missing are a few empty beer cans.

"Max?" Robert calls out. His voice echoes off the high ceiling, seemingly expanding in the emptiness and yet, paradoxically, made smaller by it. Weaker.

"It's us," he goes on. "Alice and Robert. We just wanted to check if you needed any help."

Still no reply.

I walk further into the church, even though my whole body is screaming at me to leave. The Jesus above the altar seems to be grinning mockingly. How could I ever have thought he looked like he was in pain? His eyes are cruel, there's something all-knowing and menacing in his gaze, and that thin mouth looks twisted into a frozen, self-satisfied parody of a smile.

"Maybe he's already gone," I try. "Maybe he couldn't find anything so went to find food somewhere else. Down to the square or something."

A walk to clear his head. To get the taste of me out of his mouth.

The thought sends a stab of sorrow through my chest. I'm losing everyone, one by one. But maybe it isn't Silvertjärn I've lost them to; maybe it was me all along.

"Maybe," Robert echoes. He walks forward at the same cautious, restrained pace as me.

The sun is shining through the open doors from above the distant treetops behind us, making our shadows stretch out in front of us. They turn the entire church into an eerie imitation of life. Spindly limbs extending and moving in slow motion.

"Max?" I call again, my voice curdling slightly. "Are you here?"

Robert squats down next to the extinguished fire, then stands up again.

"He's been here, at least," he says. "This is where we left the honey and the last tin of sardines this morning, and now they're gone."

I look over toward the chapel. The door is closed. Did we leave it like that, or was it open when we left?

I can't remember.

I don't say anything, but Robert's eyes follow mine. He nods.

The fear starts to dawn within me—a ringing in my ears, a film over my tongue.

We make our way past the rows of pews toward the small wooden door. Our shadows swell over it, merging together as a many-armed monster by the time we reach it. I deliberately avoid looking up at the crucifix; I'm too scared I might see the figure turn and pull a face.

Everything is too still; a sort of stillness that only comes with the subtle vibration that sets into your skin when you sense a presence.

Robert opens the door.

It's the very image of a quiet, frozen peace. The yellowed lace curtain across the window. The little table, unassuming Windsor chairs. The small, blue-and-white-striped rug by the kitchen counter. The lovely evening light that paints the room in lacy shadow patterns.

The honey jar stands, prim and proper, on the table. The glass is thick and solid, with a faint tint of green, and the odd tiny air bubble along its heavy base. One of its edges is lined with blood and hair, like sticky oil paints smeared on with clumsy fingers.

He is lying facedown, which is some sort of blessing. One of his legs is pulled up under him, his stained jeans dragged up over his pale, thin calf, and his arm is reaching out to the corner. As though he were trying to crawl away.

I don't need to wonder what has happened this time; there's no need to study faint bruises on his neck, or the color of the whites of his eyes. The back of Max's head is one big slop of blood, bone, hair, and something gray, spongy and gleaming. It wasn't one well-aimed blow, or two. No: someone stood astride his struggling, lurching body and methodically hammered the honey jar onto him until he stopped moving.

I don't scream. I'm expecting to, but it never comes.

I think of how his face had looked back at the train station, open and curious, as he had gazed down the tracks into the forest. Of his swinging gait when we first met, the awkwardness in his elbows, the oversized, ironic T-shirts he always wore. Of how his face had looked an hour ago, his eyes filled with rage, his tense lips pressed against each other.

Of how beautifully those last rays of sunshine bounce off the blond hair on the crown of his head, the part that heavy jar didn't reach where the skull has retained something of its shape.

Far, far away I hear Robert lean over and puke on the floor, a shaky, abstract shape.

The smell of his vomit pierces my haze. It's sharp and offensive, and with it comes something else; the scent of what used to be Max.

The scream builds in my chest but turns into something else, leaving my mouth as a dull groan.

I don't understand. How can he be dead? How can he be lying there with a smashed skull if Tone is locked in the house? How can he . . . Nobody could have . . .

The figure in the rain.

Emmy's sea-green eyes looking straight into mine:

"You saw somebody, didn't you?"

Tone's pain-choked voice:

"I heard something below us."

The laugh on the video.

The scream over the walkie-talkie.

Tone's hand drawing a stick figure with long, straggly hair and a black-hole mouth.

Something is very wrong.

I back away, stumble, fall out of the door, and look up, up and left, at the crucifix. Jesus hasn't turned to look at me. His dark, painted eyes are still staring straight ahead, out over the village. Out over Silvertjärn.

Robert's hand is covering his mouth. He follows me back into the church, his movements dazed and jerky, the shock written on his face in big, soundless letters.

"She was right," I say, my lips numb. "You were right. We're not alone here."

THEN

Elsa had heard the distant whistle of the train as it pulled out of the station.

She should have felt something at her last hope leaving Silvertjärn, but she found nothing. There's nothing left in her.

It's so dark down here that she can't make out anything at all. She has already felt her way along the cold, damp earth, around the rough stone walls and up the small staircase; she has pounded on the door and screamed, but it did nothing, and her pounding hands had felt weak and useless.

Where would she even go if she did manage to get out?

Before that whistle of the train, she had had no idea how much time had passed. It had felt as though she had spent several days down here in the parsonage cellar, but that shrill whistle had brought some of her senses back to her. A few hours have passed since then. It must be around five or six in the afternoon now.

What is going to happen to her?

Elsa has been trying not to dwell on that. Nor on what will become of Birgitta and Kristina. But down here her thoughts spin beyond her control. She's just as powerless to stop them as she is to break down that impenetrable door up there.

Sometimes the odd shard of hope glimmers before her.

Perhaps they're just keeping her down here until evening; perhaps Margareta will start to wonder why their letters have stopped; perhaps Staffan will listen to reason.

Perhaps, perhaps, perhaps.

Hunger has already come and gone. All that remains now is the thirst, which has gone from a dry sensation in her throat to a steady, prolonged pain in her head and stomach. It's cooler down here than out in the sun, but the August heat has nevertheless forced its way inside. When she closes her eyes now she sees silver lightning bolts before her.

The creak of the door makes her start. Dazzled by the light of the rectangular opening, she shields her eyes with her hand.

"Fru Kullman," says a young man's voice. It's dull and monotonous, unfamiliar to Elsa's ears.

Elsa tries to peer through her fingers, but against the light it's impossible to make out who it is.

"Fru Kullman," the voice repeats. "Don't make me come down there to get you."

Her ears may be unused to human voices, but Elsa can still tell a threat when she hears one.

Her legs aching, Elsa gets to her feet and climbs the staircase. They don't want to carry her, but whether that's down to the thirst, hunger, or darkness, she can't tell.

When Elsa reaches the top of the staircase she has a wild urge to try to run, but the young man—who in the light turns out to be Frank Sundin—takes a steely, painful grip of her arm. He hardly looks at Elsa before he starts walking. She feels dazed and confused, but she does her best to keep up with him and not to fall.

It seems hopeless, but she has to try:

"Frank," she begs him, "you don't have to do this. If you let me go now you can say I broke free and ran off into the forest. You don't have to . . ."

He neither replies nor looks at her. Instead he jerks her arm so hard that her shoulder almost pops out of its joint and, with a yelp like a kicked dog, she goes quiet.

Elsa can't tell where they're going. They have already passed the church, and are now walking down toward the square. Where is he taking her? The streets are eerily empty. Elsa doesn't spot a single person on the way. The windows gape darkly, and the doors stand shut, despite the hot, dry afternoon.

When they pass her house she looks away.

The murmur swells up ahead of Elsa before she sees the horde. By now she is faint from thirst and hunger, her throat is swollen, and her head is throbbing. It's only when they start to near the square, when the country lane is met by the cobblestones, that she realizes where all of Silvertjärn is.

They are all thronging into the square, spilling out into the surrounding streets and houses. When Elsa and Frank approach, the horde falls silent and makes way for them. Elsa searches for a familiar face, someone to hold on to, but by now they are all as good as strangers to her. These faces that she has known her whole life: the young men and women she cradled in her arms as babies; the friends she comforted and advised; the people who one month, one week, even one day ago would have chatted happily to her in the street, who would have asked after Margareta's news down south, and if she'd be bringing the little one up to visit anytime soon.

All of them watch Elsa in silence. All of them let them pass.

After a few steps Elsa lowers her eyes to the cobblestones and stares at her feet. The shame envelops her like a heavy blanket. It's those staring eyes. She's unsure if it's her own shame she feels or theirs; if she's ashamed of herself for letting them lead her like a dog, or of all of them. Of what they've become.

When Elsa hears the sound she looks up. She can't contain the scream that tears from her throat.

"Birgitta!"

The cobblestones in the middle of the square have been torn from the ground, exposing the earth beneath them like a sore. In the soft gash of soil stands a thick pole, a birch shorn of bark and branches.

Birgitta is tied to the pole.

Thick ropes run around her waist, binding her to the trunk. The ropes cut into the soft, tender flesh around her midriff, which, so soon after giving birth, is still bulging. It must be terribly painful. Her arms have been pulled back and bound behind the pole, and her head is lolling. Elsa can't see Birgitta's face, but she can see her bare feet and swollen ankles below the loose shift she is wearing. Blood has run down the inside of her legs, drying on her feet and pooling underneath her.

"Birgitta," Elsa repeats, this time scarce more than a whisper.

She doesn't move.

"Elsa," the pastor's soft voice greets her.

Until this point he has blended into the crowd, but now he takes a small step forward, out into the empty space that has formed around Birgitta.

"At last," he says.

His face is calm and peaceful, and this scares Elsa more than anything else so far.

"What have you done to her?" she asks. Her voice is hardly more than a croak, her tongue dry and rough. The August sun has started to drop below the horizon, but the afternoon heat is still heavy and oppressive.

"It is time now, Elsa," Pastor Mattias says softly. "It is time to take the next step. Too long have we allowed evil to live among us. To corrupt us. But no more."

Elsa wants to tell him that he's insane, out of his mind. But when she looks into his gray eyes she sees a cold light shining from within, one that silences her before she can even say a word.

If Kristina was born yesterday she must have been conceived last winter. In December. Just a few weeks after he arrived.

When had he started to whisper into his followers' ears that she was evil? That she was possessed by demons?

Even if she could speak, who would believe her? Would it not sound just like the vicious lies one might expect of one who served the devil? Just as he has always said.

Speechless, Elsa looks around at those standing closest to her. Her neighbors. Her friends.

Who of them would believe her if she tried to tell them the truth?

"You are evil," Elsa says to the pastor, her voice shaky and hoarse.

He doesn't get angry, doesn't get agitated, simply shakes his head sadly.

"Do you hear that?" he asks the congregation around them. "Do you hear how evil spreads like venom? It infects like a disease, passing from one to the other, mangling the soul until there is nothing left to save." The pastor turns his cold, calculating gaze on Elsa.

"Is there anything left in you to save, Elsa?" he asks.

She wants to spit in his face, but she can't. She's too afraid, too thirsty. Too weak. Too defeated.

"We'll soon see," he says, and it's as though none of the others are there, as though he is whispering quietly in her ear.

He looks out at the crowd.

"It is time," he says, his voice louder now, more resounding. It jangles out over the square, making even the last of the hubbub die down.

"Time to drive the evil from our midst. To receive God's light. It is time to choose—and to choose the light."

He pauses.

"Are you willing to choose the pure way?"

It starts as a whisper, uncertain and hesitant, but then it grows to a raging tempest, a preposterous cheer that verges on hysteria.

He raises his arms. The sight of his beautiful white palms immediately silences the crowd. They are as though entranced, a swaying delirium that runs like waves through the whole village.

"Kaj?" he says, and, though it's hardly louder than his normal speaking voice, in the silence it carries regardless. Elsa sees a movement in the crowd, sees it part once again.

Kaj Andersson leads the ranks. He is tall and strong now, with curly, sandy-blond hair and a square jaw, but Elsa remembers him as he used to be, when he and Margareta went to school together. All elbows and grazed knees.

There are four of them in all, all tall boys and men, with broad shoulders and bulging arms. Each of them carries a large wicker basket filled with stones.

The stones are smooth and round, water buffed. They look like they have been collected from the riverbed. Kaj and the other three put the baskets down in front of the pastor and straighten up. The pastor smiles warmly at them and gives them a small nod. Kaj nods in response and disappears back into the crowd.

Elsa catches sight of Dagny behind the pastor's back. She is standing stock-still, her eyes glassy. Frank's brother, Gösta, hovers behind her like a warning. He doesn't need to restrain her, though; she doesn't seem to be in any condition to attempt an escape.

Ingrid is standing immediately in front of Dagny. The red lipstick she always wears has been smeared around her mouth—or at least that's what Elsa thinks, until she realizes it's a nosebleed. Gösta has a tight grip on both of her shoulders, and her hands are bound before her with a tightly wound string. She is staring at the baskets of stones, eyes wide in horror.

"Who among you would like to help to cleanse our congregation?" comes the pastor's voice, and now it's a pounding waterfall, thunder rumbling across the square. "Who among you are prepared to act as Christ's hands? Step forward. Step forward and act."

At first nothing happens. But then they start to move, crowding and flocking around the baskets. Hungry, grasping hands reach like claws for the stones, at first hesitantly, then heatedly. They push and shove to get their hands on them.

"We must dare to bleed, and to spill blood," the pastor sermonizes over their free-for-all. "We must choose the light. We must choose God. We must crush the devil among us, for otherwise we shall never be whole."

The stones have started to run out. Those standing at the front start to edge back, most with two or three stones in their hands. Young and old, men and women, Elsa knows them all. One of the girls is no more than twelve years old. Greta Almqvist. She has a round, flat stone in each hand, each so big that her fingers can't close around it.

The silence envelops and swallows them. For one eternal second, nothing happens. They all stand still, waiting. The only sound is the swish of nine hundred breaths, like the soft flutter of a butterfly's wings.

"Sing with me," the pastor says calmly.

Around him they begin to sing as one. The melody is familiar.

"A mighty fortress is our God, A bulwark never failing;
Our shelter He, amid the flood Of mortal ills prevailing . . ."

Birgitta twitches when the first stone hits her thigh. When the second meets her waist over the ropes, she raises her head and howls. Elsa glimpses two swollen black eyes through her hair, a broken lip.

The howl rises to a scream when little Greta Almqvist hits her in the face with one of her stones, splitting her eyebrow so that the blood starts to flow down her face.

Her screams are swallowed by the ever-swelling hymn; they become part of the chorus. Elsa screams along with her, only vaguely aware that she is doing so.

"STOP! PLEASE, FOR THE LOVE OF GOD, STOP!"

She fights to free herself, but Frank has her in an iron grip. His melodyless voice echoes in her ears.

"And tho' this world, with devils filled, Should threaten to undo us;
We will not fear, for God hath willed His truth to triumph through us . . ."

The stones are raining down on Birgitta now. A few merciful stones miss, but most of them hit their target.

Her cries have turned into an exhausted moan, a wordless prayer, fleshy and thick.

The tears are running down Elsa's face. She can't. She can't watch. She closes her eyes.

"I'm sorry. I'm sorry. Forgive me, Birgitta. I'm sorry."

NOW

Through the silence of the church comes a sound.

It's that same humming rise and fall of our walkie-talkies.

They are lying in a pile on one of the pews. I pick up one of them, a light, ugly little device in black-and-yellow plastic. It sits in my hand like a huge, distorted wasp, ready to sting.

It's turned off. The light isn't on.

I drop it to the ground, hear the plastic crack against the stone floor with a satisfying clap.

I fumble clumsily for the other walkie-talkies, my fingers hysterical. None of their lights are on. None of them are on.

The sound continues to grow in volume, until there's no more rise and fall. This isn't interference. It's the pure tone of a song on the wind, a song that seems to rise from the ground itself in the blazing sunset.

"That word above all earthly pow'rs—No thanks to them—abideth:
The Spirit and the gifts are ours Thro' Him who with us sideth.
Let goods and kindred go, This mortal life also;
The body they may kill: God's truth abideth still,
His kingdom is forever."

"We're going to die here," Robert mumbles. "We're going to die here."

"No," I say.

My mouth tastes of iron and blood, the hymn is ringing in my ears, and the noose that is Silvertjärn is about to strangle us.

"We'll have to go through the forest. We can't wait for the police."

Robert looks almost sleepy. I realize that this is what shock must look like. I'm sure I'm shocked, too, but I feel wide awake—perhaps more than I've ever felt before.

"We can't," he says. His body seems to fold in on itself, his broad shoulders slump, and his hands dangle uselessly at his sides.

"Yes we can," I say. "We're getting out of here. We'll head to the highway. Fast—now. I don't know who's doing this, but I'm not sticking around and waiting to die. OK?"

His eyes meet mine, and he nods.

"OK."

As I run between the houses, it feels like the village itself is trying to swallow us up, as though every single house were a trap, every open door a set of gaping jaws. The quiet, distant hymn echoes through the alleys and streets.

There's something deeply wrong with this place, but I no longer have any desire to stay and try to figure out what that is.

The green door is hanging ajar. I throw it open and stumble inside.

"Tone!" I cry as Robert comes in behind me, still jittery and empty-eyed.

"Try to find something we can fill with water," I say. "Look in the kitchen. If there's anything edible left then take it."

He nods and goes into the kitchen, and I run upstairs, taking the steps two at a time.

"Tone?" I say, and open the door.

The dying sunlight filters in through the window, tinting the room a fiery red. The ripped bedspread, the desk, the floorboards. Tone's terror-stricken face.

The knife blade flashes red-hot in the light, trying to blind me.

The figure holding the knife to Tone's neck isn't much taller than she is. Its face is covered by tangles of gray-white hair. One veiny, white, bony hand is clutching at Tone's hair with sinewy, gnarled fingers, while the other is pressing the long, thin kitchen knife to her neck.

"Close the door," comes the figure's squeaky, light voice.

I turn slowly, weighing up whether to scream, but my thoughts must be obvious, because the same voice says:

"One sound and I slit her throat."

It's calm and direct, with a hint of a bite. Like the sun shining through the clouds.

I shut the door, which closes with a small click.

"Are there more of you?" she asks when I turn back to them.

I swallow, unable to find my voice.

"Just us," I say eventually.

"You and the other one downstairs?"

The flicker of hope I'd harbored that she didn't know about Robert dies. I nod.

She stands still, apparently thinking. I hardly dare look at her, so afraid I am of what she might do to Tone. Instead I look at Tone, desperately searching her eyes, trying to find some trace of her in there.

I just want someone to tell me what to do.

Then I hear footsteps coming up the stairs.

"Alice," I hear Robert call. "Are you ready?"

The woman in front of me presses the knife even harder to Tone's neck.

I hear the door open behind me.

"I couldn't find a water bottle, but I . . ."

He goes quiet.

NOW

All I can hear are Tone's shallow, panting breaths.

"Good," the woman says, and I hear something of a perverse approval in her voice. "Very good."

When she looks up, her tangle of hair falls to the side to reveal a face like carved bark, something frozen and contorted. Sun-damaged skin lying in folds over blunted features; thin lips cut by deep wrinkles flapping over yellow teeth; and, in the middle of it all, a pair of glinting, deep-set gold-brown eyes.

It isn't hard to put a word to what blazes in her eyes.

It isn't fear or worry; it's excitement. An intoxicating, radiant excitement that makes her hand tremble.

"You," she says, nodding at me. "Bind his hands."

That girlishly shrill voice again; that same rounding off of her words.

I clear my throat, afraid that my voice won't carry.

"I have nothing to tie him with," I say, trying to sound as calm as possible, keeping my voice even so as not to scare or anger her.

"There's a rope on the bed," she says, sounding almost amused.

And yes, there it is, I see, as I slowly lower my eyes. It looks old and worn.

I bend over cautiously and pick it up. The fibers scratch at my hands.

"Good," she squeaks. "Now. Bind his hands."

She moistens her lips with her dry, pointed tongue.

I turn to look at Robert. His eyes meet mine. Paradoxical as it is, he looks calmer now than he did in the church, as though he's regained his composure in the eye of the storm.

When I turn back around, I see it isn't me she's looking at, but Tone. She flashes her stained teeth in something resembling a smile.

"You thought you'd do it this time, didn't you?" she asks, and it's as though Robert and I aren't even here. "You thought you'd be free to spread your poison now, that there'd be no one left to stop you. But I'm still here. Oh, yes, I'm here."

She makes a crackling, broken sound that must be a laugh.

"I could tell who you were, even from far away. I knew you'd returned. Did you enjoy my song? Remember it? It was the hymn you died to, witch. I wanted to remind you."

The entire world is balanced on her knife-edge.

She twists her head so that her eyes land on me. Slightly more of her face is exposed now, giving me a clearer view of her. Her nose must have once been fine and chiseled, but now seems to sink down into her slack skin. Her eyelashes are short and thin. And she has a birthmark under one eye—dark, oddly elegant, like the painted-on beauty spot on an old beauty.

"It's time," she says. "This ends tonight." Her eyes pin me down as she tugs at Tone's hair, tautening her neck against the blade.

"You'll give them back to me, you hear? I know it was you," she hisses in Tone's ear. "Do you hear them singing? They're waiting for me. They're going to come back to me. I'll take you there, and then you're going to give them back. You *whore*." She spits out the last word, and it sounds unnatural, like how a child would say it—someone testing the waters, trying it on for size.

Does it dawn on me slowly, or is it those oddly childish words that peel away the years? The features start to fall into place: that intense stare; some familial likeness in the way the years have flattened and eroded the

but-what-if-everyone-hates-it? emails with far more patience than I deserve, which in and of itself should make you shoo-ins for sainthoods. I promise to write to the Vatican about this personally.

Thank you to my fantastic friends, who have put up with and supported me during this process. It isn't always easy to live with a neurotic author in full-on editing mode, but you have handled it all so well that you make it look like child's play.

Thank you to Frida and Sofia, who inspire me to be a little kinder every day, both to myself and to others. I see the fact that I have you both in my life as incontrovertible proof of good karma.

Thank you to Saga, who has been with me from the very start. That you read my very first teenage attempts at a book but are still happy to look at my new manuscripts says a lot more about your character than it does about my writing.

Thank you to Anna, who said that you loved this book again and again until I had no choice but to listen. You are still the best surprise of my life. (And thank you to Anna's partner, Matthis, for putting up with how much time I spend at your apartment.)

Thank you to my dad, who seems almost more excited than I am when I call to tell him news about the book. Thank you to my brothers, Alexander and Leo, who grew up with two writers in their midst. It was tough, I know, but I will always maintain that the experience has given you valuable life skills.

Thank you to my mom. For reading, supporting, giving the best advice, and kindly telling me what an idiot I'm being in my more ridiculous moments. Being able to share writing with you is one of the greatest things. I am so lucky to have you as a mother.

And finally, thank you to you, that rare reader who even makes it through the acknowledgments.

None of this would be possible without you reading the book. All of this is for you.

So, thank you.

THANK YOU

Every writer knows that the unsung heroes of every book are the people who lie behind it: who have given their support, read drafts and offered feedback, made tea, and—occasionally—forced the writer in question outside for some fresh air and sunlight. I, of course, am no exception; in fact, I would say that I demand more of my little circle than most, so it's only right that I make a little space here to thank everyone who helped me to write *The Lost Village*.

Thank you to my fantastic publisher, Erika, who has made this book so much more than I could ever have envisioned. You saw a potential in that first, raw draft that I don't think anyone else could have. I often say a good publisher is like a coach—someone who peps you up, supports and inspires you, but who also forces you to run until you drop, and then do another five miles. You have done both with bravura.

Thank you also to my editor, John, who has had to put up with my many passionate attempts to prove you *can* write "as to" in addition to "as if" or "as though." (I am right, as, I am sure, the world will come to see in time.)

Thank you to my agents, Anna and Johanna, who have made all my dreams come true. How many people get to say that that's all in a day's work? Not only have you made sure that Alice, Emmy, Elsa, and Aina made it out into the world; you have also handled my frenetic

bones beneath her thin skin; something that reminds me of Grandma's sagging, thin lips after her stroke.

Or maybe it's just the birthmark. Maybe that's what makes the pieces of the puzzle start to fall into place.

"Aina?" I say.

NOW

Aina's eyes rivet me to the spot. I think I see something like surprise on her face, but it vanishes just as quickly as it appeared.

"You're infected," she mutters to herself, then she repeats it, drawing out the syllables: "In-fec-ted."

What we're supposedly infected with I don't know, but I assume it's nothing good.

I gulp. The muscles in my throat feel sore and strained.

"I'm Margareta's granddaughter," I say. "Margareta is my grandma."

She licks her lips again, almost compulsively.

"Margareta?" she repeats.

"Your big sister," I whisper.

She seems to go still, and for a second I think I've reached her.

But then she clenches her jaw and bares her teeth. Her heavy eyebrows pull together, the furrow between them forming a fissure down her face.

"She left me here," she says, with a whininess that soon turns to fury. "She left me here! She abandoned me. I wrote to her, but she never came."

The last part is a scratchy whisper that ends as a sigh.

"I'm here," I say. "I came here. To find you."

There is something of a sadness about her now, a helplessness that doesn't fit with her appearance. She looks at me, and in that haggard face

with its sickly, yellowed eyes, I see my own light-brown eyes staring back at me.

"I'm here," I say again.

I hold my breath. Force myself not to shrink back, but to look at her. Her face hardens to a mask of carved wood.

"Infected," she hisses again. "You're all infected. By her." Her knife presses even harder against Tone's neck, and I see the skin beneath it give way, see a hypnotically red drop of blood make its way down her neck. A broken whimper leaves her throat.

"It's not her," I start to babble, "it's not Birgitta—Birgitta's dead. She's been dead for sixty years. That's not her, Aina, her name's Tone, and she's sick—"

"One more word and I slit her throat and send her back to the one she serves," Aina says, cutting me off. That eerie calm has returned to her.

I shut my mouth.

"You think I don't recognize her?" she asks, laughing that crackling parody of a laugh again. "You think I can't see her filth in that body? I know. I've been waiting. Oh, have I been waiting."

Her head twitches slightly.

"You're going to give them back to me," she says into Tone's ear. "Hear me, witch? I'm going to take you to them, and then you're going to give them back to me. It's over now."

The sunset outside has started to turn into twilight. The last of the pulsating redness starts to ebb out of the room, replaced by a cooler purple. Night is drawing in.

"Give what back?" a whisper rushes out of my throat. "What is she going to give back to you?"

THEN

Frank doesn't need to pull or drag her anymore; Elsa's feet are moving on their own. She is walking five steps behind the pastor, between Dagny and Ingrid, and her eyes are glued to their feet. They are at the head of the congregation, and to an outsider they might look like his most devoted followers, the ones honored enough to follow in his wake. As opposed to prisoners, crushed and broken.

Playthings.

Elsa has always believed herself a strong person, one who resists, who stands up for what's right. And where that has been proven true to some extent, by now she has no fight left in her. Only emptiness.

She has lost any illusions of escape, of persuading any of them. There is no mercy left in Silvertjärn. The last of her hope died with Birgitta in the square.

However hard Elsa tries, she can't stop herself from hearing Birgitta's dying wails. Though she had closed her eyes tightly, the sounds she had not been able to shut out.

How long does he plan to keep them alive? A few days? A week? She and Ingrid and Dagny are all still alive because the pastor takes pleasure in seeing them defeated, that much she understands. But sooner or later he will tire of it. The best they can hope for is to not end up like Birgitta. The best they can hope for is a quick death.

By now night has fallen, and darkness has sunk over the village. Elsa hardly notices when the road is replaced by a beaten track, the shrubbery around them by tall pines. With heavy, lumbering steps she trudges over roots and moss, hearing the rest of the village marching in silence behind them. There is reverence in the air.

The forest envelops them like a mother. In it their true church awaits.

The pastor looks over his shoulder. He catches Elsa's gaze, and his eyes gleam like silver. There is nothing human behind them.

The realization that comes to her is more of a caress than a blow. After all that has happened, it's almost a relief.

She will never leave this forest.

NOW

"You," she says to me, then nods at the doorway. "You first."

I turn around. Robert catches my eye and I hesitate, but then I hear Aina's dry voice behind me. She sounds calm and slightly pleased.

"If you run I'll slit her throat open." She clears her throat, then coughs. When she speaks again, her voice is quieter, softer. "And then I'll take you both, one by one. Where do you think you can go? Silvertjärn is my home. You can't hide from me here."

She's old, I think feverishly, and we're young and strong. We can run faster, can get away from her if we just make a run for it. We have a chance.

But then I hear Tone whimper quietly behind my back. Some of the seriousness of the situation must have forced its way through her haze, because so far she has done as Aina has said. I don't even want to imagine what would happen if she started kicking and fighting like she did with Robert and Max.

I think of Max's smashed-in head and outstretched hand. Of Emmy's empty, staring eyes.

I open the door and slowly step out.

"Toward the square," Aina says. "To the forest."

Is this a nightmare? Or is it really happening?

The edge of the forest looks like an impenetrable barrier, a wall to another world. The pines rise up over our heads like ancient, forbidding

divinities. Against my better judgment I stop; I get stuck between heart-beats, and suddenly I can't take another step.

I can't go in there. I can't step into that darkness.

The fear explodes in my stomach, and for a while all I can think is: *Then she can kill me.*

"Go," says Aina, and she doesn't need to use any threats, because Robert whispers my name behind me, and that single word is enough to make me move. I can throw away my own life—that much I've been prepared to do before—but not theirs.

The forest around us is coming to life in a way I've never seen before. Had Silvertjärn been a graveyard, there would be whispering and whis-tling all around us. Movement everywhere. Countless eyes tracking our last steps.

My breath stings in my throat. In the darkness I trip on a root and fall. I feel Robert's bound hands fumble to catch me, but he can't do much. I land headfirst on the heather, and my knee slams into a stone, sending a jolt of pain up into my hip. I lay there for a few seconds with my face in the moss, my leg throbbing and my heart full of something resembling hate.

"Up," Aina commands.

When at first I don't move, her voice becomes softer, slightly teasing.

"Or maybe you don't feel like it? A little sleepy, are we?" Her way of speaking is strange—both young and old at the same time. It's like hear-ing a teen try to imitate the archaic speech patterns of an old movie star.

I don't need to see what she does to be able to interpret the sound that is pressed from Tone's throat. I force myself up to my hands and feet, ignoring the shooting pain in my knee.

My eyes have adjusted enough to the shadows now to make her out in the darkness. She gives a wide, cold smile, a slash across the middle of her face.

"You two, keep walking," she says. "Straight ahead." Her smile grows, impossible as that ought to be. It looks like her face has been cleft by an ax. As though she could explode—bite—stab—at any second.

"We're getting close now."

Close to what? I have my suspicions. I know the direction we're walking in. It's the part of the forest we were warned to steer clear of, where the ground was too unstable. Due to the mine underneath.

The searches had never gone down there because the entrance was still sealed, but those tunnels run deep into the earth's underbelly. I remember some of the words I found scrawled in Pastor Mattias's sermon.

Only in silence can we become free. Only by allowing the darkness to embrace us can we step into the light.

In silence. In darkness.

I glimpse it through the trees as we approach, a hollow like an open grave, a blackness deeper than the shadows. It's wide and uneven, hardly more than a hole in the ground, but I know where it leads.

Aina doesn't need to direct me to it; I'm drawn there all by myself. I stop at the edge and look down into the hole. It's too dark for me to see how deep it goes.

"What . . ." I hear Robert mutter behind me, and I reply before she does.

"The mine," I say. "It leads to the mine."

"To our church," Aina whispers, her voice merging with the whistling treetops.

"Jump," she says, her voice harder now.

"What?" I say and start turning around, but then I feel something that makes me instantly freeze. A blade on the back of my neck.

"Jump," she says, and the pressure grows until I feel it swell to a shooting pain. "Jump, or I'll give you a little push. We must go to them."

To the choir beneath us. To the darkness of the tunnels.

"Jump!" she says, her voice piercingly shrill, and suddenly I feel a foot against my back, a quick kick that gives me no time to react.

I fall.

THEN

She climbs down the ladder, down into the darkness, her sweaty fingers gripping the rungs tightly. They are rough and prickly, and feel sloppily made.

The darkness beneath is compact, their only light that of the pastor's torch. Down in the darkness it dazzles, its shifty flicker lighting up the tunnel in both directions.

This must once have been a transport tunnel, as it is long and sloping. The walls are rugged and damp. It's already cooler down here than it was up at the surface.

The pastor starts walking down into the darkness. Elsa hurries to find her feet, stumbling after him as fast as she can into the blackness and bedrock. Anything to not lose the light; anything to not be left in the darkness with the silent hordes behind her.

Elsa has seen their true faces now. She has seen the saliva frothing at their mouths; the glint in their eyes at the sight of blood; the intoxicated joy of their breathless gasps at the crack of bones.

The dancing cone of light ahead of them moves deeper and deeper underground; he is the light they follow in darkness. Elsa can see that as a symbol it must be seductive. Surely he knows that. It must be intentional.

Although Staffan worked in the mine some twenty-four years, Elsa

has only been down here twice in her life, and never this deep. The air feels thicker and heavier, and the walls seem to press down onto them. She can feel the weight of the bedrock above her; thousands of tons of rock and ore, all held up by flimsy structures, mathematics, and goodwill.

Elsa wonders how they knew where to dig to reach the tunnels. But perhaps that's no great wonder: of all the villagers behind her, how many hundreds used to work at the mine? They knew where the tunnels ran, where it would be safe to dig and blast.

Then the tunnel opens up before them, expanding to form a cavern.

The torch isn't powerful enough to reach its furthest corners, but it's bright enough for Elsa to see that the space is large—some fifteen feet high—and long. Elsa doesn't doubt that the entire village will be able to fit in here. Whether it's a natural air pocket or one of the older shafts from when the mine was new and Silvertjärn no more than a few farmsteads out in the forest, she can't tell.

In the middle of the cavern is a shallow body of water, hardly more than a pool. That's what they are now approaching, Elsa and Ingrid and Dagny and Pastor Mattias, with the congregation behind them. He stops at the water's edge and raises the torch. At first he says nothing, just lets the light speak for itself.

Frank grabs her shoulders again, hard—so hard that her bones rub. But the pain can't reach her. He's probably expecting her to launch at the pastor, to attack him in some way. He needn't worry.

"Where will you go?" Elsa asks Pastor Mattias, and her voice sounds almost like normal. "Where will you go after this?"

It's like speaking to a statue, a quiet, forbidding monolith. But he looks at her and smiles mildly.

"Go?" he asks. "Why should I go anywhere?"

Behind her Elsa hears the steps and breaths of those who have started to throng into the cavern and push out toward the walls. Those who are watching them at a distance. Those waiting.

His voice is hardly more than an exhalation, yet still Elsa hears every word.

"I have created my Heaven on Earth," he says. "Every one of these people sees me as their prophet. Their guide. Their master. They drink the words from my lips. I have created Silvertjärn in my own image. No, I am not going anywhere. We have many lovely years ahead, Silvertjärn and I."

The light of the torch dances in his gray eyes.

"Down here I am God."

NOW

In this darkness I am blind.

With every step I take, my knee sends small streams of pain up my leg, and my back is one single aching knot. I can't tell if it's the lack of light or the blow to my head that's affecting my balance, but I keep on bumping into walls, having to catch myself with grazed palms.

I hear Robert staggering behind me. He sounds like he's doing better than me, but that isn't saying much.

When I feel the water start to seep into my shoes I don't realize what it is, I just take another step. It's the splashing sound that makes me stop.

"What . . ." I begin, but I'm cut off by Aina's hoarse, excited voice as it creeps over my shoulder.

"Here," she says, and I hear her approach, hear Robert grunt as she shoves past him, her hands still fixed on Tone.

The light dazzles my sore eyes, and I blink hard, trying to get my vision to clear.

The tunnel is small and cramped. It's a transport tunnel: behind us it's straight, but ahead it looks like it starts to dip down into a bend. The mine itself must be further down. The water has flooded the passageway up to the bend, forming a sinkhole, some sort of underground lake. It's impossible to see how deep it is, or how far down it goes.

When I turn to look at Aina and Tone, I see that Aina is holding an old kerosene lamp made of glass and steel. It looks basic, and the kerosene container is almost empty, but it's more than enough for the small tunnel. In the light of the burner the dark surface of the water looks like oil, sleek and black.

I back away from the water's edge and into Robert.

"Sorry," I whisper.

I wish I could apologize for so much more; that I could make him understand everything I regret. But my voice is broken and faint, and "sorry" will never be enough.

The hymn seems to ooze from the passage walls, trickling down the rock with the damp. Aina hums along, then sings, her voice surprisingly sweet:

"Abide with me; fast falls the eventide;
The darkness deepens; Lord, with me abide . . ."

Her voice sounds solemn despite the high-pitched hymn. It gets multiplied by the tunnel's cracks and nooks, fragmented and hurled back at us like thousands of soulless whispers. She is one of a choir.

"It's over now," she says, and she sounds on the verge of tears. "It's over. The time for the resurrection has come."

I stare at the water. At the faint rings on the surface rolling out toward us.

I don't know what it is she intends to do with us, but the deepest, most primal parts of me know that she doesn't plan to leave here with us. Whatever purpose it might serve in those rusted, meandering pathways of her brain, her intention is to kill us.

Aina fixes her eyes on me.

"He promised," she says, equal parts hopeful and aggressive. "The pastor promised he'd come back if I waited. He said it wouldn't be long. I didn't want to stay up there, but he told me to. He told me to."

She shakes her head and then mutters, despairing, to herself:

"I waited, like he told me. But it wasn't enough."

She puts the kerosene lamp down on the floor, lighting the tunnel from below. The light throws her into razor-sharp contrast against the wall of the mine.

I have to keep her talking; so long as she keeps talking, she won't use the knife squeezed so tightly in her hands.

"You want the others to come back to you," I repeat, cautiously, trying to keep up with her mutterings. My brain is working feverishly. Thoughts are trying to drag their way out of the thumping bustle that is my mind, but the blow has left it feeling swollen and foggy, and I'm finding it hard to focus.

"Yes!" she gasps. Her face seems to melt into the glare from below her. "They went underground to complete the sacrifice. We were going to be able to live in God's grace. He said I didn't need to see it. He said . . . he said . . ." She breaks off, and her face contorts into a grimace.

"That's why they didn't come back," she whispers, a sudden vulnerability to her face, a naked anxiety. "We all had to be there to witness the sacrifice, but I wasn't with them. It was going to be a new testament; we were going to be the new nation. All of the testaments must be sealed in blood, like Christ's blood on the cross. It was going to purify our sins, you see. But I wasn't there, so we weren't all present." Her thin, wrinkled bottom lip trembles.

I fight to try to find the words.

"It wasn't your fault, Aina," I say.

It's flat and empty, a cliché. But her eyes light up. She shakes her head.

"No," she says. "It wasn't my fault. It was her fault. The witch's."

I see her grip on the knife harden.

"I tried to repay the debt," she says, nodding to herself. "I tried to get rid of it, the devil's spawn. I let them take it away. But it wasn't enough." The last part is said almost conspiratorially, like a whispered confidence to a good friend.

Aina puts her other hand back on Tone's neck and nods to herself.

"The witch brought the rock down on our church. But she couldn't

silence us. Oh no, that much she couldn't do," she says, running her gawky fingers and bitten-down nails along Tone's neck.

"I know what I must do. I must wash the sin away with blood."

I hold my breath. Her hand works its way, almost tenderly, up into Tone's hair.

"I said the rites over the other two," she says. "That redhead girl and the blond boy. They didn't understand the magnitude of giving oneself to God, but I showed them. They fought it, but I was patient—I didn't judge them for their ignorance. I said the rites over them so that their sacrifices would count, too. It would have been better down here underground, of course, but God sees us all. He saw my offerings. Life by life."

The light of the kerosene lamp flickers against the dripping walls.

"I liked her eyes, you know," she says to me. "The redhead's. That's why I left them open. They reminded me a little of the pastor's eyes."

She stares at me for a few seconds, then the rest happens very quickly. Her hand turns into a claw, and she grabs Tone's hair and shoves her down to her knees by the water.

I scream "NO!" but it's drowned out by the wordless bellow of the walls and the drone of Aina's voice as she puts the knife to Tone's neck and pulls her head back:

"In the name of the Father, and of the Son, and of the Holy Spirit—"

I'm shoved into the wall by something storming past me. Robert throws himself at Aina, his bound hands raised. He slams into her forcefully, throwing her off-balance and sending her headfirst into the water.

"Robert!" I shout, and I have no time to think, no time to see anything, because then she's back above the surface again, hissing and spluttering, thigh-deep in the water.

Robert, however, is struggling to get up on the slippery bedrock; he slips and falls with his bound hands in front of him, and I see him land heavily. Aina lets go of Tone's matted hair and shoves her toward the other wall. She takes two long strides toward Robert, her teeth bared like an animal.

"You took him," she says, "you took him from me," then she shoves him underwater with one knee to his back and holds him there. I see her take his head in both hands and pound it down onto the floor beneath the surface, see the muscles in her withered arms tense and the tendons in her neck tauten, and I throw myself into the water and try to tear her away, grab hold of her arms, but her slight body is stronger than what should be possible, and she claws at my face until my blood starts to run, and when I reach for my cheek in shock she throws me off her.

Robert's flails have started to weaken. In the flickering light I see blood bloom out into the water from his face.

I get to my feet and suddenly—

everything stops.

Aina has frozen on the spot. The muscles in her arms tense up and release, tense up and . . . release.

The knifepoint that has sprung through her neck releases a trickle of blood that pools in the depression above her clavicle. She puts one hand to her neck and runs her fingertips over the blade, which glitters like a necklace beneath her jaw.

She opens her mouth as though to say something, but no sound escapes her lips.

Slowly she falls off Robert and down under the surface. I see the shadow that is Aina sink, lightly and gracefully, toward the bottom, and then start to drift toward the edge of the passage.

Tone stays standing there, her legs spread wide, her eyes on Aina's body. Her breaths are heavy, and her face is covered in sweat. The cut that has now dried on her neck is in almost exactly the same spot as where the knife pierced through Aina's.

Her hands are still clenched in front of her, as though around the handle of a knife.

My stupor is broken, and I throw myself at Robert. I grab hold of his arm and pull him up over the surface, then drag his leaden body halfway onto dry land and turn him faceup. His nose is a fleshy mess, and the

blood drips from it in slow quivers that mix with the water in his hair. His lips are slightly parted, and his eyes are closed.

"No, no, no," I whisper, hardly aware of the tears spilling from my eyes. "No. Please, no."

I lean down toward his smashed face, and my tears drip down and mix with his blood, but just as I'm about to put my hand over what remains of his nose, he makes a sound.

His eyes flutter open.

His body lurches and he coughs, a gurgling sound that brings with it a belch of water. I move back slightly, sobbing, laughing, shaking, and Robert rolls over onto his side and throws up. He makes to wipe his mouth, but his hands are still bound. Trembling, I crawl around and untie the rope.

I look out over the water and see Tone standing there, her eyes still fixed on the dark shadow about ten feet from her. It drifts ever closer to the spot where the passage turns down into the underworld, leaving a mirage of blood in its trail.

Then suddenly she's gone.

Aina has dropped over the edge.

It's completely silent. Tone clenches her fists once, twice. I hear the echo of a little sigh, and then her shoulders relax.

I think I hear something in the distance.

It sounds like tinny kids' cries.

Then Tone suddenly sinks to the floor, as though the strings holding her up have been cut.

She looks me in the eye and smiles, a small, shaky smile.

"Is she home now?" she asks quietly.

Then her eyes roll back into her head and she loses consciousness.

THEN

The pastor raises his torch high above his head.

"Today we have taken a great step," he says in his smooth, sing-song voice. "We have taken one step toward enlightenment. Toward the kingdom of heaven."

Elsa can't see the congregation behind her, but she can sense them: their glittering, staring eyes; the scent of their anxiety and excitement.

The dark water shimmers behind him, languid and impenetrable, and the air smells of clay and minerals.

"God sees our sacrifices and endeavors. But He doesn't only see those who live in His truth; He also sees those who have turned their faces from Him. He sees those who have strayed from the true way, those who have allowed themselves to be seduced by Satan's lies."

The pastor lowers his torch so that it is in line with Elsa's eyes.

"He sees them, and He welcomes their return," he says. "None of God's children are strangers to Him. Like the prodigal son, one can always return to God's embrace and be welcomed home. God is love."

Elsa hears Dagny give a quiet sob beside her. She gropes around for her hand, and when she finds it she gives it a squeeze. She gets no response. It hangs soft and limp in Elsa' fingers.

"Would you like to return to God?" he asks them, staring at Elsa. The torch's flame dances in miniature in his eyes.

"Yes," Dagny sobs sloppily. "Yes. Yes."

Ingrid says nothing. She stares resolutely ahead, down into the water. Perhaps she, like Elsa, understands what awaits them. Her face is hard and determined. Her nose is swollen, but it isn't bleeding anymore.

"God's arms are open to you," he says to them, but in a loud, vaulting voice, as though sermonizing. "You can return. You can be cleansed of your sins. You can rise anew, freed of your burdens and regrets."

Dagny's sobs intensify until her shoulders start to shake. Elsa lets go of her hand. She can't bear to feel her trembling.

"Let us help them," says Pastor Mattias, raising the torch once again so that the sharp shadows transform his lovely, androgynous features into the cruel vision of an avenging angel. "Let us restore them to our Lord. Let us cleanse them, and cleanse ourselves."

"Amen," Elsa hears behind her, nearly nine hundred whispering voices that spread in caresses along the cavern's dripping walls and tunnels. "Amen."

The pastor nods at the boys behind them. Heavy hands land on Elsa's shoulders, forcing her roughly to her knees. The rocks scrape the skin on her knees and calves.

The knife he draws from his belt is nothing special; it's a pocketknife, the type carried by every man and boy in the village. Its handle is black, and its blade glistens in the glare of the torch.

The pastor hands the torch to one of the multitude of people standing behind them and bends forward. He places his hand on Elsa's head. It's dry and warm.

"Don't worry," he says, "she isn't here." It's a whisper, directed at Elsa alone. "She's above ground with the baby. She won't see this."

Aina.

The gratitude that wells up in Elsa is perverse, a thick, sluggish delirium that mixes with the hatred she feels until she can no longer separate the two, until they become one in her body.

She looks him in the eye.

His dry lips kiss her forehead.

Dagny's sobs have risen to a full-on cry, and she is begging and pleading:

"No, please, please, let me go, I didn't mean to, I promise to never . . . never . . ."

Her voice turns into a howl, then a whimper, and Elsa doesn't get to hear what it is that she will never do.

The pastor straightens up.

"I submit this soul to You, O Lord, for You to welcome her into Your Grace and cleanse her of the sin and blackness of the world," he orates. The hand on Elsa's head grows heavier. He digs his fingers into her hair and pulls her head back, exposing her neck.

He raises the knife, a silver sword in the glare of the flickering torch.

"In the name of the Father, and of the Son, and of the Holy—" he says, but his voice is drowned out by another sound.

A rumble above their heads. It runs through the rock above them like a peal of thunder: weakened structures that have been cut and hollowed out time and again; beams that have rotted and weakened and now start to give way; thousands of tons of bedrock, buckling under the strain of its own weight.

Some of the congregation scream—short, shocked cries. Elsa hears the sound of backing, stumbling feet. Most of them can't move at all; there are too many of them, in too small a space. There is nowhere for them to go.

The pastor looks up again and opens his mouth.

"No," he says quickly. A command, not a prayer.

Elsa closes her eyes.

As the world comes crashing down the short cries turn into panicked screams, but even those are drowned out by the bellows of the bedrock as it caves in and consumes them.

How funny, Elsa thinks, the second before the world dissolves around her and everything turns to nothing.

The muffled roar of the rock above them sounds just like Birgitta.

NOW

Robert carries Tone as we limp our way back toward the village. The night sky is in full bloom above us, and the bright, glowing half moon makes the kerosene lamp redundant. Just as well: the last of the kerosene has burnt out, and the wick fades to a thin glow before going out.

"I'll leave it here," I say quietly to Robert, who nods, and I put it down by the path. There it will stay, like a little marker. A dropped bread crumb showing where we've been.

We walk toward the square, as if in silent agreement. It was where we slept when we first arrived; we can spend one last night there. One last night before they come to get us.

The square is completely still when we reach it. The April night tints the ruins of the cars dark blue, but they don't feel threatening anymore. The last of the stench of burning metal has started to pass. Robert lays Tone down carefully on the ground. She is wet and her skin feels hot, but she looks better now than before. The water washed off the worst of the blood and dirt from her face.

I stroke her head gently. Her breaths are quiet and regular. I can't tell if she's asleep or unconscious, but her facial features are calm and flat.

"Will you stay with her?" I ask Robert, and he nods. He has twisted his nose back into place as well as he can, but it still looks awful. I don't know how it's going to heal.

"Where are you going?" he asks.

"I thought I'd get some blankets and sheets from the school," I say. "We can make a fire with them. Warm ourselves up."

He nods. There's not much more to be said.

I walk around the school to reach the fire escape, then climb it carefully. It creaks, but holds. It's darker in there without the moonlight, but my eyes adjust and I find my way around.

I gather as many blankets and sheets as I can carry, and put them in a pile by the window. Then I step into the hall.

The white figure by the wall is almost invisible in the darkness, but I know where she is. I walk over and kneel down beside her, then pull back the sheet from her face.

She is cold and stiff. Her lips are frozen.

The tears well up in me again, and this time I let it all out. My sobs are quietly draining, not loud or dramatic, and I let them flow through my body until they ebb away. Then I just sit there for a few minutes, until my breathing calms, until my hands find their way into my lap and I can look at her, at her still, light face in the flimsy glow of the moonlight outside.

"I'm so sorry," I say. "I'm so, so sorry. Forgive me."

I take in a deep breath and let it out. The air tastes of dust and old sunshine.

Then I lean forward and kiss her on the forehead. Her skin is icy under my lips.

"Thank you," I whisper.

I feel my way around her neck and find the delicate gold chain. The clasp is small, and it's hard to open in the darkness. I have to use my nails to get hold of the small catch.

Then I fold the sheet back up over her head, so she can rest away from this world.

Once the fire starts to take, Tone curls up exhausted beside it and immediately falls asleep. Her chest rises and falls steadily under the blanket.

At first I hardly dare take my eyes off her, but after a while I feel some of my tension release.

Robert is gazing deeply into the fire. I clear my throat.

"Robert," I say quietly. He looks up at me.

"I have something," I say. I reach into my pocket and fish out the necklace with the gold heart.

"I got it," I say. "Up there."

His eyes follow the swinging heart in the glow of the fire.

"Her mother should have it," I say quietly. "I thought that . . . that you should give it to her."

The words sting in my throat.

At first he says nothing. But then he holds out his hand, and I let the thin necklace chain wind down into his palm. He holds it carefully, like something fragile. It almost disappears in his big hand.

Robert looks at it for a long time. I wrap my arms around my knees and sit in silence.

He closes his hand.

"She regretted it, you know," he says eventually. His voice is slightly claggy from the swelling in his nose. "She never stopped regretting it."

I try to swallow the tears that well up in my throat. My voice doesn't want to carry. I purse my lips and stare into the fire until my vision cracks into a thousand sparks.

"I know," I say, biting my cheek hard.

Then I say quietly:

"She saved my life."

The faint breeze blowing across the square is surprisingly warm, almost mild. Summer is on its way.

An unexpected sound from above makes me look up. It's light, almost warbling. It takes me a few seconds to place it, but then I see the slight break in the school's silhouette. There's a bird sitting on one of the gutters.

"That's the first bird I've seen since we got here," I say.

"Yeah," he says. "Me too."

It twitters again. I wish I were the sort of person who could identify birds by their song alone. I have no idea what type this is.

But it's beautiful.

EPILOGUE

I waited, but no one came.

I waited and waited, and I fed the child, but they never came back. So in the end I went to our church's entrance, climbed, shaking, down into the tunnel, and followed the path in the darkness. I refused to take any torch or lamp with me. Only he was allowed to do that, for he was our lightbearer.

He told me to stay above ground with the child. He told me that she was important, and that I was to stay with her. That I was to wait for them, and that they would be back soon. When I reached the rubble I didn't understand what it was; I thought I had gone the wrong way, accidentally climbed down into a different tunnel that had collapsed, and gotten myself lost. I started to panic. I thought I would die down there, alone in a secluded tunnel, with only the sound of dripping water for company.

But then I found my way back, and the exit was where it was supposed to be.

Four times I walked back and forth before I understood.

The days passed. Cars came driving into town, and I left the child to them in the school. Perhaps it was her fault that they hadn't returned, that devil-spawn. If they just took her away with them then he would have to come back to me.

I hid down in the tunnels, for I remembered what he had said: that those outside God's grace would take me from him and destroy our paradise, for they knew no better. That the woman who had been my mother would surely have fed them lies about us.

They would never understand. No one could understand.

But then the water started to rise over the rubble. And I remembered what my father had said, back when I still had a father: they used to have to pump away the groundwater, to stop the passages from flooding.

I wanted to stay down there and let the water take me, but I knew I couldn't do that. To take one's own life is a sin, and those who waste themselves are the ones who burn most furiously in hell.

I had no choice but to wait for them. I had given my word.

I knew that he would come back to me.

After a while the food ran out. I had to go into others' kitchens and start eating from their pantries. But I could never bring myself to go back into *her* house, my false mother's house. I had a feeling in my bones that this was all her fault, or at least in part. She had always loved that witch more than she loved me, in spite of everything.

I let the rest of the congregation look after me. I slept in their beds and ate of their food. We were all one, and what belonged to one of us belonged to us all, I tried to persuade myself. That was what he had told me. But it felt wrong, and I started to feel sad. At night I would cry.

Sometimes I felt the doubts creep up on me, like stinging little devils. What if they didn't come back? What if he was wrong?

But I beat them off, fiercely and furiously. He had promised. He was God's chosen one, and he had told me we would be together for all eternity. That we would create paradise on earth.

I went back out into the forest, to the path that led to our church. I took a lamp with me this time: perhaps their light had gone out, and they had gotten lost in the darkness. He used to call me his light. His divine light. His angel.

Perhaps I could show them the way out of the darkness. Perhaps I could help them to return.

I went as far down into the tunnel as I could. The water had risen so high that I couldn't even see the rubble anymore. Soon the tunnels would be completely flooded.

I sat there until the lamp burned out, and then I cried again.

But then I heard them. From out of the ground itself.

I heard them singing.

And then I cried again, but this time in relief.

I realized that my offering had not been enough. I stayed down there in the tunnels, moving upward with the water until it stopped rising, and I listened. They whispered to me at night. At first I didn't hear them so clearly, but I learned with time.

They told me what I had to do. Sin must be cleansed with blood. Sooner or later the devil whore would return, and then the price would be paid.

So I waited.